Last Mispri...

"special editi..."

CW01456237

ΩNITIUM

THE DIVINE SAGA 1

First edition.

Cover art by Sevennah Storm.

Editing by William Burkhart at SIXDOOM LITERARY LLC.

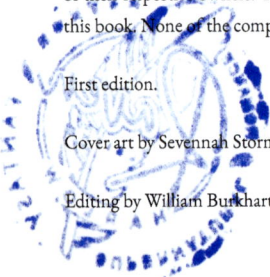

To my incredible husband, your unwavering belief in me has been my source of confidence, lifting me up whenever self-doubt crept in.

To my wonderful children, you have been an endless source of inspiration. Your encouragement has given me the determination to make you feel the same pride in me as I do in both of you.

To my dear friends and family, thank you for your continuous support throughout this incredible journey.

It is with great thanks to fellow author and graphic designer Sevennah Storm for bringing to life the fantastic cover of this book, (and subsequent installments) and to my editor William Burkhardt. This series never would have been brought to life if not for their genuine compassion and an immeasurable amount of patience.

TRIGGER WARNING

This book contains explicit sexual content, including on-screen rape and prostitution. It also addresses miscarriage and themes of depression and suicidal thoughts and actions. Additionally, it features apocalyptic scenarios that some readers may find upsetting. Please proceed with caution and prioritize your mental well-being. If these topics are distressing, consider skipping this content or ensuring you have support available.

"We are brought to an end by your anger; by your wrath we are dismayed."
  Hosea 13:11

PROLOGUE

The stench hit my nostrils before I could see the cause. Once I had a clear line of vision, it still took my brain longer than usual to comprehend what was happening. I could not make sense of it all. Everything happening all at once, too fast to keep up with.

Flames danced before my eyes, like hands reaching up to the starless black night sky. A blazing, chaotic inferno had engulfed the city.

Deafening screams of horror and despair from the injured echoing, drowning out the wails of sirens. They were beyond saving now.

People fleeing for their lives, running through the streets.

Plumes of thick, tar-like smoke. I could see them choking upon it as it filled their lungs, their panic-stricken eyes widening as they faced their untimely demise.

Heavy drops of rain had fallen from the sky; Mother Nature's feeble attempt to neutralize the flames They burned as if released from Hell itself. This small spattering of rain could never control their fiery tendrils whose wrath clawed through the earth like Hell Hounds, inflicting irreparable damage on every building they tore through,, leaving nothing but death in its wake. Anything that crossed paths with it would end up in the fiery furnace. There was no sanctuary, nobody was protected. No matter how hard they tried to hide.

Lurking in the shadows behind the thick bellows of smoke, I watched it all unfold from beyond my physical body. Relishing how I could see it all. How I could feel it all.

I had destroyed *her* hard work. I was enjoying how it was being dismantled piece by piece. Torturous for her, no doubt. For once, I was uncaring of her thoughts, her feelings. All of her creations would burn, her depiction of her perfect world shattering before her very eyes. Unable to prevent what was yet to come, the pain, the panic, the devastation.

This city was a mere snapshot of the total annihilation, the impending doom facing them all. Mirroring scenes identical to this, from all over the world, at this precise moment in time. Even if *she* could prevail through it all, there would be nothing left.

Only the desolate wasteland I had once called home.

What had taken her several millennia to fashion would take a mere matter of minutes to eradicate. Unraveling all her hard work, her labor of love, by pulling at one thread.

This would bring the end to the world, to all life as we know it. The world would burn until there was nothing left; relentless in its mission, until everything was decimated. Leaving in its wake piles of ash as tall as the buildings that had once been tall and proud. A graveyard of bones in place of the thriving societies that had once lived there. That she had once been so proud of.

All of this may have been started by her, but it will end with me.

This was not the result of the world-scale war on the cusp of fruition. No impending missile attacks threatened from beyond the seas. *No, it is not because of any of that.* The cause of this catastrophic destruction, on this worldwide magnitude, was...

Me.

ONE

Fueled by hate. Desiring to destroy. Filled with an insatiable hunger for power. I had adopted the ancient Videshan mantra; to create fights between my enemies, to divide them.

My aim is to distract my enemies from attacking me, deflect their attention to their own quarrels among themselves, weakening them so they would have no chance against me. The oldest tactic of war: divide and conquer.

I had not always been this way, had not always been so overcome with this deep loathing for the world. The people, the cruel twists and turns of life, of this predetermined fate had changed me. Had made me what I am. I had no control over it. I just had to embrace the darkness and accept who I have become.

Humans have been the same since the dawn of time. Driven by the deadly sins; pride, greed, lust, envy, gluttony, wrath, and sloth. All predestined to be self-destructive, inflicting pain and suffering on others and the cause of their own demise.

Ever since Eve tasted the forbidden fruit, humankind would fail. I should have seen it then, as I see it now. *They all need to be destroyed.* The slate needed to be wiped clean, to allow there to be a fresh start in an empty and desolate land.

Back to the drawing board, coming up with bigger and better ideas. How could I change things? To make the improvements it so desperately needs. To create an Earth 2.0.

How could I make a world free from evil? Free from suffering? Free from pain? When the pain, the suffering, the evil, was all I knew?

Alice

It was the start of winter when color drained from the world into a monotonous canvas of gray.

Gone were the songs of birds, which had become the soundtrack to life, harmonizing in the wind that fluttered the petals of blossoming flowers.

Feeling dread and sorrow as life wilted and withered under the weight of the oppressive atmosphere and the drastic change in temperature.

The wind, once gentle, now battled against branches of centuries-old trees, threatening to uproot them and destroy the wildlife hiding within. Sheltering from the bullets of ice-cold rain that would attack from all directions.

Today was an omen of what was yet to be discovered, about the world, and about me.

I always knew I was different, that I saw things that no one else did, felt things in a way which was unfathomable at first.

I am not your typical college student.

"Move over! Make some space for me," her voice called, stirring me from my reverie, from my observation of the world behind the fogged-up windows.

The damp, earthy smell radiated from her, overpowering the sweet floral perfume she wore.

I tore my eyes away from the dreary scene outside of the world beyond the bus window, to see who it was that spoke, although I knew the answer without having to look at her, but I did so.

A pair of honey gold eyes bore into me like fire. I could feel them piercing into my soul. As I studied her, I noticed that her usual platinum blonde hair was now several tones darker and clung to her face like a frame around a photograph. Water droplets beaded at the very ends of her strands of hair, clinging on to the tips, threatening to fall, unrelenting in their desperation. Or to succumb to the gravitational pull which was weighing them down.

Before me, swaying with the movements of the bus and unsteady on her feet, was Effy. My best friend, and truthfully my only friend. In some ways she was more like a sister to me, having known each other our whole lives and at one point living less than a stone's throw away from each other.

In this part of town, everyone knew everyone, and families and friendships ran generations deep. Once you were here, you spent your whole life here, stuck in limbo as if this was purgatory.

Apart from my family. My parents moved from the roughest part of town, where drunks and drug addicts made up the majority of the population, to the quiet suburbs to give their unborn child, me, the best possible upbringing. Though they had not been prepared for their frosty welcome. It became clear, as I grew up, that everyone here hates change, especially new people in the neighborhood. Not that there were many. We had been the last new faces on the street, and that was over twenty years ago.

"Are you moving or not?" She asked me, growing impatient. She had always been the bossy, domineering one between us, even though she was just as shy and as self-conscious as myself in public. I loved her dearly, and at times could be overbearing, but I missed her living so close. Living on the outskirts of the village, we no longer see each other like we used to, these small conversations to and from college, on an overcrowded, damp-smelling bus.

The one thing we could never talk about was her father, he was dead as far as she was concerned. It was his affair with a work colleague that had led to her moving house, her mother taunted by those with a poisonous tongue and a penchant for meddling in others lives. As soon as they caught a hint of the word "affair" and "divorce" they were like a pack of wolves thirsty for blood.

I shuffled closer to the window, moving my bag and coat off the seat beside me. The way she slumped down, her sigh was loud and exaggerated. Clearly indicating that I had not moved quick enough and she was annoyed to be kept waiting.

Even though I knew all there was to know about Effy Valentine, she actually knew very little of me. There were things she could never know, secrets that I buried deep.

"You OK?" I asked her, as she shrugged off her sodden backpack and flimsy denim jacket.

"Yeah," she murmured as she sat back in the seat. "You?"

I nodded, as I took in her heart-shaped face and pale complexion. There were black smudges beneath her honey gold eyes. She was the prettiest out of the two of us, with the figure, and the defined cheekbones of that of a model. There was not a warm-blooded male who would deny her beauty. Especially compared to me: the runt of the pack. Compared to her I was invisible. The only thing that people noticed about me was my wild mass of unruly, ginger curls.

Despite her stubbornness, and the pissed-off look on her face, I could feel her energy, this thrum of excitement buzzing within her. It was clear her annoyance with me was only temporary.

Within a matter of seconds, she smiled at me, unable to contain it any longer. "So…" her voice chimed, high pitched. "Have you heard about Josh?"

I rolled my eyes. I could not help it. It was my involuntary, instinctive, reflex reaction whenever his name was mentioned, which happened a lot. Effy could not stop herself; Josh has been living rent-free in her head for years. He was all she could think about, all she could talk about.

It was rather irritating, listening to the continuous documentary of his life, as if he were a celebrity. The latest news of who he was seen with, the cheating rumors, the drama that came part and parcel of being the most popular person. Not just in high school, but also the entire college campus. Hell, this entire part of town was under his spell. He has everyone eating out of the palm of his hands, holding onto his every word, as if he were God.

"Pfft. He would make a terrible god," she whispered. The little voice that plagued my every waking moment, my every dream. This voice was a part of me, but she was not me. She was a parasite, living through me.

I must have been missing some important information about him, as everyone swarmed to be his minions, as if he was some kind of king, or dictator.

One thing was for certain, regardless of who he was, or whoever he thought he was, I could see he was not a good person, and I was not going to fall for his charm like everyone else. I may have been invisible to most, but I prided myself on not being a sheep, a follower. Hell would freeze over before I became another person to pander to his already over-inflated ego.

As much as I hated to admit it, I lost a modicum of respect for Effy. When I learned of her crush, I felt a touch of disappointment towards her, as day by day she turned more into a Josh-groupie and less of the friend I once knew.

He had been her crush for what felt like forever, intensifying further when she discovered he would attend the same college as us. *"can not be that much of a somebody if he is going to a an Ivy League College,"* the voice piped up. I smirked. *Sometimes we were on the same page.*

"He broke up with Sienna!" She squealed in a childish whisper. Scared of being overheard by the other students from our college; Valkyrie's Hall, as the bus filled up.

I smiled at Effy, pitying the way she would always hope that she would become his girlfriend after he broke up with his latest victim. She was always clinging to hope, always trying to push herself into his sights. Although she did her utmost to get him to notice her, her attempts were in vain. Yet, no matter how disappointed and disheartened, she was. No matter how many times she vowed he was not worth her time or her tears, within a few days, she was obsessed with him again.

Truth be told, I was surprised that he had not taken advantage of the fact she offered herself to him. She was quite gorgeous, far better looking than any of his latest conquests.

"Perhaps he is intimidated by the pretty ones" the voice quipped. To an extent, I agree, either that or he went for the girls who were 'nobodies' in his eyes. Those girls he saw as beneath his social status, who would rely on him and revel in their newly found popularity. Those girls who would be too scared of the consequences should they wrong him, or do anything that could end up in their fall from his good graces. The girls that would never question him or his actions, and who he could use to further boost his egocentric disposition, while still being able to do whatever he wanted, whenever he pleased.

Josh was two years our senior, according to Effy he had been granted a deferred start to college following the death of his father. As heartless as it may sound, I cared very little for the details.

He was the stereotypical bad boy, who donned a devil-may-care attitude and flouted as many rules as possible. His rebellious reputation preceded him yet he had a charismatic charm that allowed him to get away with anything; as all the girls loved him, forgiving his every sin, whereas all the guys wanted to be him, envious of his carefree lifestyle.

He was the epitome of physical prowess; an athlete, always working out at the college's gym, lifting weights, and showing off his Latest achievements. He knew how to wear the crown of popularity, and despite my better judgment, I knew he wore it well.

I did not want to crush my friend's dreams, but they were not on the same planet when it came to relationships. Despite her attractiveness, she had never had a boyfriend, and romanticized the very thought of having one. Whereas Josh went through them like they were going out of fashion. Still a virgin, Effy had only gone as far as a slight drunken fumble, retaining the same view as me. Our virtue was to be saved for the right person - someone who would value it.

They were two opposites who would never work. Effy being a shy, timid girl, who always played by the rules, too scared to say the wrong thing, do anything that could offend anyone. Unlike Josh, who strives to cause as much offense as possible, loving to humiliate anyone if given the opportunity. He hated authority and saw rules as challenges, only created so that he could break them.

I despised every part of him, every fiber of his being repulsed me. Though I could never divulge the full extent of my dislike while Effy was obsessed with him. I had hoped it would have been a fleeting crush, yet I could feel as each day passed the distance in our friendship widening, fueling my hatred for him even more. There was something dark and sinister and although I was unable to pinpoint what it was exactly, I knew Effy needed to be protected from him.

"Effy," I sighed, getting to my feet as the bus drew to a stop outside the college campus. The vast buildings to the left of us towered several stories high. People in their hundreds were spilling into the main entrance already.

I looked at her, her eyes showed the determination of a hunter tracking down its prey, it was then that I had no choice but to admit defeat, accepting the fact that deep down I knew no matter how many times I told her, how many times I would warn her, she would never listen. Her rose-colored glasses were as thick as beer bottles, seeing only what she wanted to see. "Effy, you shouldn't worship him, and the ground he walks on...he is not a God," I told her, my last-ditch attempt to engage her to even listen to me.

She shrugged and looked over her shoulder. "He may not be God, but I will make him mine." She winked. "One day."

Josh

I struggled to pinpoint what it was about her, why she intrigued me so. There was something about her, something that compelled me to her.

A certain *je ne sais quoi* about her that fascinated me.

It was not her looks; quite plain, quite average, quite unforgettable. There was something else about her, almost indescribable, for there were no words that could do it justice.

You could say she had an elegance about her, a power, an aura. One that shone like a beacon, even though it was invisible to the naked eye. The warmth she radiated was like an open fire, a fire that matched the color of the tangle of curls on her head.

I liked the fact that she was unlike any of the others. She paid no interest in who I was, who my family was, ignorant of the influence that I had held because of it.

Perhaps she did not know. After all, she may have been born here, she may have lived here her entire life, but my family legacy ran deeper than just my father. Our name could get us into trouble, just as easily as getting us out of it.

Perhaps she knew I was the youngest son of Charles Morgan, of Morgan Industries. My father was a hard bastard, a cruel father, and was not one to be impressed by anything, but he garnered respect from his global success. He had inherited a small family business from his father and transformed it into a multi-billion-dollar empire.

I had been watching her from the driver's seat of my car, as she got off the bus with her irritating friend, her head down, holding onto the straps of her heavy-looking backpack. Her shoulders hunched as she battled the weather to get through the main entrance with the rest of them. There was nothing about her appearance that stood out, other than that bright shock of hair and her piercing green eyes.

Her defensive body language spoke volumes as she navigated through the crowd, her anger palpable.

I had vowed to get to know her, to convince her of my charm, but we were already nearing the end of term, and she had not engaged in my attempts of conversation with her.

Her lack of enthusiasm in getting to know me was infuriating. Everybody wanted to know me, to become friends with me. Hell, girls were backstabbing their best friends to be with me, but not her.

As frustrating as she was, it was also quite refreshing. I had been so used to everyone being friendly, offering themselves up as easy targets of my lust, that her lack of willingness to want to know me was unfamiliar territory.

She had become my next challenge, and it was not going to be easy. She was someone I would have to chase, to make more of an effort to get to know.

I was going to take her; I was going to make her mine. But I needed to take baby steps first.

I was going to ask her to be my date for the Summer Solstice Soirée at the end of the month.

"Hello?!"

"What should we do?"

"Hello?!"

"Why don't we try-"

"Hello?!"

"Do you think we should -"

"HELLO?!"

Muffled voices were suffocating me. I could feel my lungs constricting, as if the oxygen was being sucked out of them.

If I was going to die, I wanted death to hurry and consume me. I just wanted to be put out of my misery.

These voices were distant at first, but each time one of them spoke, their voices drew closer. The voices become louder, heavy with emotions, though they thought they were doing their best to conceal them.

I could hear the urgency in their hushed exchange. I could feel their uncertainty. I could taste their fear, the salty droplets of their perspiration as they leaned over me, their faces now inches from my own.

I did not need to open my eyes to know who they were, to know what they wanted. I did not need to be able to see my surroundings to know where I was or why I was there.

I knew everything and everyone. I even knew what was coming, before it happened; events that were coming, looming over us all like an oppressive cloud. A series of occurrences that no one could prevent from happening, that no one would see coming... until it was too late.

Life was always the same, like a broken record repeating itself. Born, contend, die. A continuous loop she had manifested through her creations. Every one of us had a predestined fate, me included.

Truth be told, the choices made throughout our lives were ineffectual, immaterial false hopes given to us that led us to believe that we could change our Fate.

The journey never mattered. We were all heading towards the same destination: to the dark abyss, to the finality of death.

As my consciousness returned, it became harder to block out the light, to ignore the warmth that radiated from their bodies that were too close to mine. Too hard to ignore the breath on my face as they leaned over me.

It was difficult to remain in control of the situation, knowing all that I knew, unable to prevent the sequence of events that were yet to happen. I did not want to wake up, at least not yet. I was not ready to accept my Fate. I was not prepared to face reality once I opened my eyes.

TWO

It was hard to stay focused, driven to the brink of insanity listening to the steady staccato beat of shoes on the cobblestones that lined the street outside. Everyone was going to be in attendance tonight. I needed to be sharp, focused, and on my best behavior. Valkyrie Hall, named after the local historical links to the Vikings, needed to be spectacular. It needed to live up to its name.

It was not just a party, it was a formal gala, hosted by me, the mayor, and my wife, Selene. Only the most elite and prestigious guests were invited to attend. It was all that anyone could talk about, both those invited and those not, leading up to the event.

Stirring up jealousy and envy between others was a specialty of hers, done for her amusement. Selene made no secret of how selective and how pretentious this gala was going to be. It. It was an honor to have made the guest list. It showed whose company she could tolerate, as there weren't many people of whom she liked.

It was all for show, the gala, a stage for those invited to showcase their elevated social class. To flaunt their assets and boast about their achievements.

The irony was that this was Selene's world, Selene's infamy that flocked them to this gathering, rather than mine, their mayor. It was bizarre how easily she had slipped into this pretentious way of life, this judgmental and isolated existence, dining with the upper class, the *crème de la crème* of guests, when this was not the world or the social status she had been born into.

Raised in the streets among the sewer rats, her family possessed no wealth. In fact, they held very little to their name. They could not afford to feed two hungry mouths, proffering her brother over her. When I met her, she meant nothing to no-one, not even to her own family. They showed no concern for her, could not care if she lived or died as she struggled to fend for herself. They had acted to her for all her life, but the streets were not much kinder. She was shown no compassion or concern for her.

I remembered in minuscule detail our first meeting.

Work had grown tiresome and monotonous. I had deadlines to meet and important meetings to schedule, people to butter up if I was to become the new mayor the following year. I had to think of something that made me stand out, something that my opponents did not have. So far, I was drawing a blank, unable to think straight. I decided that an evening stroll would be the best thing to clear my head.

The sun was setting in the distance, casting the sky in a sun-burnt orange hue that graduated into crimson and violet, accentuating the slate gray clouds that imposed overhead, threatening to make good of the local weather reports of out-of-season storms.

I had reached the park without realizing. It was as if an invisible hand was guiding me towards her. Compelling my feet to walk in a different direction than the usual route I would take, as if they were acting from the rest of my body, as if they had a mind of their own, taking me, yet into her path.

Selene is a big believer in the supernatural, claiming our meeting to have been written among the stars. *Fate*. Though I believe I had simply been in the right place at the right time. My father always told me, "Man makes his own Fate and his own luck. Only through hard work and sheer determination can man succeed in life." It had become my mantra in life, working as hard as I could to prove I was the best, and stay on the pedestal on which I had been placed by my peers.

That day, as I entered the park, a booming clap of thunder sounded overhead, reverberating through my body, the damp earthy smell rankled my nose. Seagulls overhead cawed as they circled in the dark and oppressive sky. An ominous sign, moments before the rain began.

Thick, heavy drops plummeted to the ground mercilessly. Its suddenness caused flooding in the streets, soaking anything and everything in its path.

Deep regret set in. My tailor-made suit was made of the finest materials, designed to emphasize my status, my power. Not to withstand this torrential downpour. What would people think if they were to see me in such a sorry state?

Head bowed low, holding onto my hat, I stomped through the park to the corner of FairGrove, a short distance from my abode. There was no way I could return to the office, not looking like this.

Perhaps an early night would do me good. Perhaps a good night's sleep was what I needed to refresh my mind. It was always best to have a fresh head for a fresh campaign.

Pushing forward, ignoring others scurrying around beside me. That was when we crashed into one another, both of us taking several steps back to see who, or what, we had encountered.

I would explode, shouting profanities and showing my aggression at the lack of respect from those of lower status. *How dare they walk in the path of me? Do they not know who I am?*

One look at her was all it took for all my words to become lost somewhere in the back of my throat. Disregarding the rags in her hair and the tattered dress she wore; she was the epitome of beauty.

She blushed, flustered, and embarrassed gathering her belongings that she dropped during our collision. It was not much, a basket of bread and fresh apples. "I'm so sorry," she gushed, avoiding my eye contact. "I was not looking, the rain- "

I smiled, a motion my face was not accustomed to. Feeling the muscles in my face ache in my efforts, I picked up a stray apple and offered it to her. "What is your name?" I had asked her.

"It does not matter, sir," she muttered, her eyes still cast to the floor.

It mattered to me. For some unknown reason, she mattered to me. I needed to know. Her beauty was so compelling, I lifted her chin so that I could see her face. Willing her to look at me for the first time. She flinched at my touch. No man had ever treated her right,

I swelled my anger at the thought of her ill treatment, at the awful life she must lead., knowing she deserved better just by looking at her.

Her eyes flickered open, revealing a set of vivid green eyes, almost too bright to be real. "What is your name?" I asked again, my voice audible over the torrential rain that drenched us. "Selene," she whispered back, her eyes never leaving mine. "My name is Selene."

Her name echoed in my head "Selene" I purred. "You are the most beautiful woman I have ever met," I watched as she grew red, blushing at my compliment. "Tell me, Selene, do you belong to someone?" She shook her head. "Good, because you do now," I said as I pulled her into my embrace. "You are mine... and you will live a wonderful life."

She looked up at me as if I was mocking her. "You have only just met me," she gasped when she stared at my face, realizing that I was not one to jest. "You do not even know me," she added.

"I shall have the rest of my life to get to know you, if you are willing to give me a chance to give you a much better, happier life?" My eyes pleaded with her. For me, it was love at first sight. It was as if she had cast a spell on me. I was never one to be this spontaneous, to admit my emotions like this.

"Are you sure?" she asked.

I nodded, bringing my lips to hers. "I am very sure that I want to make you my wife."

A sudden knock at the door snapped me out of my memory. The smile that brightens up her face that day lingered in my mind. She appeared from behind the door, looking just as beautiful now as she did back then.

"Christopher, darling, they are waiting for you," she whispered as she sauntered over to me, her dress rustling with every step as she drew closer.

Selene stood poised, half into the study, the evening dress she had been keeping a secret revealed. A deep emerald that hugged her figure and complimented her copper-colored hair. Looking every bit the part of the mayor's wife - my wife. She was elegant, graceful, looking as though she had belonged in this life. Never in a million years would you believe I had found her on the streets.

"Darling, are you okay?" She asked, her hand reaching out to my face. A slight and subtle gesture of protectiveness. "Darling. we need to discuss-"

I held up my hand, silencing her. I would not discuss her adultery before the start of the gala. I did not want to discuss her sordid affair, nor think of her spreading her legs for another man. Yet what sickened me more was that a child was now growing inside of her from that other man's seed. Hatred boiled in my blood for the child, its existence planted inside her to taunt me until the end of days. A product of wickedness and sin; even before it has been born it has managed to worm its evilness inside of me, making me lie and deceive my peers. I would have to pretend that *it* was my child. To prevent the scandal from leaking to the public and the press, I would have to convince them that I *loved* this child, until one of us perishes.

I secretly prayed it would perish within her, gone before it was fully developed, as heartless as it sounded, I wanted to save myself from living a web of lies for the rest of my life.

If the truth should ever be unveiled, it would tarnish my campaign, my reputation. Everyone would question my ability to run as mayor; how could I control public affairs if I had no control over my wife?

"We will, Selene," I composed myself, unable to look her in the eye, "but not now. As you said, darling, it is best not to keep them waiting."

I have been around for a *long* time.

It has been too long to know how many years, centuries, millennia I have wondered about this Earth.

Choosing to live among the humans, to be a parasite, to become a part of them. Invading a small fraction within their unconsciousness to control them, to manipulate their surroundings, to manipulate their Fate to my will.

To humans, the thought of immortality may be appealing, but it soon grew tiresome, lonely, monotonous. Watching those you love wither away before your eyes, becoming a frail and weak shell of the person they had once been in their youth. The heartbreak and sorrow of their loss when everyone around them succumbs to the finality of death.

I tried not to get attached, to not invest my own emotions into the lives of the vessels I possessed, but unfortunately humans are notorious for allowing their lives to be dictated by their emotions.

Yet it was their emotions that separated them from any of my other creations, and as much as their pain hurt, it made me feel alive. Their happiness made me giddy, their love encompassed me in warmth and their excitement buzzed through me like a nest of angry bees.

I knew that I could not experience the highs of their emotions without enduring the lows and none of it was possible without my vessels.

Throughout time I had countless faces and names. Regardless of gender each one was unique, different, special. I was proud of my creations; none of them looked the same, spoke the same, thought the same, and most importantly none of them *felt* the same. Love is still love, but to it was all fire and passion whereas to others it was gentle and wholesome.

Alice, on the other hand, was the most unique and special of them all. No one before her ever knew I was there hiding in their subconscious. None of them had been able to channel my power, my strength nor feel my own emotions. None of them except her.

She was by far the strongest vessel I have ever possessed, despite her slight frame. She was the descendant of my very first human vessel. By making her my *chosen* vessel, I had immortalized her for all eternity. *She just didn't know it yet.* She would remain human, fertile, young forever.

She could pull my own memories from my subconscious; snippets from the previous vessel's lives, something that none before her had done. She could harness my strength and use my power from a young age, with ease and with accuracy as if they were her own.

Anxiety gripped me as the realization dawned that I had been the one who was manipulated and controlled. I had become suspicious that it would end in a way I had not planned.

If I had known what problems would come with using her as my vessel, I would have contemplated remaining without a physical body until the end of time.

Francine – 1870

As I lay here, drawing out my last few breaths, savoring my last few moments on Earth, it seems only natural to reflect on life. To contemplate all of your decisions, all the sacrifices that had been made throughout your life.

Some in their pursuit of happiness, of love, of seeking redemption, while others could have been made in a vain attempt to prevent those whom you love around you from suffering.

It is at this moment in my life that I accepted The Divine had destined my life to be the way it was. Despite the pain and suffering, I knew she had a plan for me. Life was nothing other than a journey mapped out in the heavens above. Although we may never or understand why, we may find her cruel and wicked to test us in ways almost inhumanely possible. There was a reason for it, only she needed to know it. We were mere puzzle pieces whose lives made up the bigger picture.

My mother always said, "there are no such things as coincidences, Francine. Things happen for a reason, whether you know it at the time or not."

I had found it hard to believe that losing all my children had been for a reason. What justification could satisfy a grieving mother, a mother who has been pushed to the edge of despair, of madness, of complete devastation not once, but three times in her existence?

I think of Fredrick, George and Oliver, my dear boys who had all succumbed to various illnesses in their brief lives on Earth. How could such sweet, innocent children's deaths be predestined before they had been born?

As I struggled on, wandering the Earth without them, I had grown bitter, grown suspicious of The Divine's ways. Part of me even questioned their existence. Questioning why they had chosen me to mete out a punishment.

Now, though, I felt a comfort to know I shall join them soon, in the safe and sacred sanctuary of Heaven. I was hoping, praying to The Divine that he would be merciful and send my husband, when he perishes, straight to the dark, fiery depths of Hell.

"He? Why is it that so many humans refer to The Divine as a man? Women are not as weak or feeble as is led to believe."

This raspy voice again. I had been hearing it more frequently in the lead-up to my last day on Earth. Muttering and mumbling, sometimes it was incomprehensible and angry, and at others soothing and empathetic.

The voice, when it spoke, left a presence in the atmosphere, consoling me in my dying isolation. Even if it is a creation of my being, a figment of my imagination, designed to comfort myself in my last moments.

Just two words were all I needed before I left this world for the afterlife. Two words bringing solace in my departure from this world.

"Goodbye Francine."

Alice

I woke up and cried. Mourning for a person who I did not know, the trauma of watching her take her final breath, even though I know this all happened decades ago, did not make the pain feel any less real. When my eyes opened as the morning sun filtered into my bedroom, feeling loss still felt so raw that tears continued to flow, clinging to my eyelashes.

I was not sure if it was the loss of this elderly woman I was mourning, or whether it was the loss of my father who died when I was too young to understand, before I could mourn for all the experiences we would never get to share; such a wedding day, my children's births, all the milestones in life that you expect your parents to be a part of.

I had been staring in the mirror for a while, trying to cover these blotchy, red eyes with concealer and foundation to the best of my abilities, but I was no professional make-up artist. Usually, I wore no makeup. So, when Effy had remarked on my appearance the bus that morning, I knew my attempts had been useless.

Effy and I used to tell each other everything, and sometimes I had been indecisive about telling her about the parasite that lived within me for as long as I could remember. I knew she wouldn't believe me; she would ask me to prove it. Yet, if I was to prove to her I was The Divine's vessel, she would quake in fear. It would ruin the only friendship that I had left. Forever.

For the past few months, my dreams were no longer dreams. Instead, I was reliving scenes, memories, from past lives. Her past lives, decades, even centuries old. Each snippet was so vivid, so tangible, that upon my awakening, it had taken several moments to adjust to where I was, what century I was in, even who I was. This morning was no different.

I questioned her, as I tried to cover up my tear-stained face, why she was showing them to me now. What was the importance of me knowing her former vessel's lives; their heartaches and their pain? She refused to acknowledge my questions, almost as if she did not know the answer herself.

There was something else that I was hiding from Effy, something that I wanted, needed, to tell her. Before someone else told her. Josh had asked me out, in a round-about why.

Not only that, but now, he has kissed me. While she had been out on a field trip for her performance class. But I knew that once she knew, her jealousy, her envy, would overrule any modicum of logic and reason left within her – especially where Josh was concerned.

Over the past week, he had been trying to make conversations with me, and had been trying to come up with ridiculous excuses just to talk to me. I knew I should be flattered; I knew it evoked a lot of hate and whispers among the female population here at Valkyrie Hall College from those who were desperate for their chance with him - Effy, included.

The difference was that while they all craved his attention, I did not. He irritated me when he tried to engage me in a conversation; he repulsed me when he tried to touch my arm or my shoulder when giving me a compliment. The more I tried to ignore him, even being flat-out rude and abrupt in rejecting his advances, it seemed to spur him on more. He was not a person who took 'no' for an answer.

It had happened after my psychology lecture, the one subject that Effy and I did not share. The only subject that I did share with Josh. Throughout last week he had opted to sit beside me, claiming that I 'looked lonely.' Throughout the whole of the first year,

I had sat on my own, it gave me the space I needed to spread out the multiple textbooks, my notebook sat in the center with plenty of pens and highlighter for me to take notes.

Now with him sitting next to me, all of this space was cramped, our legs touching, as he sat with his legs so far apart it left me with the smallest gap for my own underneath the desk. His self-assured grin and playful wink belied his confidence in his own charm. Yet whenever I did not give him the response that he wanted, it would ignite a fire within him, give him further encouragement to try harder, where others would just accept the fact that I was not interested.

As the class had finished, as I tried to squeeze past him to leave the lecture hall, he had taken it upon him to snatch up my notebook, the one that contained all my annotations. Considering he was much taller than me, he held it up high, out of my reach. "Josh, please just give them back" I sighed, but when he shook his head, and kept his arm raised, I had stood on tiptoes to reach it, my fingertips just grazing the bottom of the book.

"Let me do it," the voice within me seethed. "You can get that if you want to." A few years ago she wouldn't have asked permission, she would have just taken over. I knew my strength, knew I could do some damage to him if I wanted.

But I would not cause violence, nor was I going to expose my secret, by unleashing her powers and her strength over a stupid notebook.

"Josh, just give it back," I sulked.

He wrapped his arms around me as he spun me around to face the mirrored glass panel of the door. "I think we make a great couple," he said, staring at our reflections. "a gorgeous girl like you, with a handsome chap like me," he smirked.

"That is never going to happen," I told him, trying to release myself from his grasp, but his grip on my body tightened. My notebook crashed to the floor.

"Alice, why don't you just give in? Be my girlfriend. Let me impress you, so that you can see how right we are for each other." He whispered; his mouth pressed against my ear, his voice oozing with desperation, "I promise you, you will like it."

I shook my head, "Josh n-"

His lips pressed unwanted against mine. The rest of my words, my refusal of his nonsensical idea, had gotten lost as his tongue writhed inside my mouth. No matter how hard his lips thrashed against mine, I refused to interact, to engage. I was consumed by worry the entire time, my mind racing with thoughts of how Effy would react if she discovered the truth.

I imagined the pained look on her face, how heartbroken and betrayed she would feel if she ever knew. It would destroy our friendship for good.

I let her take over. Feeling her wrath surge through me, feeling her impulse reaction to bite his bottom lip, to knee him in his crown jewels.

"Fucking bitch!" he hissed as he released me. Wounded and shocked, he staggered away from me. His eyes glinted, as a dangerous expression flashed across his face, a mix of anger and determination. I felt something within him shift. A darkness had taken hold of him as his brown eyes seemed to darken to an ominous, oppressive black hole.

"*Demon,*" she whispered, forcing me to take another step away, refusing me to reach for the notebook. It was the first time I had heard even a flicker of fear in her usual confident voice. "*We need to leave, now!*"

Before I knew what was happening, before I could even try to stop her, I bolted out of the lecture room, running as fast as my legs could manage.

"I will have you Alice!" He roared. "You mark my words, you will be mine". Even though there was a distance between us, his words still echoed in the now empty corridor. Fuck.

Tremors coursed through my body, rendering me unable to stand still as we pulled up to the bus stop. My lungs felt as though they were on fire, burning in my chest as she propelled me to run as fast as possible away from him. My breathing was heavy, my stomach twisted in knots as a wave of nausea washed over me.

I could not comprehend all of what she had been telling me in a hurried voice as we navigated through the maze of the college, not stopping for anything or anyone. Determined to put as much physical space as possible between us.

I recognized that his threat was serious, that he would be unrelenting in his advances. If he would not take no for an answer, I was worried. *How far would he go? Where would this end?*

Josh's threat had been aimed towards me, but the 'demon' inside him wanted *her*. My parasite.

This scenario was much worse than it appeared on the surface. The most popular person had chosen me to be his, and I had refused him. By doing so, not only had I made him an enemy, I had painted a large target on my back.

"*If demons are around, Lucifer must be planning something; to free himself from Hell.*" her voice was panicked. I tried to prompt her further, but she had shrunk back into the furthest corner of my mind.

I always thought that Lucifer, the Prince of Hell, was just a character created to scare people into more righteous citizens, to abide by the holy scripture. But she assured me, Lucifer was undeniably real and he was always seeking one thing.

Her.

THREE

Josh

It was difficult for me to contain my rage and fury, not to release the dark shadow that lurked within me after her rejection.

She was not being a tease. She was not playing hard to get. She did not want me, and I was not sure how to react to it. No one denied me. Ever.

Who the fuck does she think she is? Why does she think she is better than me? She is nothing! A nobody!

Yet, if that was true, why was every part of me attracted to her? She was not even that good looking compared to her friend. But her friend, Effy, was boring, predictable. Too eager and willing to give herself over to me. Alice was different. It was her inner strength, her inner power that attracted me to her.

My shadow wanted her in a way that made little sense to me. He wanted to harness her strength, wanted to wield her power as if she contained some magical abilities that would boost his own inflated ego to match that of the 'devil'. Lucifer. To overthrow him in some kind of Hellish war between them, with demons like the one inside me on either side.

☙

POV - Unknown

Lucifer was not free yet; he was still imprisoned, lurking in the shadows of Hell, biding his time while his abominations worked out a plan to free him.

But he will come for me, as he always did. No matter how hard I tried to keep him encapsulated in his own realm, he always found a way to escape.

His demons scared me, these abominations that should never have existed. They held powers of their own, dark forces to be reckoned with and some stronger than my own angels.

Alice needed to stay away from this particular demon; Asmodeus. He was up to no good. Lucifer might be evil, but this demon had an ambition to be worse. *Much worse.*

I had to give her credit, her initial instincts had been right about him from the start, but he had set his sights on her now.

He knew she was special, even if he did not know why yet, he would soon learn. The shadow that he harbored would soon enlighten him.

Bad things were on the horizon. I could feel it.

$$\mathcal{S}$$

Alice

The Summer Solstice Soirée.

As decorations and banners were being hung around the college, the halls were lined with posters advertising the event, creating a buzz like no other party has.

This was the one party each year that was not all about booze and drugs, where everyone could wear their best ball gowns and tuxedos. It was an open invitation, almost an unofficial competition, to see who would be best dressed - or who made the most effort.

It was all the students would talk about, ignoring the fact that we would sit on our most important exams the following spring. The exams would determine whether we would make it in the real world, in our chosen professions, where no one can correct our mistakes, where we had to take responsibility for the decisions we made, where we were just little fish that had become accustomed to a well-protected and looked-after tank to be dumped into a big pond where there were predators lurking in the shadows.

The Summer Solstice Soirée was the be-all and end-all, or so it would seem. Each year was bigger and better than the last.

This year, it was supposed to be epic.

Apart from one tiny snag, I did not have a date.

"Well, you could have had a date, but he was a demon," the voice in my mind reminded me.

Scowling, I pushed forward through the busy corridor, ignoring the memory of Josh's initial proposal of being his date.

"Hey wait up!" Effy shouted as she made her way through the bustling corridor. "Did you hear?" She eyed me, excitement oozing from her every pore. "Josh asked me to be his date for the Soirée!" she squealed, jumping up and down and waving her arms.

I attempted to force a smile, pretending to be filled with joy for her, but inside I felt nothing. It was a struggle to pretend, knowing that he had only asked her to get closer to me.

"So? Do you have a date yet?" she asked, realizing that I was not sharing the same level of enthusiasm as her. "You do know it is not the 18th century. Girls can ask guys to be their date now!" she elbowed me in the ribs.

I knew she meant well, but since her dream had now come true, she seemed to forget the social disposition we were both in before. We both used to share the same social awkwardness and have the same lack of self-esteem to ask someone to borrow a pen, or copy their notes in class, let alone ask them to be my date!

I was only going because Effy had been exhaustive in her efforts. Trying at every turn, having an answer for every excuse I had tried to make. Truth be told, my stomach twisted into knots just imaging about how many people would be there. The main hall is not that big considering how many students would be there. It would be loud and raucous, cramped and confined. My heart raced at the thought of trying to make small talk among the pretentious alumni and other student's I have avoided talking to so far in my academic life. I am not a social person, nor one to enjoy confined spaces, give me a book and the great outdoors and I was content.

With the added insult that if I went, I would not see Effy the entire night, wrapped up in the arms of the demon that is Josh, or worse, I would have to spend the evening with both of them. Trying to avoid Josh's flirtatious looks and remarks, while Effy's attention was averted elsewhere.

My chest tightened, my breaths grew shallow. *Not now, we will not freak out about this in public.* I told her, catching Effy's quizzical gaze.

I shrugged, trying to be nonchalant. It did not work. Instead, Effy thought I was just being overdramatic, and problematic because of Josh. She sighed and rolled her eyes, looking like a complete stranger.

Over the last few months, she had morphed into someone else. All in an attempt to become someone Josh would be attracted to. Wearing heavy set make-up, false eye-lashes and painting her lips in a red lipstick that was too harsh for her pale complexion.

Even her wardrobe had changed; no longer reserved and respectable, more skimpy outfits more suited for a woman of the night or the cliché pole dancer. I loved her, but the way she tried to embody someone who she was not, was pathetic.

Effy no longer looked like my best friend. She has changed. Her longing for Josh has changed her, I corrected myself. So absorbed in trying to fit this mold, to follow the trends of his prior girlfriends, Effy now resembled this unrecognizable creature before me. I wondered whether she had noticed a change within me too, or perhaps she was too preoccupied to notice.

She smiled, her eyes twinkling, "I have a plan."

POV - Unknown

All it takes is one moment to change the course of destiny. One harrowing choice that crosses the line rendering a person irredeemable. Once their soul was marked, they were no longer under my protection or control. That responsibility lay with *him*. Once you were marked, you were irrevocably the property of the Devil.

Without knowing it, you could have already crossed that line, and by the time you realize it, it would be too late.

It's ironic, hilarious even, to see and hear these desperate humans begging and praying for forgiveness from their deathbeds. Believing that their sins will be forgiven and they will be accepted at the gates of tranquility that is eternal peace.

Perhaps they may have been forgiven, once upon a time. But after being around for as long as I have and seeing as much as I have, these humans do not deserve The Divine's forgiveness.

Not a single one of them.

Christopher – 1988

The great hall was decorated with exquisite taste. No expense was spared for organizing this event, from the selected food being served, to the ornate napkins under the silver cutlery on every table. Each napkin was adorned with hand-embroidered initials of the guests, showing them where they were to be seated. Extravagant floral masterpieces sat at the center of every table.

All of this was because of Selene. She always had a particular eye for detail, always knew the little things, small personal touches, such as the embroidered napkins, would go a long way to impress the guests and make them more inclined to support my continuation of my role as Mayor. This was all that the gala had become this year, an unofficial campaign to wrangle their votes in my favor.

She danced and twirled across the room, welcoming and entertaining her guests. Flitting around the room like a butterfly across a bed of wildflowers. Enticing and fascinating to watch. Goddess-like in every way imaginable.

Selene had always been the perfect host for parties; she always knew the right things to say to bolster their egos, how to cater to their often-ridiculous needs. Regardless of who she had invited, Selene always stood out in the crowd.

It was easy to see why other men would find her attractive, why they would try to seek her attention, but what I could not fathom was what I had done to warrant her disrespect. I had given her everything she could have wanted, could ever have needed, and more. I had introduced her into a new society of a higher status than what she could have visualized.

Her skin was glowing in her secret pregnancy, gaining multiple compliments from the guests whom she welcomed. My chest constricted and my heart squeezed as I lamented in anguish. Envious of the nameless gentleman who fathered her unborn child.

For now, she could conceal it, capable of hiding it despite her slight frame. At the moment, she did not show she was with child, but soon it would be obvious, a barrage of questions would be asked, and it was crucial that I was prepared for them. I either needed to stand by her, prepared to raise another man's child, or shun this adulterer, publicly disgrace her and renounce her from my life.

Deep inside my heart, I knew I could not forgive her, could not ignore her indiscretion. It would soon be obvious. I could not disregard her clear lack of love for me. For if she loved me, she would never have forsaken me, our relationship no matter how temporary, for the arms of another man.

Her lost, forlorn eyes caught mine from across the room. She wore the same mask of suffering that had attracted me to her. My instinctive nature was to be her hero, to remediate her pain. She may have been smiling for the guests, but I could tell in her eyes that deep down, the weight of pretending to be happy burdened her.

I saw a flash of color flicker across her eyes, looking red in the light, lasting only a split second before returning to their usual shade of brown. I knew then, in the pit of my stomach, something was not right.

A heavy, oppressive silence fell upon the attendees, before ear-piercing screams filled the room. Terrified guests fled from the hall, running for their lives. Their movements were chaotic, uncaring of class or social standing when they were pre-occupied with their own self-preservation.

A sea of bodies, heads bobbing up and down as they flooded the two exits. Arms flailing in all directions as they tried to push and shove their way through the throng of people in a bid to escape. The shattering of glass as chairs were thrown out of windows as their panic and determination to flee outweighed any other thought. The broken shards descended to the floor like rain,

The thunderous sound of hundreds of shoes beating against the wooden floor vibrated through my skull like a baseline, replacing the soft thrum of conversation that it had been moments ago.

Then there was silence.

A metallic aroma like rust and iron permeated the air, so strong it stung my nostrils, and coated the back of my throat with its clotted, tangy taste.

I glanced down. A vibrant patch of crimson was seeping through my white dress shirt, spreading outwards.

Blood. *My* blood. I sensed it escaping my body with the ferocity of a wild boar, its unrefined strength surged through the wound rendering me exhausted and weak. The dense viscosity coasted my skin like a warm, sodden blanket.

Time stood still, as I stared at this ever-increasing stain that now spread across my entire chest. My body paralyzed as an icy grip squeezed the air from my lungs and confusion clouded my mind like fog. My pulse throbbed in my ears as the realization kicked in, I had been shot.

Quickly followed by a sudden bolt of excruciating pain, that tore mercilessly through my chest as if I had been struck by lightning.

I crumpled to my knees, pressing both hands to the wound in an incompetent attempt to staunch the blood. I understood what was happening to me, I knew I was dying.

The intense pain contorted my face, my eyes scrunched into small, narrowed slits. My vision blurred as I looked across the hall.

I saw her. Selene. My goddess, my tormentor.

In her trembling hands she held the revolver, placing the barrel to her temple. *My gun* I realized, the very gun that had fatally wounded me.

As I was bleeding out, I tried to reach out for her, tried to tell her I had forgiven her for everything, that I had always loved her, but my words died in my mouth - distorted by the blood which had poured out from it.

In those last moments, life slowly ebbed from my body. My soul was ready to depart into the afterlife, only faintly noticing that Selene had rushed to my side. The gun still pointed ay her skull.

"My darling, you must understand... the devil... he's real." She mumbled. Her cries grew louder as her body quaked turning into howls of despair.

"The seed of the devil is inside me." She whispered in my ear. "I never wanted to betray you, my love... I hope you can forgive me."

The shot sounded, echoing through the silence.

The blank glare of her lifeless eyes was the last thing I saw before the darkness consumed me.

FOUR

Blackened tower blocks and scorched skyscrapers descended to the ground like the building blocks of a toddler. The shattering of glass as it exploded from its window panes upon impact with the concrete below.

I watched as they crashed one by one into the Earth; the impact cast shock waves across the desolate, ash-laden ground. The tremors could be felt for miles, causing a domino effect of other buildings to come crumbling down to the ground.

Charred skeletal remains of those that tried to flee, of those who had gotten caught up in the wrath of the flames, littered the streets, everywhere, and anywhere. Obliterated and cremated by the unruly fires wherever they had fallen.

Sadly, they were collateral damage. These human deaths had been in vain, as it did not have to end this way. Decimating her creations and eradicating the world she created had never been in my interest. No one would survive this apocalyptic scale inferno. No one would be around to witness the aftermath of the destruction that I had caused.

Sad, perhaps a little poetic, that the one who created this earth and all the creatures within, had been the one who gave me the opportunity and the means to destroy it.

❧

Isobel

As a child, I never mattered, blending into the background, seen but not heard. I was that child that slipped under the radar, forgotten about, a child that had gone missing, never to be heard from again.

It took me by surprise to find that my deadbeat parents had actually noticed I was missing. It may have been three months too late, but who was I to judge how long it took them to sober up and realize they actually had a child in the first place? *Better late than never,* that was my parents' response to everything. Three days without electricity, *"better late than never".* Bailiffs turned up on our doorstep demanding repayment on a loan that they had snorted up their nose or injected in their veins, paying them a bare minimum amount when their state funding came in *"better late than never."*

I shouldn't have been surprised, that they had not noticed my absence, they were atrocious parents. Lying to the police the date and time of my disappearance, lying to social services that I had been happy and healthy, lying to the public that they cared for my safe return.

Even the photograph they used for the 'missing person' posters was outdated, by at least five years, taken during their last spell of sobriety. It was my last day of primary school, wearing a white shirt that was two sizes too small and a false smile on my face that never reached my eyes.

These posters were plastered everywhere; on lampposts, billboards, newspapers even on the back of milk cartons. Though despite the wide coverage, the information on there was useless, making it impossible to actually find me. *Perhaps that is their plan?*

Since that photo was taken, I had changed both physically and mentally. First, my hair was longer, curly, its natural color had darkened with age. Second, I had lost a lot of weight. The expected 'puppy fat' had fled off me as soon as puberty hit, as well as their abuse and neglect over the years. The three day stint with no food in the cupboards had helped shed that weight. My face now withdrawn and dark rings circled my eyes from lack of sleep night after night.

Though sleep was a foreign concept to me, not only did I have nowhere to go, my brain would not switch off. The constant thrum of the city and the threat of danger, I always had to be alert, keep my mind sharp and focused. I watched the world around me, wishing that I did not have to walk miles to find something almost edible or somewhere I could hide from the pitiful, hateful glares.

When I had first seen myself in the reflection of an abandoned shop window, I had not recognized the girl that was staring back at me; a street-rat, a hobo, a *junkie.* Ironically, I was probably the only sober homeless person in this state, but the irony was not lost on me that I looked more like the problem than the one I was running from.

In truth, I knew their 'concern' was merely a charade, an easy way for them to exploit my disappearance for their own benefit. For their own monetary gain. In one article, it stated that a 'collection' had been created to help fund the ongoing search, that hundreds of concerned citizens had donated to, in the hope of me being found alive. That money funded their disgusting habits, the ones I had tried to run away from.

In the whole time I had been on the streets, not one person had recognized me, not one person cared enough to ask who I was or why I was there.

On my own, from the age of fifteen, I had seen and done many things no child should have known about, let alone do, just to survive.

As a nation, we are notorious for throwing away good food at supermarkets and restaurants. Even households wasted more food so more often than not. Finding food to eat was easy as long as you had a strong stomach and did not mind salvaging them. With a mix of anxiety and disgust, she sifted through the nauseating, rotten debris, hoping to discover something edible and harmless.

The real struggles of life on the streets were trying to keep dry, trying to stay warm over the long cruel nights, exposed to the shit British weather, night upon night of relentless downpours, of gale-force winds, some so strong that it could uproot decades-old trees.

It was also important to keep the belongings you carried modest, and light, so carrying the minimum amount of clothes, blankets, and other possessions in case you needed to make a quick escape. That being said, there was one of my possessions that I could not have left behind.

Scruff. My most sentimental possession. A stuffed border collie dog, who lived up to his name. He was given to me by a social worker, one who cared about the children under their protection. I must have been five, but I remember her telling me that scruff would offer me protection, and to cuddle to Scruff if I ever felt scared, that he would always be there so I would never be alone.

Scruff now had one ear almost completely torn off and a button eye missing. His fur was now matted and sported some unidentifiable stains. He brought great comfort to me over the years, and still does to this day.

I know that a stuffed toy would not protect me from the horrors of the world. But he was a token, a reminder that there were still some good people in the world.

I just had to find them.

Some may question why I would choose to live inside a human; such pathetic lives compared to being the celestial, immortal being that I was.

Humans experience raw emotions, something that cannot be compared to any other living creation. No two humans could ever feel the same emotion in the same way. Love, hope. Happiness. As well as pain, despair and desperation were all subjective.

Feeling these emotions was like a drug to me. Addictive. No matter how many humans I have lived through. I could never get enough.

Until they became too much.

Until her emotions clouded my better judgment.

Until her emotions controlled me.

With each human I could feel their emotions, but never had they felt as strong as hers, never had they become too strong to control, too strong to take pleasure from feeling them. This vessel and her powerful surge of emotions had drained me. They had weakened me to where I questioned my choice of using a vessel.

Without a human body, though, my ethereal being drifted through time. Growing tired and bored. No reason or justification for my presence beyond the first creations.

I used to enjoy the mundane, monotonous routine of human life. The hard graft with little gratitude, and the greed of the rich, whose aim was to keep the poor in poverty. Enjoying the deceit and lies in the webs they spun, which made up their lives, until those closest to them no longer knew the truth of who they were. I reveled in the betrayals of those who were supposed to love them.

Hindsight is a wonderful but dangerous thing. Often, I question whether I would do all of this again: knowing all that I know now.

If I could go back, would I have do things differently?

I wonder whether I would have ever taken a vessel, had the first time, all those millennia ago, not been a complete accident.

Bjorn: 869 AD – The Birth.

The spring air carried the fragrance of new life. The resinous smell of the forest; damp & earthy with woody notes from the mixed spruce, fir, and pine trees.

I inhale a deep breath. This smell reminded me of home, of Norway, thousands of miles across the unforgiving sea.

It has been many years since I have been home. We traveled to England, with the hope to discover and find riches beyond our wildest dreams. We were not wrong; the churches had silver and gold. We had also discovered that the soil here was rich. It held plenty of the nutrients to support growing crops and rearing livestock.

Some of us shared the same vision, to remain here, to build settlements. To create a new prosperous life here in these foreign lands, where our people could also thrive.

The English never even saw us coming. Too preoccupied with the bickering feuds between divided nations, it made it all too easy to sneak into and invade their lands. They had already divided themselves, which had left them vulnerable for us to conquer them.

Their ports and strongholds defended themselves, they fought, determined to stop us on their borders. They were not aware of the fact that we brought great numbers of warriors in our efforts. All of my men were eager to fight for victory, soothed knowing that they would enter Valhalla should they fall in battle.

I felt a tug on the sleeve of my shirt, trying to stir me from my thoughts. I had become overwhelmed by my worries, drowning me in the sea of chaos that flooded my mind until I had lost all awareness of reality.

There was another stronger tug. This time I felt the snap of my awakening from my thoughtful trance.

I looked to see who it was, smiling when I noticed it was her Sylvi. My woman. Her stomach was swollen, ripe with my seed. We were expecting the babe to come any day now.

Fear and panic filled her bright green eyes as they swam in a sea of tears. I could feel her worry and anxiety kick in, as her contractions began, as she tried not to dwell on her loss, while that was all I could focus on.

This would be child number four.

None of our previous children had survived the night. Doubt niggled in my mind that this child would suffer the same unfortunate fate similar to its siblings before it.

My heart was shielded, it was too hard, too upsetting to watch history repeat itself. I poured out my heart in prayer, imploring the Gods to show us kindness by blessing us with a thriving and accomplished successor, hoping they would shield us from the heartbreak of another child's tragic Fate. For her sake. Sylvi could not go through this again.

I did not want to think of betraying my woman, the woman I had loved and married over a decade ago. I did not want to think of laying with another woman who could never compare to Sylvi, just to produce an heir. But that is what I would have to do, if this child should perish as its siblings did before them.

I prayed to the goddess, "Please, deliver this child in health, to save my love, to save my child," I muttered under my breath. So low and unsteady so Sylvi could not hear me. I could not show her my fear, my concern, I had to be her rock. I was a warrior, I feared nothing, yet my stomach twisted in knots at the thought of losing her.

Yet their fates were now in the hands of our gods, we had done everything we had been advised to do to ensure a smooth and healthy conception. To make love under the full moon, and to present the gods a sacrifice prior to the babe's arrival.

My gaze fell upon my woman, as the bleats of the goat echoed in the background.

"Bjorn." she whimpered, her face contorted in pain, as her trembling hand held out the silver dagger. "It's time."

I prayed to the Gods before turning to face her. "I am here, my love."

FIVE

I had been watching from above, unseen and undetected. I had become invested in this Viking couple.

Three children had perished before their lives had begun. The first born was a son, but he was born sleeping, formed, so beautiful they were beside themselves with grief.

Their second son was born deformed. He struggled to move, to writhe as a newborn babe should. It was often the Viking tradition to abandon them, to let them perish, but he had not lived long enough. He succumbed to death within two hours of his introduction to the world.

When their third child, another son, was born, their long agonizing journey to become parents, to produce an heir, was over. He seemed so promising, wailing loud and strong cries from the moment of his arrival, but he refused to suckle, refused to take the milk from her breast.

Without the nutrients, he was beginning to starve. All night they tried different ways, different methods the healer had advised to help encourage the infant to feed, but before the sun had set, to mark a new day, the child had gone. The cold winter air had whisked his spirit into the night sky to join his brothers.

I wanted to ease their suffering, to prevent further pain, but their lives had already been fated. Their children's deaths were not in vain. They were not strong enough to continue the bloodline, a bloodline that had been foretold to last generations. One that I knew I would need to continue for many centuries to come.

I could do nothing but watch Slyvi's arduous pregnancy, unable to determine if her child would be strong enough until it entered this world. But finally, after several long months, the wait was over.

The woman, Sylvi, was in labor. The miracle of life, the incredible process of childbirth, fascinating that humans can develop another human within their bodies, to be born perfect and whole.

A piercing cry reverberated in the room, I wanted to get a closer look at this child; I wanted to make sure it would survive this time.

As I gazed upon the baby, taking in the ten perfect fingers and toes, the small patch of fine blond hair, its round cheeks and little button nose.

For five years I hovered around them, watching as she grew. My attention invested solely on her whilst the world descended into chaos and war. She captivated me with her feisty spirit and strong determination. Even as a child it was clear she would be a warrior, a fierce and unyielding leader of her people, ruling with her head rather than her heart.

I wanted to feel her energy, I wanted to witness her life through those deep green eyes of hers. I was drawn to them like a magnet, hypnotized by their vivid color and intensity.

Until one day I found myself being sucked into the depths of them, my essence merging with that of her soul. My ethereal entity was no longer hovering over her. Instead I was inside her.

For several moments everything was black.

The only sounds I could hear were those of her thoughts, spiraling around me like a whirlwind. Deafening and dizzying as they thrummed in her subconsciousness.

The light was bright at first, my vision obscured, yet I soon realized that I was looking through her eyes, and she was staring up at the sun.

Her confusion swirled around me, she could sense another presence within her. Yet I was flooded by her warmth, as her mind and body accepted me, allowing me to become a part of her.

Her gaze lowered to the lake at her feet, watching the gentle ripples obscure her reflection, a small smile crept across her dainty lips.

"Hello friend," The girl said, her words directed to me. "My name is Freyja."

Francine - 1840

Queen Victoria was on the throne, seated next to her new husband, Prince Albert of Saxe-Coburg. An arranged marriage, a marriage to form an alliance. A marriage of convenience rather than love.

I knew that feeling, to be trapped. To be married to a man I neither knew nor loved. Edward.

On the outside, he was perfect. Tall, dark hair, handsome with his chiseled jaw and dark mahogany eyes. Born of wealth and status. How he loathed my company, a lady sold to his parents to enhance both of our family's wealth. We were married for our families to become allies. A pact which Edward made clear not long after we married he did not want to be a part of.

I was besotted with him at the start, as would any woman in my situation. This attractive, wealthy man was my husband, the one who promised to love and to honor me until death do us part.

At the start, it had been fun, getting to know him in every way. The way he looked at me with his smoldering eyes, lusting over the virgin that he was carrying in his arms, had eased my worry and anxiety about having sexual intercourse for the first time. I knew it would hurt, my mother had warned me, but she had also told me: "you need to push aside the pain, you might not always enjoy the deed, or the man you do it with, but you must always carry out your duty as is expected of you".

The first time, on our wedding night, had felt like pure enchantment, every touch filled with wonder. Making love with my newlywed husband was amazing. I filled every moment I could beside him, underneath him, on top of him. Reveling in the fact that he wanted me with the same intensity. During the day whilst he was at work, I longed for his return, to be swaddled in his arms, pouncing on him as soon as came home like a predator capturing its prey.

His shaft felt like it had been made to fit me. My inexperienced core welcomed him and accepted him, as he took me to ecstasy without fail every night. He had made me feel amazing, as if I was the most special person to him on Earth. It was in these moments I took great pleasure that I did not need my mother's harsh warning. Forever grateful and content that I had been blessed with the perfect gentleman. Perfect as a lover, My husband was perfect. Kind, loving inside and outside of the bedroom.

That was until I fell pregnant with his first son; when it all fell apart. Edward would get frustrated if I had been up with morning sickness, or unable to get comfortable. He was always blaming me for his tiredness. So, he soon moved into another room to sleep. Only entering mine when his sexual urges overtook him.

Being pregnant, especially further into the pregnancy, I did not always want sex, but he was relentless, forceful. Taking me against my wishes just because it was what *he* wanted. He became a different man than the one I thought I had married. This man was a monster.

It was then, in those moments, that the words my mother had once said rang true. I knew I dared not to refuse him or cry out in pain when he had become too rough, pushed too deep. There were times I thought I was going to die, when his hands held onto my throat just a bit too tight, for just that bit too long.

Perhaps prior to pregnancy that could have become a kink that I enjoyed, but with a beach ball in between us, there were very few positions that would work.

That was when he must have grown tired, gotten bored with me, for he used me when he wanted, in a quick, rough furious fuck, or he came home sporting lipstick marks on his collar of his shirt when he did not.

I struggled to swallow that he was sleeping with another woman, or many women, while his son was free inside my body, morphing it from my usual slender figure to one of a bloated beached whale.

The disgust in his eyes when he looked at me, choosing to only take me from behind on the odd occasions he did frequent my bedroom. I suppose it was so that he did not have to look at me, so that it was easier for him to imagine me being somebody else.

I knew I did not deserve this treatment, having to share my husband with whores. I should not have been his last resort when they turned him down. By the time our first son had turned one, I was pregnant again with our second child.

It was around the time when I knew, when everyone knew, that I was not enough for him, that he had given up trying to make this marriage work. No longer discreet in his extramarital affairs, he saw no shame now in his adulterous behavior.

Soon, not only was he rough in the bedroom, he became rough all the time, using me as his physical and emotional punching bag. Hiding me away in the house, often locking me in during his working day, to stop the neighbors from seeing the wounds and the bruises he inflicted upon me.

Still, I carried out my duties. I bore him three sons: heirs to Edward's empire. Security that his bloodline, his lands and his lordship's titles would be inherited. I had done all that was within my power to please him, to spare myself from punishment, but it was to no avail.

More often than not, I was locked behind closed doors, only being allowed to leave with him acting as a chaperone, redirecting their attention to him rather than me, when we went to the village market.

I had become Edward's toy to take his frustration out on; an unwilling participant in his anger games. A demon was inside him, I was sure of it. No mere mortal could inflict such suffering and pain on another. Uncaring and unsympathetic.

As the years dragged on, as he aged, he had lost his appeal; his physical attributes and sexual prowess were not what they used to be. When they failed him, and the women were no longer interested in him, I would suffer the wrath of their rebuttal that consumed him.

Soon he had swapped his urge to fuck, to his urge to indulge in alcohol and gambling.

The slippery slope he tentatively climbed had burned through his family's wealth, his inheritance and profits of the company were squandered on his habit. Even with little to our name, his worked less. Splurging what little earnings he now brought home on the races than food for his children when they were alive. There were days where I would give up my meal, just so they did not go without.

I could feel myself breaking with each day that went by, losing, losing the will to live when all three of our sons were buried in cold, lonely pauper graves.

I was a broken woman, walking around with lead in my heart, unable to pretend that our marriage was fixable, unable to afford to keep up with maintaining our house, yet he refused to sell it. He still wanted to make everyone believe he was a wealthy businessman, yet in reality he had sold his family business, had pissed the proceeds against the walls, until we were dirt poor, with not even a penny to our name.

We were living on borrowed money, and it was only a matter of time before these thugs would come to collect their repayment. Money that he had spent, and we had nothing to show for it, nor a single penny to repay.

I was worried, scared of what they might take, what they might do as their repayment. I was living in fear of my life.

The constant worry and stress drove me into an emotional breakdown point; my mind slowly became unhinged from reality and could no longer cope with the situation I found myself in.

His vows were worthless, nothing but empty promises, he had no intention to love and honor me through sickness and in health. He found himself multiple opportunities to betray and deceive me, yet none to change the error of his ways and show no remorse for his actions.

Death was coming for me, its icy tendrils slowly wrapped around my lungs, squeezing a little more air out each day and flooding my veins with ice until I could no longer move unaided.

At times my mind would wander, my speech reverted to child-like, simple sentences for the most part, but also as an incoherent babble at others. He had no patience to decipher. His lies and deceit had unhinged the rational part of my brain, it no longer functioned as it should. Information would not stick, my memories faded into nothingness.

Perhaps if he had found it within himself to change, he could have fixed me, or at least resolved some of my mental instability, but he refused. He should have repented his dishonesty, atoned for his sins, before his judgment day. Instead he broke his promise to care for me unconditionally, as he had promised all those years ago, and locked me away, at home, and then in a local mental institute.

It was lonely there, staring at the same four white walls, without anyone to come and visit me. If my boys were alive, I knew they would have come, but not once did *he*, my estranged husband, come to see me, allowing me to rot there until the end of my days.

That was when I started listening to her voice, when I had accepted what I was, how the rest of the world saw me: I was insane.

$$\mathcal{S}$$

Effy

There were no words to express my elation. My excitement built within me like a shaken soda bottle, ready to erupt at any moment.

I had waited long enough. I had tried hard enough, and now my dream had come true; Josh and I were officially dating.

It felt strange, after all this time, that I was able to call him my boyfriend. My heart fluttered every time I saw his name appear on my phone's screen. I had no misconceptions of what he expected out of a girlfriend, I had been prepared to surrender my virginity to him. I would do all it took to solidify what we had together.

I knew his relationships never lasted long, but I was determined to be the one he would not want to replace. I was going to break his cycle of flings. He was mine now - I would not let him go.

Josh's gentle snores stirred me from my sleep. His cologne still lingered in the air as I watched the rise and fall of his chest.

What is it about him that Alice hates so much?

Alice

I could have done without these flashbacks, these memories from her former vessels' lives, that flooded my sleep. I had enough dress and anxiety of my own to deal with, let alone feeling emotions from strangers who had lived decades, even centuries ago.

Last night I had felt Francine's every emotion; the love she felt for her husband, the betrayal and pain he had inflicted upon her, until she drowned in her own despair and depression. Seeing her lucid and insane thoughts near the end of her days as if they were my own.

It caused me to wake up with dark circles under my eyes. This was all I needed, to look half-dead on the day of the Summer Solstice Soirée. all lectures had been suspended today, as the college prepared and was decorated for tonight.

All day, I could not stop Francine's inner thoughts from dancing around my head. We were alike in some ways, the anxiety she felt about losing her virginity mirrored mine. Though I could never tolerate the suffering and hardship like her.

My mind flashed to the Soirée tonight as a wave of anxiety washed over me. I still had no idea who my date was. *Did he expect anything from me?* I had never been in a relationship, never kissed a boy. I was not naïve enough to believe in fairy-tale romances and remaining a virgin until I found *the one*, and I refused to rush into anything with someone I barely knew. My virtue and my dignity warranted more respect than that.

I sighed as my eyes swept over the sea of people at the campus. I was on my own, a minority cast out of society for my inexperience with relationships. Apparently, it was an alien concept for a woman in this decade to still be a virgin.

My thoughts went straight to her. *Effy.*

My heart sank; I had lost her *forever*.

She was no longer pure or innocent. Her soul had been damned the moment she had succumbed to his demonic allure and relinquished her virtue. I had warned her, I tried to protect her, but the hold he had on her outweighed the love that had once flourished in our friendship.

Gone was my best friend, replaced by a cheap imitation, one so badly misconstrued that no resemblance of the Effy I once knew remained.

Her relentless fixation on attending the Soirée had been tiresome, like a dog with a bone, it was all she spoke about until the point it had become another obsession. I found myself evading her, catching an earlier bus or hiding in the library during lunch, just so that I avoid listening to any more of her mindless chatter.

I told her for the hundredth time I was not going. Yet, three days ago morning she had caught me off guard, as the familiar purr of Josh's motorbike pulled up beside the bus stop with Effy sitting on the back of it. I squirmed at the sight of her arms wrapped around him, so close to his groin. I cracked under the pressure of their glares. I had yielded to her, submissive to her newly found dominance, intimidated by the 'popular' girl that she now was.

I instantly regretted the moment the words left my mouth in a bid to shut her up - "fine, I'll go." My insides burned as if acid had replaced the blood that pumped through my veins, and my stomach clenched in dreaded anticipation. Whereas her eyes had lit up, sparkling despite the gloomy gray clouds that smothered the sky above.

"I have the perfect date lined up for you," she squealed, her hands clapping together.

"Shame her boyfriend didn't get the memo, " the voice in my head hissed, as my eyes clocked him winking at me.

My nostrils filled with the acrid smell of sulfur and ash, it was *his* scent; the oppressive and demonic entity that lurked within Josh. It filtered my thoughts evoking a fear I had never felt before. Even after Effy had become his girlfriend, he was still making flirtatious advances.

During class he would encroach on my personal space, his hand would graze my arm as I reached for my textbook, or his fingertips brushed against my thigh knowing that my eyes would snap open wide and I would flinch at his touch. Josh Smith was not going to give up without a fight, intent on pushing the buttons that would get a reaction from me and relishing when I would snap at him, wishing him dead.

I sighed. My phone felt like lead in my hand, after reading her last message; detailing the instructions for tonight. I could not reply because her message had made me feel nauseous. *Your date will get to your house for seven, the limo will pick you two up first, and then Josh and I a little after seven-thirty.* She had ended her message with a wink-face emoji, the implication was clear. They needed some *alone* time.

There was no way I could tell her about Josh's advances without making myself sound jealous. They sounded ridiculous even to myself even though I knew them to be true. Yet I could not make her see what was glaringly obvious if she was content in being blind.

Discarding my phone on the bed, I dragged myself to the bathroom, splashed my face with cold water, wanting nothing more than its icy bite to wash away my feelings and to forget Francine's unfulfilled life.

Yet my anxiety still gnawed away at my insides like a caged beast desperate to escape. My muscles tensed and my hands trembled as I returned to the bedroom and started pulling out the items that had been hand-delivered by her less than an hour ago.

They had pulled up outside, the purr of his Harley Davidson announced their arrival before my mom could even answer the door. The sun gleamed off the polished chrome, stinging my already strained eyes.

"Oh Effy, are you going to come in? I haven't seen you in a while," my mom had said, her voice floating up the stairs.

"Sorry Mrs. Bowers, I'd love to, but I have so much I need to do before tonight," Effy had replied. "I just came by to let Alice borrow a dress for this evening."

My steps faltered and I almost stumbled, Effy's eyes locked onto mine, her genuine smile blanketed me in guilt for avoiding her. "Sorry I can't stay, Al," she muttered. I nodded, keeping my mouth pressed tightly, not trusting my voice.

"Here, you'll love it!" she squealed, handing over a black garment bag and a black cardboard box. "Complete with shoes and accessories," she added with a grin.

They felt like a ton of bricks in my arms, they may have only been a dress and shoes, but it was ladened with the promise I had made Effy; I could not back out of the Soirée now.

As I watched her walk down the path of our front yard and scramble on the back of the bike. I studied her as she slid on her pink helmet over her shiny blonde locks before weaving her arms around him effortlessly.

My heart throbbed in my ears, the air in my lungs froze as I watched her when I had watched the pair of them on the back of his motorbike until it was nothing but a dot in the distance.

"So, are we really going then?" the voice in my head whimpered. My mom gave me a curious glance.

"There is a party... at college." I told her, acting as if it didn't bother me, like it was insignificant, yet as I made my way back to my bedroom, I felt as if I was walking to my doom.

SIX

I had been waiting for her, Alice, at the coffee shop a few minutes away from the school. It was our regular meet-up point on a Thursday when we both had a free period. But she was running late. I had been staring into my coffee cup, stirring the frothy milk of my cappuccino when I felt a presence at the other end of the table. Smelled the unforgettable cologne waft in my direction.

My eyes shot up in his direction, still not quite believing he was sitting there in front of me. He had given me his gorgeous smile, flashing those straight white teeth, as he lounged in the chair opposite me.

"Hi," Josh greeted, sounding as if this was a regular, everyday occurrence. As far as I was aware, this was the first time he had spoken to me all year. He ran his hand through his jet-black hair, flexing his biceps in his pastel blue t-shirt. I could feel my pulse racing as my eyes transfixed on him before me. All I could think about was how I wanted to rip his shirt off and run my hands over his torso, while his experienced manhood ravaged my virginal slit.

I saw his eyes glisten, his smile widening, looking at me like he had access to my thoughts. My cheeks flushed scorching hot, like a fire had been ignited behind them, knowing they were as red as a tomato. I pressed my hands to my face, trying to disguise my embarrassment, casting my gaze downwards at the coffee cup, pretending it was more interesting than him.

"Ef, I have been thinking about you *a lot*," he started, taking a sip from his disposable coffee cup. "I know that we don't share any classes, but I see you with Alice a lot, and I have to say that you are very attractive," he said with a sexy smile, revealing his pearly white teeth. I wondered when he had first noticed me; what had I been wearing? How did I style my hair? What were Alice and I talking about?

I felt the heat in my cheeks intensify, as his smoldering gaze remained fixed on me. I still could not believe he was actually talking to me, that he had called me *very attractive*. It was like a song to my ears.

"So I was wondering if you wanted to accompany me to the Summer Solstice Soirée?" he asked, his velvet words wrapping around me. "That is, if you don't already have a date?"

I shook my head from side to side, my insides numb.

"So, you will go with me?" he asked, his tongue licked his lips as I squealed like a piglet in delight, much to my own embarrassment.

Be cool Effy, I warned myself, before hastily composing myself. With a deep breath I steadied my nerves, worried that my voice would crack and return to the high-pitched shriek. "Yes, Josh. I would like that very much."

"Good," he said, leaning forward in his chair. His finger traced small spirals on the back of my hand. "Ef, I was thinking, perhaps we could, you know, hang out a bit, before then, get to know each other better," he winked.

He did not need to spell it out. I may have been a virgin, a lot more inexperienced than the other girls he had been with before me, but I knew what he was talking about. I nodded my head, trying to be nonchalant. My previous pep-talk repeating itself in my head.

"Sure, sounds like it could be fun," I replied, giving him a coy smile. "Let me know when."

With a small chuckle, he got to his feet. "How about tonight?" he asked with a devilish glint in his eye.

What about tonight? I wondered stupidly, my eyes staring at him blankly. He smiled, as he walked around the table, wrapping his arm around my shoulder. "I'm free tonight if you want to hang out," he whispered in my ear.

His breath was hot, the vibration of his words sent small shivers through my body. I nodded, dumbfounded. I felt his teeth graze my earlobe before he started speaking again.

"Good. Do you know where I live?" he asked.

I swallowed the lump that had formed at the back of my throat and my stomach twisted into a mass of tight knots. I nodded once more as my heart raced.

"My place at six? I will order us a pizza, perhaps we could watch a movie?"

He did not hang around for an answer, my eyes followed him as he gracefully maneuvered through the bustling coffee shop. No girl ever 'just chilled' with Josh Smith, and there may have been a movie on his TV, but I doubted any of it was actually watched.

I pinched myself to make sure this had not been a dream. My fingernails bit into my skin leaving small white crescents indented into my arm.

Nope, I am definitely not dreaming.

I ditched my lectures for the rest of the day, texting Alice pretending to be sick. She would not understand if I told her the truth, her focus was always academic, and she hated Josh with a passion I could not understand. As far as I was aware, they had never uttered a single word to each other.

First stop, the waxing salon.

My core dampened just at the thought of him touching me there, my skin tingled at the thought of his fingertips dancing across my now smooth mound. I was nervous, unsure what to expect. He was rumored to be *large*, I sniggered as I tried to imagine it, the feel of it in my hands. My mind clouded with doubt, I was inexperienced, I had never seen one in real life before, what am I supposed to do? I suddenly felt queasy, as my fear gripped me in a chokehold. What if I do something wrong? What if I don't make him *hard?*

So many doubtful thoughts swirled in my head as I scrambled around in my wardrobe, looking for something to wear. Finally settling on a denim skirt, one my mother definitely would not approve of, a pale pink blouse with the top buttons left undone, paired with my knee-high boots.

My eyes locked onto the clock behind me; it was time to go.

I made my way to his house; he did not live too far, just on the outskirts of the village, like me, but he was in the upper-class area. Where the houses were bigger, grander, with large drives and electric gates.

Being the youngest child of a multi-billionaire appeared to have quite some perks.

My mouth felt dry as I approached his electric gate, pressing the intercom button with a shaky finger. *Pull yourself together Effy*, I told myself, *you cannot afford to fuck this opportunity up.*

His face flashed on the LED screen; his handsome smile greeted me. "Gates are opening for you Ef" he said, just as the electric gates clicked into motion, opening inwards. I slipped through, admiring the vast lawn of cut grass, cut into neat vertical lines. Trees lined either side of the drive, the gravel crunching under my boots, as I approached the large house that loomed ahead of me.

I did not have time to admire how large it was or how the exterior looked, as I saw him leaning against the door frame, wearing nothing but a pair of cargo shorts.

My heart skipped a beat. He seemed to be more handsome, more sexually attractive in the comfort of his own home.

I felt like a child, still living at home with my mom, while he was in this place all to himself.

What have I gotten myself into?

"Hi" I said, standing in front of him, his eyes scanning me from head to toe.

"Hey" he breathed, as he wrapped me in his arms. My face pressed against his bare chest. I felt my insides melt as his muscles enveloped me.

"Um, I brought some snacks, and some wine," I said once he released me, holding up the canvas shopping bag I had hitched over my shoulder. He took the bag like a gentleman, placing it on the side unit in the hallway after closing the door behind me.

My eyes widened as I took in the high ceilings, the modern spacious, almost fully open plan layout of the ground floor. There was an open fire in the living room. I could feel its warmth radiating from where I stood.

"Effy…" he purred, his body behind my back, his mouth against the nape of my neck. "You have no idea how hot you look"

My knees felt weak as his mouth planted tantalizing kisses along my collarbone, working his way up to my jawline, his mouth pressed to my ear. "I will be gentle with you," he whispered, his lips grazing my earlobe. "I know this is your first time"

I swallowed as he spun me around to face him, his chest pressed close against my breasts, his hands now placed on my buttocks. He drew his mouth closed to mine, allowing his words to tickle my lips, "I am going to make sure this is an experience you will never forget".

I made an involuntary whimper as he drew my body even closer to his, so that his erect member pressed against me. I tried to steady my breathing, tried not to let my anxiety set in. It has to go someday, may as well be with the crush as I had envisioned so many times in the past few months.

His tongue teased my lips. "Are you ready?" he asked, his voice almost inaudible. I nodded my head, unable to trust my voice. "Good, because I want you so fucking much"

In one swift motion he swept my feet from beneath me, carrying me to his living room, laying me down on the floor in front of the fire. Blankets upon blankets had been scattered on the floor, with throw cushions dotted around to make it more comfortable.

I squealed a little as his hand slid between my thighs, toying with my new lace underwear underneath my skirt. "We can stop if you want to?" he murmured, without removing his hand, cupping my smooth and now damp heat.

I shook my head, smelling the mint toothpaste on his breath as he spoke. "I want to, Josh." I declared in a husky voice, a small smile playing on his lips as he leaned forward.

"I want you," he said, his hands grasping my underwear, hearing it rip as he yanked at it, feeling the fabric give way in his grasp.

There was no build-up, no teasing, just his deep, passionate kisses as he positioned his tip against my entrance, inserting it inside of me. My core was on fire, as the burning sensation spread an uncomfortable heat through my body. At one point I thought I was going to rip.

"Relax," he kept repeating, thrusting, "Just allow yourself to enjoy it," he moaned, feeling the resistance give way,

He moaned as he thrust through the resistance. I felt something snap, as his entire shaft was now inside me. A white-hot searing pain surged through my core. I cried out, my nails dug into his back.

He did not stop, as I thought he might have. "It will pass soon Ef," he whispered as his hips continued to drive against mine. I did not doubt him, but it had taken a while for the pain to subdue.

When it did, it was replaced by a pleasure I had never experienced before, this urgency to release this build-up of pressure that was bottled up inside me, like an active volcano waiting to erupt. Within moments I caved to the sensations, unable to hold back the flood of ecstasy any longer. My body convulsed as his name rolled off my tongue in a loud cry. My heat pulsed around his member as his own guttural moan broke out. "Next time, it won't hurt so much," he whispered, as he crushed his lips against mine.

As he pulled out, I felt hot liquid seep between my legs. I heard the snap of the condom being taken off. "It's okay, it's only a small bit of blood," he said, pecking me on the forehead. "A bath will stop you from feeling too sore."

I did not even register his words after he had said 'next time', feeling my heart flutter at those words, relieving me from my anxiety and removing my doubts that he would ditch me.

As he helped me into his bath upstairs, moments later, I knew then there this was more than a crush. I loved him. I knew I had reserved my virginity for him, as if this was how it was all along. It was Fate.

I could not picture a better way or a better person to lose my virginity to.

It baffled me why Alice held such a strong dislike for him, underneath his rebellious persona lay a kind and empathetic soul. She just refused to see it.

Alice

I paced the house nervously, unable to settle on the book I had been trying to read to distract my thoughts. Now, as I stared at my phone screen, it was the dreaded time to get ready.

As I stepped in the shower, I allowed the thick billows of steam to embrace me, the aroma of lavender filled my lungs as I tried to take deep breaths. Meticulously going over the plan Effy had formulated.

My mystery date was going to knock on my door at seven, though in her text she had not revealed whom my date was.

I needed to be ready in the next hour and a half, before whoever my date was would arrive. Then the limo is going to pick us both up from my house at seven o'clock. Where Effy and Josh would already be inside, waiting for us to attend the Soirée together.

I missed our routine, Effy's and mine: getting ready together at one of our houses, checking each other's outfits with immense scrutiny, choosing accessories that would go well with what we were wearing. Applying each other's make-up, fixing each other's hair.

All while sipping on pre-drinks, which were a bottle of wine or some mixers, whatever we could smuggle without our parents noticing. Where we would dance away any nerves to party-vibe music. It has always been our tradition.

Now though, she had organized everything because she had planned to spend as much time as she could with Josh, disregarding our tradition. It stung, knowing that my company now comes in second place to *Josh*.

It should not have come as a surprise, her life now orientated around him, making herself available for his every whim.

I felt jealous, not because she was with Josh, but because she had a boyfriend, because she was so caught up in this 'whirlwind romance' that she had forgotten about me. Her best friend. I longed for her to find happiness, and for a moment, she had. However, I could not shake the feeling that her joy would be short-lived. We had both watched it play out, many times over the years, the girl always ended up heartbroken. I did not want that Fate for my best friend.

Anxiety bubbled in the pit of my stomach as I watched my mother try to tame my fiery and unruly mass of copper curls into a chignon bun, leaving a few curls loose to frame my face. "I'm sorry I can not see you leave in the Limousine" she had apologized as she put in the last few pins to hold it all in place.

"Make sure you take some photos," she said, kissing my forehead as she left for her night shift. I nodded in response, knowing how guilty she felt for not being around as much as she wanted to be. Mom had been working as many shifts as she could just to make ends meet. I had even picked up a weekend job just so that I could chip in. I felt guilty for still living here and for relying on her as if I was still a child.

I glanced at my phone, as a message notification popped up:

18:15 - Effy: *slight change of plan, all thx 2 my mom! Ne way, I will meet u all @ prom.*

I squinted at the message, checking I had read it right: I was going to be alone in a limo with two guys, one I did not know, and Josh.

My heart sank even further, and my stomach twisted into more knots as I studied myself in the mirror. Admiring Effy's handiwork, her inexplicable taste and eye for detail.

The dress she had picked out was slim and elegant. Deep burgundy in color, hugging my curves and pooling around my ankles. Effy knew my style, knew what would work with my pale freckled complexion and my ginger hair. Even though she was now wearing more daring ensembles, she still knew what length of dress I would feel comfortable in. The more covered up, the better.

"You look-" the voice gasped. "You look so much like her, my first vessel," she added. We both stared at my reflection in the full-length mirror.

I shut her out, apologizing, explaining how important it was to be in control of her tonight. The necessity of keeping her prisoner inside my head, to ensure my secret I had been harboring for my entire life would not be revealed tonight.

I made my way downstairs, the matching burgundy clutch bag and gold heels in one hand, and the golden accessories she had given to me in the other. I used the small mirror in the hallway to put in the gold drop earrings, and was just putting the necklace on, with infuriating difficulty, when there was a knock at the door.

Startling me, causing me to drop the damned thing on the floor, the heart-shaped pendant slid off the chain. It was impossible to find on the soft-pile carpet. *Shit!*

I swung open the door, my words caught in my throat when I realized who it was standing before me.

"Josh?"

Josh

This was my opportunity, the only one that had opened since getting with Effy. The darkness within me had hoped that by taking her best friend, it would have gotten us closer to Alice, but if anything, it had distanced us further.

I had become distracted by her. I was developing genuine feelings for her, but my shadow was still obsessed with Alice. *"We must have her,"* he growled. His desire was insatiable.

Before his infatuation with Alice, all he wanted was sex. Lots of it, enjoying taking the virtues of each girl. Demanding a new playmate every few months, one of his own choosing, so when he had chosen Effy, I had been excited, yet cautious.

I had always found her attractive. With her slim figure, blonde hair, angelic face, always looking innocent and charming. I found her more interesting without the make-up and the clothes, yet with them she was tantalizing and sexy.

That was until he became gripped with his urge for Alice.

Over the course of the three weeks, I imagined a potential future with Effy. But Asmodeus, the shadow that loomed within me, had other ideas. His plan, should he succeed, would shatter all these notions of a future with Effy, should she ever find out.

He had canceled the limo when he had read her text message, explaining the change of plans. He was buzzing, knowing this opportunity to get Alice alone may not present itself again. I had sent a text out to Alice's date, Max, a friend of mine from the village football team. Lying to him about the canceled limo, I told him to make his own way to the Soirée where we would meet outside.

Asmodeus guided my feet to her house, I begged him to reconsider his actions, to reason with him, but he was not listening to me.

I felt his lust stirring beneath my skin, as he used my eyes to scan her curvaceous body, lingering on her breasts as his desire burned, before reaching her face. Her eyebrows were knitted together in confusion as a scowl spread across her face.

'Josh?' she asked, glancing at the clock over her shoulder. "You're early... Where is the limo? Where is Effy... and my date?"

I was unable to reply, *he* had taken over, slamming the door shut, he took hold of her shoulders and slammed her against the wall.

I tried to block it out, to not be a witness of what was to come, trying to detach myself from the situation that was unfolding before me. Alice would not know the difference, that It was not I who was carrying out this vile deed. All she would see was my face. Feel my body pressed against hers, my hands as they pinned her wrists above her head against the wall.

I felt powerless against him, knowing that there was nothing I could do to stop him. Once he had control of me, he would only relinquish his power once he had used my body for his intended purpose. *To capture and kill Alice Bowers.*

Alice

My heart was frantic, my eyes wild. I knew Josh did not like to take no for an answer, but never had I thought he would have resulted in this.

"Josh," I cried, "please!" My words had fallen on deaf ears. His face was determined, angry even.

"Where is she?" his voice snarled; small specks of spit landed on my face.

"Who?" I asked, confused. "Effy?" He snarled in response, huffing as if I was stupid, squeezing my wrists tight above my head. "I don't know where she is, she just told me plans changed because of her mom"

He gripped both my wrists in one of his hands, while the other closed in around my throat, pressing against my windpipe.

"Help!" called to her. *"Please help me!"* I begged her, as I felt lightheaded and giddy. She did not stir, did not come forward, even though I could still feel her there, hiding in the shadows.

"Josh!" I cried, "what are you doing?"

His mouth curled up into a menacing snarl, "where is that bitch inside you?" My eyes snapped open in fear, noticing the black orbs for eyes penetrating my own. How does he know about her?

I shook my head, feigning innocence, hoping this would help my cause. "I don't know what you are talking about," I lied. "Josh, have you been drinking? Please Josh, please let me go... I won't say anything about this...to anyone... Please...Please stop."

"Lying bitch" he spat. I could smell it then, the alcohol in his breath, noticing the slight slur in his voice. "You are both lying bitches. She has three seconds to surface, to surrender herself to me"

He muttered something under his breath, something incomprehensible, in another language, *"tu nunc sub imperio meo es, eam mihi dona aut corpus tuum et virtutem tuam"* his eyes never left mine.

He let go of my wrists once he had stopped his mutterings. I tried to attack him, willing my hands to push him away from me, but they refused to move. I realized then, whatever he had said, had paralyzed me, controlled my every move. Whatever Josh was, it was not human. It was only then that I remembered her words *"Demon"*.

Shit.

He pushed me to the ground, pressing his hands down on my shoulders. My panic and fear were bubbling inside of me, I tried to scream, to wriggle out from his grasp. I had no way of defending myself unless she came forward.

"Fucking do something!" I yelled at her, *"before he goes any further"* I felt her refusal stab me like a knife to the heart. She would not suppress her stubbornness, her unwillingness to prevent this from happening to me.

All I got in response was her silence.

The sound of the zipper of his suit pants being undone, the feel of his hands snaking their way under my dress made my stomach churn. My blood ran cold, my head spinning from oxygen deprivation as his other hand returned once again to my neck.

This couldn't be happening.

She could not forsake me now, in my time of need; when only she held the power to stop this, whether by force or by her surrender.

She refused to help. She was prepared, willing even, to sacrifice my body, to allow him to steal my virtue, to protect herself.

Time seemed to freeze, as did my body, all that could be heard was the persistent sound of the minute hand as it worked its way around the clock's face. Tick, tick, tick, tick.

I tried to concentrate on the sound, trying to remove myself from what was happening, as I felt his hand tear away my underwear, as easily as breaking a spider's web. Exposing my delicate flower to his touch.

Please don't let this happen!

SEVEN

I am referenced to by many names throughout the various religions and cultures that have transcended across the Earth throughout time. Such as 'The Almighty', 'The Savior', 'The Creator of Life' but my favorite was 'The Divine'.

Some scriptures I find oversimplify my abilities, while others over-complicate them. Some believe there are multiple ethereal beings like me, several gods, each one having a purpose.

Perhaps this is easier than explaining my multiple personalities.

Many ask how I can be called righteous when I allow evil to corrupt the world, to allow my innocent creations to suffer needlessly. Why do I not intervene when natural disasters kill innocent people and cause species to become extinct?

It is straightforward when you think about it - balance and sustainability.

Earth functions on a precarious equilibrium of good and evil. Once, I harbored this balance, the good and evil in me; my many personalities. Although I had not intended to create one of the evilest creatures to grace the Earth, it happened, like two sides to a coin.

When I created angels, formed from each of my personalities; righteous, brave, intelligent, resilient, loving. They took heed of who their master, their creator, was.

"I am The Divine, but you can also call me Freyja."

Yet from the ashes of their creation, coiled from the deepest and darkest part of my existence that I refused to admit I held, the Devil; Lucifer, was born.

Alice

His hands were planted on either side of my head, his lifeless black eyes locked onto mine. I refused to accept this was happening as his manhood brushed against my slit.

As he held me down, my wrists now in his vice-like grip, his knees pushed my legs outwards. He was strong, too strong, and I was paralyzed. He had done something to me that had made me incapable of controlling my body.

All I could do was scream at her, call her name in helplessness *"Freyja, please don't let this happen!"*

My words echoed in my mind. I was on my own, despite her still being there. She was allowing this to happen.

All I could feel was my weakness, my vulnerability.

I closed my eyes, tried not to let myself feel what was happening, what he was doing to me. But he had released some of this anesthetic hold he had on me. I tried to free myself, tried to push away from him, using the heels of my feet to dig into the ground, but his hands grasped hold of my dress, pulling me back towards him.

The fabric was torn in the struggle, but I was no match for him without her powers. His muscular physique overpowered me. He forced his shaft into me, hard. I exploded in unbearable pain. I tasted blood, realizing I had bitten my tongue as I had cried out.

My whole body was burning, from my slit outwards, the resistance that had objected to his manhood being inside me had shattered. My hymen had been torn by his member. It was official; I was no longer a virgin.

Every thrust brought tears to my eyes as the pain ripped through my body. My inner walls tightened around him, rejecting his every move. I felt him push through it regardless.

I opened my eyes, seeing his satisfied smirk, feeling sick as he groaned at his release. I felt it as his seed left his body, filling my sore, aching entrance. I whimpered as he withdrew from me. A small menacing chuckle escaped him.

"You should have chosen the easy way, Alice."

He left me lying there, cold, abused, broken on the floor. This entire ordeal had lasted ten minutes, but it felt like it would never end. I had been trapped in my personal Hell; with a demon she had warned me to stay away from.

I waited until I heard the door slam shut in his wake, too frozen with fear, too embarrassed, too ashamed to move while I was still in his presence.

Silent tears rolled down my eyes as I struggled to get to my feet, seeing my reflection in the mirror. My hair was ruined, my mascara smudged, streaks of it from my tears ran down my face. My lipstick had been wiped across my face by his forced kisses. I stared at myself in a trance, my mind reliving the entire ordeal, until the nausea overtook me, tasting the bile in the back of my throat.

The climb up the stairs to the bathroom was like ascending a treacherous mountain. My legs were heavy and my knees weak. Stumbling several times as my cumbersome gait led me to the bathroom, only just making it to the toilet in time to vomit. My hands trembled as I reached for the tissue, my vision still blurry from my tears.

Hurriedly I locked the door, before climbing into the shower, turning it on. Letting the water cascade over me, as I sat on the floor of the cubicle, still dressed.

I was hoping it would wash away his touch. Hoping it would wash away my shame. Wishing that this had all just been a nightmare that I would wake up from soon. I pinched myself, just to check, but what had happened was real.

What Josh had done to me was real.

I felt dirty, used. He had stolen my virtue, my virginity. That was something that should never have been taken by force. I had held onto it, waiting to offer it to the right person at the right time.

I could feel the blood seeping from between my legs, could see it mixing with the water as it flowed to the drain. I cried. *How could I have let this happen? How could she have let this happen?*

My actions were automatic, verging on robotic, as I towel dried myself and put on clean pajamas. Covering myself in the oldest and biggest of them all. I tucked myself into bed and laid gazing at the ceiling. Allowing all my thoughts to swirl around my head, dizzying and disorientating. Asking questions, I did not know the answers to, remembering every tiny detail and trying to lay blame. Blaming him, and then blaming myself for being so pathetic and weak.

Tears flowed like a burst dam, as my sobs rattled my whole body, until I succumbed to a disturbed, unsettled slumber.

In my dream, I was falling. My arms flailing, trying to find anything to grasp hold of.

As I continued to fall deeper and deeper. Visions of Josh's smirking face loomed over me, his demonic, beady black eyes flaring at me. Sucking out my soul as he tore at my insides. My screams, begging, pleading with him were drowned by his sadistic laugh that was echoing in my ears.

All I could see was his smug face. Hearing those final words, *"you should have chosen the easy way Alice."*

Freyja

I could swap from vessel to vessel as and when I wanted, unlike my angels, who had to stay with that vessel until their life had ended. They could flit between possession and their ethereal form, but they could not enter another human body.

Sadly, the same could not be said for Lucifer's abominations - demons.

For some of them I flitted, enjoying the happier parts of their lives, but others I had become invested in the paths they had chosen, wondering if they would fulfill the Fates they were predestined to live, or if their choices had veered them along the wrong path.

But those fatalities were not on my conscience. My vessel Christopher was destined for great things, accompanied by his beloved wife, Selene. That was until Lucifer came along.

He had wrangled his way into Selene's subconsciousness. In his attempt to get to me, even I had not known it.

My heart dropped and my jaw hung open in disbelief as he coerced her into taking the life of her own husband, her lover, her savior.

He took great pleasure in twisting things, destroying things, especially toying with human lives, poking and prodding them the way an inquisitive child would play with a worm in the garden.

"What was the point of humans, if not for my personal entertainment?" he had asked me once. It was the reason we were not compatible. It was the reason he was in this infinite pursuit of me. I would never surrender to him. We had one thing in common, though: *we were drawn to Power*, like a moth to a flame or an addict to drugs, the hunger, the strife to become more powerful, to be desired and feared above all others.

I felt an indescribable surge of power, surpassing the limits of human understanding. But that feeling was lost on me in my ethereal form. I needed a human to feel my power course through their veins. I hoped that one day, I would feel it, like thousands of fireworks erupting all over their body, consuming me.

Yet the burden of such strength and power could be too much to bear.

It came with a responsibility that I had never imagined or prepared for. My absence, my lack of support, left Alice vulnerable and feeble. I knew I should have prevented what happened to her, but my self-preservation prevailed. Instead I had stripped of her own strength to protect mine.

This human would want to seek revenge one day, and I would be more than happy to oblige.

$$\clubsuit$$

Alice

The moment I opened my eyes, I knew it had not been a nightmare.

I was unable to lift my head off the pillow, despite the blinding morning sun filtering through the room. I had already silenced my alarm once by throwing it across the room, but now as it was ringing out again, louder this time. It was giving me my final wake-up call before I would be late for my shift. It was at this moment I regretted catapulting the thing across the room.

I winced in pain as I tried to move, as every muscle in my body cried in protest. Every limb felt like they were made of lead, too heavy and cumbersome to move. My whole body was in agony, feeling battered and bruised. Sore and aching, as if I had been on the losing end of a boxing match.

My head felt too heavy on my shoulders as I shifted my weight, trying to get up from my bed to reach my damned alarm clock that was still shrilling in the far corner of my room.

I peeled the duvet from my body, feeling a dampness between my thighs that was not there. I tried to swing my legs off the bed, my core was on fire, my thigh muscles screamed with the movement.

That was when I saw it, a large dark red-brown stain across the crotch of my pajamas. It had seeped through and puddled underneath me, ruining the fitted sheet and duvet covers. I groaned, not just because I was in pain. How was I going to explain this to my mom?

Images of his assault on my body came crashing through me like violent, tsunami-scale waves. Unable to think of anything else other than him pinning me against the wall, against the floor, seeing the anger, the sheer determination on his face as his knees forced my legs wider. Feeling myself screaming and writhing in pain as he violated me. Every thrust, every grunt, forever imprinted. Forever haunted by his laugh once the deed had been done.

My chest tightened and my lungs burned as I tried to gasp for air. I was drowning in my fear. The walls were closing in; the floor was spinning. Disoriented and dizzy, my brain pounded as his cackle continued to reverberate inside my skull. The nausea hit me without warning and I vomited all over myself.

The alarm clock was still ringing. Its shrill, piercing sound was the only thing that had kept me grounded, something that was from reality that prevented me from falling any deeper into my horrific memory.

The rational part of my brain knew I needed to clean myself up, to pull myself together, but my body refused to move and my mind kept repeating the questions I did not have the answers to. Why did he do this to me? Why didn't Freya stop him?

In my mind I thought that if I disposed of everything from yesterday, anything that might trigger flashbacks, I would feel better. Including Effy's dress.

I was wrong.

I gathered up the sodden and tattered mass that was the dress, dumped beside my wardrobe, looking like a ball of gum that had been chewed up and spat back out. I felt the darkness overwhelm me.

I was not sure how long I had been curled on the floor in the fetal position, hugging the sodden dress, but the sound of the front door opening, and the distinct sound of my mother shuffling around downstairs after returning from her night shift flipped a switch in my mind.

I have to move. Now.

I moved automatically, as if I was in autopilot mode. Yanking the bedding free from my bed, ignoring the roaring pain that surged through every part of my body and replacing it with fresh bedding that still smelled of the jasmine and honeysuckle laundry detergent my mom always used. I gathered up the dress and stripped my stained pajamas, balling them up in the bedding and unceremoniously shoving them in an old gym bag.

Its actual use had been for sleepovers at Effy's house, it had been months since I had used it. Wrappers littered the inside of the bag and a couple of old DVDs rattled around, remnants from the last time I had slept over at Effy's. It was the night after her mom had tried to commit suicide. I had gone to her in her time of need, ladened with cheesy films and snacks to help her shelter her younger brother from the reality of her mother's actions. I had been her shoulder to cry on, and her jester to cheer her up.

A pang of sadness flooded me, I missed her, though it was clear she did not miss me. A bitter taste lingered in my mouth as my anger swelled in my chest. We were like strangers now, distant and cold.

I tugged at the zipper, silently cursing as it buckled under strain of its bulging contents. The seams were at breaking point and the handles left deep grooves in my hand as I carried it over to my wardrobe.

It was bursting at the seams and the zip looked like it would break at any given moment, but for now it would have to do. I stowed it in the back of my wardrobe, with the intent to dispose of them when my mom was next at work.

I forced myself into the shower, allowing the hot water to cascade over my face, over my pained body, noticing bruises forming on my wrists and inner thighs. I allowed my tears to flow, allowing them to be washed away by the running water. Watching as the water escaped down the drain, wishing that my memories would slip away with them.

"You are a strong, independent woman," Freya whispered to me, her words soft and gentle.

"Fuck off," I muttered aloud, blocking her out.

She did not get to comfort me, not when she could have prevented any of it from happening. *She is The-Fucking-Divine! She has the power to smite him where he stood yet she let it happen!*

I was still in the shower, allowing the steamy jets of water to lash against my body, trying to focus only on the sprays of water touching my skin, not his hands. Trying to forget his forceful knees spreading my thighs apart, forget his manhood violating me, forcing its way inside my objecting core, when there was a faint knocking at the door.

I bit down on my bottom lip, stifling my sobs, warning myself over and over again. *Do. Not. Cry.*

EIGHT

I am a mother, I knew instantly when something was wrong. From the moment she was born it had become second nature to know when my daughter needed me. So I knew there was something wrong as soon as I noticed the absence of her sing-song voice that usually drowned out the sound of the shower.

Instead, soft whimpers that she thought I was unable to hear, accompanied her morning shower. With each small sniff, a small piece of my heart broke. I wanted to comfort her, to right the wrongs, to shelter her from whatever it was that upset her.

"Alice, honey? Are you okay?" I asked, gently knocking on the door for the second time. There was no response, as she turned off the shower. Behind the door the soft padding of her bare feet on the tiles could be heard, the scuffling of toiletry bottles as she put them back in their place.

I heard her sigh, as the lock on the door clicked, moments before the door swung open. Something was definitely wrong.

Alice looked awful, her porcelain skin had a sickly, jaundice hue which made her red, swollen eyes look more severe and prominent. She refused to make eye contact, instead keeping her eyes on her knuckles that had gone white under the tight grip that she held on her towel.

"Oh, Alice, honey," I cooed, wrapping my arms around her, holding her tightly against me. I felt her stiffen beneath my touch. "Sweetheart, what's wrong?"

She shook her head, stepping backwards. "Nothing, I'm fine." Her voice was small and quiet. Her chin tucked into her neck, her eyes fixed to the floor.

I stared at her, giving her that look, all mothers do it. It's the look that says, 'I'm here for you, you can tell me anything.' But the silence continued to stretch between us.

"Mom, I'm fine!" She gasped, storming away into her bedroom, leaving wet footprints on the plush beige carpet. A memory flooded my mind, our last vacation as a complete family unit, months before Adam was killed. My heart stopped for a moment, as I recalled their wet footprints, side by side, in the soft white sand.

My breath caught in my throat, I missed him. He has been dead over ten years, but the pain of losing him was still fresh and raw.

The bedroom door slammed shut, snapping me out of my reverie. My shoulders slumped as I admitted defeat. I missed the days she would crumple in my arms and pour her heart out to me, the days where she needed me to reassure her as my hand smoothed the small of her back.

Those days are long gone now.

I walked past her room, intending to flop onto my own bed and sleep after my draining night shift at the hospital. My feet ached and my back hurt, but hearing her still sniffling, banging and crashing around behind her shut door.

Suddenly I found myself at her door, my hand knocking frantically against the white-glossy wood. "Alice, what the hell is wrong?" My voice was harsh and demanding, I did not sound like myself. I had become the stubborn mama bear who would not leave without answers.

"Alice Elizabeth Bowers. I demand you open this door." Nothing, just infuriating silence, so quiet I could hear the ticking of the minute hand on the clock downstairs in the hallway. "I just saw Effy on my way in, she was concerned about you. She said you didn't go to the party last night. If I'm honest she looked rather pissed-"

The door swung open, revealing her dressed in baggy pajamas several sizes too big, a thick robe wrapped around her with the hood pulled up.

"She's not downstairs is she?" Alice asked hurriedly. It clicked, that was the problem. They had yet another argument. It had to be something big, *perhaps Effy's new boyfriend?*

"No," I replied, my voice softening, I watched her head slowly bow, her shoulders relaxed slightly as she shuffled back to her bed. "Do you want to tell me what happened?"

Her eyes flew up at me, her lips trembled as she pressed them together. She opened her mouth as if she was going to say something, before shutting it tightly once more.

"I just... I don't feel well." Her voice was but a whisper. "I wasn't well last night, that's-that's why I didn't go." Alice looked uncomfortable, "I should have called her, but-"

"Is that what you have fallen out about? Over a party?" I asked, sitting beside her on the bed, the soft mattress sunk beneath my weight, like a giant fluffy cloud.

Alice shifted slightly and when I reached for her hand she flinched and drew it back quickly. My eyes narrowed. "Alice, I'm trying to help here."

"I don't need your help mom. Please, just go."

I recoiled at her sharp tone, a fierce fire glinted in her eyes. Something more serious was going on, there was something she was not telling me.

"Is that what you want?" I asked, getting to my feet, hoping that she was not too old for reverse psychology to work. I took several steps towards her door, slowly accepting that she was not going to say anything further with each step.

I sighed, "you know where I am if you want to talk." I said, looking over my shoulder as I opened her door.

"Thank you, mom," she whispered, her voice so quiet I had barely heard it. I spun on my heel, my eyes sweeping over her as she wrapped her arms around her knees protectively. She tried to crack a smile, I could tell it was forced, but I smiled back.

"I love you, Alice," I murmured. "I am always here if you want to talk about anything, okay?"

She nodded slowly, swiping the back of her hand across her eyes. "I know mom..." she took a deep breath, "I love you too."

I had fallen into a restless sleep, my worried mind running through scenarios that could be going on in her life. *Was it her part-time job? Was it too much with college? Was she struggling in college? Had she and Effy fallen out about something more serious?*

All day I waited for her to approach me, to tell me what was wrong, but she stayed in her room all day. She had refused her favorite meal and even turned her nose up at a steaming hot mug of cocoa.

I glanced at the clock; time to go to work again.

I made myself a sandwich to take to work, and made one for Alice too, but when I had gone up to her room, she was asleep, curled tightly in the fetal position, the bedding swaddled her like a giant cocoon.

The sinking feeling returned, as I placed the sandwich and glass of water on the top of her bedside drawers. I frowned as I looked at her sleep, noticing the scrunched up face, almost contorted in pain.

What is going on with her? What is my daughter hiding from me?

☘

I knew Cole was trouble when I met him. Our friendship had been built out of necessity rather than by choice.

Some would say Fate had brought us together, that our meeting in a dark alley behind a popular fast-food restaurant had been predestined to happen. Personally, I thought it was just coincidental. Our situations were similar; Neither of us had anywhere to go, both of us were trying to go about surviving the streets.

To this day, neither of us has ever admitted to each other what our reasons were for being in that alley on those nights, we both had our secrets, and we were both determined to keep it that way.

There in that alley, we had stuck together for survival. He refused to let me out of his sight. He had welcomed me into his company; he gave me a choice to stick with him for survival. He took me under his wing, almost like he had adopted me as his younger sister, taking on the responsibility of keeping me safe and fed.

It was now several months on from that day, the day that had changed my life. We were in sync with one another, as if we had known each other our whole lives, we knew things about each other that no one else did.

Not long after meeting, we discovered an abandoned warehouse not too far from the city. It was somewhere we could stay undetected and out of the blistering winter that was upon us, coming in thick and fast. There was no running water or electricity, but it had walls and a roof. It was enough to keep us sheltered from the treacherous elements.

At the very top of the warehouse, we discovered a small office, which was where we set up our squatter's camp. Using stolen candles from a nearby shop to provide us with a little light, it was enough to keep us going for now. This, for now, was our makeshift home.

Near the warehouse was a very upmarket, posh, residential estate. Neat white fences lined their immaculate rectangle gardens. The scent of the freshly mown lawns and blooming flowers tickled my nostrils as my eyes were mesmerized by the vibrant colors each garden held. Reds and purples, oranges and yellows, not a weed in sight. Each house looked like a duplicate of the last. Crisp white paint, clean window sills, and each garden pruned to perfection.

Personally, I found great comfort in wandering their streets, in the shadows of late evening, their houses lit up with signs of life, TVs flickering, fish tanks glowing. Especially now, in the run-up to Christmas.

It is easy, when you are on the streets, to forget what day or month it is, they all seem to drag on, a blur, each day a struggle to survive. But from this little estate, the evidence was clear from the way each house was decorated with twinkling multi-color lights, and the way their ornamental garden trees had also been decorated in the festive spirit.

Candy canes and small plastic baubles hanging on the branches, placed to the point of perfectionism, not too cluttered and not too sparse. I reached out to one ornament; it was that of a tiny angel, white with a shock of gold for the hair and glitter on the wings and halo.

It was a stark difference from the flamboyant and glowing baubles and decorations that my parents would exhibit if they were not inebriated. The red and gold foil ceiling decorations that would succumb to gravity, and fall to the floor and the decades-old glass fairy lights that were now considered fire hazards.

I turned on my heel, the glorious waft of baked goods, cinnamon rolls, gingerbread, and fresh loaves of bread filling the air. The scent alone made my mouth water and stomach grumble. The angel clutched tightly in my hand.

It was easy for me to succumb to fantasy, wandering these streets, imagining what life would be like inside one of these homes. But there are reminders, no matter how big or small, like the stab of hunger on an empty stomach that would wake me out of my fantasy-world and prompt me to return to our makeshift home in the warehouse. Or as we referred to it, The Loft.

It was in this makeshift home we used whatever we could salvage to improve our living quarters, to make the best out of the situation we were in. Trying to cover the mold spores and dull gray paint that peeled off the walls with posters and photos that we had ripped out of our stolen magazines. Discarded newspapers littered the floor, alongside some rugs that had been rescued from landfill that would help take away the chill of the concrete floor.

We, well I, got most of our items like blankets, throws, pillows and even some items of clothing from the residents' bins of that estate nearby. Everyone was always so wasteful. Too quick to throw out items when they showed little wear or use. The coat and my ankle boots I wore had been discarded like trash, despite the designer labels. I was always the one to collect such items. Cole never wanted to go there.

His brow would crease, scowling if I even suggested he should come along with me one day. I assumed it may have been too difficult for him to return to this rundown warehouse after being among the rich, or it was too sad to be around those loving families in their homes while we were here with no one else other than each other to depend on.

The door to the loft swung open, creaking on its hinges, as Cole rented the loft. His cut nod to me was a signal, his silent way of saying "I'm not in the mood to talk".

I nodded back, giving him a faint smile of understanding, having learned the ability to sense his mood after months of living like this. If he was not in the mood to talk, I had to respect his silence.

It was hard becoming accustomed to his coldness at first, but sometimes I felt at peace in the silence that loomed over us. Able to continue living in my fantasy world. Only talking to him when he spoke to me first.

Cole, or the dark silhouette of him, was huddled over the two camping stoves. These were some of the few items I have salvaged; survivors from the fated destiny of the landfill. I had found these along with some other camping gear and sleeping bags discarded in the estate. Their previous owners must have discarded them when camping because "unfashionable" or when they had found out that camping was hard work without electricity and all the other luxuries they were accustomed to. For us, these items had made our survival that little easier.

The familiar scent of baked beans and blackened sausages lingered in the air. Taking me back to a time before Cole and I had stumbled upon the warehouse, where we had lived in a makeshift shanty town of tents and cardboard constructions on the outskirts of a different town. It was always loud and crowded.

The night was filled with snores, drunken conversations several decibels too high, fights over scraps of food or looted alcohol and drugs, anything they could score to keep them numb. It was there that I had learned how to make a living, how to survive.

I shook my head, trying to clear those memories, taking off my coat like the most prized possession and nestling into my sleeping bag and blankets. Musty smelling, but warm.

"I picked up some supplies," Cole muttered. By this he meant he went to the homeless shelter where food parcels were handed out and other items such as hats and scarves were also donated to be issued to us who are living rough. He hated going there, they always asked too many questions, forcing a cheery smile and a "let's be friends" attitude. I also hated it there.

"I would have come with you," I said as I snuggled deeper into my sleeping bag. My hand searched for Scruff. His one remaining ear bristled against my fingertips, and I instantly felt more relaxed knowing he was there.

"I tried to find you." Cole said, his voice held an icy chill. as his gaze pierced through the dark in my direction. The dim light of the candles marked him as nothing more than a shadow, as their wicks were drowned in the melted wax.

Moments passed with us just looking at each other through the darkness, neither of us moving. The tension in the atmosphere was palpable, as I realized I had missed the opportunity to meet him after work. Our chances of smuggling more supplies from his workplace and the shelter were better when there were two of us.

Instead, I had lingered too long in the housing estate, caught up with admiring the angel ornament I had stashed in my coat pocket. "Cole, I'm sor- "

"Don't. We have enough for now." He snapped. "Come. Eat."

We ate the sausages and beans in silence, not bothering to replace the candles, allowing the darkness to encompass us.

Freyja

I'm not sure what it was about her, about Alice. I grew bored with the monotony of human life, but living through her was fascinating.

Perhaps it was because she could channel my strength, my powers. Her heart overflowed with kindness and purity, mirroring my essence in human form.

Now though, I could feel her body was tainted as a darkness grew within her.

The seed of a demon.

I knew I could have prevented it from coming to be there in the first place, but there would have been another time, another opportunity where this would have arisen.

There was a bigger picture, a predestined plan, devised a millennium before she had even been born.

Lucifer's downfall was happening, right now, inside of her. The dark fetus inside her will destroy Lucifer, and all his demons, soon.

The irony that a creature with half of their blood would work against them, would lead to their ultimate demise was not lost on me.

I was not aware at the time of choosing her as my vessel that she would be the bearer of such a creature, would harbor such power. I had tried to leave her before she was attacked by him, Asmodeus.

That was when I discovered I was stuck here. Unable to release myself from her subconscious no matter how many times she willed it, no matter how many times she tried to expel me from her being.

The darkness that grew within her had held me captive.

Trapped inside a cell of my making.

By making her my *chosen* vessel, she had become my only vessel, my only entity.

We were now one.

NINE

"What are you doing?"

A timid voice, a whisper came from the slightest crack at the door frame.

Whipping my head around, I saw my mom peeking from behind the door, only her head and shoulders visible. Her usual smiley and warm face had soured, her face a puzzle of emotions I could not understand.

The Barbie doll fell from mid-air with a crash as her body fell through the air, her legs and arms colliding with various levels of neon pink walls and floor of her doll's house.

"Just playing," I replied, picking up the Barbie doll and brushing her hair.

"How many times have I told you" she whispered, tiptoeing a little further into my bedroom. Her bare feet were silent on the deep plush carpet.

I wanted to keep eye contact, maintain control and be defiant, but I lowered my head, so my gaze fell into my lap. "But I was just playing" I muttered, my voice audible over the voice in my head.

"Be strong, have no fear, I'm beside you. She is wrong, shed no tear, good is inside you" the voice kept repeating, song-like. A lullaby for only me to hear. The voice was soothing, calming and kind.

"Alice, listen, we need to talk" my mom said as she kneeled beside me. She seemed to struggle to be too close to me these days, like I was a monster or worse, *vegetables!*

My trail of thought distracted me, reminded me of the disgusting vegetables always served with every meal, mom always watching me, pointing out that they would make me big and strong! Their taste repulsed me, but the voice convinced me to eat them, mouthful at a time until they were gone. "Not so bad, were they?" mom would always ask, to which I would never reply.

"Alice, you know you should not do that" my mom said, taking the Barbie from my relaxed grasp. She admired it, turning it around, looking for something, before placing my barbie into the doll-size bed on the top floor of the dollhouse.

"Mom, I am just playing with Freyja,"

Her fingers froze, mid-tucking the doll under the pink and white crochet blanket that she had made for the dollhouse. Her body was stiff, like Barbie's.

"Freyja? Again," she hushed, whipping around to face me. "Alice, you must not play with Freyja anymore. She must leave you alone."

My eyes swept over her face, eyes deep green, like the color of seaweed we saw when we visited the beach in the summer. Her hair was brown and shiny, like slippery wet mud and her lips as red as the roses that used to grow in Nana Bowie's Garden. That was until she 'passed on' and papa Bowie could not look after them like she did, saying it used to upset him too much, so he dug them all up.

"Alice" my mom whispered, placing a tender hand on the side of my face "do you understand?"

I nodded, even though I did not understand at all. Freyja was my friend, she never bossed me around like Effy did, and there was no way I wanted her to leave me alone.

Her rose-red lips brushed against my forehead; I could feel her inhaling the fragrance of my apple shampoo. She seemed to relax a little, her body more human like that of a doll. "I love you Alice" she smiled, wrapping her arms around me.

I hugged her back, feeling the warmth of her body against the side of my face, both of us kneeling on the plush carpet.

When she had left a few moments later, I took the Barbie doll back out of the bed, wishing her to become animated, suspended alone in mid-air. I loved to admire her this way, the way her dress fluttered, and her hair swayed with the slightest movements.

I would have to try harder to keep Freyja a secret.

Isobel

The howls of the wind whipped through the empty warehouse, rattling the metal panels on the side of the building, the rusty chain-link fence groaning in agony, as the rain hammered on the metal roof. The storm was still yet to pass, and we were running out of food and candles.

Alone, and with weather like this, I could slip into my fantasy world, a world where my parents were different, better. They cared about me, looked after me and raised me how every parent should. Perhaps we would have lived in a house on that estate, a home to be proud of, where we would have guests who were not ashamed to be associated with us, who would grimace at the piles of dirty plates and stained upholstery. How the social workers never took me away from my parents after their many visits I will never understand, the last before my disappearance refusing to step any further than the hallway, tucking herself in small, not to touch the walls or using her hand to reopen the handle on her exit.

I still remember the way her nose was scrunched up, the putrid, rotten smell offensive to anyone, sickening despite my attempts to clean and mask the odor with sprays.

My life could have been so different if my parents had not been addicts. But they will never change, they tried and failed at every opportunity presented to them. I wondered if I was being punished, if my character was being tested. But the only person who can change, and has changed, is me.

I peered out the small window, seeing if I could spot Cole on his return from work. The window was too small and too high to look out of. It was much smaller than the TVs that hung in the houses in the estate nearby. Occupants inside, enchanted by them, sat in a trance-like state. Too absorbed in the moving images to notice the scrawny girl peeking through their window.

There was no sign of Cole, even though evening was more settling in, some street lights flickered to life. He was back by now. He had been working in a local restaurant as a 'pot wash' a couple of days a week, in cash. Untraceable.

It was measly pay for the grueling work, but Cole never complained. Even when he came home with sore and dry hands from using the harsh chemicals used to clean the plates for hours at a time.

I sighed. I wanted to help, but there weren't many places wanting to hire a young girl, to pay cash and not ask questions. Questions I did not want to tell them; my living arrangements, parents, *my name.*

I had a way of making money, but I did not want to resort to *that* again. The thought sent a shiver through my body, my stomach tightening into knots.

The only way I could help was to go to the shelter to collect some more supplies, there would be more available and more on offer given the weather outside.

I pulled on a denim jacket; scruffy, stained and several sizes too big. It was a donated item from the shelter, as there was no way I could wear any of the items I had scavenged from the estate. Not only was it asking for trouble, but I also did not want anyone else to go there. I felt protective and possessive of that area, like it was my sanctuary.

Marching through the downpour, I focused on putting one foot in front of the other, forcing myself to walk toward the shelter. Stealing a quick glance over my shoulder, I could see the housing estate, it had been over two weeks since I had been there last. Cole did not like me going there too often, and I did not want to be another reason to darken his mood further.

As I pushed forward, towards the city center, the scenery looked more gritty, more familiar. This city center was like any others I had been to. Graffiti scribbled on buildings, bus shelters and boards over the windows of vacant shops. Glass debris crunching under my too small and battered trainers.

The shelter was in the church's basement lodged in the very heart of the city, it would be quicker to walk through the alleys and back streets to get there, but being alone at this time, I was not brave enough to wander there. So, I stuck to the main roads, lit up by neon shop fronts and a couple of scattered streetlights. It added an extra ten to fifteen minutes on the journey, but it gave me time to reflect on Cole.

These past few weeks he had been in one of his dark moods, battling with his inner demons more than before. He would come back to the loft after his long shifts, tired, smelling like a mixture of grease and pine-fresh dish soap, and unmoving from his sleeping bag.

We had spoke no more than a few words to each other; I did not know whether I should try to engage him in conversation or remain silent. It had been almost six months since we found this warehouse, and almost eight months since we agreed to stick together for survival. Yet I still never knew the correct way to react when he was like this, though I always had an inkling that his sour mood was because of me.

There was nothing romantic about our relationship, I'm sure he only saw me as a kid-sister, as he must have been around at least three, maybe four years my senior. He must have felt compelled to help me, and to continue to help me.

Perhaps I am the reason for his bad moods?
Perhaps I am too much of a burden for him to bear.

TEN

Emily

I needed sleep, my body was tense and achy from my night shift, but my mind would not settle. Worry and concern for Alice spun like a whirlpool in my head. I was slipping in and out of restless sleep.

I was running. The hallway seemed to stretch forever. The more I ran, the longer it became. Alice's sobs grew louder, but I could not reach her. The bathroom door opened and I saw her withdrawn face, her blotchy red eyes. I held out my hand to reach her.

Suddenly I was falling through darkness. My hands clutching at thin air, feeling the wisps of it flutter between my fingers.

The end was coming, even though I could not see it. My momentum was rapid, plummeting to the ground that I could feel getting closer.

The sound of an alarm pierced my dream.

My eyes snapped open, my blurry vision adjusting to the familiarity of my surroundings: the crisp white walls dotted with family photographs, the hazy sunlight filtering through the blinds, the smell of the bedding I had cocooned myself in.

It had just been a dream, a manifestation of my concern. Yet my heart was pounding erratically in my chest. A gray cloud of worry was surrounding my brain.

Alice.

Her alarm was still echoing down the hall, followed by the sounds of frantic footsteps and the crashing of her drawers.

"Shit I'm going to be late." I heard Alice mutter as she hurried past my bedroom door, her steps thundered down the stairs. It took a few moments for my brain to register that she was going to work.

Launching myself out of bed and pulling my door open wide, I startled her as she stood on the top of the stairs.

Dressed in her work uniform, a dark navy polo top with a small embroidered logo that said 'J R News' in white, and a pair of black trousers. I smiled at her, watching her as she tied her copper curls into a loose ponytail.

Her face was pale and gaunt, and I noticed some bruising on her arms. Her eyes flashed towards me, shoving on her jacket to cover them. "I'm sorry I woke you," she said hurriedly, taking off down the stairs quicker than I could stop her.

Where had those bruises come from?

As I followed her, I caught a glimpse of myself in the mirror, my own orange curls resembled a bird's nest on top of my head, dark shadows formed under my eyes. I was still in my disheveled and creased clothes from the day before. I looked as awful as I felt.

The distinct sounds of plates clattering and cutlery rattling came from the kitchen. As I neared, I held my breath, praying not to start an argument.

"How are you feeling today?" I asked, watching her pour the carton of orange juice into a glass and taking a sip to delay her reply. Her hands were slightly trembling.

"I...um- I have to go," she mumbled, downing the last of her drink and placing the glass on the side.

"Alice, do you really think you should go in today? You still don't look-"

"I'm fine mom!" she snapped, pushing past me, her footsteps echoed in my skull as she walked to the door. She hastily slipped her feet into a pair of trainers and scooped up her old gym bag from the floor.

I scowled, I could not remember the last time she had used it, it looked full and heavy. "What's in the bag?" I asked, moving closer to her.

Without another word she left, slamming the door behind her.

How had she gotten those bruises?

Something else niggled in my brain as my eyes slowly dropped as I stretched across the sofa, too tired to traipse back to my bedroom.

The spacing between the bruises that wrapped around her wrists were large - *a hand-print?*

What the hell is going on?

Freyja

I could feel Alice's energy like a ball of white-hot electricity, sizzling away, waiting for the right moment to explode. I could sense the chemical imbalance of her hormones, could see the way her emotions were overpowering her.

It was too early for humans to detect, but I could feel the darkness already growing within her. The poison was already spreading, altering her in ways that were not physical *yet*, but her anger raged inside her.

There will come a time, in the *very* near future, when Alice will realize what has happened, when the damage has already been done. Asmodeus has sealed her fate.

Soon, she may be too strong for me to control.

☙

Alice

She realized that I had shut her out. I felt her despair and desperation as she clawed at the barriers I had put up around her in my mind.

Josh's attack was still raw, and the bruises on my wrist and neck were angry; deep purple and yellow. I had no explanation for them. None that I wanted to give anyway.

This morning had been a close call; I had not been expecting her to be awake so I knew she had caught a glimpse of my bruised wrists, so I know I would not be so lucky next time. If my mum knew the full extent of my bruising on other places of my body; she would be like a dog with a bone. Relentless in her barrage of questions that would put the Spanish Inquisition to shame.

My alarm had startled me this morning, though I had not slept. Instead I had reflected on the options available to her. Narrowing down to the three easiest ways in which she could have stopped it, all three of which require very little effort on her part.

Telekinesis. The power to move objects with the mind. She could have pushed him when he was on top of me, flying him through the air and crashing into the wall at the other end of the room, giving me some extra time to call someone, the police, Effy, my mom. Or it could have given me a brief window of opportunity to run.

Better yet, she could use it to control him, to force him to put one foot in front of the other and leave my house, to put as much distance between us as possible. Using her power of mind-control on him, like she had when I was younger, when we would play with my Barbie dolls. He could have become my puppet.

Telepathy. The ability to read people's minds, or to communicate with them without speaking. Often people don't realize it's another person talking to them, they believe it is their "conscience" trying to coax them out of doing something they shouldn't or to make them feel guilty afterwards when they don't listen. She could have done that, she could have been his conscience telling him to stop, to think this situation through. Or at the very least she could have read his mind and given me a warning.

Mental Manipulation. The ability to control someone's thoughts, to implant ideas into someone's head, nurturing the odds until they believe it was their own thought. She could have manipulated, could have changed, his original intentions or wipe them from his memories. Better yet, she could have just fed him the notion to leave me alone. To drop this obsession. To forget all about me. For good.

Why didn't she do something?

When my alarm rang off for the second time that morning all I wanted to do was hit snooze and bury deep underneath the covers, but I know that if I avoided work for a second day in a row, not only would I have to put up with my mom's merciless interrogation, but my boss would also start asking questions too. I could not afford to lose this job, it was easy and was relatively well paying considering the low-skill required. I stacked shelves, I served customers, I had zero stress, but it meant that I had to face the world. Walk beyond these four walls that I had imprisoned myself in.

The thought made my stomach churn, and the encounter with my mom before I left had not helped, I was so scared about her finding out the truth of what happened, I panicked and fled.

My flippancy and anger had not gone unnoticed by her, but I had no time to dwell on it. I had walked less than a hundred yards from my house, the real fear kicked in.

My heart was palpitating, fast and irregular, a bitter taste filled my mouth as my eyes scanned the streets for any sign of him. Paranoid I kept looking over my shoulder every time I heard a scuffle, the sound of a car passing by would make me jump.

I was not ready to face the world, but it was too late. I had to get rid of this gym bag, and the only place I knew it would go unnoticed was the commercial bins around the back of the shop where I worked. Everyone dumped their rubbish there, and it was collected every Monday, so by tomorrow all evidence of his attack would be long gone.

The alley was dark and dreary, smelling of urine, but I was determined to get rid of this bag that had been burning a hole through my palm since I left the house. Graffiti plastered the walls, and food debris littered the floor. The smell made me want to heave, lobbing the bag into the open bin, I then ran as fast as I could out of there, hoping the smell would not linger on my skin.

Hot, sweaty and out of breath, I practically fell through the door. A bell chimed announcing my arrival. I froze. My eyes fixated not on my boss, but who he was talking to.

"Ah Alice, I hope you are feeling better this morning." My boss greeted me as he emerged from the storage room. "I have just been telling your friends here that you weren't in yesterday because you were unwell... I wasn't sure if you would have been in today either to be honest with y- where are you going?"

The world was spinning too fast, Josh and Effy were standing before me, staring at me in shock. I knew I looked dreadful, Effy's eyes told me as such. Gathering the last of my strength I pushed through to the back room, I needed to escape, but I could not return home either.

"Alice?" My boss called after me, "Alice, are you alright?"

My heart was beating too fast, I slammed the door of the stockroom closed and leaned against it. *What the fuck am I going to do?* Heat crept along my neck until my cheeks flushed, my head dizzy and my vision blurred. *What the fuck is he doing here?*

Loud knocks on the door behind my head made me shriek, I felt like I was a victim in a horror movie, where they lock themselves in a room with no escape. I was doomed.

"Alice, I am worried about you, please... let me in." Effy's voice cooed from behind the door. "I promise I'm not mad at you for not going to the Soirée!"

Her annoyance was the last thing on my mind, I was trying to control my body from not vomiting in the stockroom. As I swallowed back bile, stooped over clutching at my abdomen, I heard the click of the lock. *Shit.*

Suddenly Effy's perfume filled the small room, the door pushing me aside easily, allowing her to enter. She wrapped her arms around me, turning me around to face her. I was numb, frozen by the glare Josh was giving me over her shoulder.

"Alice, you look dreadful-"

My knees crumpled and I fell to the ground as darkness enveloped me.

⚇

Josh

I had felt him take control, as Effy was helping her to regulate her breathing. Asmodeus was relishing in the torment, in the suffering, he inflicted.

"Can you feel that?" he asked me. *"That is fear; pure, unadulterated fear,"* he cackled. As he squeezed into the small stockroom and stood next to Effy. She was sitting on the floor, her friend's head in her lap and holding onto her hands. She was oblivious to the bruises, but I had noticed them instantly. My stomach twisted into knots, knowing it had been me, *him*, that bad caused them.

Alice's eyes flickered open, blinking wildly as she tried to take in her surroundings from her perspective on the ground. They locked onto mine, I thought for a moment they were going to pop out of her skull when all of a sudden she went limp and lifeless. *"She was so scared she fainted!"* Asmodeus smirked.

"Alice!" Effy screamed. "Josh, do something!"

He growled something incoherent and released his control on me. My eyes snapped back to focus just as Effy started talking once more. "Josh, she fainted! Where's her boss? I need to go and find her boss!" I obeyed her commands, but I did not trust myself, did not trust *him* to be close to her.

I gazed at the peacefulness in her face, a stark contrast to moments before. I stared at her luscious lips, full and pink against her pale skin. After a few moments *he* resurfaced, unable to refuse touching her hand, running his fingers along one of her wrists, she tried to hide the marks with some scrunchies on one wrist, and a large cuff bracelet on the other, but we knew they were there.

I felt sick, as his thoughts re-lived those moments. He was enjoying taking her by force over and over in his mind, regretting not prolonging it when he had the chance.

He leaned over her, his voice low and sinister as he whispered in her ear, tearing himself away from her at the sound of Effy's footsteps. Behind her, a man in his late fifties wheezed, his bald head glistened with beads of sweat which he quickly dabbed at from a handkerchief stored in the breast pocket of his grubby shirt.

Asmodeus smirked before relinquishing his control on my body and skulked back into the corner of my mind. My stomach lurched, a lingering feeling that this was not over. His words repeated themselves in my mind. *"The seed will take root."*

Asmodeus

It was hard to contain my happiness, feeling absolute elation knowing that the Seer had been right all along. She had appeared before meal most five years ago, had sought me out to explain in detail a vision she had that explained the fall of Lucifer, the end of his reign of Hell.

It would all start with a child. Not just any human child. A child born of light and dark; a demon father and a mother containing the purest ethereal being to have ever existed: The Divine.

She had refused to give me specific details; she had given me no hints as to where I could find The Divine's vessel, but when I stumbled upon her, I knew what I had to do.

I had tried the conventional way, to lure her vessel into a relationship, to consummate the child that would be born. However, when her human vessel rejected him; *rejected my advances*, I had been left with no choice.

I had always taken great pleasure in taking the virtue of damsels, if consensual, so to find out I could kill two birds with one stone; that I could fulfill the required steps for the Seer's vision to come to life, and to please my ego, had been too tempting to ignore.

Over the years, there had been many who had claimed many prophecies that would cause the destruction of Lucifer.

Yet, none of them had ever come to fruition, instead all that their claims had brought about was their own demise, courtesy of Lucifer himself - until now. I could feel the seed taking root in her womb, I could feel the change in her chemistry, the change in her aura. It was still fresh, recent, too soon for her to know.

I knew, and that was all that mattered. I would be the one to take down Lucifer. I would be the one to challenge his authority over the infernal fiery pit of Hell.

If the prophecy is indeed true, this unborn child within her would be the key to my success. Only time would tell, but I was here for the long-haul.

I was in no rush to help Alice nor The Divine, but Effy's persistent rattle of words were infuriating.

Effy was talking to me, to him, but I had not been paying attention, staring at Alice's inanimate body, imagining what she must bethinking, reminiscing on her feelings of fear and panic in the moments before her collapse.

"Josh, take her into the back room, we need to get her somewhere more comfortable... There is a sofa in the employee area." She said with annoyance. She had already issued these directions, the ones I did not listen to the first time around. "Don't take your eyes off of her!" she demanded "I need to call her mom. as well".

I scooped her up in my arms, feeling the thrum of her changing body, of her body's acceptance to the foreign seed that resided in her. My lips curled into a smile as I walked away, from them, had my back towards them, my mind creating images of how easily it would have been to kill her; to snap her neck, to start another frenzy of Lucifer's searching for The Divine considering he was so close.

If I could have severed her head from her neck, preventing The Divine from being able to escape her vessel. I did not know if she would perish like the other 'lower' ethereal beings, such as us Demons, when our vessels were dispatched in this manner. Yet, it could be assumed that she would rot in an empty shell. It was the ideology behind Purgatory; being stuck in a place that no longer existed, with no escape.

The knowledge that I had violated Lucifer's soulmate, that the child that grew within him would be the one who would orchestrate his downfall brought a smile to my lips. "Well done Alice," I purred, "you are playing your part so well."

Alice's eyes flickered open, as I sat down on the sofa in the employee's 'canteen'. It was nothing more than a box room, big enough for a small TV and sofa. There were no windows and only one door leading in and out. A smirk flickered across my lips, being alone with her in a room that had no escape.

At first it took her several blinks for her eyes to make sense of her unusual perspective, to realize that she was in my arms, being cradled like a baby. I chuckled as she squirmed, as I kept my grip on her tight.

"Get off me!..." she protested. "Get your fucking hands off me!" she hissed. She continued to writhe, to break free from my vice-like grip, even though she knew it was in vain. I was under strict orders 'not to take my eyes off her' so I was not allowing her to make a run for it, to give her the opportunity to leave my presence.

"Nuh-uh-uh" I sighed, shaking my head from side to side. Watching her terrified eyes follow my movements. She screamed out, to which I tutted her, before readjusting my grip so that I could pull at her hair hard.

"You will keep your mouth shut, and stay quiet, if you know what's good for you" I warned in a low growl, checking the room for cameras. Her fear was delectable, delicious.

"I cannot let you go," I whispered in her ear. "You are bound to me, though you may not know it yet."

$$\text{☙}$$

Alice

He released me , allowing me to move away from him, moments before Effy and my boss Robert entered the room.

My head flitted between them all, feeling like a trapped animal with no means of escape. I could feel my breathing growing heavy, I could feel my body trembling with fear at the thought of being so close to him, at the thought that he had been touching my body while I was unconscious. *Had he done anything?*

"Alice, you fainted, you need to calm down" Effy said approaching me, I held my hands out to her, to stop her coming near me. "Stop being silly" she said, grabbing my wrists, her annoyance and frustration clear on her face.

I snatched my arm away from her. "Don't touch me," I whimpered, as tears sprung to my eyes, as my wrist beneath her hand throbbed beneath the scrunchies. I had tried to use them to cover up the bruises that marked the spot where he had crushed my wrists only days before.

"Just leave me alone!" I added, darting through the small parting that Effy had created by moving closer to me. I was too fast for either of them to stop me, too little too late when Effy finally gave chase as she called after me.

"Alice, your mom is coming here!" she shouted, "Al- "she gave up as she saw me whiz past the outside of the shop window, head bent low, running as if my life depended on it. In my eyes, it did. I needed to stay away from him. I need to stay away from them both.

I was less than five minutes away from my home when my mother's car pulled up beside me, her red, ballooned face told me she was furious. "What the fuck, Alice!" she screeched as she wound the window down. "Get in the car."

I got in the passenger side, remaining silent. I could feel her explosive energy, knowing that at any moment she will burst.

"I was sick with worry!" She screeched, pulling up the handbrake, making it clear we were not going anywhere until she had said her piece. "Effy told me you fainted! That you freaked out and ran out when they were trying to help you..."

Her voice lowered from a shrill ear-piercing shriek to a gentle, calm tone when she noticed my body shaking with my sobs. I had tried so hard to contain them.

I knew I could not tell her the truth; I knew she would want to get the police involved. She believed in the judicial system, as did I, but I knew it would only make things worse. They would make me relive every detail for their records, would interview me, would take him in for questioning.

But what if he could convince them I was lying? Everyone seems to worship him, it would not be a far stretch to assume that others would be willing to believe him over a nobody like me.

I took several deep breaths, inhaling through the nose and out through the mouth, to calm my sobs. "I keep having panic attacks," I told her. "I don't know what triggers them, but they make me feel ill. They prevented me from going to the Soirée... what happened at work today was another one."

I glanced over to her, her mouth hanging open, I had stunned her with my confession. She had no words of wisdom, no response prepared.

"Is...is that why you don't want to see Effy? Because she doesn't understand? Or she doesn't know?"

I put my head in my hands, "she knows now." I sighed. "Not that it makes it any easier to cope with."

She nodded her head, her lips clamped shut, her eyes had become glassy as she took off the handbrake and headed home. "Alice, we will get through this, okay. It's just stress about your exams." she muttered, seeming to convince herself rather than trying to convince me.

Weeks, months even, have now passed since that night, yet it all still feels so raw. My body, tender, aching because of the changes that were happening inside of me. I have grown tired of trying to pretend that it never happened, that I was fine. Yet these unrelenting panic attacks still troubled me, my vivid flashbacks still haunting me in my waking hours and in my nightmares.

Several long, tiresome weeks of just going through the motions of life, automated by habit, while inside I was numb, lifeless, unable to feel any other emotions other than pain and sadness.

There had been many days where I woke up feeling conflicted between wanting to barricade myself in my room, never to resurface, and at my lowest to end it all. While others, I felt the compulsion to continue to act like nothing happened, to not allow him to have any hold over me.

Despite my inner turmoil, I felt as though my performance was award-winning. I had convinced everyone that I had been struck by a case of severe panic attacks with no known cause. Everyone, including the doctor and psychiatrist my mom insisted I saw, categorized these "episodes" down to the stress of my impending exams.

It had been a stroke of genius blaming the panic attacks for my non-attendance to The Summer solstice Soirée, for them causing me to be ill. These "episodes" gave me an excuse, a free pass, to get out of college whenever I wanted to. Whenever I needed to, especially if he came too close for my comfort.

I wondered if my mom's background as a nurse would have made her skeptical about the legitimacy of my panic attacks. I thought she might have interrogated me further, over the apparent lack of knowledge of what was causing them. The thing with mental health is that often there is no explanation, there is no way to determine the authenticity or to prove the severity of it.

It benefited me and no one, not even my mother, could accuse me of lying as they at one point or smother everyone had witnessed one of my panic attacks,

She had interrogated me about it, often in the days following, as I returned from the doctor's appointment, or as I returned from the psychiatrist. Almost expecting some tangible answers after visiting either of them - answers that could 'fix me'.

Perhaps, had I told either of the professionals the truth, they may have been able to make an informed decision, may have been able to offer ways to deal with the body-quaking, nerve-shattering panic attacks when they happened in full force. Perhaps they may have been able to offer something other than taking more medication to deal with it.

It had taken Effy a little while longer than most to believe they were to blame for my non-attendance to the Soirée, and even longer to forgive me after all the hard work and effort she had put into my preparations. "Do you know how much effort went into designing your outfit?" she had yelled at me a few days afterwards, "how many hours I sat looking at dresses online for you? Let alone how much they cost!"

I prayed she wouldn't ask for it back because she wanted to return it. Visions of my old gym bag lying in the shop's dumpster behind the shop. It was long gone now, in a landfill somewhere. along with the other sodden and stained reminders of that night.

All of which could have incriminated him, should I have contacted the police; had I come forward about his assault. But in my head, I knew he would get away with it. If I had reported him, it would only make my life more difficult and hellish than what it already was. She never brought it up again, thinking she was punishing me by giving me the silent treatment, focusing all her energy on her repulsive, sadistic boyfriend of hers.

What she did not realize was that she was doing me a huge favor. The further away the 'incident' became with time, the more introverted I had become. Finding it difficult to even hold a small talk with my classmates, the harder it was to be social, to even pretend I had anything to say to people. I had lost all interest in leaving my house most days, especially losing my job at the village shop. I no longer had a reason, aside from college, to leave the house. Much to my mother's despair.

On that traumatic day, Josh had not only destroyed my hymen, but he had also destroyed a huge part of me along with it.

Now I had become isolated from the world and the people in it. I no longer felt joy in the things that I used to, like music and art. I had lost my personality, no longer knew my identity.

I no longer took no comfort in being alone in my house on my own, instead feeling vulnerable and paranoid. Though I had not told her, my mother seemed to know that I hated being at home alone. She never asked why, but I knew she tried to schedule her work so that I was left on my own for as little time as possible, even though when she was home I still shut myself away from her.

I was being watched; monitored zealously by my mother whenever I was in her company, and *his* whenever I was at college. Paranoia gripped me in a relentless chokehold.

I was the prey and he the stealthy predator that lingered in the shadows waiting for the perfect opportunity to strike once more. His attack had already filled me with venom, weakening me ready for his next fatal move.

As hard as I tried to maintain some normality, feigning a smile, trying to attend classes as usual, I would sneak off when it became too exhausting to don fake smiles and cheerful façade, pretending everything was as normal, as if the entire ordeal never happened.

As the weeks progressed, it became more of a struggle, as the burden of the ordeal had snowballed. I had bigger problems than just my insomnia, paranoia, and panic attacks. I was pregnant.

It was not something I had contemplated, too wrapped up in my emotions. I had assumed the nausea I felt each morning was the aftermath of the nightmares that flooded my dreams, but I could not explain the sensation of vertigo and the loss of balance that would overcome me throughout the day. It was only when my period never came did the thought cross my mind.

I had been in denial, unwilling to accept that pregnancy hormones were causing my erratic mood swings and emotional unbalance. I took test after test in the hope that the next one would have the answer I wanted to no avail. Even as the seventh pregnancy test came back positive, I refused to accept it. No matter how hard I tried, I could not wish it away. I could not make it any less real.

As soon as I found out, I avoided Effy like the plague. I ignored her texts and dodged her calls. I even avoided contact with my mom as much as I possibly could. Keeping myself locked in my room whenever I was at home, evading her hawk-like eyes. I could never tell either of them the truth, *but how am I going to hide it? What am I going to do with this thing inside me?*

My stomach lurched, I could not bring myself to call it a fetus, a small bean that would grow into a fully-formed baby, with limbs and its own heartbeat. Instead I saw it as one more parasite inside me, using my body to garner its strength while slowly depleting my energy and strength.

Despite the fact I could not tell them the truth, it was impossible to evade everyone forever. Not in this small town. There were little options for me to choose from. Two to be precise; either everyone had to find out about my pregnancy, which would lead to a full-scale interrogation, or I had to leave everything and everyone here. *Fuck.*

I forced myself to attend all my exams, despite missing huge chunks of revision lectures in the past few weeks. In each exam the clock's ticking penetrated the silence, taunting me that my time was slowly running out. I sat there reading the questions over and over again. Each paper was a blur, my mind unable to recall the answers as my agitated thoughts swirled in my head, scared beyond belief of the *thing* that was growing inside me. *Not that the results of these exams matter now.*

My plan was simple. Once my results came back, I would disappear. I would go as far away from here as possible. As far away from *him* as possible. I did not want him to find out. I did not want him to stake his claim on *it*. Josh would have no further involvement in my life.

Today was the last day of term and the last of my exams were over. I knew as soon as I had left the final one, psychology, that I had failed miserably. I had been aware of him sitting several cows behind me, the feel of his glare prickling the back of my neck, causing every hair to stand on end. My mind was blank, the questions glaring up at me from the paper, the words dancing before my eyes, taunting me as I failed to recall anything other than his close proximity.

As I left the examination hall, returning to the locker to collect my belongings, I had never felt so relieved to go home to an empty house. I had planned to have a nice relaxing bath where I could mull over my future, to construct a plan.

I had no idea what I was going to do. I was too scared to consult my doctor. Dr. Elliot had been my doctor since my birth, he knew every illness and ailment I had suffered with over the years, and he used to be my father's golf buddy.

I knew my condition would be secure under doctor-patient confidentiality; *but would someone recognize me there?* His doctor's clinic was the only one nearby, so it would be evitable to bump into someone who knew me, and *who might alert my mother.*

I knew the cut-off point for a termination was drawing close and I had been meaning to do some research into it, but I had procrastinated. The thought of the process, the destruction of a life made my nausea return with a vengeance. The realization weighed on my chest, I did not want to consider that as an option.

Silence suddenly enveloped me, jerking me back from my thoughts. The throng of people had cleared, Everyone had already fled from college like a mass exodus, grabbing their belongings as quickly as possible so that they could get ready for the 'Farewell Ball' tonight, one last party for the students in their final year.

I was not going, so I was in no rush to collect my belongings, loitering until I was the only one left in the corridor. The silence was comforting, freeing, giving me the opportunity to consider my next move.

I was checking I had everything in my backpack, my focus on the contents of the locker when I felt a firm hand tighten around my throat from behind.

"What are you going to do about that?" That growl, dangerous and stern, the voice from my nightmares.

My heart froze as the air was squeezed from my lungs and my words clogged my throat. His grasp tightened, my pulse throbbing against his fingertips.

I felt him drag me around the corner, into a small part of the hallway not monitored by CCTV, his forceful shove and my lack of balance made me stumble with a deafening crash into the metal lockers. In the blink of an eye he had closed the gap, his hand once again crushing my windpipe as he pinned me against them. The coolness of the metal spread across my spine, but it was fear that caused goosebumps to prick my skin.

All the memories I tried to block from my mind resurfaced as my eyes filled with tears. I could feel a panic attack brewing deep inside my chest.

"I said... what are you going to do about that?" He asked, releasing his grip on my neck, placing them on my waist instead.

I followed his line of vision; the small swell of my stomach. Even beneath the baggy clothes and my arm that was instinctively wrapped around it, I could see it in his eyes, he knew.

The muscles in his jaw tensed, the vein at his temple protruded from his skin, dark purple against his otherwise pale complexion. Josh's eyes still fixated on the bump that had resulted from his actions. Undeniable proof of what he had done. How in one moment he had changed my life and shattered all prospects of my future.

I had told no one. Not a soul.

So how does he know?

ELEVEN

Maxine

The fluorescent lights in the homeless shelter were jarringly bright. My eyes stung as they tried to get accustomed to the artificial lighting.

The hall was bustling and crowded, the sea of gaunt, unwashed faces seeking shelter from the stormy weather outside. A wave of gratitude washed over me as I contemplated the modest one-bedroom apartment I would retreat to once my obligatory shift of court-ordered community service had been served.

Pouring out a bowl of stew, which contained more water than anything else, with some day-old stale bread, I contemplated my life choices. Pitiful food for pitiful people. My life was not so different from theirs, I was hopeless and lost, my future lay in the hands of those who judged me. The sense of regret filled me as I recalled the mistakes I had made that had led me to be here and my daughter taken out of my care.

I knew that I could have easily been on the other side of this counter. The stupidity that addiction brings, the recklessness. I had been so consumed by the stress of being a single parent, I sought solace at the bottom of a bottle.

The moment they told me I could lose my daughter for good, I was determined to sober up. I had attended counseling to confront the reasons for my dependency. They all stemmed from my ex-boyfriend, a dead-beat father who vetoed his responsibilities at every opportunity. Being her sole provider was emotionally challenging, and I had crumbled under the pressure.

As my eyes scanned the room, taking in the paint peeling from the walls and the grubby, dysfunctional throng that sat around the tables slurping loudly at the stew, I knew how easy it was to fall back into old habits; one glass of wine, had turned into one bottle, which eventually became more and more. I just wanted a good night's sleep without the worries flitting through my head.

The acrid stench of rot and urine snapped me out of my thoughts, my stomach flipped as the smell clogged my throat. I tried not to show my feelings, but my face was as transparent as a sheet of glass, my repulsion and pity etched across it.

Why did they not use the facilities the shelter provided to have a nice hot shower, to be clean?

Some of them didn't view being clean something worthy of the money the shelter charged for using this facility. A lot of them were making the choice between eating and sleeping that night on the streets, or not eating and sleeping in a warm bed in the shelter.

I tried to stop myself from recoiling when their skin grazed mine as they collected their bowls of soup. I could not help but feel ashamed of myself for being so judgmental, for the sudden urge to douse myself in bleach and burn my clothes.

There was one person who I always looked out for, a young teenage girl, though I had not seen her in days. I hoped that she had found somewhere warm and safe to go.

My heart felt for her, being a mother, albeit not a very good one, I could not help but feel sorry for her. I wanted to help her, she should be at home with a family who loves her, who cares for her, not here with these unsavory characters and lost souls.

This shift marked the half-way point of my mandatory community service; grateful that helping in the shelter had been available over scrubbing graffiti from the abandoned shop or picking up trash from the streets.

A cold wind whipped through the air as the door burst open. The girl, bedraggled and drowned like a sewer rat, tentatively walked towards the counter.

She stood before me now, her eyes skittish framed with dark rings. Her cheeks were sallow and gaunt and she trembled as she picked up the silver foil take-away container. "Can I have this to go please?" she asked, her voice barely a whisper.

I nodded as my eyes swept over her. She bore the obvious traits of being homeless. The ill-fitting, stained clothes, the smudges of grime on her face. My heart ached for her, but in a way I was relieved to find that unlike most of the others she was sober.

The rain still dripped from her hair, trickling down her face and pooled on the floor, she was shivering but did not voice her complaints. She was defiant and stubborn, refusing to allow her teeth to chatter as she bit her bottom lip.

She kept looking over her shoulder, weary of the other people here, flinching at the sounds of shouting that was coming from a particularly rowdy drunk. She would flee as soon as she could.

Where are her parents?

"Let me get you a blanket, or a change of clothes." I offered, handing her the container complete with lid.

She shook her head. "I'm fine."

My brows furrowed at her stubbornness, it was obvious she was cold. That she needed something if she was to go back outside.

"Why don't you stay here for a little while, dry off then." I suggested. "We have tea or coffee."

She shook her head once more, her lips drawn into a thin line. I stared at her, not backing down, my maternal instincts took control of the situation. "At least let me get you a coat." I sighed, as I handed her the plate of bread.

She nodded this time, causing a small smirk of triumph to flicker across my face. "Stay there." I said, catching her swipe a few extra pieces of bread from the basket. I ignored it, although I shouldn't have. There were still others who were hungry and needed feeding just as much as her.

I hurried to the supply room, unlocking the door before flicking on the light. My heart dropped, the shelves were almost bare, all the coats had already been issued. My mind racing, I fled to the office. I was going to give her a coat. Even if it was my own.

As I rushed back to her, I removed my keys and mobile from its pockets and gave it a quick brush off, *it should be a perfect fit*. When I returned less than five minutes later, I thought she had taken her opportunity to leave, but my eyes found her a few moments later by the supplies counter. Rob must have snuck out for a cigarette while there was a break in the relentless rain, leaving the supplies cupboard unattended.

He too was here for mandatory community service, so he cared little about the rules we had both been given. No extra food, No extra supplies and no personal questions.

It was obvious this girl was an opportunist, sneaking behind the desk undetected by the others, and stowing a few extra cans of food and bottles of water.

"Hear you go, one nice dry coat." My voice startled her, she jumped almost a foot in the air. She eyed it suspiciously, her nose wrinkled as she smelled the garment.

"This is your coat." she said, a flash of confusion crossed her face.

"It *was* my coat, it's now *yours*. You need it more than me."

She turned her back on me as she put the coat on. Just as I thought, it fit her frame well, a little big around the bust, but otherwise perfect. She picked up her rucksack her eyes caught mine. "What's your name?" I asked, the words just tumbling out of my mouth.

"Um... Thanks." Her voice cracked and tears filled her eyes, revealing that she had never known true kindness before. I noticed she did not answer my question.

It was just such a shame that there was no one looking after her, an anger surged through my veins at her parents.

How dare they let her fend for herself like this. How dare they abandon her.

Isobel

When I got back to the loft, Cole had fallen asleep still wearing his shoes and work apron, his body hanging off his sleeping bag and no candles had been lit. He had just collapsed, exhaustion had overwhelmed him before he could remove them or get the place warm. *How long has he been like this? How long ago did he get back?*

I placed the tin foil container on the middle of the camping stove, reheating its contents, stirring, and listening to the soft snores coming from Cole's sleeping bag.

There were no words to describe how much I loathed going to the shelter. The volunteers strained to maintain an upbeat façade, engaging in forced small talk while concealing their critical thoughts behind artificial smiles.

The horrid stench of body odor, piss, and feces assaulted my nostrils as soon as I walked in the place. Seeing all those faces covered with scars and mouths full of decaying teeth made me shudder. That was what awaited me, my future, if we continued to live on the streets.

No matter their reason for being on the street, we were all in the same boat, all trying to survive the shit show. Yet, being there made me feel vulnerable, not only because I was the youngest, but because of the realization that the shelter was our lifeline. Not just for these people, but for me and Cole too.

What would happen to us if the shelter did not exist? If the shelter shut its doors tomorrow, we would all be up shit's creek without a paddle.

A memory returned to the surface, a part of my past I had tried to bury deep, the grunts of the man who took my virginity, who paid well for the privilege. His calloused hands roamed my body as I lay looking at his contorted face, stiff and numb. I shook my head to clear the vision, but his grunts still lingered in my ears, suddenly I no longer felt hungry.

"You shouldn't have gone on your own, Bel." Cole's voice grumbled, sounding half asleep. There was an unmistakable tone of protectiveness in his voice. I shrugged, a pointless gesture, given that he could not see me in the dark.

"You should eat before it gets cold." I said as I held out a spoon in his direction.

"Aren't you eating?" He asked, as he shuffled over and took the spoon. My stomach churned, the man's face still etched into my memory. I shook my head.

Cole scowled, forcing a piece of bread in my hands. "Bel, you need to eat." His eyes were soft as they locked onto mine illuminated only by the orange glow of the camping stove.

"I ate at the shelter." I lied, casting my gaze to the floor.

I nibbled at the bread while Cole ate in silence, I could feel the intensity of his eyes on me. He knew I had lied and that I was keeping something from him, but was too courteous to ask about it.

"Do you know it's Christmas Day tomorrow, Bel?" Cole asked once he had finished eating, his eyes scanning the almost intact piece of bread still clutched in my hands. I smiled when he said my name.

Cole has always addressed me as Bel, it was a pet name my parents coined when I was little, though it had been years since anyone had called me it. It evoked happier memories, a time when I had been loved, I saw it as a term of endearment rather than an abbreviated version of my name.

I shook my head, even though I had overheard conversations about it while at the shelter. Apparently, it was the one day of the year where rations were not as limited, and 'real' food was served.

"I want you to have something," Cole whispered as he put down his bread and rustled around in the camping pack beside him. Within a few seconds he had retrieved whatever it was with a sigh.

As he placed the object in my hand, he pulled my hand closer to the stove, so that the small flames illuminated the object. A small delicate silver necklace with a small cubic zirconia stone pendant that was shaped like a heart. It was not expensive or of any great monetary value. But it was obvious the item held great sentimental value to him.

"My parents died in a fire in our apartment," he started. I could feel his gaze upon me as I admired the necklace. "This is all I have left of them." I wanted to give him back the necklace. The sentiment was too heavy, and I was unsure what to say. He closed my hand with his; the necklace secured in our hands. "Merry Christmas Bel" he murmured, as he retreated to his sleeping bag in silence. No longer interested in the watery contents of the container on the stove.

$$\sideset{}{}\bigoplus$$

Francine - 1842

My boys. My sweet, heavenly boys. Fredrick, George, and Oliver. Their gravestones stood side by side and were aligned in the same pattern in which I would call them to the table for supper. As one by one, with very little time between, and in that order, they were laid to rest here.

I had wanted to pick the most beautiful spot, on top of the hill with beautiful scenic views, where ancient and towering trees could provide shelter from all the elements, where the wildflowers bloomed in the height of spring and where wildlife could roam from the nearby fields and forestry. It was a nice and unexpected sight to see a wild deer wander among the land of the dead.

But they were dumped here, abandoned here in pauper graves. Left here to rot and be forgotten about in the remotest part of the church cemetery. Hidden behind the abandoned ruins of the old church. My boys, my departed children, faced an eternity of staying in the dark. Plagued by shadows even in the height of summer and drowning in murky pools of water on the stormiest of days.

Wildlife was not to be spotted here, nor would humans venture here - for all the souls buried here were long forgotten. Their gravestones stood at crooked angles, weather-worn, the lichen free to cover and annihilate them. Names and dates were no longer legible, some gravestones had crumbled.

It broke my heart knowing my sons would remain here forever, knowing that when I die there will be no space for me beside them. What gave me strength knew that at least they would be together, the three of them, even if I would be alone.

It was a dry October day, but there was a bitter chill in the air which froze my lungs with every breath I took. Accompanied by a bitter wind that would cause my hair to whip its tendrils in my face. It could have been raining fire and I still would have come. I had never missed a birthday, whether they were dead or alive, and I was not about to start now.

I almost forgot about the small bundle of wool in my hands as I became too concerned about my displeasure of the location of their last resting places. I noticed my knuckles had turned white from the tight grasp I had on it in my ice-cold hands.

I placed it in the center of his grave, as the memories flooded my mind, tears blurring my vision. Memories of the many painstaking months it had taken me to complete this gift for him. The agony of continuing to create something that Oliver would never wear.

The blue wool that I had dyed by hand, unable to afford the blue wool that I fell in love with at the local market, had been knitted with the greatest detail and with my utmost care. I had unpicked buttons from old garments, trying to match as many as I could to incorporate onto Oliver's present.

Today he would have been two years old. Today he would have worn this cardigan. He would have laughed and loved the item, knowing I had made it for him. However, life could be cruel, and he will forever be eighteen-months old, under the guardianship of Fredrick, my forever nine-year-old eldest son and his other brother George, who would forever be six.

None of us deserved this life, forced into poverty by my husband's hand, his love for ale, his terrible habit of making poor decisions and his desire to gamble our money away. I wanted more for my boys, I wanted more for me, but it was never written in our stars. It was never meant to be.

I wondered what I had done to deserve such a terrible, lonely life full of nothing but sadness and hardship. I must have done something terrible to suffer as such under the watch of The Almighty.

ॐ

Alice

If I had to sum up how I felt in one word - I was *tired*. I was tired of the exhausting self-loathing. I was tired of trying to keep a secret that was becoming too big and too noticeable to hide. I was tired of dealing with this alone and pretending I was fine.

I am far from fine.

I was drowning from the inside, my lungs burned as they filled with all the emotions I was trying to contain. My head was hurting from worrying about the future; the birth and all the responsibilities that followed after, as well as feeling the pain and suffering from her former vessels. One human can only feel so much before going insane.

Days went by since my confrontation with him, scared to venture any further than the bathroom to vomit. *If he knows, then who else does?*

I had convinced my mother to delay another doctor's appointment, stating that the nausea was caused by my recurrent panic attacks, which was not a complete lie. But I knew that this excuse would not work for much longer, seeing her concern growing more and more each day, as did my stomach.

I was loathing the way she would stare at me for too long, as if I was a puzzle that needed to be solved. Hating the unconvinced nod of her head as I made my excuses not to leave the house, not to go anywhere with her, not to leave the comfort of my room.

Today she had walked away defeated, her footsteps padding away from the other side of the locked bathroom door. Her head bowed to her chest, knowing I would not give any more details on this matter, but there would come a time where she will stand her ground, where she will demand answers.

I could not hide this ever-expanding waistline, especially from her beady, hawk-like eyes. Thankfully, she had been working so much and did not have the time or the energy to weasel the truth out of me, like I knew she would have had she been at home more. Nothing ever used to get past her, my dad had always joked that she should have become a detective because of her fine-tuned intuition and impeccable observation skills.

As I rested my head against the cold-tiled wall of the bathroom, I was contemplating my options. I did not have many; only two viable options. One: Tell her the truth, open a can of worms and ruin my whole life. Two: Leave with no explanation. Disappearing with no idea where I was going, or how I was going to support this child. There was a third 'option', but the thought of it made me vomit once more.

I sighed, allowing my eyes to close, shielding them from the brightness of the brilliant white tiles that sparkled and gleamed under the LED lights overhead. They were blinding in comparison from my curtain-drawn dark, dense room from which I had resurfaced from.

I needed to leave, and soon. I would have to figure the rest of it out along the way. Though, before I could do anything, I needed money.

TWELVE

Isobel

It was funny that despite the time we had been living in each other's company. Christmas Day was the first time I had heard Cole speak of his past – about his parents. He never indulged my curiosity when I had asked him about them before, and I learned to stop bringing up the subject.

On the many cold, dark nights we spent on the streets, sheltering from the awful British weather, our go-to topic of conversation would be about how terrible my parents were. Night after night, I would pour my heart out to him about my parents, and how I had no choice but to run away.

I would rather starve on the streets than spend another sorry moment looking after them when they were too drunk to function. Yet Cole was harboring the ache of sorrow, shielding his grief over losing his parents and was forced into being homeless because he had lost everything.

I felt like a terrible human being. I had parents I did not want, and he missed and wanted his back.

"Did your family ever have any Christmas traditions?" Cole asked as he stirred the spaghetti hoops on the camp stove, his eyes flashed up at mine from the pan, a small smile played on his face, up his eyes showed a deep sadness lurking within them.

I shrugged, unable to maintain his expectant gaze. "Perhaps when I was younger..." I sighed, my family was too dysfunctional to celebrate things like Christmas or birthdays, "I doubted they knew what day of the week it was, let alone when it was a Christmas."

"What you did not have a tree? Or go Christmas caroling?" He asked, bewildered. "One year my father and I went to a local place to select our own Christmas tree, there were hundreds of them all in rows, a man nearby with an ax to chop down the one we decided on. But I could not bring myself to do it; to choose to cut down a tree that had been growing for years, decades even. It seemed cruel, wasteful, even then at the age of seven, just to chop a tree down for the benefit of a few days."

He turned off the stove and poured our portions into small metal cups, placing a spoon in each one, before tearing off the rest of yesterday's bread to accompany it, "I opted for a small tree that was in a giant plant pot instead. It was a dwarf variant of the traditional Christmas tree, every year after that the tree would be rolled in from the back garden, to be decorated with lights and tinsel... then after the holidays it would be rolled back outside so it could continue to grow in the pot."

I smiled, this was a side to Cole that I had not seen before, a reminiscent, happy side. "I remember my mother was fascinated by angels, she always had one at the top of the tree looking down over all of us, 'protecting us' she used to say. There were some plastic ones which she would put near the bottom of the tree, not too worried if we accidentally broke them..."

An enormous smile broke out across his face "and they got broke *a lot*... I was a clumsy child!" he chuckled before returning to his story. "But my mom had some more intricate glass, crystal ones that she would place near the top," his eyes seemed to have glazed over as he recalled the memory, "I used to love the way the colors would reflect off of them, casting mini rainbows on the wall."

I got up and walked over to my coat pocket, digging around for the ornament I had taken from the tree, remembering my fascination with it. "Like this?" I asked, holding it out to him.

He nodded, "almost identical." He sighed, holding it over the candle, allowing watching the light refracting off the ornament bouncing onto the walls in different colors. "Where did you find this?"

"On a tree in the estate..." I replied, too busy focusing on the lights on the wall, fixated on the patterns and colors, unaware that he was trying to give it back to me. I shook my head as he tried to force it into my hand. "No, Cole.. you should have it. To help you remember the good times."

"I can't, it's yours-"

I put my finger to his lips. "Consider it a present from me," I told him, curling the angel into his hand. "It's not much, but I hope it brings you happiness."

"It's perfect" he beamed, embracing me into a hug.

I could have sworn I saw a tear in his eye, but when we broke apart moments later, it was gone. "Talking of presents..." I said filling the silence. "Your gift yesterday... I never had the chance to say thanks." I carefully fished the necklace from the pocket of my jeans. "It's beautiful, but I can not accept it…it belongs to you, it's all that you have left of your family…"

"You *are* my family now Bel." He said in a low voice. "I want you to have it."

I nodded, staying silent as he clasped it around my neck. Butterflies were fluttering around in my stomach; my heart was beating as fast as their little wings. Cole had let his guard down, had allowed me to see a different side to him.

He leaned forward, his mouth was inches from mine, his eyes were staring at me.

"Do you know what is ironic about my family's Christmas tradition?" He asked me, oblivious about this sudden switch in my feelings towards him. unaware that I longed for him to kiss me.

Several long moments went by as we remained poised this close to each other, I could feel his hot and heavy breath on my lips, my heart was drawing me closer, I was just about to kiss him when he began talking once more, I pulled away from him.

"Christmas morning, before we opened any presents, we always used to help out at a soup kitchen…my mother never felt right if we all tucked into our Christmas dinner while others went hungry," his smile faltered a little, his voice so low it was a whisper. "Oh how the tables have turned."

Alice

Christmas Day in our household always felt awkward, forced without my father being there to celebrate it with us. We still went through the motions, but it felt wrong.

At Christmas, he transformed into a big kid, set on decorating the tree with popcorn hand-strung, like he had when he was a child, instead of tinsel. Helping with baking cookies and watching Christmas films. We would always play board games and sing Christmas songs, and if the weather was on our side, we would go outside to build snowmen and create snow angels.

Ever since he had passed, it never seemed to snow on Christmas anymore. It was as if Mother Nature had decided not to be so cruel to remind us even more of his passing.

Today was just awkward, neither of us talking, neither of us eating. Both of us wallowed in self-pity, grieving for my father, feeling the pain of his absence grow bigger with each year that passed.

Since I became a teenager, my mom would opt to work overnight on the children's ward, doing her bit to spread some Christmas cheer by taking in some freshly baked gingerbread men. It was her tradition to hand them out to the children and their parents; this year was no different.

Her shift would start soon, which meant I would be home alone. Instead of feeling liberated, I felt vulnerable and scared. Anxious that it may happen again.

"Alice, you know I love you, don't you?" she said to me, before she got up from the dining table. "You know that you can tell me anything, right?" I nodded my head, unable to meet her eyes. I could feel them as if they were burning into my skin. *"Tell her,"* Freyja urged, *"she will understand. She will help you. You don't have to do this alone."*

I felt my anger prickle inside, *"I wouldn't have had to go through this at all... you could have stopped this!"* I hissed at her, clamping my mouth shut. *"Now leave me alone!"*

The opportunity to tell her passed, as she waited in silence removing the gingerbread creations from the oven. A strong waft of the heavenly scent of gingerbread filled my nostrils, but I refused to say the words out loud, unable to bear the shame and disgrace of being a teenage mother with no sign of the child's father in sight.

We stayed in silence for a few moments longer, until she accepted defeat dumping them unceremoniously into a Tupperware, excusing herself to get ready for work. I remained seated at the dining room table, waiting for her to leave before I moved. Scared that today of all days she may notice the bump protruding underneath my dressing gown.

"Don't worry about clearing up" she said as she re-entered, her work uniform on, her take tied back in a ponytail. "Merry Christmas Alice," she said as she left with her tub of baked gingerbread men. I noticed once she had left, that for the first time, she did not leave me any.

Isobel

In the days following Christmas, Cole and I fell back into our usual ways of surviving. I was trying to pretend that our 'moment' never happened; that I had not wanted to kiss him, and Cole said nothing further about his past, closing himself off from me, as if those words had never been said: *"You are my family now Bel...you and I, against the world..."* Yet the lingered in my mind and tugged at my heartstrings.

The days bled into weeks; and as quickly as the atmosphere had changed on Christmas, it had reversed itself back to what it had been before. Or at least that was what I was trying to convince myself.

I kept noticing little things about him that would make my heart flutter, such as the small smile that would curl his lips whenever he caught a glimmer of the necklace around my neck. I wore it with pride and it brought me comfort. When I held the heart-shaped stone between my fingers, it brought me inner peace like Scruff did.

A few days ago, I discovered a clock while exploring the outbuildings of the disused warehouse we called home. Despite the glass face being cracked, and the frame buckled, it still counted down the hours of the day.

Now, the second hand was ticking, echoing in the vast emptiness, as if it was taunting me in my loneliness. Almost mocking the fact that time seemed to stand still whenever I was alone; waiting for Cole to finish work.

Cole. My heart and body ached for his company, ever since he had given me this sentimental gift, ever since seeing a side of him I had never seen before I had looked at him, and felt differently towards him, seeing him more than just being brotherly figure, wanting him to be more than just a companion of survival.

I shook my head; I would not allow myself to succumb to silly, girlish feelings. Feelings that he would never reciprocate anyway. It would be a waste of my time and energy to convince myself that he would ever feel the same way.

I needed to focus on staying alive. January was cold, the harsh icy breeze tore through the warehouse, making it harder for us to keep warm. The shelter had been running low on provisions of tinned food, so we had tried to make our potions smaller so that they would stretch further. My stomach growled as a testament to my hunger.

Trying to occupy myself, I made a list in my head of the items I needed; extra blankets, more candles and something that could block the draft that had billowed from underneath the old, heavy office door.

I looked at the clock again, even though the hands had moved since I had last looked at it. I sighed as I recalled the other items that I had salvaged from the outbuilding at the same time as the clock: an old office chair and a couple of old paperback books.

The book covers were faded, torn and moldy, but the pages inside, while yellow and discolored, were still legible. I had been proud of my findings and was filled with the ambition to read their contents as a productive way of filling my days. But every time I tried, as I did most days, I could not focus on the words. My brain would disengage from the contents, I would become too distracted in my thoughts of Cole.

I smiled to myself as I remembered the delight that lit up Cole's face that day, as he began spinning himself around on the office chair until he would feel dizzy, afterwards inviting me to do the same. At the time I thought he never noticed the other items I had brought back to our living quarters, especially the books.

Yet, as I glanced around the room now, I spotted a corner of a book poking out from beneath his sleeping bag, piquing my curiosity. My mind raced with questions about the book's title, its plot, and my own misguided judgment of him as someone who did not seem like a passionate reader. Though I knew better than to go rifling through his minimal belongings.

The vibrant red sky outside was visible through the small window, the sunset was often beautiful from up here, looking out over the top of all the buildings. It also showed that I did not have too long of a wait now until Cole would finish.

I made my way out of the warehouse, wrapped in a long coat, which was several sizes too big, but was perfect for fending off the cold. I replaced the broken metal sheet that blocked our entrance to the warehouse, before making my way towards the housing estate.

The sun had retreated in the time it had taken me to reach the estate. Darkness blanketed the neighborhood, for the few brief moments before the streetlights would flicker to life. I was careful not to be seen as I walked through the streets. My heart raced, fearing that any attention drawn to myself would cause alarm among the residents, prompting them to call the authorities.

Neatly arranged and patiently awaiting, their recycling bins brimmed with shimmering wrapping paper, while abandoned Christmas trees leaned against the fences, ready for collection. I thought back to what Cole had said about Christmas trees, which chopping them down was so wasteful just for a few days of celebration, as I looked along here, I could understand why he would feel that way. Dozens of them all brittle and dry. Dead.

The smell of the decaying pine trees was strong, heady, satisfying considering that if we ever had a Christmas tree up it was the same old plastic tree that smelled musty and damp, with branches that were so dusty, they had always made me sneeze.

I observed the boxes of donations that sat beside the recycling bins, a local charity's logo printed on the side of these plastic lidded containers. I tried to see if there was anything of use, not at all feeling guilty for taking items that were being donated to a charity. I figured we were less fortunate than those who would end up buying these donated items at the charity's shop in the town center.

Inside each box I passed was an abundance of toys, suitable for various age ranges, most of which looked almost brand new. Toys that I would have loved growing up, along with more Christmas baubles than I had ever seen in my life. After a quick scan, however, there were no glass angels among them.

In all honesty, there was nothing that would be useful to us on this occasion until I came to the last house just before the gates to the old cemetery. Outside was a neat stack of items, all folded and clean. These had not been left out for long, still warm to the touch, nor were they placed in the donation box that contained a lot of crockery and bakery tins.

I looked around to see if anyone was watching; in case they had been dropped or forgotten, but the street was empty. I did not want to get caught stealing, especially in a place I frequented often.

The pile held a few coats and jackets in various sizes, folded blankets in an assortment of colors, and several pairs of hats and gloves. None of them bore stains or holes like the ones the shelter would issue. These all looked new, or as good as, including the small black backpack with embroidered hearts scattered across the front, which had been carefully placed beside the pile.

It was like a present, like someone had left it here for me to find. I looked around again, suspecting that someone would be nearby, yet there was no one to be found. After checking that the coast was clear, I scooped the items up and squashed them into the bag. There was too much inside for it to close, but I had pulled the zip across just enough to stop anything from falling out.

I pulled on a hat and a pair of gloves, wrapped a scarf around my neck and headed for the cemetery. It was the quickest route to Cole's work.

As I made my way towards the cemetery, I could feel eyes on the back of my head. That distinctive sense that someone was watching, but every time I glanced around, there was no one there. I stepped over the ruin of an old stone wall, chancing one last look behind me. A flicker of movement caught my eye, but it was too dark to have seen what it was. It moved too fast, as soon as I blinked it was gone.

I gripped the backpack straps that rested on my shoulders, as I pushed my way through the overgrown cemetery, being careful where I stepped trying to avoid standing on any gravestones.

Despite my homelessness, I maintained a dignified demeanor. They may have been gone and forgotten about, but I was not about to stomp all over their resting places. They were the lucky ones, at least at one point they had family who had cared enough about them to lay them to rest, to mark and attend their graveside many years ago.

It was much more than what could be said for me.

Alice – FLASHBACK: Fourteen years old.

It had become second nature, the older I got, to keep Freyja a secret. Easier to hide my ever-developing abilities and lie to all those around me.

I discovered my passion for arts and crafts. I found it seemingly effortless to create beautiful paintings and pottery, in art class I excelled above the other students. I could mold and turn my creative vision into reality. How much of that was my doing or Freyja's abilities is still unknown.

I found I could do anything I put my mind to. No obstacles could deter me. If I wanted something I would get it, as if conjured out of nothingness. My wish for it to be so, would make it so. It was frustrating not knowing if without Freyja, would I be the same person, or would I have achieved all that I have so far. Would I have won the nation's youngest artist award? Or the best youth author, become the best youth baker or won the spelling bee against college level opponents?

It was hard not knowing who I was without her. Who I am, without her constant influence. It was a relief to remain grounded, humble. Knowing that Freyja would let me know when I had gone too far or become overconfident. She would freeze me out, ignore me. desert me until I had corrected my mistakes.

It was during these phases that I would be filled with dread, worried that this time she was gone for good. That one constant being, who I grew to love and understand, to accept as a part of me, would be gone forever. Then she would welcome me back, start talking to me again and point me in the right direction.

It had been Freyja who had alerted me to this girl who would wander the streets, forlorn and lost, taking items that were donated for charity. When I first saw her, I was annoyed. How *dare she steal from the needy!* It had been Freyja that prompted me to pay closer attention to the girl, pointing out the sorry state that she was in. It was obvious the more I noticed her in the estate that she needed these items.

Last night I had placed some items that I thought might have been useful to her over our fence. I spotted her at the top of the street through my bedroom window. Watching her with piqued interest, taking in her ill-fitting clothes; the zip up hoodie several sizes too big and jeans that were a few inches too short.

As she walked under the streetlights, trying to avoid being spotted, you could see the skinniness of her ankles. Her face was gaunt and withdrawn, dark circles under her eyes and her hair a replica of a bird's nest.

I hoped the items would bring her warmth, feeling ashamed that I was here alone in this huge house with the central heating pumping out on full blast, while she was down there, relying on the donations from others just to survive.

I wanted to help her, but I did not want her to catch me watching her. I did not want to scare her away, or make her feel ashamed for needing help.

I continued watching her, through a slit of my curtains. I wanted to decipher if she visited for any other reasons, if her visits had any regularity or pattern, but it turned out it was just random.

I knew I had to help her, in any way that I could, but the question was always the same: *how can I help someone who doesn't want to be seen? How can I help her other than leaving things outside for her to find?*

THIRTEEN

She was late. Again. A loud yawn erupted from me,

That damned clock is supposed to help with her timekeeping, but all it is doing is disturbing my sleep with its incessant ticking.

The rain was pouring down, the brown paper bag that held a couple of sesame-donated chicken burgers and sweet potato fries Mr. Banerjee had let me take, were absorbing the rainwater. The giant paper cup of fizzy cola was beginning to sag because of the excess moisture. She had better turn up soon, or I will eat her share.

I perched on a bin that sat next to the fire escape of the restaurant, the only entrance and exit my boss permitted I use. I understood, I was not a good look for the restaurant, the sight of me left his customers with a bitter taste in their mouths, vowing never to return. I did not argue when he first told me, I was just appreciative of the paid work. Thankful for the scraps of cash issued on a semi-regular basis.

I looked at the alley behind the restaurant, it looked similar to the alley where I first bumped into her. *Bel.*

I had not paid attention as I walked through it daily, but now that I had a few moments it brought back memories from that day.

What struck me first was her outfit, a skimpy red leather skirt, black blouse with too many buttons undone and long knee-high boots. All of it hanging off her skeletal frame. It was easy to tell that those clothes did not belong to her.

Her face was withdrawn, mascara streaking and red lipstick smudged. Her face should have been the picture of radiance and of youth, but dark circles lay heavy under her eyes and healing bruises on her left cheek.

She seemed unaware of the aura she wore; that had been abused and neglected for as many years as she had been alive. A child that should have been in a warm and loving home, not wearing skimpy outfits, scrounging for food, and looking for someone to love her in all the wrong ways. Then, there was that awkward moment when she noticed me.

As I tried to lurk in the shows to remain hidden, to keep my demons that brought me here, a secret. Her eyes flung themselves open.

I gritted my teeth, not because of the cold and damp, because even to this day knowing the true reason she was there made my blood boil. The way people took advantage of her, how there was no other way, or so she must have felt, to survive. To make cash to live, to pay for a shelter, or worse. She certainly was no child; I supposed she never had the opportunity to have a normal childhood, but even so she should never have been in *that* game.

Meeting her back then, I had this instinct, this urge that I had never felt before. I knew I had to protect her, show her there was another way to survive. I could not leave her to continue turning tricks just to stay alive. I changed that day. She had changed me, and I still was not sure how I felt about that.

Footsteps running, growing louder as they approached, distracted me from my thoughts. They were around the corner, gaining momentum. If this was an attacker, I was in no position to defend myself with both my hands full. "Cole?" I heard her gasp, as she appeared around the corner. Breathless and doubled over. Instant relief washed over me, followed by anger.

"Where the *Hell* have you been?"

Isobel

I knew I was going to be late. I had lost my footing and tripped on a crooked headstone. Some items had fallen out of the bag, but with the dark and overgrown bushes, I could not see enough to collect them all, and some would have been so sodden with mud and rain that they would have been useless anyway. I scrambled back to my feet and tiptoed through the rest of the cemetery. Once I was out of the worst of it, my feet on solid ground, I ran as fast as I could toward the restaurant.

My heart was thudding in my ears, my lungs were sore, and I had an intense pain in my ankle, but I did not have time to dwell on it. I had to push through the pain and try to pick up the pace. I had promised to meet Cole when he finished his shift, and so far this week, I have been late every day.

As I rounded the corner, seeing him with his arms full of sodden food, I could have cried. "I'm so sorry" I babbled, hobbling over to him. "I fell in the cemetery." He took a step forward, offering me the paper cup.

"Are you okay?" His free hand now held my chin, as his eyes studied my face. I nodded,

"I will survive," I muttered, bringing the straw of the cup to my lips, savoring the sugary sweet cola.

"Come, let's get you out of the rain," he said, dumping the saturated bags of food in the dumpster before putting his arm over my shoulder, "Use me to support your weight, I think you may have sprained your ankle."

I tried not to read into the situation too much as we headed back to the loft. My right arm wrapped around his waist, clutching at his top while his left arm draped over my shoulder. I could feel the heat radiating from him. It sent goosebumps up my arm. The way his muscles in his torso rippled underneath my touch was difficult to ignore as we stumbled along in silence.

Maxine

They looked like drowned rats, or as my late grandmother would say: *'They were in such a sorry state'.* Their arms wrapped around each other, hair stuck to their faces, looking wind-battered and drenched. The girl looked pained as they collapsed down onto the cafeteria chairs.

I did not recognize the young man she was with. At a first glance, he appeared to be very controlling and possessive of her, as he took off his jacket and draped it over her shoulders. His gaze never left her despite walking towards me.

"Do you have any hot food left?" he muttered, his eyes scanning the kitchen behind me. "She has hurt herself and has been in this weather for too long."

I know we had served the last of our stew hours ago. I was here to clear up and help any wanderers who may stumble in to escape the weather. "I could make you both a cup of tea or coffee."

He snarled, "tea will be fine," he glanced over his shoulder towards the girl. His body softened a little, "can you put plenty of sugar in hers please." When I returned from the kitchen with mugs of sweet tea, her head was resting on his shoulder. Her eyes closed. He nodded thanks, before he told me they would not be here long, just enough for her to dry off and warm up. Her eyes flickered open when he whispered in her ear and placed the hot beverage in her hand.

Her hands cradled the cup to absorb the warmth. Inhaling the steam as she held her face over the hot mug of tea. She gave me an awkward smile. "Let me grab some biscuits" I chirped, heading over to the pantry and storage room area. It was supposed to be off-limits right now as items are only issued at set times each day. But I had keys "in case of an emergency." I classed this as an emergency. I rooted around for some toiletries, towels, fresh sets of clothes for them both, a roll of fabric bandages and a packet of digestive biscuits.

"We have bathrooms just down the corridor, ladies to the left, gents to the right, have a hot shower, get cleaned up and put on these dry clothes." I instructed, placing the items on the table in front of them. "I'm Maxine, by the way."

In the space of five minutes, I had broken every rule and guideline I had been instructed while undertaking my community service here, but I did not give a damn. I was here to help, she needed my help. *Who the fuck cares if I had to break some rules to help her?*

My heart raced as my maternal instincts went into overdrive, desperate to ensure her safety and protection. I wanted her to feel kindness and love.

☙

Isobel

The scorching water hammered against my skin, creating an overwhelming sensation. The scents of apples and coconuts from the shampoo and shower gel stuck in my nose. It was nice to feel clean again. I scrubbed and rinsed and scrubbed some more, a little uneasy on my feet, but determined not to waste a single moment under the luxurious hot shower.

Once finished and dressed in the new clothes, I reached up to hold my necklace, but it was gone. I searched the bathroom, shook out my old clothes - *I must find that necklace!*

Defeated when it was nowhere to be found, I hobbled back to the cafeteria area, where Cole would be waiting for me. Tears welled in my eyes. *How had I lost his sentimental gift? One of my most important possessions?*

I zipped the jacket all the way up as I approached him, not ready to admit the loss yet. Maxine was sitting at the same table as him, they were talking while dunking biscuits in another fresh cup of tea in front of them, the steam rising from the three cups.

"Feeling a bit better?" she asked, her eyes soft and friendly.

She looked different today than what she had when I first glanced at her when I was in the shelter before Christmas. Her face no longer contorted in discomfort or disgust. Her hair was tied up in a messy bun, her face wore no make-up and sported casual blue jeans and plain white t-shirt underneath a powder blue jacket.

As they sat side-by-side, they both appeared to be around the same age, a few years my senior. If I was to hazard a rough guess I would say early to mid-twenties. My gaze lingered on Cole, admiring his shock of black hair that hung limp and wet against his neck, and the clean black t-shirt and tan cargo pants.

Jealousy washed over me. He did not look homeless any longer, in fact he looked even more handsome. With washed hair and clean clothes it was easy to see that he was attractive, and why she had been flirting with him.

Stupid girl, I told myself, *he will never like you.*

I could not bring myself to look in Cole's direction, but I could smell the men's deodorant and body wash coming from his skin. It made me feel giddy and weak at the knees. He smelled just as good as he looked.

As I sat down, I nodded my head, the carrier bag of wet clothes dumped by my feet. Maxine was asking us about our lives, how we were coping. "Do you or your sister need anything?" she asked, her gaze directed at Cole. He shook his head as we both said at the same time.

"She's not my-"

"I'm not his-"

Our eyes locked. A small smile curled at his lips. Maxine shifted in her seat, a shy smile on her face.

"Sorry I just assumed." She bit her lip. "Do you or your *girlfriend* need anything else?" Cole shook his head. I noticed he also did not correct her, to tell her we were just friends. A small smile flickered across my face as butterflies fluttered anxiously in my stomach.

"Um... Are there any candles and matches?" I asked.

❦

Bjorn: 885 AD – The Rise of a Warrior.

She had the grace of a goddess, but the attitude of a warrior.

Her eyes sparkled dangerously; her lips pulled into a confident smirk as she swung the sword. Her hair an uncontrollable sea of fire as she swirled, following the blade as it hit the intended target. She had the poise of a lady who had no business on a battlefield, but she harnessed the strength of Odin. The way she wielded any weapon was effortless, her weapon of choice, a simple ax.

With a long handle made of ash wood and the blade made of one amateur lump of metal welded to it. It may have been basic, and brutish, but she could handle the ax. It was no easy feat to swing such a heavy weapon, sharp yet sturdy enough to crack open a skull. But she made it look easy, as if it had been made from feathers, her techniques even putting some of our best warriors to shame.

I taught her every combat method and technique with all the weapons we had in our arsenal. She was an excellent archer; every arrow flew with accurate precision. Her defensive skills with a wooden shield were flawless; it is a difficult skill to develop, but she had mastered it. Her timing was impeccable, just before her enemy could recover from their last failed attack, she would strike with vicious certainty. It was clear, however, that although it may not have been her favorite to satisfy her blood lust on a battlefield, her destined weapon was a sword. Watching her spar, she resembled her namesake, embodying the goddess of battle.

Freyja was not only a goddess of battle, but of love, fertility, beauty, as well as sex and pleasure. Deemed as Odin's equal, selecting her chosen from the fallen warriors, her Valkyries would lead them to her great hall of Fólkvangr,. It was a great honor for any Viking to be chosen by Freyja in death. Those who were not chosen, but who also fought but were slain in battle, would be welcomed with open arms by Odin, where they would drown ale and feast forever in the hall of Valhalla.

This girl in front of me, her fight was a dance, it was mesmerizing. She knew where to hold her weight so she could outmaneuver her opponent. She knew where to strike. She was mindful not to waste energy or lose her momentum. Each thrust of her sword was fatal.

Her finishing touch was a sheathed dagger plunged into the neck. Under the base of a helmet and above any armor, one of the most vulnerable places of a man amid a battle. She relished her victory, paraded in the square, blood running down her blade and along her forearm as she raised her sword high for all to see.

I was certain that Freyja, my daughter, could win the war with her sword-bearing skills and her brilliant mind. Though I prayed to the gods that it would not come to that.

FOURTEEN

Marcus

My phone was ringing. Even though it was on silent mode, the noise of the vibration against the oak side table woke me from my slumber.

"What do you want?" I asked, my voice a harsh whisper. I did not even bother to look at the caller ID. I already knew who it would be.

"I have fucked up," he slurred.

"It's three-fucking- A.M. I don't need your school drama waking me up before work!"

"I've fucked up bro, I need you."

I rolled my eyes - he always needed me.

I clambered out of my bed. Stepping over the piles of clothes that had been discarded in haste last night. Pulling out a clean set of clothes from the drawers. Trying to be as silent as I could, careful not to wake the girl in my bed, Jessica? Janice? Whatever her name was, it was unimportant, she would be gone before I got back. I grabbed my phone, wallet, and keys before shutting my apartment door, I clambered into my car, heading toward Jay's, a seedy hovel of a bar, to get my brother.

Josh

The music here was awful. But it was loud enough to drown out the thoughts that were swirling in my head. Dizzying. Although that may have been down to the whisky.

Sometimes I could justify my actions. My impulsive behavior, my sudden outbursts of anger. Other times I looked for answers, or someone else to blame, but when that fell flat, I knew one thing that could wash it all away. Drowning my sorrows as they say, until I could no longer feel the guilt.

I lifted my glass to my lips, only to realize that it was empty. Was this my fifth? My sixth? Or was I in the double figures now? I wondered admiring the empty glass, the ice clinking inside. "Get me another" I ordered slamming the glass down on the bar.

"I think you have had enough." The bartender faced me. Her blonde hair pulled up into a tight ponytail, her uniform hugging her delicious curves and leaving little to my imagination. She crossed her arms. "I think you need to go home."

I stifled a laugh. "Now why would I do that?"

"Because you need to sober up."

"I'm waiting for someone" I slurred, trying to keep my eyes open.

Although being the stupid idiot that I am, he was here because I called him. I hated dealing with him, his self-righteous, self-absorbed attitude with his pretentious mannerisms, the way he always looked at me with disdain and intolerance. He learned all of that from our father.

But despite all of that, I still needed his help. He leaned closer to me, his gaze intense and stern. "What have you done now?"

Isobel

Back at the loft there was an air of awkwardness between Cole and me. He had helped bandage my ankle up to give it extra support. Maxine did not want us to leave, although she promised we could pop by and use the facilities free-of-charge on the days she had listed, on a scrap of paper, those were the days when she would be there.

He lit the candles in silence, rolled up one of the spare blankets from my backpack into what resembled a sausage and placed it in front of the door to block out most of the draft. It was not perfect, but it made a massive improvement. He then took an extra candle over to his sleeping bag, pulling out the book he had hidden underneath.

I watched as he flicked through the pages, turning away when he noticed me watching him.

"Bel, are you alright?" he asked, glancing in my direction. I was sitting upright, my knees tucked up underneath my chin with my arms wrapped around them. My face now staring at the blank wall, mortified that I had been caught staring at him.

"I'm fine Cole. Just a bit cold. I'll warm up soon."

Without hesitation, he was on his feet, heading over to me with an extra blanket. I thought he was just going to give it to me. Shock coursed through my body as he sat beside me and slid his legs into my sleeping bag. "Lean into me Bel, let me keep you warm."

Numb and a little awkward, I did as he instructed. I uncoiled myself from hugging my legs and laid down with my head resting on him. I could feel the rise and fall of his chest. I felt his breath as he raised his mouth to the top of my head. "Try to get some sleep" he whispered, his breath hot against my scalp.

His fresh, clean scent along with the regular rise and fall of his chest with every breath was soothing. His heart was beating fast, I assumed whatever he was reading in his book had been interesting or intense.

I tried to slow my pulse, taking a few slow, deep breaths, I had never been this close and intimate before, especially with Cole. Even my prior experiences were never this intimate; I was just there for the cash, distracted and disengaged from the situation and the stranger who was just there for their release.

I felt something cold slide over my collarbone. "I believe you dropped this," he murmured.

My hand flew up to the necklace, my fingers fiddling with the heart-shaped stone. Tears welled in my eyes and my chest grew tight as my sobs swelled inside me.

I turned so that I could look up at him, to tell him I was sorry and to thank him for finding it, but his face was closer to mine than I realized. His hand brushed the side of my cheek, before resting under my chin. His lips were hovering over me, intending to brush against my forehead had I not moved at the same time. Instead our lips grazed against each other, sending a ripple of goosebumps along my body.

For a moment we hesitated, his eyes were wide and his facial expressions appeared to be shocked in the dim glow of the candlelight.

I closed my eyes, wishing the ground would swallow me whole, as I braced myself for the embarrassment of the rejection I knew would come. I went to move my head away when I felt his lips lock onto mine. This time they were purposeful, intentional, his tongue parted my lips so he could deepen the kiss.

Time seemed to have stopped, the ticking of the clock disappeared along with everything else. All of it was irrelevant, all that mattered was him and this kiss.

We may have been homeless, with nothing to our names, but in this moment I had found somewhere I belonged. Something that ignited a flicker of hope for our future.

FIFTEEN

Josh

Marcus refused to look at me from the moment he escorted me into the office and threw me into the chair opposite him, to the moment I held my head in my hands, tears and snot running down my face as I told him what I had done. Only meeting my gaze once I had finished answering his interrogation style questions; the who, what, where, and how. A deathly silence fell over us when he asked me why I had done it. I felt his eyes bore into me, a fierce and intense gaze that pricked at my skin.

I shrugged. "I was drunk." My face looked up to meet his glare.

His balled fist connected with my jaw. The metallic taste of blood instantly filled my mouth. His mouth snarled into a grimace. "You are a stupid son-of-a-bi-"

I cut him off as I flew to my feet squaring up to him, my fists raised ready to fight. He may have been my older brother, may have inherited dad's business and wealth, but I was sure as hell going to knock his lights out. *Smug asshole*, he was always sitting on the moral high ground as if he could do no wrong.

Marcus stepped forward, hands on my shoulders pressing hard on them until my knees buckled underneath me and I crumpled back into the chair.

"I suggest you sit the fuck down, and shut the fuck up." He warned, his voice oozing with repulsion, his disgust apparent when he began to avoid eye contact once more.

Even though I could only see his profile, I could see the muscles in his jaw tighten, his fists clenched into fists until his knuckles turned white.

My alcohol-induced cockiness evaporated when he stopped pacing. He was trying to surmise a suitable plan to elevate the serious repercussions that my actions had caused. Something my father referred to as "damage control". A plan that would mitigate any loss or harm caused by my unfavorable behaviors and rebellious actions.

"You are a real piece of shit. Did you not learn from the last time? Or the time before that?" His clenched fist slammed down on the desk beside him.

There was nothing I could say, too ashamed to admit how many times I had been here, listening to the names he called me as time after time my actions got me into trouble. Trouble only his help could resolve. The shadow within me stirred, chuckling to himself at my desperate pleas for help. *"Nothing your brother can do about it if she wants to keep it."* He smirked.

Marcus' voice snapped me back to his attention, "This time Josh, you have really fucked up." He sighed, sitting in a chair the furthest away from mine. Hunched forward with his elbows on his knees. "And now she's pregnant?" He asked. I nodded, unable to speak. "But she isn't trying to blackmail you?" I shook my head. "How certain are you that it's yours?"

I knew it, the shadow knew it, I had been her first, though I could not bring myself to say the words. I remained silent for a few more moments.

"I know it's mine Marcus," I muttered. "She is not that type of girl."

I thought back to the coincidences, a long line of them to be exact, but at the time, each one seemed insignificant. It was not until Effy planted the thought in my head. It sprouted like a tree, the thought continued to grow as I stalked her, watching her demeanor and body change despite the baggy clothes she tried to hide behind. Until its roots ran too deep, I could not ignore the inevitable truth, which set to destroy the foundations of my life, and uproot my future.

That was why I confronted her, her reaction confirmed it. The way she wrapped her arm around her stomach protectively and stared at me in defiance. She would not get rid of it out of her own free will. I had no choice but to request Marcus' help. Perhaps the persuasion and lure of a huge sum of money would rid me of this problem, and would part her from the child.

⛢

I felt like an over inflated balloon, threatening to burst at any moment. Day by day, week by week, my stomach grew. It became more and more difficult trying to hide the watermelon I was smuggling beneath my abdominal muscles. No matter how baggy the clothes I wore were, they were always snug around my torso.

I needed to get away from here, as loving and as understanding as my mom was, she could barely provide for the two of us on her wage alone. I refused to put any more of a burden on her.

I pulled out items from my drawers, stuffing them into a new weekend bag I had ordered online. My thoughts filled with questions, questions that only one person could answer: Freyja.

Why had she abandoned me in my time of need? I needed her to protect me. I needed her strength and her power, I could have stopped this from happening. If only she had intercepted, I would not be in this position now.

It was agonizing to accept I was powerless, too feeble and weak to have prevented Josh from violating my body without her help. I no longer knew who I was without her, I no longer knew where my entity stopped and hers began. We had always been in sync, she had always had my best interests at heart, until now.

A sudden knock at my bedroom door disturbed my thoughts, my hands stilled for a moment. "What is it mom?" I asked, as the knock grew louder and more impatient.

Cursing under my breath I shoved the weekend bag under my bed and I climbed under the duvet, ensuring the bedding covered me fully. "Mom, you can come in," I called.

The door opened with a creak, slowly the light from the hallway filtered through the gap, casting the figure in the doorway as nothing more than a dark silhouette.

It was too tall and too broad-shouldered to be my mom.

"Um... who are you?"

Freyja

It was as though he were a magnet, and we were mere shards of metal being drawn to him. His aura was compelling and strong.

The stranger who stood before us, his floppy dark blond hair brushed to one side. His hands pushed into the pockets of his gray fitted suit pants. I observed every miniscule detail of him.

He wore black pointed shoes, so shiny you could see your reflection in them. The black shirt he wore was sharp and crisp, not a crease in sight. His tie fastened with intricate precision, its color matching the small triangle of lavender handkerchief that poked out of his gray blazer pocket. The hint of a tattoo that snaked around his neck was only just visible beneath his collar

This stranger was a man who commanded respect and conveyed an undeniable sense of power.

Though what I was trying to determine was: *should we feel safe, or afraid of him?*

Marcus

I was determined to be as callous as my father, to put the family name and reputation above all else, but I knew as soon as I pulled up outside her house it would be easier said than done. This was a girl, a young woman, who had done nothing to provoke his advances, who did not deserve for him to force himself upon her because he was drunk and handled her rejection badly.

I liked this girl already; there were few who would refuse Josh, so I knew she had to be someone special, someone out of his league, either in physical appearance or in mental capacity. I hedged a bet with myself that it was both.

The house was dark inside, no lights were on, no windows were open, and the curtains were all drawn. I glanced at the clock on the dash of my Volvo, 09:45. This girl had to be awake by now. I crept around to the back of the house. I was a recognizable person, the wealthy CEO of Morgan Industries, it would do more harm than good to be seen knocking on her front door.

As I walked through the overgrown yard to the rear of her house, I noticed the back door was left ajar. Instantly it set off alarm bells in my head, my heart thumped in my chest. *What if someone else already knew? Already got to her to use as blackmail?*

I let myself in, trying not to touch anything with my bare hands. The place was neat and tidy, no obvious signs of a struggle or burglary. I did my best to sneak around the house, but my shoes squeaked against the tiles of the kitchen with every step I took.

I cursed my choice of attire, wondering why I had let my father's words persuade me to wear a damn suit. *"If you are dealing with business, you must look like you mean business."* A saying my father always lived by. Even so, I questioned whether he would even wear a suit to bribe this young woman into terminating her unborn child.

It seemed that the house was empty, the lounge was dark, there were no shoes by the front door, nor any keys hung up on the small hooks anchored to the wall. I paused on the bottom step of the staircase at the sound of soft creaking floorboards, the crunch of bed springs, and padded footsteps.

So, someone is home. I had no doubts about it, that person upstairs would be her.

I trundled up the staircase, finding it hard to ignore the family photos lined the walls, all of them showing this beautiful red-haired child, with big green eyes smiling at the camera. Each frame showing more curls and freckles than the last, her facial features changing from a cute and childish girl, into a woman who appeared to embody a goddess. She had elegance and poise in these older snapshots, though sadness behind her piercing green eyes that seemed to imprint themselves in my mind. There was something special about her, something that I could not shake off.

A hard lump formed in the back of my throat along with a pit in my stomach as the realization dawned on me, this red-haired young woman was the one he had violated. She was the one who was pregnant with his child.

The girl looked like an ambitious, kind-hearted person, definitely out of Josh's league. My stomach tightened into knots, *how would she handle being a mother so young? How many of her hopes and dreams would be ruined by keeping this child?*

My heart was beating as I stood outside her door, unsure what I was going to walk into, how she would react to my presence. I even doubted myself whether I could follow through with the plan I had concocted. On paper, it seemed reasonable, the most beneficial for all parties. But now, in the silence of her house, hearing her soft whimpering sobs, I felt more compelled to help her than I did my own brother.

If I had been my father, ever the ruthless brute, he would never have doubted himself, but that was where we were different. I had a heart, it was just buried deep, and I kept it heavily guarded. It had to be, being the CEO of a multi-billion company there were some things you could not do on a whim. I could not just let anyone into my life, I could not just allow myself to love anyone, unless they had been vetted first.

I took a deep breath to steady my nerves as I opened her bedroom door. Her room was stuffy and hot to where I could already feel beads of sweat on my brow. I stood in the doorframe, waiting for my eyes to adjust to the darkness.

A minute or so passed, but all I could see was the outline of her sitting beneath her duvet, clutching it tightly to her chest. Her green eyes shone in both surprise and fear by my intrusion.

I could taste the stale air in the back of my throat, every breath hung heavy in the room. She must not have left here, out of choice, for a while. The overwhelming guilt crashed down on me, I needed to get some fresh air and allow some light into the room. I was uncaring at this point if she protested as I made my way over to the window, throwing open the curtains and pushing the window as far open as it would go.

Inhaling a deep breath of the fresh, crisp air that filtered in from the outside, I felt a little calmer. Even though I could feel her watching me, her eyes burning the back of my head, watching my every movement. *I would too if a stranger barged into my bedroom.*

"Who...who are y-you?" She asked once more, trying to make her voice louder, sterner, but her fear was getting the better of her, indicated by the cracking and faltering of her voice as she spoke.

I could see from the small sliver of light that this pregnancy, or rather the secrecy of the pregnancy, was already taking its toll on her. It was not healthy to keep herself shut up in her bedroom all day. I wondered what she had been doing, moments before I entered her room. My eyes scanned around, noticing empty drawers were left open and there was a scuff in the carpet as if something had been dragged out, *no shoved underneath* the bed.

My stomach churned, *was she planning on leaving?*

My eyes locked onto her, noticing the way she cradled her arms around her torso, protective of the cargo she was carrying.

Shit.

It was then I knew I could not ask that of her, I would not impose the initial plan on her, at least not directly. I perched on the end of her bed, careful not to sit on her feet, and faced her. For the first time I could distinguish her facial features, the deep green color of her eyes, the smattering of freckles across her cheeks and nose. Her hair was the color of my favorite season; fall, reminding me of the vibrant ambers and oranges of fallen leaves.

Her hair was scraped back into a bun, messy, half-hearted as a few strands of curls straggled free and fell in front of her face.

It was clear she was not one to spend hours on her appearance with heavy make-up, her vanity table was empty apart from a few lip glosses and mascara. This girl was a natural beauty, she did not need make-up. Even in this unkempt and disheveled state, she was gorgeous. One of the most beautiful girls, I mean *women,* I had ever seen. How timid and shy she had looked both in her photos and in real life. Modesty was something that could not be taught.

I clenched my jaw, unable to understand how or why my brother had committed such an atrocity against her. I knew she was not the first girl he had raped, but she was the first who had gotten pregnant from his actions.

It made me feel sick - *why her?* He had girls lining up for his attention, he could have had anyone of them whenever he desired. Yet he chose to force himself on the one girl that did not want him, *because she refused him.*

I reached under the bed, finding the handle of a bag. I tugged at it, dumping it on the bed between us. My eyes stared straight at hers. "Going somewhere?" I asked, as I pulled out the envelope from the inside of my blazer, handing it out to her.

Her eyes flitted from the envelope to me several times, her breaths short and shallow. Though she did not speak, her eyes were wide and glassy.

I tried to give her my most charming, welcoming smile, but even to me it felt forced. Instead I allowed my face to soften as my eyes danced over her,

"Alice, I'm here to help you with your little *situation.*"

SIXTEEN

She never could deal with demanding or difficult situations. She had been eight when her mother Sylvi died, succumbing to the treacherous peril that all women face amid childbirth.

Freyja was my only daughter, my only heir, yet she retreated into herself. Refusing to talk to anyone, unable to look at anyone. For months, a year almost, she had become a shadow of herself. Almost as if she too had become a ghost.

Even now, with her hand bound with linen, a crown of daisies nested on her head, taming the sea of fire that flowed beneath it, she was here in body but not in spirit. The Gothi performed the ceremony that would bind Freyja and Erik as man and wife. Only I seemed to be able to see she was hiding in the depths of her subconsciousness.

With the weight of our situation burdened upon her shoulders, despite her firm disapproval of this arrangement, she had accepted this matrimony only out of her undying loyalty for me, her father. I was the leader of our people and we both knew this joining of armies was in the best interests for our clan.

Erik's reputation had preceded him; a ruthless and barbaric warrior. Victorious in every battle he had fought in, evading the halls of Valhalla each and every time as if the gods favored him here on and were not ready to welcome him into their halls yet.

As the leader of another clan, a larger group of trained Viking Warriors, he had shown his strength and his numbers when he landed in Mercia, setting out to invade the lands and rule them.

Freyja was aware of our vulnerability and the desperate need for their alliance in the face of a potential Saxon attack. She agreed to the marriage knowing that she would never set foot in these lands once the ritual was complete. Her wedding gift, a white mare, prepared for their immediate journey to the new Mercian lands.

I could see Gunnar in the crowds, watching while the woman he thought of as his being bound to another man. His jaw was clenched, he was unable to take his eyes off her. I moved closer to him, ready to pounce should he make any attempt to interrupt the ritual, but he never did. Instead, he lowered his head and returned to his empty tent.

She stood there, her dress flowing in the spring breeze, stunning just like her mother during our hand-fasting ceremony. But unlike her mother, her mind was not here, enjoying this moment. I assumed it was elsewhere, amid the clashing of swords and the chaos of a battle that I hoped she would never be a part of.

In stunned silence I watched as Freyja went through the motions; the exchange of rings made by our finest blacksmith, Leif. She never could cope with her feelings, shutting us all out when they had become too much instead.

I knew she did not love Erik, that it was Gunnar her heart yearned for, whom she had envisioned to be her hūsbōndi. Her Fate had been carved in a different direction.

I had failed her, I could tell from her eyes she was now lost to me.

Isobel

On the few occasions I had allowed myself to imagine what kissing him would be like, never had I imagined it would have felt like this. Hot, intense and wild. It was as though the dam that had held all of his pent up emotions had burst. The dividing wall that had separated us crumbled and there was nothing stopping either of us from taking what we wanted.

When we eventually pulled apart, he hugged me close to his chest. "Good night, Bel" he whispered into the top of my hair, feeling his lips against my scalp, his words muffled.

My heart was hammering, my mind was reeling, I was too awake, too alive with energy to try and sleep. Thoughts and feelings whirred around in my head that had surfaced from his kiss. Reminding me of the scale-electric set my friend used to have when we were younger. We would make the car speed around the same continuous loop, increasing speed until it spun off course and collided into the wall with a crash.

I must have eventually fallen asleep, though I was not sure for how long, because when I finally opened my eyes, I was alone. Cole was nowhere to be seen in the loft.

I felt a pang of sadness, does he regret what had happened? Does he not feel the same for me as I do for him? Did he not enjoy the kiss like I did? Does he think the kiss was a mistake?

My mind panicked over what had happened and how he must have sneaked out to start his shift without waking me. I glanced at the time, it was ten o'clock. His shift would have started at nine.

I got to my feet, relieved to see all of his belongings still in the loft. My heart raced with worry, fearing he may have abandoned me after that kiss.

The pain in my ankle snapped me out of my thoughts. Fuck! I winced but continued to keep myself busy by tidying the small space we called home, throwing out the used matches and the burned-out candles.

That was when I noticed the angel ornament I had given him, sitting on top of the book he had been reading, beside my sleeping bag, The angel had been facing me, as if looking over me as I slept. I turned to his sleeping bag, still zipped up and left how it had been the day before.

A sense of warmth flooded me, comforted in the knowledge that he had slept beside me, cuddled into me, for the rest of last night. I was too eager to stay in all day, I needed to go out to feel the fresh air against my face. A clear head and an open mind, ready to embrace whatever Cole's reaction is when he comes home later. I hoped the feelings were mutual, though I could have been mistaken, but that kiss. No one can fake feelings like that, can they?

I took a steady stroll through the town, ignoring the pain in my ankle. My presence went unnoticed, as I blended into the background of the busy crowds that gathered in the town center flooding in and out of the shops. It must have been a Sunday as it appeared most of the shops were only just opening, the sounds of the shutters winding up from over the windows and doors. There was a digital clock in one of them, which also displayed the date. Sunday 5th February; forty-two days after Christmas day.

The town was buzzing; crowded and loud. A group of girls, younger than myself, waltzed through the center with their arms laden with shopping bags, gossiping, and living in their own contented bubble. I watched in envy as they took selfies with their iced coffees and screwed their faces up in laughter looking at the image afterwards without a care in the world. For a split second, I wished I was one of them. What would my life be like?

I shuddered, a sudden chill washing over me, if I had been one of them, I would never have met Cole. I shook the thought from my head, as I scurried away from them, my eyes glancing in shop windows at clothes I could not afford to buy, and smelling the freshly ground coffee and freshly baked cakes from the coffeehouse.

Today was a special day, which was why I knew how many days it had been since Christmas Day. Today was my birthday. Not a "milestone" birthday, I was only turning seventeen, but it meant I was one year closer to being an "adult".

I was counting down, biding my time, until I no longer required parental consent to do anything. I could change my name, or get a tattoo if I wanted, but I was just looking forward to being free to live my life without the burden of my parents having any control over me. If I was to be found now, they could still dictate how I lived myself, if they were sober enough.

Not only that, but today marked the date that exactly a year ago I had first met Cole. I doubted he would remember, since then he had had the burden of looking after us both. His mind was likely too busy to remember such tedious things. But I remembered, because it was the day that he changed my life, for the better.

It marked the day where I had escaped the hellish underbelly of the world accompanied by strange men, breathing over me as they worked themselves up for their release. My stomach churned, the smell of coffee and cakes as I walked past the coffeehouse made me feel nauseous as more memories from the past I was running from played through my mind like a cinematic reel.

I could never truly enjoy my freedom from the past though, not while I lived in constant fear of the monster who 'owned' me; the master that controlled it all. A shudder ran though my body as I recalled his frequent personal visits and being on the tail-end of his wrath; learning it was not just a myth. I was lucky to have survived this long, no other girls who ran had lived to tell the tale.

Today was an enormous deal to me, but I knew that to Cole, it was just another day of survival.

Freyja

Without sorrow, you could never experience the magnificence of love.

Without despair, you could never understand the feeling of hope.

Without darkness, you could never appreciate the power of light.

I contemplated this strange man's words as he left Alice's room, the demure and humble way he spoke. The tone of his voice as he spoke to her, as if he truly cared.

"I want you to call me, when you have decided what is best for you. Especially if you decide to leave."

The room was still and quiet after he left, cold and empty. Alice felt it too, her trembling hand clutched at the envelope, staring at it as if it would spontaneously combust at any moment.

A check, hers to cash and do with as she pleases, with an unsaid agreement, the identity of the father would never be revealed.

SEVENTEEN

Darkness covered the Earth like a blanket. Smothering all light and noise from the ground below. Obscuring my vision of the damage that I had caused. It gave me a brief respite to reflect on all that had happened so far. I did not want a world to exist where she did not belong, it was not fair: all the heartache, all the pain, all the trauma I had endured to keep her healthy and protected. I would not show mercy on those who had not shown it to me, *why should I?* Only one person had been my savior, had been my light through those trialing times, but *he* could not save me from myself. Not this time.

Pain, spite, and rage engulfed me. These actions were not for the 'greater good', they were mine, and mine alone. Destroying Earth with the fires of Hell was my choice, not hers. She may have hated who I have now become, yet she was the one who created this, who made me this monster. She had plenty of opportunities to correct me, plenty of opportunities to prevent this from happening.

I was now the bringer of death, the creator of chaos. I refused to run from myself any longer. Never have I felt more alive, never have I felt more powerful than now, surrounded by the massacre of my making. I had brought about the feared apocalypse.

'The Divine' must have foreseen this future. *Did she know all along this would happen?* Perhaps she wanted to see the end of this Earth as much as I did.

I had erased all of her wrongs from the world - she now had a blank page to start afresh. She could learn from her mistakes if she was not so stubborn to admit them. If she could take responsibility for them, she would know how to do things differently the next time around.

The Divine would be able to mold her creations, harden them to ward of the evilness that had affected them in this one. She could prevent the atrocious actions that humans inflicted upon the world and each other. Once she had mastered it all, perhaps she would think twice about taking another human as a vessel.

As the flames danced closer, licking my skin and stinging with their bites, I opened my arms wide to embrace them. The Divine would not keep me captive in a world where I do not belong. A world without the one thing I never thought I could love, but wanted more than anything else possible.

I would rather burn now, than be her puppet for all eternity.

$$\text{⳥}$$

Francine - 1870

Today I was going to end it all.

I could no longer live this way. I did not want to live with him, or live without my children. Relentless pain and suffering on a continuous loop of misery was all that my life had become. It was too overwhelming, too lonely. This world held no solace for me, I no longer wanted to scrape by in the toxicity of this existence. There was no point, no reason for my being on this Earth.

The voice in my head tried to persuade me to rethink, but no matter what she had said to me, she could not change my mind, she could not stop me.

I was waiting for him to come home, drunk as always, after work. The table was prepared, and our food was cooking away on the stove. Two glasses of wine sat on the table waiting for us to drink. I had already finished my third glass before topping it up again, he would be home any minute now.

I was ready.

"What are you doing woman?" He yelled, crashing through the door. The wine must have sent me to sleep, sat at the table, waiting. "Smells like supper is burning!"

The scent hit my nostrils; it did smell like something was burning. The aroma of charred flesh and soot clung to my nostrils, making my eyes water. I fled to the kitchen and opened the oven door, a billow of smoke engulfed me, causing me to choke.

A layer of crispy blackened skin coated the whole chicken, but thankfully it was salvageable. I dished up our meal, boiled potatoes and seasonal vegetables onto the plate before adding the special ingredient. The finishing touch, the means to an end.

My hand trembled, as I hesitated. The voice questioned me *"are you sure you want to do this?"* it said. *"Are you sure you want to damn your soul?"*

I shrugged, I am already living in Hell, the devil can do no worse than my husband.

I smiled as I took the plates to the dining room table, placing the first plate before my husband. "Enjoy" I said, as I took my seat opposite him, my heart hammering so loudly in my chest I thought for a moment he could hear it.

I watched him devour the food before eating my own.

Like the pig he is, he was soon shoveling mouthfuls of roast chicken, potatoes, and vegetables into his mouth. only stopping for gasping breaths. When suddenly, his cutlery fell out of his hands with a clatter, his hands gripped the edge of the table as he gasped for breath. His facial expressions hardened as if he was turning to stone.

I watched with morbid curiosity and inhuman satisfaction while his eyes opened wide, almost popping out from his skull, as the realization set in. He was going to die.

A laugh escaped me as I watched him flail around, as he tried to stand but his legs were too weak to hold him. This monstrously obese figure swaying, his fingers unable to support his ghastly weight on the edge of the table.

My laugh deepened as he crumpled to the floor like the sack of potatoes I had dumped in the pantry earlier. The harsh thump as his head hit the floor filled me with childish glee, excited by the way he tried to reach out to me, his hand clutching at thin air and his mouth open, trying to beg for my help.

He knew it was too late. I had bested him.

I had tricked him into his own demise, though his own sin of gluttony. Thrilled that my new best friend had not failed me. Strychnine. A readily available vermin killer. I had bought it earlier from the market. It whispered to me, called to me from across the busy crowds.

I had chuckled when the vendor had remarked "you must have a lot of rats" when I handed over the last of our coins to pay for it. It had been a stroke of genius to mix the white powder into the home-made gravy, watching and stirring as every minuscule speck had dissolved. Strychnine was odorless but was said to have a bitter taste. As a precautionary measure, I had added a few spoonful's of sugar just to counterbalance the bitterness. I did not want to raise any suspicions too early into my plan. Failure was not an option.

As I continued to watch him writhe in pain, a line from a Shakespearean play entered my mind: "shuffling of his mortal coil." It was fitting, given the circumstances.

I had read a lot of Shakespearean works. With no children to fuss over and only the house to clean and husband to tidy up after, I was free to fill my day reading his words, over and over. Memorizing my favorite lines from his plays and sonnets. There were many of his quotes that would still fit scenarios in our modern society, and surely for many centuries to come.

"And all the men and women players; They have their exits and their entrances, and one man in his time plays many parts."

∾

Josh

Alice tried to evade everyone as much as possible, she tried to fade into the background, so no one would notice her. Wearing baggy, shapeless clothes to swallow her up, trying to make herself seem invisible. She also stopped working at the shop.

I had noticed, *Asmodeus* had noticed.

I tried not to pay attention to her, my guilt and remorse had led me down the slippery slope of obsessing over her once again. The fear of her speaking out against me had caused me to be aware of her, of her whereabouts, as much as possible.

She was carrying *my* child.

Besides my own feelings, Asmodeus had become fixated with Alice. Recalling his forceful act upon her body, reliving it in my mind over and over. He had become as happy as a pig in shit over how miserable she was, how much he had broken her.

I wished it had never happened, I wished the shadow never found me. It had always been him, controlling and manipulating me into behaviors beyond my control, and at one point I had enjoyed it, reveling in the power I held over them.

But now it had gone too far, the others did not suffer as she was suffering. None of the others had gotten pregnant, *so why her?*

"Josh, I'm worried about Alice," she sighed, her hand resting on my shoulder, a gentle action, but it snapped me back to reality.

We were walking towards my car, the 1985 Chevy Impala. Marcus was guilt-tripped into buying it for me when he found out our father left me out of the inheritance. It was my pride and joy, rarely used but Effy refused to get on my motorbike in fear it would mess up her hair before our date.

"She isn't herself... well you saw her at the shop...I- I cannot get to open up to me- she won't even answer my calls." Effy started sobbing as she got into the passenger seat of my car. I sighed as I got into the driver's seat. "I don't know what to do, Josh, we used to be best friends, now she won't even talk to me."

Asmodeus wanted to respond, to tell her that if she was a better friend she would have already known the truth. She would have been around Alice more to notice the changes, the swollen stomach and the enlarged breasts. He wanted to tell Effy that she had no one other than herself to blame, she had discarded Alice like trash the moment she became my girlfriend.

I managed to refrain him from letting him speak, though my hands were sweaty against the steering wheel. I hated keeping this secret from Effy, I could feel it spiraling out of control.

I knew what was wrong with Alice. I was the reason Alice had not gone to the Summer Solstice Soirée. Effy had been bitter, pinning the blame on Alice being ungrateful and unappreciative of her efforts. I knew the truth, but there was no way Effy could ever find out about it.

It was a night I regretted, but Asmodeus had planned it all along. Every detail he had manifested, down to the shadow that lurked inside Effy's mother, the one who would whisper to her, encouraging her to take her own life.

All it took was a stupid overreaction to a comment made by Effy's younger brother. My stupid insecurities, my stupid ego, my paranoia had brought the worst out in me as did the alcohol I had turned to. Asmodeus had taken advantage, he knew what was going to happen. I had no control over him, especially when I was intoxicated.

Pushing away the thoughts of that night, I tried to focus on the road ahead of me. The winter sun was low, glaring off any reflective surface, blinding even beneath the black shades I was wearing.

Effy had started talking again, but so was the voice in my head.

Freyja

I was helpless and weak, as a wall of darkness surrounded me. I had felt her disconnection and how she had shut me out and pushed me aside.

She could not expel me from her consciousness, despite her continuous attempts, so instead, she had shunned me.

I had avoided her and evaded answering her questions for too long,

I betrayed her.

How could I tell her that this was Fate? How could I tell her that all of this was to rid me of my unwanted soulmate?

Alice would not believe that the child she carries is the key to eradicating all evil from this world.

There had been no easy way for me to tell her the truth, in fact the truth would only raise more questions that I was not prepared to answer, so I remained quiet, waiting for the inevitable to happen.

I have known Alice all of her life, I knew she would grow to love the child inside her, despite the traumatic way it had come into existence. I knew that the child had her protection and she would not allow any harm to come to it.

Even though I was blinded to what was happening, I knew Alice would not terminate this child no matter how much money she had been offered. Her maternal instincts were already in motion. She was a descendant of fierce warriors, she would fight tooth and nail for the protection of her child, of this much I was certain.

Alice did not need to know that she was protecting the future of the Earth in her womb, to love it and cherish its existence.

All that mattered was that this child lived, so that it could destroy my most monstrous creation. Lucifer.

EIGHTEEN

Crystal

"Fuck..."

The phone flew, shattering on impact as it collided with the wall, next to the bed. I flinched. Johnny's fury was like a storm brewing, ready to unleash its destructive force. He was pacing the room, naked. He was already annoyed at me as I was short again this month. But business had been slow, and I had a child to feed. He wanted repayment, now. So, I gave him something that I knew would appease him, to buy me some extra time.

There was only one thing I was good at, one thing that he wanted almost as much as the money: *Sex.*

It seemed to have been working until he received a phone call. Whatever had happened, whatever it was the conversation was about, had darkened his mood. His eyes were murderous.

I was terrified of him, whenever he was in this mood, it resulted in pain being inflicted upon whoever was near him. That was not good news for me.

"That's another one gone," he mumbled, sitting on the bed, pulling on his clothes with conviction. I could feel the anger radiating from him, a silent seething as his mind raced.

"Another fucking OD" he sighed as he held his head in his hands, clutching fistfuls of his hair.

Overdose? Shit. Another one of us girls was dead. That would make it the third in less than two months. It meant triple the loss of his earnings. *How much harder am I going to have to work to cover his losses?* When the first one died, he expected me and the other remaining girls to make up for his economic loss, which had increased when the second perished. And now, there was a third.

I already did not see my child as much as I wanted to. Yet keeping a roof over her head and food in her belly was my only priority. It was the driving force, my motivation, the one and only reason I kept continuing to do this disgusting work. I feared for our safety if

I ever tried to run from him. No one could escape him or his spies, no one *except for her. Lily-*

"Crystal" he looked at me, snapping me out of my thoughts. His expression was not what I had been expecting; soft and pained. He was worried. *Very* worried, and he had a good reason to be.

These deaths were causing suspicion, among the police force. They could uncover the grand scale of his sordid organization, along with all the other illegal sidelines he was juggling, at any moment.

'Crystal' was the name he gave me as my pimp. All those years ago when he had scouted me when I worked as an 'exotic dancer' who provided 'alternative entertainment' in the VIP lounges at the gentleman's club in the local town.

It had been my first job after giving birth, unable to hold down a typical nine-to-five job because of the cost of childcare. Even after working with him for so many years, I still refused to disclose my real name or give him any information about my personal life; my family, my home address.

I thought that by keeping this information a secret, I had something over him, somewhere I could vanish when it came time to quit. Though I soon learned that this was not a job you could walk away from, there was no way you were tendering your resignation and living a normal life afterwards. Many girls had tried and failed. Once you were one of his girls, especially one of his prized 'cash-cows' with plenty of regular clients, you could never leave. Johnny would hunt you to the ends of the Earth if you tried to run from him.

"I need you to do something for me," he said, breaking my trail of thought once more. I noticed he was now dressed and staring at me. My mouth was dry and my chest grew tight. Nothing good ever came from his demands.

He moved as sleek as a fox, hovering over me and straddling me on the bed, asserting his dominance. As he climbed further up the bed, the duvet slipped from my grasp exposing my bare breasts to him once more.

Licking his lips as he held one, pinching my nipple between his thumb and forefinger. He pulled and twisted it hard until I winced in pain. I tried to cover them back up, but he grabbed both my wrists in a swift motion, holding them in one hand, above my head. His other hand closed around my throat, pressing against my windpipe.

"You are going to find me new recruits," he said leaned closer, putting more pressure on my neck. I could feel myself struggling under the weight of him, as he lowered his body onto my legs, his nose now pressed against mine. I had no escape, all I could do was succumb to his demands.

Forcing myself not to panic, telling myself not to make any sudden movements, as I began nodding my head, in my attempt to show him my willingness. I was in no power to object or refuse to obey. I tried to speak, though only, and a croak came out of my mouth.

He released his grip around my throat. I tried not to gasp for breath. His smile was lopsided, as he ran a hand through hair, the color of thick, oily tar. "That's a good girl" he said, as he lowered his hand from my neck to the other breast. Both of his hands squeezed them hard, too hard. I winced.

I knew better than to cower, yet at the slightest hint of pain he yearned to inflict more. His hands crushed them as tight as he could, the enjoyment of my suffering etched across his face. "Please, Johnny!" I pleaded. "You're hurting me."

He let go after a few moments of prolonging the pain, pleased with himself for making me beg. Johnny was as sadistic as they come, relishing in the pain he inflicted upon others. I could see he was hard once more as he got to his feet. He was off to pay another girl a visit, to give them the same demand he had given me.

I watched him as he walked towards the door, pulling the duvet up around me, to cover me as his back was turned to me. He stopped and glanced over his shoulder.

"You have two weeks to find me two girls for my payroll. You'll get a bigger cut if you can get me a third girl." I nodded my head. "You better get to your darling daughter, while you have a couple of hours free" he remarked, looking at his phone.

"Your daughter is called Roxanne, isn't she?" He paused, enjoying the look of horror that flashed across my face. "I wonder if she will follow in the footsteps of her mother." He smirked as he stepped out of the door, slamming it shut behind him.

I shuddered, my blood running cold through my veins. *How did he know my daughters' name?* I panicked, knowing that I had never told him any personal information, especially about my daughter.

What else does he know about me?

I had never got dressed and rushed out of his premises so fast in my life. Over my dead body would I allow my daughter to live this way. I forced myself to move fast, despite the pain in my nether regions from the brutal way he had fucked me earlier.

No daughter of mine will work for someone like him. But the reality was I had to find at least two women who would. Two women that were other peoples' daughters, so that he could replenish his assets, as if we were livestock.

I had to go against my better judgment and sign them up for a life of Hell, convince them to sign their bodies and their souls to the living, breathing devil that was Johnny Malone.

$$\mathcal{S}$$

Josh – FLASHBACK: The Summer Solstice Soirée.
I glanced at my watch as I swaggered up the path to her front door. 17:25.

Smiling to myself, knowing that I had made it early enough to avoid an argument, knowing the hours of organization she had put into this night had stressed her out. *Perhaps there was time to help her relax a little.* I thought to myself as I hardened at the thought of burying myself deep into her tight slit, I was sure she would not refuse me so long as I did not mess up her hair.

I knocked on the door, clasping my hands together, blocking my arousal from view. Trying to tame down my thoughts, my devious plan of seduction. Even though everyone loved me and worshiped the ground I walked on, as if I was God, I still thought better than displaying my sexual prowess to someone such as her mother, should she answer the door instead of Effy.

I was fiddling with my tie when the door opened, revealing a scrawny boy, who appeared to be no older than thirteen. His blond hair was scruffy, and he wore an old, faded t-shirt emblazoned with the words "Screaming Orgasms" above a picture of a long-haired, all scantily-clad female band that I never knew existed.

"Hi. I'm here to see Effy," I said, my confidence oozing with every word, my charming smile creeping onto my face. "Are you Effy's brother?"

He nodded "James" he replied standing up a little taller, a little straighter, trying to mimic my confident stance as his eyes looked me over from head to foot. This was the first time I had come to her home, I had not yet met anyone from her family.

I was suited to perfection, on Effy's orders. None of my other girlfriends dared to dress me, to boss me around or try to control me. I was not even sure why I let her or why I cared about her feelings. I did not for any of the others.

"She's not here," he replied, shutting the door. I held my hand out to stop him.

"Don't mess about, James," I warned, "she told me to pick her up at half-past six."

"She is not here," James snapped, rolling his eyes in impatience. Boredom etched all over his face. Either he was an Oscar-winning actor, or he was telling the truth.

"Well, if she isn't here, where is she then?"

He pulled an exasperated face, shrugging his shoulders. "I dunno. She said something about checking in on Alice... or was it checking in on Alice's date?", he shrugged, a false apologetic smile flicked across his face.

I have a knack for telling when someone is lying. Typically they avoid eye contact, but his gaze bore straight into mine, he was challenging me. A smirk curled at his lips, knowing I had taken the bait.

"I've noticed she seems to use that excuse a lot," he said as he pulled his phone out of his pocket, and then slipped it back into his jeans, "and I noticed she has been coming home rather late too."

James lifted his chin in the air and sniffed in the gap between us. "Is that your usual cologne, Paul?" He asked. I stepped back, trying not to let my anger or shock show on my face.

Who the fuck is Paul?

"I'm not Paul." I remarked, trying to harness my anger. "I'm Effy's boyfriend, *Josh.*"

His brow furrowed as he shook his head. "I don't think I've heard that name... I definitely recall her saying her boyfriend was called Paul... it's not a code name for you, is it?" He smirked as he sniffed the air once more, I was losing my grasp of my rage, I could feel it slipping out of my pores quicker than I could try and compose myself. My muscles were shaking and my nails dug into the palms of my hands.

"It is definitely a different cologne she smells of when she does *eventually* come home."

His words hit me like a punch to the gut. *Is she seeing someone else? Would Effy have the bollocks to cheat on me?*

I stood there too stunned to move as he slammed the door shut in my face.

Growling to myself, I headed to Jay's Jazz bar, a terrible decision. I should have just waited for her outside of college, at least that way I could have gotten some answers.

I cared about her, more than I had anyone else before. I felt betrayed, her brother's words hurt more than they should have.

I was always the one who cheated. Feeling used and abandoned was not a feeling I was accustomed to. *Did she even realize how lucky she was?*

After Asmodeus had taken his opportunity with Alice, we returned to the bar. I had no intentions of going to the Soirée after that. I would rather stay here and drink until I could no longer remember my own name. Hoping that the bottom of a bottle of whisky or two would help drown these thoughts and feelings that lived inside me.

Who the fuck is Paul? Who the fuck does she think she is? No one cheats on me!

Without realizing, I stood outside the main entrance to the college, with an urgent need for answers. I was two hours late.

My fists clenched, my jaw tightened as I tried to scout her among the students, dancing too close on the makeshift dance floor or kissing and groping in the darkest corners. *Was she among them? Was she here with him? Had she sought comfort from him instead of me?*

She found me, all disheveled and drunk, sitting at the make-shift bar where only non-alcoholic drinks were being served. Thankfully, I had snuck in my hip flask filled with whisky.

Effy tapped me on the shoulder, I tried to ignore her, but she was persistent.

"Josh? What's going on?"

"Who the...f- fuck is P-P-Paul?" I stuttered, "are...you...f-fucking...someone...e-else?" I demanded, though my words were nothing more than a slur.

Her slap across my check caught me off guard. The skin stung from where her hand had made contact. She tried to push me away from her when I grabbed her wrists. "Your brother told me..." I started, my words sounding more coherent, as if the slap had sobered me up.

She was furious, "That little shit!" She scowled, before bursting into tears. "I would never. I haven't been... He's lying!" She sobbed, as my hands still held her wrists.

"My mum... she is *ill,* I try to keep as much of it from him. Sheltering him from seeing her when her mind is in a *bad place,*" her voice cracked.

Something about her reaction made me believe her, using her wrists in my grasp to pull her closer to me. Our faces inches apart, I could see it in her eyes, the truth of her words.

"Effy..." I breathed, my lips brushing against hers, feeling her bottom lip tremble. I let go of her wrists. "Effy... I'm sorry" I mumbled, brushing my thumbs under her eyes, wiping away her black mascara-stained tears.

I cupped her head in my hands and kissed her, a hard, passionate, *fuck-what-people-think* kiss. Smiling as I felt her arms snake around my neck as she pressed her body against mine.

My member stirred at her closeness, her heat teasing the tip purposely. "I have wanted to be with you for such a long time Josh... I would never, ever do that..." she whimpered as she broke the kiss, her nose brushed against mine. "I love you."

I froze at her words, I had heard them before from the other girls I had been with, all of them at one point told me they loved me, but hearing them from her felt different.

Something stirred inside me, a desire to hear her say them over and over, an urge overcome me to say it back. Never had I told a girl *that*, because it was never love only lust, but Effy had taken me by surprise. I felt different when I was in her presence.

Do I love her? I asked myself, as another kiss ensued.

"Yes... yes you do" the darkness inside hissed angrily. My stomach churned, not sure whether to feel elated or scared.

Joy coursed through my veins, savoring the discovery of something real and significant, while my fear lurked within, stemming from my insecurities, a childhood that lacked love and compassion. *How can I love her when I do not know what love is?*

Asmodeus stirred within, his voice cutting through my thoughts. *"As long as Effy remains open to trying new things, I have no plans to break up your relationship. Besides, her eagerness to please you is... delicious."* He paused as a shudder rippled though my body. *" I am finished with Alice...for now."*

Silence blanketed us, my voice faltered as I spoke. "Effy, I-" A lock of her blonde hair untangled itself and fell in front of her eyes. I swept it back, so that I could stare into them unobstructed. I studied her face; her eyes were ringed with smudged black eyeliner, her foundation streaked with pale tear tracks and her lipstick had now worn off. But she still looked beautiful.

"Effy, I'm sorry for ruining your night," I told her "You look amazing."

Her gaze dropped to the floor, unable to shield the disappointment from flickering over her face. She was desperate to hear those three little words come out of my mouth. She bit her bottom lip as it started to quiver.

"Effy, I have never said this to anyone..." I pressed my mouth to her ear, as if I feared other people overhearing me admit my weakness, my true feelings. "I love you too".

There was a sudden intake of breath before she crushed her lips against mine, I could feel her desire burning through her skin, her need and her want matching my own.

We slipped out of the decorated hall, finding a quiet, unlocked storage room. "I want you Josh," she whispered, her hand reaching under the waistband of my pants. "I need you. Now."

It took no persuasion on my part, as I lifted her dress to reveal her black lace underwear, my member bulging until it was uncomfortable. I pulled at her lacy undergarments until they tore off in my hands. She squealed in delight as my fingers explored her excited slit.

I threw her against the wall, as she used the shelving rack beside us as a foothold, I took her, hard and deep and fast. My urgency to mark her as mine, my desire to fill her with my seed overwhelmed me.

Effy's small gasps quickly turned into loud throaty cries as she failed to control her pleasure. I could feel her inner walls tightening around me feeling the softness of her flesh against my balls as she took my full length.

I could feel the muscles in her body tightening, embracing themselves for the impact of her climax. "Come for me," I moaned, as my release was building. I could feel myself slipping, losing control, as my seed swelled in my balls. Soon I was observing the scene, no longer in control of my body.

"*Come for me...*" Asmodeus growled, as he drove his hips into her harder and rougher. One of my hands was around her throat, the other holding both of her wrists above her head as he continued to thrust deep into her warmth.

It seemed too familiar; the control of a defenseless woman; realization hit me like I had just been hit by a truck. *He is trying to recreate the scene with Alice.*

"I'm... I'm coming!" she gasped, her eyes squeezed shut as she rode her wave of pleasure, "Fuck, Josh don't stop!" Her body bucked against mine, her walls clenching my shaft, milking me for my seed.

"That's a good girl...*Alice.*" Asmodeus purred as my load shot forcefully inside her.

Her eyes snapped back open, just as he released his control on me. Gasping from the orgasm, my member still inside her I was too stunned to comprehend what he had said.

She pushed me away, hard, my back hitting the shelving racking. "What the FUCK!" She shrieked, her voice angry, but raspy from her climax. "Did you... did you just call me fucking *Alice?*"

Tears had sprung into her eyes, rolling down her cheeks within seconds. "You said you loved me!" She shouted, pulling down her dress. Anger rose within me, "*what the fuck? Why did you fucking do that?*" I yelled at him, as she continued to stand there in silence, staring at me.

"*I got carried away,*" Asmodeus replied, his breath unmistakably heavy, his tone was uncaring. "*You can not deny that it was not the best orgasm you have ever had though?*" He chuckled.

I stood stock still, the last of my load still dripping from my manhood, as I tried to catch my breath. *Fuck you.* I cursed trying to block him out.

I shoved my limp shaft back into my boxers and done up my pants, just as Effy had decided to leave, giving up on getting any explanations from me.

"Effy... I-"

"Don't!" She cried, leaning against the back of the door. "Everyone has always wanted *her and not me,*" she sobbed. "I should have expected that you were only using me to get to her." Her voice was low and quiet. She too was broken because of *me* and my shadow.

"Effy, that's not true." I tried to reason with her, my hands gripping her wrists once more. "I do love you, Effy." My words, even to my own ears, sounded pathetic. This situation did not look good.

I knew then that I had lost her, the only person that I had truly cared about. The only *woman* I had ever loved, all because of *Asmodeus.*

Her eyes flickered up into mine, she was scared of me, my hands were too tight around her wrists. "Please Josh, let me go."

Effy - FLASHBACK: Two Days After The Summer Solstice Soirée.

I was lost without him. I felt as if a huge part of me was missing. It was devastating to be called her name as I passed the very peak of my climax. Distraught to feel his load pumping inside of me, as he imagined he was fucking her.

I was unable to sleep, or eat, or even continue to function with my day-to-day life without him. It hurt to ignore his calls, to not respond to his messages when they appeared on my phone, but every time I saw his name flash up on the screen, the flashback of that moment would resurface.

An image of the two of them sneaking around behind my back filled me with rage, but I loved him, and I had believed him when he had said mere moments before that he loved me too. *So why was he thinking of fucking my best friend?*

I had heard the rumors, heard that he had tried to charm her, had asked her to be his date to the Soirée, on the same day that he had asked me. I thought she hated him; she had shown such distaste towards him throughout my crush on him. *Was that all for show?*

I did not want to believe that she had betrayed me like that, but I was not sure of anything anymore. I had tried calling her, I had even popped over to her house the next day, but her mom had told me she was not well.

I needed answers almost as much as I needed him.

As I looked at my phone, my finger hovering over the call button beside his name, it sprang to life. *Think of the devil, and the devil will appear* I thought as his name flashed up on my screen. Josh - BF.

I snatched it up to my ear, hitting the accept button, desperate to hear his voice.

"Effy?" He asked, sounding unsure and broken, "Effy... please forgive me... I- I dunno what happened, why I said her name..." he mumbled, his words almost too fast to comprehend.

"Josh, I have some questions, can I see you?" I asked.

"Yes! Of course! Come now!" He said, his voice sounding excited, hopeful.

Within an hour we were fucking on his sofa, almost as if that ordeal had never happened. He had sworn an oath on my life that he had never been with her. I had allowed myself to believe his lies, allowed myself to get caught up in the moment.

"Effy, I don't know why, but I don't even find her attractive... see...feel... this right here, this is all because of you".

He had pushed my hand inside his boxers, sliding his rock-solid shaft against my palm. instinctively it wrapped around it. I heard his groan as I slowly slid it along his length.

His words became heavy pants as I increased my rhythm. "Why would I want her... when I already have you?"

His breath was hot against my ear. He claimed he loved me over and over, as I ran my hand along his length. He practically shouted it at the top of his lungs when I took it in my mouth, allowing my lips to stretch around him, forming the tight seal that I knew he loved, allowing him to thrust against me until the tip reached the back of my throat.

"Fuck Effy, I love you so much." *Perhaps the more he said it, I more I would actually believe it.*

I had swallowed his excuses and lies as I swallowed his load, trying not to think too much about it. Burying my repulsion and jealous feelings deep within me. If I wanted to keep him, I had to learn to accept I was always going to be second best.

If I can keep him wanting me, and not her, and he truly is not fucking her behind my back, then I can try to forget it ever happened. Of course, there was always going to be that flicker of doubt that would lurk in the dark depths of my mind, but I knew I either had to deal with it and move on or end it for good.

I knew I could not do the latter.

"Effy, I love you" he purred as he nuzzled my neck, his hands cupping my breasts as he took me from behind. His thrusts were long and hard, the need to please me, to make me forgive him spurned him on. Every time he entered me, I felt his hips smack into my buttocks, I would expel a cry of pleasure. I could not control it, *he was so fucking good.*

I gripped onto the back of his leather sofa, digging my nails in leaving faint crescent marks indented in the brown material.

Second best never felt so good.

NINETEEN

Josh

I could hear Effy talking now, as we drove, my mind thinking about how lucky I had been to keep her, how he had given me the green light to tell her my true feelings moments before fucking it all up by saying Alice's name as I'd ejaculated inside Effy.

I looked across at Effy and smiled, amazed that she had forgiven me. The quizzical look on her face made me realize that everything she had said had not registered, it had all just sounded like a babble of unfamiliar sounds.

"I mean, if it was anyone else, I'd think she was pregnant!"

"What-?" I spluttered, slamming me back into the here and now with such force that I slammed my foot down on the brake. The car screeched to a sudden halt. My heart was in my mouth.

"Josh? What are you doing?" She asked confused, "are you dropping me home?"

"Effy, did you just say that Alice is pregnant?" I asked, as I drove through the town center.

She chuckled "Alice has never had a boyfriend, let alone had sex with someone... unless there is something you're not telling me?" Her eyes narrowed as she looked at me, I shook my head, trying to control my shock. For a moment I thought she knew the truth, that she was going to blurt out my disgusting secret.

She seemed content with my reaction, turning to look out the window, as an awkward silence fell between us. I grabbed her hand, brushing my lips against the back of it, before returning to the steering wheel.

That seemed to appease her further, she smiled and looked back at me. "We may no longer be as close as we once were, but I'm sure she would tell me if she was pregnant. We are like sisters, so I will get the truth out of her..."

She looked at me then, her eyelashes fluttering, "Josh, please tell me the truth, did anything happen with you... and Alice?"

I shook my head, leaning over to the passenger seat to kiss her firmly on the lips, to reaffirm my innocence. "Effy, since being with you, I have been faithful to you... I haven't fucked *her* or anyone else; I swear... that is something I cannot say about many of my past relationships." A lump formed in the back of my throat, my lie slowly choking me.

I returned to focusing on the road ahead, as we rolled to a stop at another set of traffic lights. "I want to be the boyfriend you deserve. I want to be with you, and only you."

That little smile she gave made my heart leap, I never thought that I, Josh Smith, would have been smitten in my life, yet here I was. Effy had given me her heart and had captured mine along the way. I had no intention of breaking either of them. But I did not trust myself whilst Asmodeus was still inside me.

"Well, I think it's all just a coincidence, I doubt if she has even kissed a boy, to be honest!" she chuckled. "But I'm worried about her, about what others will think of her...and I'm struggling to reach her, to help her, but I don't know what I have done wrong!"

She pouted, staring out of the window in silence, watching as the raindrops trickled down, on the outside.

Coincidences. My father always warned me: "there is no such thing as a coincidence."

I knew one day the truth would be uncovered, unless my brother could get through to her, make her get rid of the child before it is too late.

Fuck. My future once again is beyond my control.

෩

Maxine

She had come into the shelter earlier today than she usually would, so it surprised me to see her.

"It's not quite time yet," I said, pointing to the clock. It had sections painted yellow to show when the pantry and storeroom were open.

I saw her shake her head and motion to the bathroom. I nodded and turned my back to feign ignorance. I could not get in trouble if she snuck in while I was not looking. I knew we were supposed to charge for use of the showers, it was one of the main rules, but I never did, not just for her, but for anyone who needed it. *It would be much easier to talk to them if I couldn't smell them as soon as they walked through the door.*

I had been counting down the hours of community service I had left; I only had a little over thirty-five hours until I had fulfilled my court order. One more week of being here, until I could push forward with my plans to get my daughter back.

A massive part of me felt relieved as I would no longer have to come here and be reminded of how close I had come to becoming like them, but another part of me wondered what would happen to *her*. *I wish I had reached out to her sooner, perhaps I could have been more help to get her out of this situation.*

I shook my head, scolding myself. Hearing my mother's harsh words when I spoke to her on the phone the other evening. She was less than empathetic.

"Max, focus on yourself, focus on getting Laurie back. This homeless girl is not your responsibility, but Laurie is." Her voice was clipped, trying to hold back her annoyance and disappointment in my actions that had led to her taking custody of my daughter. "You owe it to Laurie to make amends, to do right by her. You do not owe this girl anything but the service you provide in your mandatory community service order."

I watched the girl, whose name I still didn't know, reappear, all clean and sparkling. If I had passed her walking along the street, I would not have known she was homeless.

Can I really turn my back on her?

$$\text{❦}$$

Freyja

Soulmates.

Everyone is predestined to have at least one, me included, though my soulmate bond was more of an accidental happenstance of my doing, rather than destiny.

For some humans, who lived with their hearts and minds open, finding them was easy, but for those who did not, they found it difficult, if not impossible. Those that were conceited and arrogant, malicious, and violent or manipulative and dishonest; they had no room in their hearts for anyone other than themselves.

Although those who were shy and suspicious of people also found it difficult to find their soulmates, too scared to wander too close to the flame that is love, for fear of getting burned. It may not have seemed fair, but that was the grueling reality of life.

Life is not always fair.

To live a life without feeling that bond of pure unadulterated love was not a life not worth living, nor was any human life if they did not seize every opportunity thrown their way, or to climb over an obstacle in their path.

This girl, my vessel, was a fighter. Her ancestors had been fighters too, strong-willed, weapon-bearing, and valiant Vikings, who loved just as hard as they fought. The Vikings cherished and respected nothing more so than the Gods, followed by their hyski - their family.

Her soulmates were out there, but her path to them would not be easy. For around every corner in her life there would be trialing obstacles, destined to test her, to test her soulmates' resilience and strength of love for one another.

Throughout time, many humans failed to find their soulmate, or keep them, because of the path they chose. Opting for the easiest route, to walk away rather than stand and fight, which would lead them to a life of unfulfillment and unhappiness.

I may have had a wicked sense of humor. Yet, I gave all my creations a chance of true happiness and love. In fact most humans had multiple soulmates that traversed their lifetimes. But choice lay with them. They needed to decide whether they felt it was worth their time and effort, which would lead to another harsh reality of life.

Life was never meant to be easy.

Alice

I was still sitting staring at the envelope in the bed, my breath baited and my heart and pounding, long after he had left. I was still trying to get my mind around the implied ultimatum that lay within the envelope. Get rid of my baby or leave.

If was to leave, I would lose any connections to friends and family and could never return. That part he had made crystal clear. If I left, Alice Bowers would cease to exist. With a new name, new identity, I would have to disappear without a trace, vanish like a ghost.

Inside the envelope was a check, for a sum of money my brain struggled to comprehend. A vast sum of money that I would never earn in my lifetime. Three-million dollars. A large amount of money doesn't seem real, but that was what they felt my baby or my silence was worth.

I should have asked who he was, or how he knew Josh, but my mind was too stunned at the check that he was offering me. *Three-million dollars.*

The stranger had explained it was more than enough to cover the costs of private medical treatment, such as a termination and to pay off my mother's debts. There was even enough to pay off my student loans and live comfortably for the rest of our lives.

"My mom wouldn't have to work as hard" I had mumbled, taking my eyes off of the check for a moment to look at him.

"Your mom wouldn't have to work at all, if it's properly invested," he sighed.

I had studied his face, there was a softness within him, as if he was trying to hold back from saying what he truly wanted to. Every now and then his jaw would clench and he would tear his eyes away from me, fiddling with the handkerchief or his tie to distract himself.

I looked back at the check to the bag that was still open on my bed, untouched from when he had put it there. On the back of an envelope was his name, and a telephone number. His words echoed in my mind; *"I want you to call me when you have decided what is best for you. Especially if you decide to leave."* He had made me promise to call him, no matter the time of day or night.

My jaw dropped when I finally plucked up the courage to look at it: *Marcus Morgan.*

The check and envelope fell out of my hand, fluttering like feathers into the bag, his name blazing up at me from his neat italic scrawl. I didn't need to search him on the internet to know who he was, but I did it anyway. *No way was that him.* But photo after photo confirmed that Marcus Morgan had been in my house, in my room, and offered me money to get rid of this baby or keep quiet and leave.

What business does the CEO of Morgan Industries have with my unplanned pregnancy? What was his connection to Josh Smith?

I stowed the back in the back of my wardrobe, scared that if he had found it so easily, so would my mom. I needed time to contemplate, to figure things out, but I knew time was not on my side.

How will I even explain to my mom how I got the money from? Even if I claim to have won the lottery, she will still ask questions.

I was already living a tangle of lies regarding Freyja, so I would struggle to cope with any new ones woven into it. Lying was not in my nature, I struggled to keep track of them.

By accepting this money, it would either sentence me to a lifetime of banishment from my mother, or sentence my baby, which has been growing rapidly inside me for weeks, to death.

No. Not even an option. I never thought I could feel love for something that was created in such a heinous and malicious way. But I did. I have developed a love so blindingly fierce and protective as it grew inside me. *A termination is completely out of the question.*

Three-million dollars would be enough to start a new life to purchase a new legal identity. But it would be just me and my baby. I would have to cut everyone out of my life, including my mom.

I was not sure if I could do that either. *How am I supposed to do this all on my own?*

Isobel

I gave Maxine a quick smile before I left the shelter, though she never returned it, her eyes were glazed over as she stared at me, as if she was lost in her own thoughts.

The smell of coconut shampoo filled my nostrils as I headed back to the loft, taking the shortcut through the cemetery and along the housing estate.

The air seemed to have dropped at least two degrees here, the sun that shone brilliantly in the sky was blocked by the towering church, leaving the ground here cast in its shadow.

The ruins of the old church had almost corroded into nothing but piles of rocks covered with thick green moss. The gravestones were wonky and irregular in this part of the cemetery, part of the old church.

Time and weather had eroded most of the gravestones, yellow lichen spread over the surfaces making it difficult to make out the names and dates. It was a stark contrast to the front of the church, with all the pristine graves, polished marble and granite headstones with gold engraved lettering.

These people had been forgotten about over time. I gulped at my own impending demise; this is what my grave would look like, if I even got a grave at all.

I paused as I noticed two unmarked graves, only indicated by two simple stone crosses that bore no writing that I could see. They were isolated from the others. Over time the crosses had cracked and parts were beginning to crumble.

Curious and intrigued, I studied their graves. Forever to remain unknown.

"Legend has it that they were part of a murder-suicide pact..." I turned on my heel, losing my balance, to see where the voice had come from.

"The wife is said to have killed her wealthy and gentlemanly husband before killing herself. Legend states that she was insane." She paused, "Personally, I just think she had had enough of his shit."

A girl stood before me, a little over a few feet, though I had not heard her approach. She smiled once she realized she had my full attention. "I'm Alice by the way" she said as took another step forward. Even though her smile and her body language was friendly and welcoming, I made it clear that I was suspicious of her. In all fairness I suspected everyone, apart from Cole, of wanting something from me or to do me harm.

She stopped a foot or so away from me, her outstretched hand reaching in my direction. "I want to help you." The girl, Alice, as the wind whipped her fiery red-hair into her face, and in front of her like more hands reaching towards me. She had a delicate heart-shaped face and her green eyes shone like beacons, revealing nothing but warmth and kindness behind them.

Alice wore a denim knee-length skirt and a white blouse which had small orange and daisies embroidered around the collar and hem. The buttons were small gold-colored daisies with small diamante gems in a cluster at the center of the flower.

She did not look all that much younger than me.

I looked down at my own clothes, feeling embarrassed and scruffy, wearing baggy jeans with tears and rips, a faded gray T-shirt, accompanied with a black jacket that had a hole in the pocket. I kept my gaze fixated on the pair of old grubby pink converses that were on my feet. Everything I was wearing had been donations given to the Shelter, items that Maxine had set aside prior to my shower earlier.

My appearance compared to hers was like that of complete opposites. Chalk and cheese. Black and white. Clean and Dirty. Loved and unloved.

"What's your name?" she asked.

I was thrown off by her directness, and as I stared at her I felt compelled to tell her.

"Isobel," I mumbled, scuffing my feet, as I kept my eyes lowered to the floor. I felt as though I was not worthy of being in her presence, let alone talking to her.

"Come with me Isobel," she smiled, linking her arm with mine. "We are going to be good friends."

I walked in silence, allowing her to lead the way.

TWENTY

I could not get the image out of my head. Seeing him violating her body tormented my thoughts. It had even crept into my dreams. Every time I recalled her face seeing how broken she looked it caused my anger to flare up inside me. It made my blood boil as I remembered the look of pain in her dark-green eyes.

To see her like that had ignited a fresh wave of hatred towards my brother as bile rose in the back of my throat. She was beautiful. Even though she had messy hair and wore no make-up, she was still gorgeous. Even more beautiful than the woman who was softly snoring beside me. A woman I had taken as a distraction to get Alice out of my head, even if only for a few moments. *What is her name again? Lucy? Lauren?*

It did not work. Instead my mind was playing twisted fantasies in my head. Last night this woman's face morphed into Alice's as I drove my shaft so hard and fast into her that she screamed so loudly the people in the apartment below banged on the ceiling. I cringed as I recalled the moment I had murmured Alice's name. The woman underneath me had stilled, before she responded. "I can be anyone you want me to be, *Mr. Morgan.*"

Fuck. What is wrong with me? I have done my part, she had the check, now all I need to do is wait for her decision and make the necessary arrangements.

I was once told how pregnancy induces hormones that can make them appear to 'glow' yet I had never believed it. I had never understood how that was possible considering the additional strain on their bodies and the additional weight gain. I had envisioned pregnant women to swell like a balloon, to be repugnant, not radiant and alluring. That was until I met her. Alice made me realize how wrong my thoughts had been, not just about pregnant women, but about all women in general.

What a chauvinistic, shallow prick I had been.

When I had been sitting opposite Alice on her bed, I could not stop staring at her, from feeling attracted to her. Thinking of how much I wanted to cup her face in my hands and kiss that plump mouth of hers, to cuddle her, to show her what it felt like to be with someone who cared for her. *What am I thinking?*

I would not jeopardize the plan, not for any personal desire, fleeting or otherwise, that I may harbor for her. Alice had been hurt enough by one of us Morgan men, she did not need any more trouble in her life.

My reputation has preceded me; forever immortalized on the internet. Reporters were quick to report that I had nothing but a string of love interests and meaningless one-night stands. The last thing Alice needs is paparazzi hovering around her ass like flies on shit.

When I looked at her that day, I could not help but question: How was my brother capable of inflicting such horror upon her?

The woman beside me stirred, her arm draped over me as if she had some kind of hold on me. I shoved it off, laying there, staring at the ceiling as I recalled meeting Alice for the first time.

She had not been who I had expected to see when I entered her house; someone pure and innocent and so far from his usual taste in women. I knew she had to be different when I learned she had rejected him, on multiple occasions. But even the ones I had to pay for their silence had been vain and confident. Most of the girls were determined to milk the Morgan empire for all it was worth because they had been raped by the youngest family member. By Josh. I could not blame them for wanting compensation.

But not her.

I had read her facial expressions and body language like an open book. Her surprise and her unexpectedness of the situation was genuine. She had not been looking for a payout. It was almost as if she had no idea who Josh was, who I was, and what legacy we had derived from.

Before I had visited her, I had hired a private investigator to run a full background check on her. I wanted as much information as possible, a way for me to understand her and her background before I met her. It held no recent photos of her, apparently she was not present on any social media platforms. The only photo they had pulled up was her college yearbook photo, but that had not been the girl I had seen, this photo was a shell of her, her eyes had no spark, no life to them.

I clocked the date on the timestamp, three days after Josh raped her.

I crawled out from my bed, and headed into the small office I had in the adjacent room, her file still sitting in the drawer. Her name was staring up at me: Alice Bowers, and was thin and flimsy, containing notes from years ago when she had tonsillitis and had her tonsils removed. Her cell phone call and text logs, her emails - which were few and far between, and her educational reports.

There had been nothing of any substance there, no criminal records or anything that showed up as instant red flags, only her lack of social media, which was rare in this day and age. Everyone, even myself, was lured into the craze of social media. I had been looking for signs she had any ulterior motives, but Alice was as clean and as innocent as they came.

There was not much to learn about her from those pages of information that I had paid a large sum of money for. My short, succinct notes glared at me from the notebook in my hand.

- Alice Bowers.

- Twenty years old.

- Lives at home with her mom.

- Her father died in a vehicle collision when she was a child.

- No social media presence.

- Large student loan, used to pay her tuition and paid into her mom's bank account to cover bills.

- No social life outside of college - no records of her at any parties or bars since she first started college.

- She had a part-time job in a small village shop - but had been let go recently because of 'habitual sickness', for undisclosed medical reasons.

- Nothing apparent in her medical records, also no repeat prescription for birth control.

- She held a full driving license but did not have her own car.

- No obvious boyfriend or love interests from her calls or text exchanges.

- She only seemed to contact two numbers - her mom Elizabeth and one close friend, Stephanie, though Alice not responded to text messages or calls for weeks.

I made these notes before I visited her, with the help of my most trusted advisor, we based the plan on what seemed like the best incentive. What could we offer her that would entice her to keep her silent? Or better yet, to terminate her pregnancy?

Offering her money seemed to be the best plan of action, agreeing to pay her more than enough to cover a private abortion and to settle all of their financial woes. But when I came face-to-face with her, I could not bring myself to suggest such a thing.

It seemed almost absurd to think that money could resolve the situation for her. She had made it very clear that she had no intention of using this child as a weapon for monetary gain.

I smiled as I recalled the moment she opened the envelope, her hand trembling when she saw that sum of money. She instantly shoved it back in my direction and refused to accept it. "I can't take this." Alice had whimpered.

"It's not a mistake, Alice, that money is yours. All three-million dollars of it." I had insisted, placing it back into her hand.

I had not needed to say the words aloud, it was already clear that she would not disclose who the father of her child was. If she wanted the world to know how disgusting my brother was, she would have squealed to all of the papers by now.

No, she was embarrassed. Too ashamed of what Josh had done to her to talk. The reality of her suffering and of her fear. made my anger and loathing towards him surge through me like a white-hit electrical current. I slammed my fist on the desk in front of me, there was not enough money in the world that would compensate for the suffering she has endured. There was also no way I could put a fair price on her unborn child's life.

I was intrigued by her, invested in her, feeling compelled to help her. I had never felt this way with any of the others who had fallen victim to his vile acts. I tried to tell myself that it was because she was the only one who had fallen pregnant, but I knew the truth was a lot more complex than that.

There was a soft padding of footsteps, leading from the bedroom. I imagined the woman I brought back gathering up her clothes that had been whipped off and abandoned in various places in my apartment, before hearing the lock clicking of her heels as the door slammed shut behind her.

My mind snapped back to Alice, as it had for the past week. I struggled to think of anything else. I found I could not focus on anything else other than my compulsion to her.

Unwilling to admit the full extent of these feelings, I tried to suppress them by working longer hours, but no matter what I had been doing, Alice Bowers was living rent free in my mind for this last week; her, and the child she was carrying inside of her. I struggled to comprehend the tough decisions that lay before her.

There was also something else stirring inside me, the attraction towards her - like a magnetic pull. So far I had resisted the temptation to check in on her, but the urge to see her again was becoming too strong to keep ignoring. The longing to see her face - those piercing green eyes. I yearned to see her smile, to make her life better, to help her however I could.

I flicked through the file, hoping to find something I had not seen before, but the girl was a mystery to me. *Who are you, Alice Bowers?*

I snapped the file shut and shoved it back in the drawer, slamming it shut as if that would remove the imprinted image of her from my mind. I stumbled back to my bed, the sickly, sweet perfume of the woman who had just left still clung to the fibers of my mattress.

I was grateful for the distraction, even momentarily, but it was not long until my mind wandered back to Alice, thinking of her sleeping wondering what was going through her mind. Had *the check made her decision easier? Did it take away some of her worries?*

I made a mental note to look into whether she had cashed it in, knowing that over a week had passed yet I had not heard from her. *Had she panicked because of who I was?*

I questioned whether I should have given her my real name, whether I should have used an alias as my advisor had recommended. Yet I wanted to be truthful so that I could gain her trust. *Why?* I asked myself, as I buried my head under the duvet. *Why do I want Alive Bowers to trust me?*

I closed my eyes, determined not to allow myself to fall victim to these feelings that were laying heavy on my chest, crushing the air from my lungs. Though I feared I was already too late. Alice Bowers was under my skin, inside my head.

I knew I should not have wanted her, I should have been running in the opposite direction, but there was something about her pulling me back to her. An unseen force that was dragging me deeper and deeper into the twisted fantasy of making Alice Bowers mine.

❦

Alice – FLASHBACK: Fourteen years old.

I could not contain my happiness. I breathed a sigh of relief, grateful that she did not run off after my introduction at the cemetery. All I wanted to do was help her. Now, she was next to me, our arms linked as we trudged through the cemetery. She was silent, as I told her all about my life; talking to her as if we were old friends, not a stranger I had just met.

I led her to my house, where she stopped. Her eyes swept across the garden, recognition flickered in her eyes as she studied the wall where I had left some blankets and backpack a little while ago for her. I could see the pieces of the puzzle clicking together in her mind, as her facial features softened a little.

"It was you?" she whispered, her eyes fixed on mine. I nodded, giving her a small smile as I slipped my arm out of hers to unlock the front door.

My mom was working, but the smell of the stew in the crock-pot, along with the delicious, unmistakable smell of freshly-baked bread greeted us. I heard her stomach growl.

"Are you hungry Isobel?" I asked, leading the way to the kitchen. "My mom is at work, so she made me some stew in the slow cooker for lunch. Do you want some?"

Isobel raised her eyebrow questioning why I was left on my own, though she remained quiet I felt compelled to explain the situation.

"My father died a couple of years ago..." I said, retrieving two bowls from the cupboard. "She still has to work, so I am left for a few hours here and there. She has no choice, I know she doesn't want to... she makes sure I have everything I could possibly want or need." I smiled.

I got out some spoons and a knife and placed them on the dining table, "It's fine, I'm used to it...I am old enough, mature enough and independent enough to fend for myself" I told her.

"Besides, she always makes me some food so I don't starve while she's out." I stopped myself, *what a stupid thing to say! When was the last time this girl in front of me ate a proper meal?* "Sorry," I apologized, my voice small and pathetic, "please, take a seat".

I dug out the ladle and scooped the stew into the bowls in silence. Only talking once I had placed her bowl in front of her on the table. "Can I get you a drink? Lemonade? Water? Squash?"

"Umm... I don't mind" she replied with a small awkward shrug. I cursed myself again. *Of course she was not fussy like Effy.*

I brought over two glasses of freshly squeezed orange juice and two ice-cold bottles of water. I motioned for her to eat. She smiled before picking up the spoon and eating. Dunking the buttered bread into the contents of her bowl. Nibbling away at it as if she needed to make it last, savoring every small mouthful.

"This is delicious" she smiled after a few moments.

"You can take some with you later. There's still loads left." I saw her shake her head in politeness. I reached my hand out to her, placing it on top of hers,

"I insist, it would only be thrown out otherwise." I lied, I knew we could not afford to waste food. But she needed it more than we did.

"Your house is amazing," Isobel said in admiration as we headed up the stairs to my bedroom. She stopped to look at the photograph that hung on the walls as we walked by them. I always stopped to look at one photo as I made my way to my room. It was a picture taken by a random stranger of the three of us; mom, dad, and me. Smiling as we lounged by a pool in some Spanish holiday resort. It reminded me of a time when we never used to struggle, when our family was complete.

"We used to go every year before my dad died. This photo was taken on our last holiday together. I was only ten." I told her, trying not to let my voice crack. I smiled at her, I did not mind the nosiness, the intrusiveness as she studied them.

"I'm sorry about your dad," she whispered as we entered my room.

The pinkness of the room blinded her; she shielded her eyes as the light flickered on.

It was a bit much, I will admit, as my eyes cast around the room. Pink paint on the walls, the thick plush carpet under our feet, curtains, not even the bedding and curtains could escape the pink hues. It was a little childish, but I didn't have the heart to change it. My father had decorated it for my tenth birthday, as a surprise while I was on a school trip.

I had definitely been surprised, considering my favorite color has always been lavender, but his eyes lit up and his smile spread from ear to ear, proud to have given me a birthday present I had not been expecting,

My hand lingered on the light switch, as my eyes found the handprint. It was faint, but it was there; an imprint of his hand left there. I imagined him leaning against it while it was still drying, when I had chuckled and pointed it out to him, he had been mortified. He had promised to repaint it one evening after work; he was gone before he even had the chance.

I'm glad that he never did. I thought as I pressed my hand against it. My hand was dwarfed by his. Placing my hand there made me feel sad, as memories of his loss resurfaced. They made me miss him even more, but it also brought me comfort, feeling as though he was still close to me. A small connection to him. I vowed never to paint over it.

I looked at Isobel, realizing she was not paying me any attention, rather looking out of my bedroom window, gazing at the street below and then out towards the industrial estate that loomed in the distance. It had long been abandoned,

"Is that where you live Isobel? Is that your home?"

Isobel

The inside of her house had been almost exactly as I had imagined it would be. Large spacious rooms, filled with lots of ornaments. Neat and tidy, the odd disorganized pile of paperwork, or too many shoes by the front door, just the typical chaos that formed a part of everyday life.

I pinched myself, in case I was dreaming, the surreal sensation of being inside one of these houses, that I had fantasized about for months. Alice's house. Alice, a teenage girl who wanted to help *me*, who had been leaving items outside on her fence for *me*.

I gazed out of her bedroom window, she had a good view of the path I would take from the loft. *Was it eyes that I could feel watching me whenever I came here?* My eyes shifted to the loft, the warehouse from the outside was rusted and in places corroded, some of the outbuildings were nothing but sheets of metal and rock, like a scene post-apocalypse. I knew it was not somewhere we could stay forever, but for now it was our safe space, the shelter from the forecast cold and wet winter. *It is home.*

Isobel had asked me moments before if that was home, as she stood beside me now, both of our reflections in the window, her arm linked into mine once more. We looked as though we could have been friends from school or neighbors, not a homeless girl and a kind-hearted stranger who had welcomed her into her house without knowing a single thing about me. Alice may have been younger than me, but she had shown me a kindness that no one else had before, even those twice her age.

"Alice, why do you want to help me?" I asked her, my gaze focused on her reflection rather than the world outside. "I mean, I'm appreciative of it, don't get me wrong, but not many people would you know, let a stranger into their home."

"Isobel, you are not a stranger." She replied with a smile, "you are my friend, and friends help each other wherever they can."

A warmth flooded my chest at her word, as it had when Maxine had given me her own coat. *A friend?* I never had a real friend before, perhaps when I was in primary school I had some, but I could barely recall their names or faces. I had seen so many come and go, so many sneers and grimaces thrown at me that for the past few years of being on the streets, I had grown unaccustomed to genuine kindness. There had only ever been Cole, though I used to question whether his hospitality was sometimes out of obligation.

I shook my head, clearing away that last thought. *Cole kissed me. That second kiss, he instigated it, that must mean something-*

I whipped my head around at the clock, panic made my heart race, the sky was darkening outside as the impending rain loomed over in the dark heavy clouds. It was hard to gauge what the time was. I sighed when I saw that the digital display showed 14:12. *I still have a few hours until I need to leave.*

"Right, let's see what we can find for you." Alice chirped, pulling me away from the window over to her wardrobe. I studied her as she pulled open the door revealing a wardrobe bursting with an assortment of dresses and t-shirts, jackets and a mountain of shoes at the bottom. The scent of fabric softener and laundry detergent hit my nose, it was a smell I had forgotten about. She took items off of hangers and neatly folded them in a pile on her bed.

"These should fit you." she smiled, turning to look at me.

"I couldn't." I said, shaking my head, there were at least twelve t-shirts, some still had price tags on. "Really, Alice, I can't take all of that."

Her brows knitted together, as she pulled open a drawer, completely ignoring me, "You're a bit taller than me, wider hips... I don't think any of my jeans will fit."

"Alice, honestly-"

"Isobel, I'm not likely to wear any of this, I *want* you to have them," Her green eyes shone with determination, "Most of these colors clash with my hair anyway," she giggled as she tugged at a curl. It sprung back like a coil the moment she let go.

I smiled, my cheeks ached. It had been such a long time since I had smiled so much.

She pouted as she eyed a pair of black jeans, sizing me up against them, when her eyes suddenly flickered open as if she had just had an ingenious idea.

"Follow me."

Tentatively, I followed, walking past those happy family photographs that lined the halls. I recalled the shabby two bedroom apartment I had lived in with my parents, there had only been one photograph that was hung askew on the wall in the lounge. It was of my christening, my parents were much younger then, holding me as a baby, dressed in a frilly lace dress over a basin of water in the church that was a few hundred yards from our apartment block. A lump formed in my throat, *how different would my life have been if they never surrendered to their addictions?*

Alice was talking once more as she opened the door to another room, it was slightly bigger and a lot brighter. The room was decorated in crisp whites; the walls, the bedding with only a few accents of purple dotted around such as the scatter cushions on the bed, and a canvas of lavender in a field above the bed.

A large, mirrored door stood opposite us. "Come" she beckoned as she rushed over to it.

We had stepped into another world, a place more fitting for a department store or clothing boutique than a wardrobe. It was almost as big as the loft in size, and each wall held rails and shelves full of neatly stacked clothes. Apart from one which was dedicated to shoes and purses.

My hand brushed over the rails as I explored it in awe, never in all of my life had I seen anything like it. I noted that some of these clothes were designer brands, still sporting the eye-watering price tags. "Wow" was the only word I could say.

I had never been one to follow fashion, I used to envy all the girls in school who all flaunted the latest trends as shown in their magazines, but my parents were never able to afford more than a few outfits. *Well they could have if they didn't use their state benefits to fund their habits.* Being homeless then, I had no choice in what I wore, essential clothes that provided warmth, ones that had been donated. But this wardrobe sent that little girl inside of me to heaven.

Alice simply shrugged. "This is only a small portion of what she used to have, though I don't remember the last time she wore half of this stuff." She picked up a black lace dress by the hanger, holding it up to herself. It pooled on the floor at her feet and she twirled on the spot. "I'm hoping she will let me wear some of this one day, it seems such a shame that they are just sitting here."

Alice put it back and picked up another one, a sleek emerald green gown, she held it up to her, looking at herself in the reflection. Her eyes sparkled and her hair looked more vibrant and orange than before. "This was a dress my father bought for my mother. Most of the stuff in here were gifts for her."

I recalled the family photos, her mother had straight dark ginger hair and her eyes were a pale green. I wondered where her crazy curls had come from as her dad's hair was poker straight and muddy brown. *What happened to her father?*

"Here, try these on" Alice said, yanking me out of my thoughts, holding up a pair of stone-washed denim jeans, "If they fit I have put aside some other pants for you to have."

I stared in awe at the pile she had made on top of the vanity unit in the center of the room, at least five pairs of jeans and a pair of gray sweatpants. "Alice, won't your mom notice some of her clothes are missing?" I asked.

She shook her head, her gaze dropped to the floor. "After my father died, she never goes out anywhere to wear most of this stuff." She added another pair of sweatpants to the pile. "These days all she seems to wear are her nurse scrubs."

I caught the hint of sadness in her voice and in her eyes, though she tried to disguise it by giving me another smile. "Isobel, you will make much better use out of them, than my mom ever would."

Emily

I always felt guilty when I had to leave her alone so I could work. It was becoming more frequent. As bills were mounting up, the less my salary was covering them. More and more we were dipping into the savings Adam had left for us, with little to show for it, other than scraping through the month.

When I chose my career, I was never driven by wealth. The idea of being rich never appealed to me, if it had I never would have chosen to become a pediatric nurse. Instead of a high-earning salary, I was rewarded with a sense of fulfillment that came from the ability to help people. I wanted to give these children who suffered the care they deserved, as well as a friendly and comforting face for their parents to approach.

So when I became a mother *and* a nurse, it made me even more empathetic and I struggled to get through the day without shedding a tear. It was difficult especially with some of the terminally ill children, those whose entire childhoods were spent in and out of hospital beds, hooked up to IV drips and would never experience a normal childhood. It broke my heart when I learned that most of them would never reach adulthood.

Then, when I found myself in the position I was now, trying to juggle the two responsibilities on my own, I knew that at some point one would take precedence over the other. I was trying my hardest not to let her slip through my fingertips, but I already knew that I was losing Alice, even at the age of twenty, she was still my baby, but these past few weeks I knew I had lost focus on being a parent, and like a stray ball she was lost to me.

As the days went by I felt like I was grieving for my loss all over again. That feeling of isolation and loneliness would creep into my mind during the darkest hours. When Adam was killed, it felt like someone had removed the rug from beneath my feet, it shattered my whole world as I once knew it. But losing Alice was worse, watching as she slowly disappeared, fading away from me, being beyond my reach, felt like I was being suffocated while parts of my heart were being ripped away.

When I left the house that morning, I reflected on my decision not to move after Adam's death. There was a part of me that regretted not finding a place smaller, more affordable on my singular income, but another part of me could not bear to part from this house.

This was the first house Adam, and I had viewed, when I was pregnant with Alice. We had fallen in love with it straight away, we had already picked our paint colors and interior designs for every room as we traveled back to his flat in the city. Together we worked hard to make this house a home, to set aside the ghosts of our past and make our family of three as perfect and as loving as possible.

Everything in this house reminded me of him.

Straight after the reality of his death sunk in, I found it unbearable being reminded of Adam constantly. Expecting him to be sitting in the living room, tinkering on something in the shed or waiting for him to walk through the doors after work on an evening. Each day that he was not there seemed to hurt more and more. Every day the realization that he would never come home hit me like a ton of bricks.

They say time is a great healer, but truth be told, it never gets easier. You just learn to adapt to the loss, to the constant ache in your heart. Life continues regardless.

I had to continue, to push through all the pain and sorrow, I had Alice to think of. She was a part of Adam that I never wanted to let go. Yet here she was slipping through my hands like minuscule grains of sand.

Alice had been a part of me and as I watched her grow up I learned all her little personality traits, the ticks that showed her happiness, her excitement and her fear. But for as long as she had been alive, I had tried to shield her from pain and from suffering. Even when her father died, I had tried to ease her grief as much as possible.

I rested my head against the steering wheel of my car once I had finally found a parking space outside the hospital, taking deep breaths to control my racing heart. It was torture to see Alice shut herself away from the world, suffering from sudden panic attacks without knowing what caused them. I had no idea what was going on in that pretty head of hers. I was beside myself, unable to sleep these past few weeks. I found myself thinking back to her younger years, remembering when she used to claim she had someone inside of her, a special friend. Freyja.

I had chalked it up to the vivid imagination of an only child, yet when things were happening, things beyond human capacity I knew I could no longer ignore the situation. *What if Freyja actually existed? What if she was a malevolent ghost?*

The day I saw her barbie floating in mid air, suspended as I spoke to her, it freaked me out. That night I researched paranormal activities, the history of the house, *spiritual possession*, but the next day Alice stopped talking about her, as if none of it had ever happened.

I never pressed the subject, but it made me think; *Who was Freyja? Was she more than just an imaginary friend? If not, had she ever left Alice? Could this be what was causing this change in her now?*

TWENTY-ONE

Crystal

When I first started working for Johnny Malone, I needed money. I was out of work, pregnant by a man who ditched me as soon as he found out and had no way to support either of us. I still needed money, Johnny made sure that we only received enough to get us through week by week.

That was why I was here, sucking on a regular's cock as if it was a lollipop. Ignoring the sounds of his animalistic grunts as I worked his length. Matthew, although I doubted that was his real name, came by every Thursday without fail. His regular six-thirty slot. I soon learned what he liked, what made him come, and within less than five minutes his hot, salty load had shot down the back of my throat in three quick bursts. I tried not to gag as I felt it slide down the back of my throat, I tried not to taste it, though it was difficult to remain eye contact as he insisted.

His bearded face contorted in pleasure as the last of his seed erupted from him. His smile was hidden behind his facial hair, but his eyes creased and his hand ran through my hair. "Crystal, as always that was fucking fantastic." He murmured as he threw himself back on the bed, panting heavily.

Being in his mid-twenties he recovered from his orgasm quickly, though he was never in a rush. Without fail every week he booked an hour slot and negotiated special terms with Johnny. I was his to do with as he wished for all of that time.

"Play with yourself," he demanded, as he stroked his limp shaft, his eyes watching as my two fingers entered my slit, slowly sliding in and out, feeling my entrance stretch as I pushed them inside up to my knuckles.

Why had I made such bad choices in life? I asked myself, *Why couldn't I have chosen a man who would have stuck around and helped support his child?*

He grabbed my other hand, wanting me to coax his member back to life. I stroked him to the same rhythm as my fingers slid in and out of me. He enjoyed watching me writhe and buck against them, hearing me moan in pleasure. It was all fake, a show I put on, not once had I experienced a real orgasm in front of or with my clients.

I felt his shaft harden beneath my fingertips within minutes, yet he was not ready *just yet*, so the show continued, as I slipped in a third finger taking my time to work them in and out of my heat.

Matthew was different to my other clients, most could never get another erection so soon after they had ejaculated, no matter how hard they tried. But not Matthew, his libido and stamina was something different entirely. Without fail every week he would be ready in less than ten minutes to fuck and come once more.

He smirked as me yanked me on top of him, my cue that he was ready to fuck.

I lowered myself down onto him, allowing my thoughts to wander elsewhere as I rode him; slow and steady as he preferred. He wanted to make use of the last half hour of his session.

I recalled how difficult it had been to get a regular job, no one wanted to hire a pregnant woman. I had no contact with my daughter's father, Ethan, he disappeared without a trace, no doubt using his bad-boy charms on some other poor unfortunate girl, who would fall into the same trap.

I remembered sitting in the launderette washing a load of newborn clothes a neighbor had donated to me, when a woman sat beside me. She looked professional dressed in a skirt suit, her hair and make-up was flawless. She spoke about how stressful her work had become as someone had left suddenly, and whether I knew anyone looking for work.

As I drove my hips hard against Matthew, I regretted telling her those two words that had forever changed my life, and not for the better. "I am." She had whisked me away for a formal interview the following day, a towering office block in the center of town.

"It's a personal assistant role," she had said to me, and when I arrived there, all seemed by the book. Dahlia, her name was, had escorted me to Johnny's office. Except that Hot Ticket Publishing was a fully operational and legitimate business in the porn industry, it also acted as a façade for the biggest prostitution business in the US.

Before I had realized I had signed my soul to the devil, the contract had already been signed that entitled Johnny to a percentage of my earnings each month without fail, in return he would provide all the essentials for me to carry out my role.

It was only when Johnny showed me my 'office' complete with a four-poster bed, handcuffs, strippers pole and a cupboard full of condoms and sex toys that I knew what I had signed myself up for.

Matthew rolled on the bed, one hand pinned my wrists, as the other slapped me hard across the face. A stinging handprint left on my his face angry as he shoved his shaft deep inside my unexpecting ass. I yelped in pain though he didn't seem to notice. His grunts deeper as they rolled off his chest. "You were away with the fairies" He groaned. "I thought this would snap you out of it."

His chuckle reverberated along my spine, I tried to make the right noises, to pretend as if I was enjoying it, after all this was my job, this was what he was paying me for. He smiled once again, as I convinced him of my undivided attention, though in my head all I could think about was how much I wanted out of this business for good.

"It's a shame I have to come here every week." Matthew groaned, "It would be so much easier and hotter to meet you in the hotel closer to my work, I would have so much more time to pleasure you."

Pleasure me? I almost scoffed, but I played along with his fantasy, moaning as he thrust deeper and increased his rhythm. I knew it was a risky business trying to freelance this sort of work, Johnny had spies everywhere, all clients who come here had been vetted, their credit card details taken and each transaction went directly to Johnny. He paid us cash every Friday, so I never really knew how much of a cut he took from each client, but I knew it was a lot.

"How about it? Sidestepping Britany and scheduling me in your diary, off the records?" Matthew's shaft throbbed, before another load exploded inside me. I whimpered as he finally withdrew, which Matthew smirked at.

"You know the rules, Matthew." I gasped, pretending to be breathless after my fake orgasm. The clients were well aware that transactions outside of the office were forbidden. Johnny was meticulous as well as clever, using Britany as a secretary to arrange everyone's weekly schedules and book clients in for appointments. As if on cue, there was a knock on the door, her girlish high-pitched voice rang out. "Time's up. Crystal, your next client will be here in ten minutes."

Matthew left moments later, "think about it." He said with a wink before the door shut behind him. I flopped on the bed, feeling his seed oozing out of my body, my hands roamed over the scars on my abdomen and thighs that Johnny had inflicted the last time I had been caught freelancing.

I shook my head. I wanted out of this game completely. Most girls here were homeless, this opportunity benefited them more than it did me. I may have been a single parent, but I had a home and a daughter to go back to, that last time I had feared for my life. Johnny had beaten me to a pulp and left me in the ER room, I had lied about what had happened, and he left a concerned citizen who found me after a mugging had gone horribly wrong.

Everything I did was for my daughter. All I wanted was to provide for her every need. That night had shook me, had made me more compliant. I no longer raged about quitting when a client got too rough, nor complained when I had to call a babysitter to look after my sick child. Johnny had shown me his wrath, and had threatened not to hold back next time I tried anything as stupid or reckless again.

I showered in silence, taking these few quiet moments in between clients to clear my head, to try and forget that I was failing in all aspects of parenthood. All the school plays I missed out on, all the times I had to rely on her friend's parents to take her to and from school. Johnny's words whirred around my head as the hot jets of water cascaded over my body.

"You knew this was not a regular nine-to-five job." He had said one evening after he visited me when all my clients for the day had finished. "You knew what you were getting yourself into."

Johnny knew full well I had no idea of the true job role until it was too late. I had no idea that my body would be his to take whenever he desired. The only saving grace was that with Johnny, even though he petrified the living shit out of me, at least my orgasms were real. Intense and as mind-blowing as they were, it was not worth living in constant fear of being found out by neighbors or other parents exactly what I did for a living.

I hated it, leaving my daughter in other people's care, putting Johnny's and my client's needs over Roxanne's. But this was the only way I managed to cover bills paid and keep the roof over my daughter's head. It was the only way I knew how; by selling my body to men and my soul to the devil.

☙

Marcus

Alice had not cashed in the check. Nor had I received any call or message from her with her decision. Frustration pulsed through my veins as I constantly checked my phone for notifications, growling when there were none.

I made sure my writing was legible when I gave her the envelope, I had specifically stated to contact me as soon as she had made the decision. Alice had been told very clearly that the money was hers regardless of what she chose to do with the child. I had a trusted team in a private hospital that would cater for a termination, or a team of trusted legal advisors who could arrange a new identity for her. All I needed was confirmation of what she wanted to do, and within minutes the relevant arrangements would be made.

I leaned back at my desk, admiring the view from my office at the top of Morgan Industries Headquarters, trying to distract my mind and my hands from checking my phone once more. I failed, snatching up my phone from the desk. I saw that there was still no call or text from her. *Nada.*

Suddenly the thought gripped me, *what if she tries to do it all by herself? What if she has refused my help and is struggling?* Not only would she be putting herself at harm, but it blew a hole in the plan and exposed the reputation of the family and business should anyone find out the truth.

I hit the call button on the only number I had saved in my personal phone's contact log, cursing myself for not obtaining Alice's number before I left. My father's voice chided me in my head. *"Rookie mistake son, it just may cost you."*

The call was answered within three rings. "Josh. Have you heard from her?"

"Have I heard from who?"

I rolled my eyes, frustrated with his idiocy. "Who do you think? *The queen.* No, Alice you twit, you remember her, don't you?"

"No. I haven't seen her around." He paused; his tone became lighter, happier. "I think she's left."

I cut off the call. My mind was nothing but a blur. *Has she really just left?*

I got in my car and drove to her house, ignoring the speed limits and swerving in and out of traffic like a madman. I had to see for myself. When I pulled up, once again there was no car on the drive.

There was also no sign of life inside the house, although it had also been that way last time. The curtains were drawn and the porch light was on, obvious signs that her mom wouldn't be returning until it was dark. I tried not to be too alarmed, remembering the first time I had come, when she had holed herself up in her bedroom. *Perhaps she is still suffering in the dark on her own? Still trying to come to terms with it all.*

I parked my car in the same spot as before, and snuck through the back yard. The closer I got to her back door, the heavier my heart thumped in my chest. *Why was I feeling this way towards a woman I did not know? The one who was pregnant with my brother's child?*

Last time I went through the unlocked back door, so I tried it again, this time it was locked. *Shit.*

I glanced around, seeing if there was any other way of getting in. I spotted a window open on the floor above, big enough for me to crawl through. Unperturbed by the climb, my need to find out what was going on with Alice overtook any kind of rationale.

In an instant all of my father's training was forgotten: *"do nothing to put yourself in danger, or to draw attention to yourself."* I smirked as I climbed the trellis that was intertwined with ivy on the back of the house, *If only my father saw me now.*

I fell into the room with an undignified crash; taking some toiletries and toothbrushes with me as I fell onto the white tiled bathroom floor. I quickly got to my feet, shoving the items that fell back into their place and brushed myself off, all while listening for any signs of movement. But the house was silent.

My heart felt like it was going to erupt from my chest and my stomach churned as I made my way down the hall, heading to the room I had found her in last time. As I approached, my footsteps tentative, I could see the door was partially open. As I peered through the gap, it was obvious no one was inside.

The room was neat and tidy, a stark contrast to my last visit here. *Where the fuck is she?* I launched myself towards the wardrobe, there were no clothes hung up. I tugged at the drawers; they were empty too. I looked under the bed to find the bag was gone. *Fuck.*

I sunk down on the edge of her bed, *I have lost her.* Glancing up briefly catching a glimpse of myself in the mirror of her vanity table, I no longer recognized the man staring back at me. I looked like a lost puppy, heart-sick and devastated.

That was when I noticed it, her vanity table was just as it had been before, lip glosses and a hair brush still sat where they always had been, except in the center of it all was a folded piece of paper tucked underneath a cell phone. I snatched up the note, my mind jumping to the worst-case scenario.

Shit, please don't let her have done that... anything but that.

Alice

It was heart-breaking to write the note. To tell her I had to leave, for reasons she will never understand. For reasons she will never know. Encouraging her to live her life without stress, and to not waste her time trying to find me. I did not want to be found.

I wanted to leave her some money, a check of my own, to help cover her finances, but I needed to be selfish. I had to ensure I had more than enough to fund this new life. On my own. I knew I needed to call him, but I had taken the opportunity that had presented itself to me on a whim.

A half price one-way coach ticket to the coast. I had enough in my account to cover the cost, I knew I needed a new account under a new identity to cash Marcus' check, so I had no option but to call him once I got there instead of before.

My heart jumped at the thought of him, as the coach trundled along through the traffic out of the city, my head whirred with conflicted thoughts and feelings. The envelope was scrunched up in my jacket pocket, my hand clutching it for dear life. His name seemed to burn underneath my fingertips.

I felt myself nod off as the coach entered its second hour of traveling, along the freeway, unable to keep my eyes open as the vast open fields all blurred into one. I thought about my future, about the new identity I would have. *Would Marcus still keep in contact?* In my dream he had, though in my dream he was much more than some stranger who offered me money for my silence. He was a gentleman who swept me off my feet and promised to love me and my child.

My eyes jolted open, as the coach came to an abrupt stop. I shook my head, *you do not live inside the romance novels you read Alice,* I told myself. *Not everyone had a happy ever after.*

The coach depot was loud, bustling with a sea of people moving in all directions, barely hearing the faint announcements from the speakers overhead as the thrum of chatter and footsteps echoed in the lobby. I had not really thought this plan through, I had no idea where I was going once I got off the coach.

I scrunched the envelope tighter in my pocket as my other hand hoisted the bulging bag onto my shoulder. I dodged in the gaps of the throng of people, making my way to the exit. I had no clue where I was going, other than the fact that I was tired and achy and I needed to find a place to stay for at least tonight.

A cab driver hailed me over, asking if I needed a ride. I nodded, though I stupidly told him I had no destination in mind. "Just a B&B somewhere." I mumbled as I clambered into the back seat. I could hear Freyja's voice, cursing and calling me stupid. I had seen horror movies, I knew that you irrevocably refuse to give such vulnerabilities away to strangers.

I sighed, *it is too late now.*

I stared at the cab driver in the rear view mirror, his face was wrinkled and his eyes looked as though he had lived a hard life. Washed-out brown eyes that had seen many things, a pregnant teenager in the back of his cab had come as no shock to him. In a way he reminded me of a grandparent, his eyes glancing at me and asking if I was okay after a few minutes. His voice sounded genuinely concerned. although I knew it was possible he was pretending.

"There are a few B&B's just up here." He said as he slowed down the cab, his eyes scanning the neon signs in the windows. 'No Vacancies' illuminated harshly in the darkness that had suddenly crept over the sky.

"What about here?" He asked, stopping outside a three story building, with peeling paint and floral net curtains in the window. It looked run-down and in desperate need of modernization, but I nodded my head. I handed him his fare and quickly got out of the cab.

I watched it disappear down the street until it became nothing but a yellow dot in the distance before I turned to face the B&B behind me.

The Last Inn. *The last hope more like,* I thought, as I took in the shabby decor and the overgrown yard at the front, the sign said it had vacancies and it was no wonder why. It was the last place anyone wanted to stay, but I was desperate.

I held my breath as I knocked on the door, suddenly overwhelmed by two frail arms as she embraced me, ushering me into the hallway. "Oh, my dear..." she flustered, grabbing a set of keys and ushering me straight into a room. "You can stay here for as long as you need."

"Um, how much are the rooms?" I asked, my voice fainting and cracking at her unexpected hospitality. She drew the curtains and straightened up the pillows on the bed. All I could see was floral patterns everywhere I looked, and in the few places they were absent, it was different shades of beige and brown.

"My dear, please call me Beatrice. It's fifty-five ninety-nine a night." Her frail voice croaked. "But pay me in the morning, you look like you have traveled for a long time and in your condition, you must rest."

She took the bag from me and placed it on the brown wing-backed chair that sat beside the bay window which looked out across the seafront. "Press number one, if you need anything." Beatrice added, pointing to the phone on the vanity desk. "Sweet dreams dear."

With that she quietly closed the door and left me to my thoughts. My hand trembled, as I pulled out the new cell I had purchased in town before getting on the coach. My fingers dialed his number clumsily and my head was giddy with thoughts of him.

Marcus. A guy I didn't really know anything about, other than the brief internet searches I had made back at home cooped up in my room. It held no answers about his connection to Josh, nor why it was important to keep hush on my unborn child. *What does it matter to a tycoon known all around the globe?*

I had scrolled through article after article about him, knowing that I shouldn't care, I should just take the money, use his services to create a new life and never look back. Yet I was drawn to him, his persona was mesmerizing, his handsome appearance was alluring. I recalled one particular headline which had imprinted word for word in my mind.

'Hot Ticket's No.1 heart-breaker is awarded to Marcus Morgan for the third year running'

Of course he was.

"At least he isn't married." Freyja chirped in.

I had no idea how she managed to free herself from the barricade I had put around her, but strangely her voice was comforting. At least I was not fully alone.

Josh

Questions kept throwing themselves at me, while I tried to focus on the results paper in front of me. *Where is Alice?* She should have been here along with everyone else collecting their results, but I had not seen her in weeks.

Where the fuck had she gone? What had my brother planned? Why did he care where she was? I knew I should have been elated that she was not here, that her absence made life bearable, I had found it easier to breathe knowing that wherever she was I was not. Yet there was a sinking pit in my stomach which said otherwise.

I picked up my paper for the third time, rereading what was typed on there. One sentence, which told me I had passed all my exams, but I could not focus on it, unable to feel the relief and appreciation of all the hard work I had put into getting these results. The proof that I had proven my brother wrong, that I could amount to something. But my brain was not retaining the information, instead my imagination was running amok.

What if she kept the baby? What if she told the press? Was that why Marcus was looking for her? Fuck. My life is over. My relationship with Effy will be finished.

I scrunched up the piece of paper and stowed it in my pocket. Walking out of the large hall, averting eye contact and avoiding conversations.

I did not want to talk to anyone. Not even Effy. *Especially not Effy.*

TWENTY-TWO

Marcus

My schedule for the day looked too busy for a Friday afternoon; an appointment with a potential client, the financial review with my company advisors, and a video call to some of our suppliers abroad. I welcomed the chaos, the business for once - less time to think about Alice.

On my way back to the office I instructed my private detective to search for her, treating Alice's case as a missing person of high importance. Within minutes he called back to say the last time her card was used was in the city that morning, she purchased a cell phone and a one-way coach ticket at a travel agent. Though he would need more time to do some digging to see what destination the coach was heading to. I ended the call, dreading heavily on my shoulders. *She could be halfway across the country by now.*

I tried to study the times of these meetings, making notes for each one, when my mobile started ringing. I was so engrossed in my schedule that I barely heard it. It was only after it vibrated off the edge of the desk and fell with a loud thump and vibrated loudly against the wooden floor that I snatched it up.

The cell phone number was not one I recognized, only two people had this number: Josh and my father. It was not likely to be the latter considering he was dead. It could have been Josh calling from a friend's phone, but who remembers phone numbers nowadays? It was all stored on your phone and accessible at the touch of a button, or a voice command. It was too soon to fuck up again. Even for him.

Then her face popped into my mind, *Alice.*

My heart was beating in my chest and my fingers were too fatty and clumsy as I fumbled with the phone, trying to hit the accept button. I almost dropped the phone in my efforts. *Get it together Marcus*, I told myself as I answered the call.

"Hello?" The sound of her voice gave me goosebumps. "Hello, Marcus...are... are you there?"

My heart was still pounding, I was sure she could hear it from the other end of the phone, my breathing was heavy, and I felt paralyzed as I tried to answer. "Yes, yes I'm here." I replied, trying to keep my voice calm and level, my hands slick with sweat. Leaning my elbow into the desk, propping the phone to my ear to prevent the damn thing from slipping from my sweaty grasp again.

"It's me...Alice." There was a long pause, I could hear the pounding of my heart and the whooshing of the blood in my ears, "um...you wanted me to call you when I had decided."

I stood up and went into the back room of my office. A quieter, more secluded place to talk, was often used for secret hook-ups with secretaries or other office clerks. I scowled as my mind thought of taking Alice in this very room.

"Yes." I mumbled, shaking my head, trying to remove the image of bending Alice over the chaise longue, driving my shaft into her tight, inexperienced slit as my hands roamed her milky-white body. I cleared my throat, tugging at my erect member that was fighting against the tight material of my pants.

I tried to stay focused on the call, in the background I could hear the faint cries of seagulls. "Where are you, Alice?"

"Um, I'm near the sea," she replied, hesitation and distrust clear in her voice. "I have just found somewhere to stay for tonight... I had to go, Marcus, I just got on the first coach that had a seat available. I- I just had to get away from there when the opportunity became available."

Fuck. How far did she go?

"Why did you leave without telling me?" I asked, trying to remain calm and in control of my voice quickly adding, "that was part of our agreement, Alice."

The line was silent for a while, I thought she may have hung up. "Alice? Are you still there?" Another wail of seagulls pierced my ear confirming that the call was still connected. "Alice, are you okay?"

"Yep." Her response, only a clipped one-word response but it was enough to tell that she was definitely not okay. "Alice, are you alone?" I needed to know that she held up to at least the term we agreed on.

A small whimper sounded before she spoke. "That's what you told me to do," her voice quivered, obviously she was trying to suppress her sobs. The sniffing and a rustling of tissue filled the lingering silence.

"Alice, send me your location. I can leave now."

"Why? Why do you need to come here?" Her voice was panicked and scared.

I tried to remain calm, professional. "We have details to finalize and if you have already left, we need to do it as soon as possible. Share your location through your GPS app, it will pinpoint your exact location."

"Um... how do I do that? I got a new phone, and it's a model I don't know how to use yet."

I took a deep breath, thankfully aware of most models and their differing apps. It was part of my job to be on top of it all. I slowly talked her through the process, step at a time, all while trying to keep my concern in check. Yet my chest tightened at the thought of her pretty face with those dazzling green eyes and that crazy head of copper coils, crying somewhere she did not know, being alone and scared.

"There... I think I have done it.

An alert deafened me as her location popped up on my phone through my GPS app. My heart plummeted into my stomach, as I ran down the corridor, got in the lift to the ground. I punched the ground floor button hard and persistently, as if it would make the lift go any faster. Watching her location pin, appear as a solid red dot, jumping up and down on the spot. Over 200 miles away. *Fucking Hell.*

She was still on the line, her sobs muffled as if she was holding the phone away from her face. "Alice, I am on my way. Do. Not. Go. Anywhere."

A small sniff came from her end, "okay" she whimpered before the line went dead.

I had no moment to lose, dashing up to the receptionist's crescent-shaped desk I skidded to a halt. "Julie, " I gasped, leaning over the desk. "Cancel all my appointments for the rest of the day."

Her amber eyes pierced mine, her face frowned as she flicked her jet-black glossy hair like a whip, as she spun from her computer to face me. "Um, okay...?"

I watched as she typed furiously, bringing up my schedule for the rest of the day. "Marcus, I mean, Mr. Morgan...these are important meetings...." she batted her eyelashes at me. I hated to admit that on more than one occasion, she had accompanied me in my back office, seduced by her. She was every part the woman I craved. defined cheekbones, slim and dark haired.

Another one of my father's lessons I had ignored; *"never mix business with pleasure, unless you want to shit where you eat."*

Julie was beautiful, the grace and elegance of a model as she sauntered around in her short skirts and sky-scraper stilettos, showing off her elongated legs that I loved to bury myself between. But as I looked at her now, I felt nothing, no spark, no chemistry, not even a flicker of attraction to her. As if her allure had suddenly worn off, I was no longer under her enchanting spell.

All I could think about was the pregnant red-haired girl who was carrying my brother's child. *What the fuck is wrong with me?* I knew by going after her I could be losing high-earning clients, fucking up a big deal I had been working months to seal.

Yet strangely, I was still determined to go to her, this damsel in distress needed my help, and I was only too willing to give it.

Julie was speaking, though I only caught a part of her sentence, "...months to speak to Mr Chang and even longer to finalize the purchase of X.Y. Tech," she was scowling, realizing her charms were not working and neither were her words. She changed tack, leaning on the desk, her face close to mine and her cleavage on full display. "You know how much your father wanted to work with them. and how much you enjoy our Friday evenings in this empty office."

She licked her glossy lips, but still my shaft did not twinge, not even a little. I backed off and stood away from the desk, facing the door. I felt a sting of regret knowing how important these meetings were for the future of the business and how much each one cost to arrange but I merely shrugged. *Fuck. But there are some things more important than money, and Alice has quickly become one of them.*

"It's an emergency." I told her already on the move to the rotating doors of the main entrance, I quickly glanced at her over my shoulder, "Reschedule if possible."

In my Volvo I quickly started up the GPS system that linked to my cell, it showed I should make it to her by eight o'clock, almost a six-hour car ride. I slammed my hands against the steering wheel, wishing I had some way to teleport to her. *As long as I don't stop, and if I break a few speed limits I could probably reduce the time, though not by much.*

The engine growled as I shifted the stick into drive, *Fuck, what am I doing?* I glanced at the dials on my dash; a full tank of fuel. *Well, at least that's a good start.*

Accelerating hard, I flew through the city, avoiding as much traffic as I possibly could by sticking to the back roads, until the city disappeared in my rear-view mirror and I was on the open stretch of the freeway.

My pulse raced, almost as much as my turbo diesel engine.

$$\mathcal{S}$$

Bjorn: 891 AD – The First Battle.

Blood rained down on them all. The fierce sounds of the battle were deafening. The thundering of hooves, metal attacking metal, the cheers of the victorious and the cries of the wounded. The silence of the slain.

We were tactical in our approach, choosing where we would confront them on the back of our scouts information. They had learned as much as they could of their plans, spying on nearby villages, bribing wenches in taverns to relay information discussed in the midst of drunken slurs - for a hefty price, of course.

Their information was undeniably helpful and true. We found the reinforcements of the Saxon army on their journey to join forces with a much larger army. Not only did the high valley peak give us a good vantage point to see the battle, but the thick forests within the valley also sheltered our men below. It was the perfect place for an ambush.

Up in the valley, we watched. It would only be on my orders to get involved in the fight if we were needed, should the tables turn on my men. We watched with bated breath, as the fight unfolded before us, as horses bolted in all directions and men thrown from their backs, landing onto the forceful blades of my warriors. Each and every one of them fought valiantly, some would grace the halls of Valhalla upon this very night, but overall, our losses were light.

The gods had been on our side, we had been victorious, *this time.* But this was only one small battle. One in a long line of battles yet to come.

The war was coming between us and the Saxons, and it would be coming soon.

As I stared out across the bloody fields, a messenger appeared by my side, holding a scroll in his hands. His horse was ragged, and the messenger boy looked half-dead, but the letter he contained was too important for him to fail to deliver to me.

I unraveled it, my eyes scanning the scratchy writing briefly, picking out the important words, resting on the signatory at the bottom of the letter. "Always yours, Freyja."

This letter left a bittersweet taste in my mouth. After four long years I would see my daughter once more, though I wished it had been under better circumstances.

Crystal

The next day I was out, during clients, searching for new recruits. I did not have the luxury of time on my side. With the extra clients I had booked it made me run late to collect Roxanne from her friend's house.

I was out of breath and sweaty when I finally picked her up, rushing as if my life depended on it, embarrassed to be collecting her nearly an hour later than originally planned. The mother, Leanne, looked at me with sadness in her eyes as she revealed my daughter asleep on her couch. "She can stay the night here, if you need her to," she said, her mouth turning into a small, pitiful smile.

I shook my head, as helpful as that might have been, I spent very little time with my daughter as it was. So, I cradled her in my arms and bundled her into the back of my dilapidated Ford.

I kept staring at her in the rear-view mirror, worrying what she must think of her absentee mum. My heart broke to know that in the course of the week I spent very little time with her when she was awake. I was missing her growing up, soon it would be her sixth birthday, and I knew I would not be able to get the day off to celebrate it with her. *Especially not now.*

I glanced at my handbag, the sight of the letters and posters made my stomach churn, the advertisements for the new vacancies available, supposedly inside Hot Ticket Publishing. It was the same ones that had drawn me in all those years ago.

Silent tears rolled down my face, leaving black trails in their wake. Once again, I was failing as a mother. I tried to suppress my sobs as I tucked my daughter into her bed, only when I was in the shower did, I allow my cries to escape me.

I allowed the sprays of hot water to wash over my body, mixing with the salty tears, wishing for a different life, a different way to make ends meet. I tried to shelter my daughter from our problems, from my way of life, but she would be asking questions soon, difficult ones that would uncover the truth and forever tarnish her view of me.

My cell rang from down the hall, my work phone, I knew this by the different notification sounds. This incessant beeping was a message from Johnny; a prompt that I had a last minute client booking.

Clive, 21:50, HQ.

Shit.

My mind raced as I frantically asked my regular babysitter for a last minute request, grateful that she had not already gone out or gone to bed for the night. *I can't keep doing this, taking on extra clients.*

I was dressed in black jeans and plain white t-shirt when I greeted the babysitter thirty minutes later, Tanya, was young, nineteen, the same age I was when I had Roxanne, she was a godsend, I relied on her more than I ought to, and I paid her as much as I could afford which would never be enough. Her ebony skin was like velvet, her braided hair tied up on top of her head. She could easily make Johnny's highest-earner ranks, but I shook that thought from my head instantly. I needed her more than Johnny did. Tanya was too nice of a girl to lure into this hell that I lived in.

"What's the emergency?" she asked as soon as she stepped into the living room. I hugged her, unable to look her in the eye as I lied.

"My mom has been rushed into the hospital." I said, quickly releasing her and grabbing my bag. "I'm sorry it's such short notice."

Tanya's plump lips curled into a pitiful smile which revealed her straight white teeth. "I can stay and take her to school in the morning if that helps?" She said, "So you don't have to rush back."

I nodded, leaving the credit card on the side. It was nearing its limit, but I guessed by the rumble of her stomach she hadn't eaten.

"Get yourself some food, and transport for the morning." I told her as I bustled out the front door, "Thank you, Tanya, I don't know what I would do without you."

I watched as my house disappeared from view in my rear-view mirror, my stomach churning as I desperately tried to think of ways to get these vacancies filled.

Where am I going to find these girls?

TWENTY-THREE

As the sun rose, casting its light across the land. All that remained was smoldering embers and a desert of ash. Gone were the luscious green trees that once covered this land. Gone was the thrum of wildlife that lived there. Gone was all life as we knew it.

"What have you done?" he questioned, walking across the wasteland in my direction. The sternness in his voice left no room for doubt, yet there was a tinge of disappointment rather than anger.

As I glanced around at the ruins of my once thriving Earth, I felt more than disappointment, I felt her despair, I felt her unforgiving self-loathing, her remorse for the damage she had done.

She believed that by destroying everything; by trying to destroy herself, she would find peace. She would be reunited with her child, but I had not let her go. I had not let her walk toward the light. She wanted this post-apocalyptic world, now she would have to wander it alone. She would have to grieve the lover she had thrown away, would have to live with her guilt for all of those who had perished by her hands. Alice would repent for her sins, until her body was too weak and frail to continue.

As my gaze focused back on him, I looked at my angel in his new vessel. His hair was golden, as were his eyes. Chiseled cheekbones and a sharp jawline. As I stared at him, he stretched out two giant white feathered wings on either side of him. *A far cry from the chubby cherubs that angels were often confused with.*

"Why?" he asked, as more people like him surrounded me, as their wings formed a circle around me. I knew they were not protecting me, which should have been in their nature, instead they were imprisoning me, containing me within their wall of white feathers.

My creations had turned against me. All because of her. The vessel who became too strong for me to control. She had destroyed everything, and I had let her.

He had asked an excellent question, one I could not answer.

Why had I allowed this to happen?

꛷

Emily

I was expecting the house to be silent when I returned from work. It was the early hours of the morning. My preferred time of the day, where the rest of the world is sleeping, even the birds had not yet stirred, their cheerful chorus noticeably absent. All I could hear alongside the soft thrum of my heartbeat was the rustle leaves and the whistle of the wind as it whipped through the trees as I got out of my car.

I felt the hair on the back of my neck rise as I stepped into the house. I could tell in an instant that something was not right. It was too quiet. The air was too still and heavy. An ominous feeling of emptiness consumed me as soon as I shut the door behind me.

It was hard to pinpoint why I felt this way when it was almost always this silent when I came home at this time, but I could feel it that something had changed. This house felt devoid of life.

My body was drained, every aching muscle rebelled as I forced myself to climb the stairs, my weary body craving the solace of my bed. I longed to flop down on the crisp sheets and allow my body to sink into the soft, cloud-like mattress. I was so close to making that a reality when I saw out of the corner of my eye Alice's door was left ajar.

I felt a sudden urge to go there, to check in on her. For the past weeks her door had remained closed, shielding her from me, but I was being pulled there by unseen hands, as a gnawing feeling ate away at my insides.

As I tiptoed down the hall, I could hear the creaking of my tired joints match those of the old floorboards underfoot. I would never normally intrude, especially as early as this, but something was telling me to go inside, like a whisper in my ear.

My worries and concerns resurfacing as I recalled how out of character she had been acting, more withdrawn, flightier, becoming more of a recluse as the days went by. I knew teenagers often went through these phases, even as adults it was easy to slip into this anti-social habit, but it was not like her, it was not her typical behavior. I could feel it, deep in the pit of my stomach, that something had happened. Something bad had triggered these panic attacks, but she would not confide in me. I did not want to push the matter too hard - she would tell me when she was ready.

Though I was beginning to think that time may never come.

I took a deep breath as the hinges creaked as I pushed the door open a few more inches, pausing when a faint, unfamiliar scent of cologne tickled my nostrils.

That's strange, Alice never mentioned she has a boyfriend, A stab of guilt pierced my chest. *Alice never tells me anything anymore.*

My hand stilled on the door handle, questioning whether I should intrude in case he was still there. Though I could hear no sounds of snoring, nor scrunching of the duvet. I narrowed my eyes, trying to squint through the darkness, trying to make out her outline in her bed. Partially expecting to see two figures in the bed instead of one.

But there was nothing.

Panic flooded every fiber in my body, my muscles suddenly rejuvenated by adrenaline as I threw her door open wide and flicked on the light. My heart dropped. Her bed was made with all her odd, mismatched scatter cushions pumped and neatly positioned. Alice's room was spotless, not a single item of clothing strewn on the floor as it had been when I had left earlier yesterday afternoon.

Everything appeared as it should, her phone charger cable still hanging off her bedside table, the paperback book she had been reading still sat beside it. Everything was in its place, apart from Alice. *Where the fuck is she?*

In a trance I clicked on Alice's name at the top of my contact list, frantically searching her room as I waited for her to pick up. As I pulled open drawers and flung open her wardrobe I began to panic when I found they were all empty. My heart froze when the familiar ringtone sounded from within the room. Alice *never* went anywhere without it.

I saw the light of her screen flashing and the vibrations of the phone against her wooden vanity desk, "MOM" displayed as the caller ID. I held it in my hands for a few moments, watching it ring until the familiar voicemail message sounded from my phone.

"Hi, this is Alice, sorry I can't pick up the phone right now, please leave a message!"

My tears fell at the sound of the usual happy and cheerful Alice. I could not make sense of this scene. Even if she had gone to Effy's house, she would leave a note or text me. But I had nothing. That was when I had noticed it, a folded-up piece of paper that her phone had been placed on top of.

With shaky hands I unfolded it, my tears burned as they pooled in my eyes as I read the words no mother wants to see.

Please don't try looking for me, I have left to start my own life. One without you in it.

☙

I was not expecting him to come, to travel all this way when I called him. I had assumed some details we could discuss on the phone, but I clung onto the hope, to the last words he had said to me. *"Alice, I am coming. Don't go anywhere."*

As time crept by, I knew it would be hours until he reached me, I sat and waited patiently, looking out of the bay window, watching the world continue outside, the waves crashing against the pebbled beach as I clutched this new phone. I felt the familiar pang of resentment towards Josh.

Why should I be the one that is being punished? Why should I be the one that is shunned, and isolated, when I was not the one in the wrong? Yet Josh gets to swan around back home unpunished?

Obeying Marcus' demand, I stayed where I was, bored and lonely in this floral-patterned room that was stuck in the eighties. I curled up on the bed, hoping that I could sleep some of the time away.

A loud thump woke me up with a fright, causing me to sit bolt upright, the bed creaked loudly and my eyes strained to comprehend the unfamiliar surroundings. Slowly as my brain woke up, I recalled where I was and the reason for me being here.

I glanced at the old digital alarm clock that sat on the bedside table, wondering when it had become outdated to own one of these, *do they even make these anymore?* I asked myself before I had registered the time. 21:00.

He isn't coming. I told myself, feeling stupid for thinking he would. *Why would he drive hundreds of miles to me?*

"Give him time," Freyja whispered, *"It is a long journey."*

I blocked her out once more, not allowing myself to be filled with false hope. He was not coming and I shouldn't care.

I swung my legs out of bed, no longer able to resist the urge to go to the bathroom. My swollen belly made walking uncomfortable and my whole body felt as heavy as lead as I shuffled away from the bed.

Suddenly I felt something shiny and cold touch my foot, accidentally kicking it away from me. I glanced down to see the new cellphone that I purchased earlier today slide along the thin brown carpet.

It was the cheap smartphone, an unknown Chinese brand that was being sold at a discounted price in the small department store next to the travel agents back in the city.

A new shitty phone, for a new shitty life.

Picking it up I noticed there were some unread notifications. Twelve missed calls, seven voicemails and five texts. All from one number.

I did not recognize the number at first glance, it was only when I clicked on the option to listen to my voicemails, hearing his dulcet tones frantic with worry, did I know who it was.

The only person who had this number.

Marcus.

Isobel

For the first time in a long time, I felt truly happy away from Cole's presence. I basked in the cozy warmth that Alice's kindness had provided, feeling a sense of comfort and contentment.

I had a friend. Someone other than Cole. Someone who I could talk to, who seemed to listen without passing judgment. "So, what happens when you... you know, have lady problems?" she asked, as I allowed her to paint my nails a very girly pink.

"The shelter will hand out supplies. But sometimes, I steal them." I replied, shrugging my shoulders. She was quiet, pondering, deciding whether my nails needed another coat of polish. Her lips pouted as she held my hand up to the light.

I looked at the mirror I was sitting in front of, the lightbulbs were dotted around the edge, illuminating my face. Earlier, she had the idea that she was going to give me a makeover. I groaned, but she had been persistent. "Okay," I groaned. enjoying the girlish camaraderie I had never experienced before. "But definitely no make-up"

She frowned, pulling her signature pout, her eyes opened wide in false sadness. "Not even a little?" She asked, sulking when I shook my head. "Fine..." she huffed as she screwed the lid back on the nail polish. "I suppose we could do your hair."

I did not have any reservations about make-up, I used to love trying out my mom's until my father caught me one day, in his drunken state, called me a *'slapper'* and a *'whore'* but I was too young to understand what they were, but I knew by his reaction and venom in his voice that they were not terms of endearment.

When I was old enough to discover their meanings, it turned out that those names he had called me, was what I had become. Make-up had become my war-paint, a mask that I donned when it came to turning tricks. I vowed once leaving that place, that I would never wear make-up again.

Of course, I could not entrust these details to my newly found friend, instead I allowed her to brush my hair and style it into two French braids along either side of my head. Two small fluffy pink scrunchies at the ends.

"I can not remember the last time anyone other than myself brushed or styled my hair," I said, turning my head from side to side as I looked at myself in the mirror. Her face lit up with glee.

The person looking back at me was unfamiliar, she was clean, well-groomed, not looking like the homeless girl I truly was. I almost believed for a moment that the girl in the mirror was someone else entirely.

"There, all done!" She chirped. Her face resting on my shoulder, her piercing green eyes staring at our reflection. "So, what do you think?"

I was more concerned about what Cole would think. My eyes glanced at the time in the reflection once more. I had an hour before I needed to go. *Would Cole like this look on me?*

TWENTY-FOUR

Marcus

After so many attempts to call her, I panicked. *Shit, shit, shit.*

There was traffic everywhere, the motorway was grid locked because of an accident, the alternative route on my GPS had gotten me getting stuck in temporary traffic lights, with a learner driver in front of me that had stalled so many times when it was our turn to go, that by the time they could pull away, the lights had turned back to red. Everything was against me, every obstacle possible had popped up to prolong my journey.

Fuck, I am going to be late! I was never late. Ever. Dialing her number again using the screen of my car, I kept repeating the same two words, "pick up". Every time I uttered them, I got more and more worried. *Why is she not picking up the damn phone?*

"This number is unavailable, please try again later or leave a message after the tone."

"Alice! I am almost there..." I paused, glancing at my estimated arrival time on the GPS. "Fifteen minutes away." I paused once more, as I approached a roundabout with several exits, trying to figure out which lane I needed to be in.

I was hot and sticky, beads of sweat had formed on my forehead, I could feel my clothes sticking to my skin. It was not ideal driving for hours straight while wearing my best suit, but there had been no time to change. Even with the air conditioning on full blast in the car, my skin was still dewy with sweat.

What a great impression I will make. I thought as I approached her little red dot on the GPS. *You are here to take care of business, not to make a good impression.* I reminded myself.

Yet, I still popped a piece of chewing gum in my mouth, gave my armpits a quick burst of deodorant before a small spritz of my cologne after pulling up on the side of the road.

This was as close as I could get to her red dot by car. I glanced out of the window, to my left I could just about make out the waves of the sea as they tumbled onto the beach.

On my right was a large illuminated wooden sign standing on the land in front of an old, run-down, Bed & Breakfast. 'The Last Inn' the sign read.

With all that money I gave her, she could have chosen somewhere a bit nicer than this. I thought as I got out of the car. Hauling the overnight bag I always kept in the car. My father's voice sounded in my ears, another one of his rules; *"always be prepared."*

It was a good rule to live by, especially in my line of business, and with my reputation. I never knew when I needed a fresh set of clothes, for a business trip, or a spontaneous encounter.

I tried to quash the nervousness that had overcome me, pulsating through my body like an electrical current, my stomach clenching and my palms sweaty as I carried the bag up to the steps.

I was not accustomed to feeling like this, especially not over a woman, but she is not just any woman, Alice Bowers was special - and not just because my brother had ruined her life.

I looked at my GPS one last time as I stood outside the entrance, my blue dot was now underneath her bouncing red one. I smirked, *if only.*

I took a couple of deep breaths as I chewed on the gum, before I knocked on the door.

Unable to hide my impatient growl when after the fifth knock the door opened, revealing an elderly woman with white-gray hair. She was staring at me over the top of the half-moon glasses that were perched on the bridge of her nose.

"Can I help you?" she asked in a frail, croaky voice, the skin around the corners of her eyes and mouth, creased as she spoke. "I am afraid I cannot accept a new guest at this late hour." She added.

"I'm looking for Alice." I said, my voice firm and authoritative, straightening my suit and slicking my hair to the side but the wind kept blowing one piece back into my face.

The lady before me looked puzzled, as if she had no recollection of the name.

Shit. Perhaps she used a fake name. Fuck, fuck, fu-

"It's fine, Beatrice, I have been waiting for him." Alice's voice filtered down the stairs behind the frail woman. I studied her, from over Beatrice's hunched shoulders, her stomach was poking out a little from underneath her T-shirt, and her ponytail askew. She yawned loudly and stretched her arms above her head a little which revealed more of her pregnant bump.

My heart fluttered at the sight of her, my nerves finally calmed down knowing she was safe and well.

The woman she called Beatrice, followed my gaze as I watched as she descended the stairs and stood next to the elderly woman. Beatrice wrapped her arm around her waist, her eyes narrowed at me. "I thought he might have wanted to cause you trouble, dear." She scowled.

Alice laughed. "No, Beatrice, at least I don't think he is," she said with a slight twinkle in her eye. Beatrice turned to Alice, her face solemn.

"Alice dear, if he is staying the night, I'm afraid I will have to charge you extra for *your* room." A small apologetic look flickered across her wrinkled face. Alice's eyebrows furrowed.

"I'll take care of that" I retorted, stepping closer to Alice, dumping my bag by my feet and pulling out my wallet. I offered the woman a small wad of notes.

She snatched it and tucked it inside her cardigan pocket. "I'm sorry but there are no spare rooms, but there may be some spare bedding in the closet... unless the intent was to share Alice's..." she gave Alice a mischievous wink before adding a quiet, "good night, dear." before leaving us alone in an awkward silence.

My undivided attention was fixated on Alice, yearning to hold her and gently tuck away those stray curls behind her ears so I could see her face more clearly. I reached my hand out to her when I saw her wince, before she cowered away from me.

I snatched my hand away, clasping it behind my back. My anger boiled the blood as it coursed around my body, my hand clenched in a fist as I picked up the bag at my feet. I was not angry at her. Not in the slightest, I was furious with my brother for putting that flicker of fear in her eyes.

I tried to avert my gaze, to not stare at her peachy buttocks as she climbed the stairs. It was hard not to when it was almost in my face. I held back a few steps, as we reached her room, trying to focus on the outdated decor rather than on her curvaceous behind.

When I stepped into her room, I could see why it was called 'The Last Inn'. It was the last Bed and Breakfast still decorated as if it was the early eighties. Stuck in a time warp, where everything was a different shade of shit. Anything that was not brown, was a hideous floral pattern, all of which were different. *This is the last place a CEO of a multi-billion company would stay.*

"I thought this place was a bit, you know... not the first place my mom would look," she mumbled, as she sat on the edge of the bed, biting her bottom lip, "it was also the cheapest option."

"I'm so-" I started to speak, shutting the door behind us. Stopping when I noticed her quietly sobbing, her arms hugging her stomach. "Oh, Alice!" I hushed, sitting beside her, not wanting to touch her out of fear of her reaction.

"I- I don't know if I can do this" she sobbed, her fingers trying to wipe away her tears. "I'm scared Marcus." She sniffed. I fought back the urge to hug her, instead placing my hands on my knees.

"I'm not going to pretend to you that I understand your pain and the sacrifices you have had to make." I said, my voice soft as I felt my heartstrings being pulled with every sob she tried to stifle.

I looked sideways at her, noticing that she had lifted her head to look at me, just as a couple of tears rolled down her cheeks. The compulsion to wipe them away took over, as I brushed them away with my fingers. I could see her trying not to flinch under my touch.

"I'm not going to hurt you, Alice." My whispered words felt as if I was shouting them over the thrum of my racing pulse. "I just... I just want to help."

Emily

The note trembled in my hand. My vision blurred by white-hot tears as they filled my eyes. Sobs choked me as the room started spinning beneath my feet.

I crumpled on her bed, inhaling the lingering scent of her as my sobs finally broke free, my grief consumed me in thick, heavy and unyielding waves.

My baby has left me. She was my world, my everything and I had lost her. *Alice is the last part of Adam I had left, but now she is gone too.*

All the pain and sorrow bottled up from the loss of Adam erupted along with my sense of loss over Alice. I had lost the only other thing I cherished more than life itself.

I had worked so hard to keep us living in the house she had always known, to maintain a lifestyle she had been accustomed to, but working all these hours had created a rift between us. My absence had created a void that had distanced her from me. I was not around when she needed me. I was not there to help her. Alice felt she could no longer confide in me anymore.

Now it was too late. She was gone and I was not sure if I would ever see her again.

Crystal

I decided I would not spend the night searching for recruits, I would start afresh in the morning before my first client. I just wanted to be at home with my daughter. To watch as she slept, blissfully unaware of the darkness that lurked this world and how close we were from being made homeless.

Suddenly, the doorbell rang. I had been startled awake by the noise, even though it was nothing unusual, I knew I was not waiting on a parcel, and being the weekend, I knew that this was not regular mail.

Perhaps it's a parcel for a neighbor, I thought as I approached the communal front door of the apartment block. When I opened the door, the courier was nowhere to be seen, leaving a brown box on the step outside. I looked at the label.

FAO Crystal Reigns.

I snatched the parcel up, returning to my apartment upstairs. My arms trying to shield the box as best as I could. *What the fuck was this? Who the fuck knows I live here?*

I tore open the parcel, finding yet more headed letters, official vacancy posters, and business cards inside.

Shit.

There was also a small envelope envelope addressed to me, sat on top of it all, it was addressed to my 'professional name' Crystal Reigns

Crystal,

As discussed, please distribute these along with the others I have already given to you. There are two vacancies that need to be filled within the set deadline of two weeks.

J

Shit. This was bad. Fuck.

Bile rose to the back of my throat, my palms were sweaty and I dropped the box to the ground. *Bollocks. I am in too deep now.*

"Mommy?" Roxanne called, her footsteps shuffling out of her bedroom, her hands rubbing her eyes. My eyes passed over her cappuccino skin and her soft, wiry hair which was sticking out at every angle.

I rushed to her, embracing her in my arms so tight she tried to wriggle out from underneath them. "I love you Roxy," I murmured kissing the top of her head, as tears streamed down my face. "No matter what, I will always love you."

I released her from my embrace, her fingers interlocked with mine. "I love you too. Mommy...why do you have to work so much?"

My heart fluttered and my mouth failed to find the words, opening and shutting silently reminding myself of the pet goldfish Roxanne used to have. My eyes followed her as she ran to the TV, turning it on before throwing herself down on the couch.

"Is Tanya coming over today?" she asked. "She normally makes pancakes for breakfast." Her eyes lit up with excitement. "Then we play dress up and go to the park dressed as princesses."

A pang of guilt hit me square in the chest. *I suck at being a mother.*

I let my eyes wander from Roxanne to the box I had dropped by the dining table, I had more pressing matters to focus on.

How the fuck does he know where I live?

Alice

The scene before me was surreal. The CEO of one of the biggest companies in the world was sitting beside me on this bed of floral nightmares, in a room that resembled the contents of the many nappies I would change in the foreseeable future.

Not only was he here beside me, he was also wiping away my tears with his fingertips.

As I stared at him incredulously, I found it difficult not to admire him. He was handsome, looking more attractive in person than in any of the articles I had stumbled across online. More handsome now that I knew who he was - *sort of.*

The main thing that had been ill-portrayed in all the photographs of him were his eyes. Those brilliant piercing azure blue eyes of his. They demanded my attention. The sort of eyes I found myself getting lost in as soon as I succumbed to the compulsion.

His dark-blonde hair had once been slicked to the right professional, and business-like, but his hair products had not lasted for the duration of the long car ride, as his hair now fell floppy in his face, looking tousled and disheveled. It looked as if he had just woken up rather than sitting in a car driving here to me for the last several hours.

I still can't believe he came.

As his fingers brushed against my cheeks, I glanced at his chiseled face which now showed signs of stubble, his eyes showed he was tired after a long day, not helped by the drive and the apparent worry I had put him under. I had listened to the voicemails, his voice had quivered, he had sounded genuinely concerned that I was not answering his calls.

"I'm sorry... I fell asleep," I murmured, my skin tingling when he moved his hands from my face to remove his tie and loosen his cuffs. I watched as he fiddled with his sleeve, as if he was trying to keep his hands busy. He undid the top buttons of his black shirt, revealing a sizable chunk of the tattoo that spanned from his chest up to the base of his neck.

I glanced away from him, catching a designer label poking out of the jacket he had strewn on the other side of the bed. It reaffirmed the question that had been eating away at me since he told me he was on his way.

Why had he come here personally when he could have sent one of his trusted advisors?

"Marcus. Why did you come?" I asked, not able to look into his eyes. "And why pretend to care?" I tried to keep my emotions in check, but my voice broke as another sob choked me.

His eyes flashed up to mine, his gaze intense, a flicker of annoyance and hurt lingered in those blue eyes of his.

"Believe it or not, Alice, I *do* care." he sighed, "I wanted to-" He shut his mouth firmly, his jaw muscles tightened as he swallowed the rest of his sentence. "My brother... he should never-"

"Your brother?" I interrupted; my hand placed on his knee. "No... no, no, no!"

My breathing had become rapid and fast, small quick breaths, the room was spinning. I was on my feet, trying to back away from him, disorientated by his words. I could feel myself falling, as my legs gave way beneath me. I braced myself for the hard landing, waiting for my body to hit the floor, but it never did.

Suddenly I was aware of his arms around me, his strong muscular arms holding me as if I was weightless, he cradled me for a few moments as he stared at me.

"I am *nothing* like my brother" he whispered, as he carried me over to the bed. Instead of stiffening at his touch, I felt my body relax in his arms,

His jaw clenched as his muscles tightened, a small vein popped up by his temple, his anger flickered once again across his eyes as he carefully placed me down on the bed.

"You should rest, Alice," he said, sitting with his back to me. I watched the muscles in his back ripple under his shirt as he stood up and walked away. My eyes tried to follow him, but they were becoming heavy. I tried not to panic, I did not want to be vulnerable and left alone with this stranger.

"He doesn't want to hurt you," Freyja's voice soothed, *"just try to trust him, if you can not trust me. He would not have driven all this way if he didn't care about you."*

"We will talk more in the morning." he said, moving my bag onto the floor and sitting in the chair beside the window. His eyes now fixed on the world outside.

"Where...will...you sleep? "I asked, my voice thick and heavy, slowly succumbing to the darkness as it washed over me.

Only catching flickers of words. I heard him say something else, though I could not tell if it was real, or if I had dreamed them.

"I would never harm you, Alice, and I will make sure no one ever will."

TWENTY-FIVE

I turned on the spot, taking in all their faces. Studying each one, as they continued to surround me, moving closer together to close any gaps with their outstretched wings to trap me further.

Their faces may not have been the ones I had given them, yet I knew each of them I did not need to study their faces to know they were unhappy.

"Why?" they asked in unison.

How can I explain it had to be this way?

One decision made in haste was the catalyst that destroyed not just humankind, but all life on Earth.

How could I explain to them that all of this was my fault? How could I explain to them I had been powerless against my own vessel to stop any of it?

I refused to admit that I; The Divine, The Almighty, The Creator of All Life, could not stop her. I refused to admit I had become consumed by her hate and her rage. That I had become so motivated by revenge that I had actually wanted this to happen.

The darkness that had created Lucifer, had ruled against my better judgment.

In those moments, I had been no better than him.

⦆

Cole

A part of me thought I had dreamed of the kiss between us, but when I opened my eyes and saw her cuddled into me, I knew we could not revert to how things had been before.

I refused to perpetuate the distance between us, I had pent up my feelings for her for too long, and there was no going back.

The kiss was something that I had not been expecting. Although I was overcome with the need to feel her soft skin on my lips, I was going to kiss her on the forehead, a protectorate kiss, nothing more. Then she moved, my lips grazed hers, and I knew I had two options. I could pretend forever more that she meant nothing more than a friend, or I could give in to my feelings. *My head versus my heart.*

I had pulled her chin closer to me with my fingertips as my lips crashed against hers for the second time, allowing the waves of my desire, my longing, my love for her to envelope us. It was easier to show her my true feelings than say them. For the first time I chose to follow my heart and throw caution to the wind.

She was the reason I worked so hard to keep her fed and warm, why I would do whatever it took to keep her happy and to keep her safe. Isobel was my number one priority and without her, I knew I would have succumbed to the demons that lurked within me.

I reluctantly slipped out from underneath her when it was time for me to go to work. I wanted her to wake up, so that I could kiss her once more, but at the same time I was nervous, *what if she only went along with it? What if the feelings aren't mutual?*

I left, but only after I placed a quick kiss on her forehead and removed the tendrils of hair that had fallen across her face. There was a slight smile on her face that had never been there before.

I felt light as a feather as I practically skipped out of the loft, eager to get my shift over with so I could return to her. But my happiness was short-lived.

A lump formed in my throat when I spotted the signpost as I crept out of our secret entrance, a loose piece of chain link fence that surrounded the warehouse.

I knew this day would come; I knew we could not live here forever. But I had hoped I would have had more time to scrape together some savings from my work.

I read the sign in shock, my eyes scanning over the black writing.

Demolition Notice - section 80.

The town & country council planning committee has agreed for the proposal of the demolition of these units to be demolished, with the use of the land being repurposed for residential purposes.

Proposed date of demolition: 1st April.

Duration: four weeks of demolition works.

Building works are proposed to begin within two weeks after demolition works are completed.

Shit.

I prayed Bel wouldn't leave the loft today, I needed to think of a plan and fast. I had very little time to find somewhere else for us to stay.

I would not see her back on the streets. *My girl will not turn tricks again, nor will we live like this any more.*

☉

Effy

"No!" I cried the moment Mrs. Bowers told me. I refused to believe her. Her mom was lying, she had to be. *Alice would never leave without saying goodbye.*

"Stephanie, Alice is not here." Mrs. Bowers sighed, she never used my full name. I had been Effy since Alice could talk, when we both struggled to say my name. We had been in kindergarten.

My eyes snapped up to hers, shaking my head, denial consumed me as my tears started to fall. She had said the same thing several times before, but her words had not registered, I still hadn't believed them, until that moment. The seriousness in her eyes as she said my name.

It had taken a few days for me to summon the courage to come here, to swallow my pride and ignore my jealousy to visit Alice. I wanted us to be friends like we had always been, I prayed she would forgive my abandonment of her. Yet, here I was, learning that *she* had abandoned *me.*

Mrs Bowers tried to calmly explain that Alice had just left, without telling anyone. Leaving behind no trace of her or no hints to where she may have gone.

"Can't you track her, using her cell?" I asked, my voice high-pitched as my panic set in. "She can not have gone far".

Mrs Bowers shook her head, placing Alice's cell phone on the table before me. "Stephanie, now would be a good time to tell me if Alice had a boyfriend, or had mentioned going anywhere to you in the past few weeks."

I shook my head frantically, scrabbling at her keypad entering her passcode. *Incorrect pin?* I glanced up at Mrs. Bowers, taking in her defeated posture, her swollen red eyes. "She left it in her room." She sighed, "along with this letter." Her hand holding onto mine. "She doesn't want to be found, Effy".

I entered her passcode again, thinking I had typed in a wrong digit in my haste, yet still it did not unlock. 'Incorrect pin' flashed on the screen for a second time. It had always been the same code, she never changed it. Not since school. It was our first locker combination at school. The locker we both shared. She had used it for all her phones, as I did with mine.

What was she hiding?

"Mrs. Bowers- "

"Please call me Emily."

"Mrs... I mean, Emily. Do you know why she- she avoided *me?* Or why she never went to the Summer Solstice Soirée?"

I bit my lip as her mom shook her head slowly.

Her mom looked at me, her eyes brimming with tears. "Effy, did she tell *you* the reason she started suffering from panic attacks?"

It was my turn to shake my head, feeling the sting of more tears prickle in my eyes.

Emily's shoulders sagged as she exhaled deeply. "I've been a terrible mother... I have been working too much. Our bills... they have been increasing so I've had to put in a few extra night shifts," she sighed. "Perhaps if I had been around more, she would have been able to confide in me. Tell me what had been going on..." her voice crumbled as her sobs escaped her lips.

"She did not tell me anything, she couldn't...." Her teary eyes focused on mine. "I was never around for her to talk to, about any of it."

I got to my feet and wrapped my arms around her, feeling our body quake as we sobbed in unison. "Mrs. Bowers- I mean, *Emily*, I have been a terrible friend, Alice... she couldn't talk to me either... I was too busy with Josh."

I was not sure how long we cried for, in her dining room, but I knew it had been light when I had gone to Alice's house, now the moon was out, casting the world in a silvery iridescence.

I called Josh, trying to hold back my tears, my mind fearing the worst.

Had they run away together?

☙

Like a guard dog, I tried to get comfortable on the floor near the foot of the bed. My jacket acted as a pillow, and I had grabbed a spare blanket from the wardrobe, positioning myself between the bed and the door. *She was not leaving me again.*

Distanced from her, I could still see the rise and fall of the duvet as she slept. My eyes flickered wider every time she tossed and turned in her sleep. The room, despite its revolting decor, was quiet. There was no noise from the outside world or any neighbors within the other rooms. Sleep washed over me relatively quickly once I was sure Alice was too deep into her sleep to run once more.

The sun peaked its way through the gap of the floral curtains, I heard and felt footsteps as they tiptoed around me. I woke up with a start sitting bolt upright. "Alice?" I asked. Rubbing my eyes, trying to clear my vision.

The smell of lavender soap filled my nostrils. There she was, rummaging through her bag, a towel wrapped around her hair, wearing a fresh set of clothes. Her bump poked out over the top of her jeans and below her t-shirt as she continued to rummage through her belongings.

"Shit" she cursed in a low whisper. I smirked, unsure if that was shock from seeing me awake, or whether she was frustrated because she had not found what she was looking for.

"Alice? Is everything okay?" I yawned, stretching my arms up to the ceiling, my back was stiff and my neck was sore. I was too old for sleeping on the ground,

She gave me a strange look, one that was a mixture of both sympathy and appreciation.

"Sorry, that must have been uncomfortable... sleeping down there," she said, her head tilting towards my makeshift bed on the floor. I shrugged, I would not let her feel any guilt for my sleeping arrangements.

She moved her focus back to her bag, rummaging around a little more, when she spoke again her tone was annoyed,

"Oh, it's nothing...I just... I forgot to pack my hairbrush."

The image of her vanity table flashed in my mind, her hairbrush abandoned not far from the note and her cell phone. A twang of guilt hit me as I imagined her hasty departure.

I clambered to my feet and went to my own overnight bag, retrieving a comb. Smirking as I handed it to her, imagining how it would fare against her unruly mass of curls.

"Will this work for now?" I asked, handing it to her.

She eyed it, "It's worth a shot." she replied, taking it carefully from my hands, her fingertips brushed against my hand. I felt a surge of energy ripple along my skin from where her finger had made contact with mine.

My eyes were glued to her as she teased her wild curls with the comb, giving up halfway through and scrunching it up into a ponytail. Her T-shirt rose as she lifted her arms, exposing the silver streaks that stretched across her stomach, faint but still there. Proof that her body was changing to accommodate the child my brother had forced inside her.

"Um... were you never taught it is rude to stare?" she pointed out, a small smile on her face, as she pulled at her top.

Blushing profusely I averted my gaze, mortified that I had been caught staring at her.

"Sorry," I mumbled, backing away from her, when suddenly she appeared inches from me, handing back the comb.

Alice's face was smiling, a genuine smile that creased the corners of her eyes. "It's fine... it... it takes some getting used to" she said, as she rubbed her stomach in a slow circle, her eyes trained on me. "I'm still getting used to it myself," she chuckled.

She is beautiful. The thought flashed through my mind, *her smile is magnificent, I want to see her smile more often.*

My heart started pounding, every nerve within my body awoke with a jolt as her hand grazed mine once more as I took the comb from her proffered hand. *What was I thinking?*

She's twenty years old, five years my junior, and she is pregnant with my brother's child. I cursed at myself for slipping back into my old way of thinking. *Alice will have enough people judging her without me being one of them.*

I knew she needed someone to support her, to rely on. I was that person - she had no one else to confide in. She was here, in this mess, because my brother had forced himself on her, unprotected. Josh had ruined her life, and all I needed to do was help her make the most out of the pieces she had left.

I looked up to see that she was staring at me, biting her lip as if she wanted to say something. It was her turn to blush and look away.

"Um... thank you for staying here with me," she muffled, "for driving all this way." Her arms suddenly wrapped around my waist, her head tucked into the crook of my neck. Her breath was hot on my skin and her heart was beating fast against my chest.

"I'm glad you came," her words were muffled, but they sounded like a song to my ears.

My arms slid around her back, embracing her warmth, enjoying this moment more than I knew I should have. I had expected her to flinch under my touch, but when she did not, I held onto her a little tighter, smiling like a child who had gotten his way. I was grateful she could not see my face, though I felt the corner of her lip curl upwards.

Her hair radiated the lavender scent from underneath the towel and I knew very well that I was still in yesterday's clothes, I could feel the stubble growing on my chin and I prayed that she could not smell the stale sweat that lingered on my skin.

"I'd better have a shower," I mumbled, breaking the embrace and grabbing my bag from beside the bedroom door, hastily positioning it so she could not see the erection that was forcing itself against my zipper. "We can talk over some breakfast."

Alice threw me another one of her heart-stopping smiles, I felt my whole body prickle with goosebumps and my member throb against its restraints.

Never has a short, innocent hug made me so damn hard before.

I stepped into the shower. The water pressure was weaker than what I was used to, but I allowed the heat of the faint sprays to relax my tense muscles, but my shaft remained solid and firm. I wrapped my palm around it, even in my big hands it was monstrous. At nine inches a lot of women struggled to wrap their hands around it, let alone take its full length.

I worked my length in long, hard strokes as I imagined how small Alice's hand would look holding it. Imagining how much of it would fit into that pretty mouth of hers. *How tight would her slit be around it?*

I stifled my groan as my seed erupted from the tip, thick white strands landing close to my feet. *Fuck.* My shaft pulsated in my hand, but it was still as stiff as a board.

I pumped harder and faster, as I envisioned taking her on that floral bedding in her room, as I held onto her widened hips, as she rode my shaft. I longed to mess her hair up, to kiss and lick those full breasts of hers. The urge to hold her swollen belly in my palms as I thrust into her from behind.

I thought of her sitting in the room, blissfully unaware I was masturbating to her, my guilt gnawed at my insides. She trusted me to help her, not to seduce her. *What if she heard my groans? What if she felt it against her thighs earlier?*

The thought of her knowing how much she turned me on, the smile on her lips teasing, as if she knew exactly what I was going to do. I bit down on my fist as another wave of cum shot from my thick shaft, harder and more forceful than before.

Part of me wanted her to know, to hear me pleasuring myself to her. Another part of me wished I was man enough to just tell her how I felt about her.

Yet my head was telling me it was best for her not to know. It was better for both parties to pretend Alice did not affect me this way. I shook my head, it would be easier said than done. *How am I supposed to cope spending the day with her without getting an erection every time I look at her?*

I wrapped the towel around me as I stared at my obscured reflection in the fogged up mirror. *Alice Bowers, you are going to be the death of me.*

Josh

I followed Effy to Alice's house. Effy had sent me a text, revealing her plan to confront Alice and find out what was going on.

My heart raced as I watched her walking along the street, her fierce determination showing in her brisk walk. I loved it when she was feisty, when she was headstrong, but my guilty conscience wished this was the one thing she would not fixate on.

A shiver ran along my spine as I panicked, *what if Alice tells her the truth?*

Effy came to a stop, her knocking on the door too impatient to be called polite. She waited, hand on hip, every bit as angry as she was concerned. Yet when the door opened, her demeanor changed almost instantly. Her hands fell from her hip, and she was shaking her head furiously.

I held my breath as a flash of copper hair emerged before Effy, her arms embraced her as they hugged on the doorstep, it was an older lady, her hair too dark, too limp to be Alice. I figured it was her elusive mother.

Only when the door closed did I move closer to the house, crouching low beneath the kitchen window, trying to listen in to their conversation.

"Stephanie, Alice isn't here... She doesn't want to be found."

I crawled away from the house and jumped back on my motorbike with a skip in my step. *Alice was gone!*

My chest felt like it had been released from the vice-like grip it had been in for so long. I could finally breathe once again.

Yet, the question still ate away at me; *where the fuck did she go?*

TWENTY-SIX

Isobel

Time flew by too fast. One minute we were reading magazines and the sun was still high in the sky, the next thing we were surrounded by darkness as the streetlights outside started flickering to life. Their dim orange glow filtered in through her bedroom window, causing my heart to race. *Shit, what time is it?*

Panic flooded my body, as my eyes snapped to her clock. 18:45.

"Shit!" I cursed, scrambling to my feet, the magazine we had been looking over fluttered to the floor, a few pages had dislodged and scattered across the floor. Alice was looking at me in shock.

"I'm sorry Alice, but I- I have to go." I snatched up the backpack, and the carrier bag of clothes "Thanks again for these." I murmured, glancing over my shoulder quickly before racing down her stairs.

"Wait... Isobel!" she called, hot on my heels. "Don't forget this!" she said, gasping for breath as she handed me the Tupperware as I opened her front door.

I glanced down at the stew, still hot from the slow cooker, the smell of beef and dumplings wafted up my nose and made my mouth water.

"Come by tomorrow, around two o'clock, yeah?"

I nodded, a small smile flickered on my face, before slipping out of her home and running through the estate. Thankfully, Alice didn't live too far away and I did not need to meet Cole at his workplace. The weekends were always busy, there was usually little to no food left for him to bring home, so I had fifteen minutes until his shift finished and then an additional ten for him to walk back.

As I ran, the streetlights overhead illuminated a large red and white signpost. It caught my eye as I sprinted towards it. I slowed down my pace so I could read it.

Say No to Ugly Homes!

I furrowed my brow, noticing several more had popped up out of nowhere. I had not noticed them earlier when I had looked out of Alice's bedroom window.

Save our Heritage. Keep our value!

Then there was another, this one was a lot less cryptic.

Stop the demolition!

It was the start of a protest.

Demolition? Demolition of what? I asked myself, as I ran the last stretch to the warehouse. My eyes caught several more signs that I no longer bothered to read, time was slowly ticking away. *I need to get in before-*

The sign caught my attention, fixed to the loose piece of fence Cole and I use as our unofficial entrance to the Loft.

No Trespassers - Unsafe building - High risk of collapse!

Next to it was a demolition notice. I strained my eyes to read it in the dimly lit area. Tears welled my eyes, blurring the words on the paper even further.

There was no need for me to read it all, the first few paragraphs told me all I needed to know. In less than one month's time, this place that we called home would be gone. There would be nothing but rubble and dust left of the loft. Mine and Cole's safe space.

I could not help but wonder; *what will happen between Cole and me?*

Alice

I stood in silence, smiling at him until the door closed with a faint click. I collapsed on the bed, wanting to scream out loud. *What was I doing? Was I flirting with him?*

Not only was he completely out of my league, but he was Josh's brother.

Josh. His name alone scared and repulsed me as my chest tightened and my heart started palpitating rapidly against my ribcage. My stomach clenched angrily. *I'm going to be sick.*

I burst into the bathroom, and threw up unceremoniously into the toilet. It was only then, as I pulled my head out of the bowl that I saw him from the corner of my eye, only then had I realized I had interrupted his shower as he now stood wrapped in only a towel.

I groaned as I buried my head in my arms. "I'm so sorry-"

"Alice," he said, one hand holding the towel around his waist, and his other holding my hair back. He was so close to me. I could smell the soap on his skin and the fresh mint on his breath. I reached for a handful of tissue, dabbing at my mouth.

"Thanks" I murmured, only moving away from the toilet once I felt the wave of nausea subside. "I'm sorry... sorry that you had to see that"

Marcus chuckled. "I can assure you; I have seen much worse." He offered his hand to help me to my feet. I took it, still a little lightheaded, both of his hands held me to steady my balance. I cast my gaze down to the floor, trying not to envision his naked body beneath the towel and how easily it could unravel at any moment.

I felt the flames burn behind my cheeks, and my head felt giddy once again. *I should not be this close to him, I cannot trust my hands to keep to themselves.* I inhaled a deep breath, the scent of him filled my lungs as I backed away from him slowly., slowly lowering the toilet seat and perching on the closest lid.

"Stay here... I'll be back" he said, dashing out of the room taking his bag with him. Within moments he returned, dressed in a plain white t-shirt which allowed his dark tattoos to bleed through the light fabric. It was tight around his biceps and his chest, I could see every muscle ripple with every movement he made. I noticed that he had also swapped suit pants for a pair of dark denim jeans and his formal shoes for white trainers.

He looked like a different person. My core tingled at the sight of him, sending goosebumps along my body. My eyes flew up to his face, noticing his stubble was gone and he had left his hair floppy and untamed as water droplets clung to the tips, threatening to fall on his shirt at any moment.

Damn. No wonder why he had won the title of Hot Ticket's No. 1 heart-breaker.

A subtle cough brought me back to attention, I dropped my gaze from his face, my cheeks on fire as I blushed profusely. I could still smell him, as he helped me get to my feet, his arm wrapped by back to support me as I tried to take tentative steps towards the wash basin. All I could think about was how good he smelled, and how hot he looked.

"Morning sickness" I mumbled. I needed to get him away from me, mortified by the sickly after-taste in my mouth. "Could you pass me my toothbrush and toothpaste?"

He backed away, only after he was sure I was not likely to crumple into a heap without his support. He pulled out the new toothbrush and toothpaste, leaning against the doorframe as I brushed my teeth. Walking over to me once I had finished, his arm returning to the small of my back.

I felt the warmth radiating through his hand, sending goosebumps prickling across my skin. I was too aware that his body was close to mine, too close to wanting to inhale his skin and pull his body against mine.

"Do you like coffee?" he asked, as I took my seat back on the bed, trying to put on my shoes. It was getting harder now, with this beach ball stopping me from bending over properly.

"I mean, are you allowed to have coffee?" He corrected as he knelt down and helped me slide on my trainers, tying up the laces without looking at me.

My hand fluttered across his shoulder. "Thank you." I murmured once he had fastened them both. "Um, I can always have decaf."

He pulled a face at me as he opened the door to the room. "Decaf- I can think of nothing worse." Marcus chuckled, waiting for me to lead the way. As we descended the stairs Beatrice's eyes were focused on the pair of us, a small mischievous glint flashed in her eyes. I could tell she suspected something was going on between Marcus and me. *Does she think Marcus is the father?* My cheeks flushed as I dropped my gaze to the floor, trying not to watch him as he walked up to her at the reception desk.

I watched as Marcus walked up to the desk, pulling out his wallet. "Do you have a spare room for a few nights?" He asked, his eyes studying Beatrice as she flicked through the paper diary on the desk.

She nodded her head as he handed her a wedge of notes. "Is that enough?" Marcus asked, his eyes no longer on Beatrice but fixated on me.

"I'm afraid we have stopped serving breakfast now." Beatrice's apologetic smile graced us both, as her eyes darted from the pair of us. "It's gone nine-thirty, but there should be some coffee-houses along the beachfront where you can grab something."

Marcus nodded as he opened the main door waiting for me to leave first. *A true gentleman.*

I felt my heart beating, as we strolled into the little seaside town, going into the first café we came across.

"So, you're planning to stay for a few days?" I inquired, trying to be nonchalant, despite my thumping heart that boomed in my ears.

"Yeah, well we have got some details to discuss and arrangements to make." he said, pulling out a chair for me. I tried to swallow my disappointment in his answer. *What else was I expecting him to say?* I felt stupid, my gaze lingering on the table before me, my fingers running over the various dark coffee ring stains on the Formica table.

"Besides" he said, surprising me by taking one of my hands that were placed on the table. "I quite like it here."

I tried not to make eye contact, but I could feel his eyes sweeping my face. "And I'd quite like to get to know more about you."

My eyes caught his charming smile again, the one that melted my insides. *Remember the plan, Alice, you only need his help,* I told myself.

I may have only *needed* his help, but I could not deny what my body and my heart yearned for, no matter how hard I tried to fight it.

I want Marcus Morgan.

☉

Marcus

I swear I felt her pulse racing underneath my fingertips, *or is that my own?*

I could not fathom out what it was about her, but I was compelled to touch her hand, to feel her skin against mine. I wanted to know her in ways I had never bothered with any other woman before.

She's carrying your brother's child, my thoughts screamed at me, like a little voice in my head. It would usually sway me into temptation, but this time it was trying to avoid it. *You cannot get involved with her, or worse, fall for her.*

One small smile from Alice and I was putty in her hand. She was shy, innocent, and definitely not like any of the other women I had ever been with. A flash of my fantasy from the shower sliced through my mind, imagining her on all fours, taking my shaft into that pretty mouth of hers whilst I stared into those deep emerald eyes of hers.

I shifted uncomfortably in my seat, signaling for the waitress, desperate for some sort of distraction.

She came at once, fluttering her eyelashes in my direction, ignoring Alice completely. The waitress leaned forward, revealing her cleavage, her dark hair falling across her face as she pouted with her lip pressed against her lips whilst she waited for my order.

"Two decaf coffees please." I said, barely looking at her.

The waitress scribbled down the order on the small notepad, her eyes never leaving me, her lump lips still pouted. "Anything else you like the look of?" She asked, sounding breathless and seductive.

I saw a flicker in Alice's eyes as they narrowed at the waitress, I bit back a smile as I shook my head, my gaze locked onto Alice, my hand squeezed hers. A blush deepened across her cheeks, as she realized I had been staring at her the whole time.

"No. We are good, thanks," I replied.

There was a time where I would have flirted with her, I would have teased her and made her beg to crawl into my bed. But that no longer interested me, there was only one person I wanted in my bed, and it was the fiery redhead sitting opposite me. The woman I know I should not want.

The waitress looked at me confused, "Why decaf?"

"If she has to suffer, so do I" I chuckled, drawing the waitress' attention to Alice. It was the first time she looked in her direction, her eyes scanned from Alice's wild curls, down to the swell of her stomach. Her eyes darted to me, then to our hands on the table. She backed away without another word.

Alice pulled her hand away from me, it felt cold without her touch. "Don't let me get in the way," she whispered, her arms crossed over the top of her stomach. "I don't want anyone to get the wrong impression... that you're the father, or something."

The thought had crossed my mind, but I shrugged. For the first time in my life, I no longer cared what the whispers said or what other people thought. My only concern was to make Alice see I was not interested in this waitress, or anyone else. I came here for *her*, whether that was in a romantic sense or not, Alice had my undivided attention.

I kept my hands on the table, though I could feel my shaft growing harder beneath the table, seeing that flicker of anger, of jealousy, riled me up. I watched as she picked up the menu, flicking through it as if she was set on ignoring me.

"Alice-"

"I got the impression you did not like decaf," she interjected, her eyes narrowing at mine over the top of her menu.

I shrugged. "It is only fair, if you have to put up with it, then so do I." Her face blushed once more, as she tried to hide it behind the menu she was holding. I took it from her hands, pretending to look through it.

Alice let her hair tumble from the hairband, I felt my mouth curl into a smile, mesmerized by the shimmering curls as they fell down upon her shoulder. For a few moments we sat in silence as I eyed her over the top of the menu, feeling my heart beating wildly and my shaft harden further.

It was only when the waitress returned with our coffees that Alice spoke once more.

"So, you're Josh's brother?" she stirred her coffee, keeping her eyes fixed upon the dark liquid in her cup. "I never knew he had any siblings... especially not a CEO or Hot Ticket's number one heartbreaker," her eyes twinkled again, teasing and playful.

"We are not close, especially after father died-"

"But you're close enough to help him now?" She quipped, her eyes suddenly on me. I opened my mouth to speak, but I could not find any words. "Why are you really here Marcus? If you're not close, once you give me the check and sort out a new identity, what happens next? You wait around for him to fuck up again and use your money to make it go away again?"

Alice's nostrils flared, her gaze bore into my soul, she had every right to be angry. She had every right to distrust me and hate me. Covering up his disgusting acts, I had become no better than him.

"That was how it used to be." I muttered. my eyes never leaving Alice's. "Until he got you pregnant."

Her eyes dropped momentarily, as her brows furrowed and she squirmed in her seat, trying to cross her legs before giving up when her bump got in the way.

"Alice, I'm not *proud* of any of that." I muttered, pulling a face before the coffee touched my lips. Surprisingly, it tasted *normal*. I took a big gulp feeling her eyes trained on me the whole time.

"Not too bad is it?" She smirked, her green eyes flashed, her annoyance was gone.

"My brother's *actions* reflect badly on the company, on everything I have built... everything I have worked my ass off for... I don't want him to reflect badly on *me*..."

Alice went to speak, but then changed her mind, taking a sip from her cup instead. I took a deep breath. "Alice, what my brother did to you, not *just* because he got you - I don't condone his actions... and I should never have gotten involved trying to cover up what he did."

But then I would never have met you, I added silently.

"I suppose I felt guilty; when my father died, he left everything to me and nothing to Josh. It opened the rift between us wider... I guess I felt that I owed him... it was my responsibility to help keep him out of trouble." I sighed. "In any way possible."

I felt her hands grasp mine. Her thumbs rubbing the back of my hand. "Josh is an adult, it isn't your responsibility to keep bailing out of these situations." The atmosphere grew thick and heavy between us, we had entered the deep stuff - treading unknown waters. I had never spoken so openly about my family or my feelings before.

I felt as though I could not breathe, I didn't trust my voice to say anything.

Alice's eyebrows knitted together as she leaned forward on the table, her curls tumbling forward obscuring her face. "I hope you think twice next time Josh's actions *reflect badly* on the company... on *you*... I-" she paused, leaning back slightly, using the back of her hand to wipe away a tear that rolled down her cheek. "I hope you remember me and the shitty life I have to live, *thanks* to him."

I don't want to ever forget you. I knew I was going to regret it, but I was already in too deep.

"Alice, I didn't just come here to make arrangements, nor out of a guilty conscience on behalf of my brother- "

My lips grazed the back of her hand, I had no recollection of bringing her hand to my lips, but the way her eyes shone, there was a flicker behind them, a longing that reflected mine.

In a split second the moment was over, our hands had returned to our coffee cups, and an awkward silence ensued. My eyes wandered around the coffeeshop, taking in the canvases hanging on the walls of large frothy cappuccinos and mouth-watering cakes, the ceiling tiles were yellowing and there were deep grooves in the wooden floor from the relentless scraping of the metal chair legs against it.

When my eyes snapped back to her, I smiled when I found her studying me intently, her lips pouting on the rim of her coffee cup. "Why did your father leave everything to you?" she asked.

My smile faltered a little, "It appears, my father was a clever man, but a proud and stubborn man. My mother died when I was five, and her death scared him. He wrote a will and left it with our family lawyer. A few years later he got another woman pregnant and remarried, she refused to take his last name and insisted Josh took her name too when he was born. She claimed she wanted to protect him from the media and the publicity." I paused, taking a sip of my coffee as I gauged her reaction.

"I don't blame her." Alice murmured under her breath.

"It seemed my father's pride was hurt, her rejection of the empire he built from scratch so he set them up for life, but was too bitter to include either of them in his will."

I could not hold back my smile, finding that hers mirrored mine almost immediately. The tension was lifted. I felt I could breathe again. "Alice, tell me a bit about you."

She took a sip of her coffee before speaking, her voice was tentative. I could see her calculating what she should or shouldn't say. Weighing whether she could trust me or not. It seemed she trusted me enough to tell me the unfiltered truth.

"My father died in a car accident when I was ten, my mom struggled as a single parent, her own parents died when she was younger too, so she had no support. My father's life insurance didn't cover much, so mom worked hard to provide for me nearly all my life on her own... I tried to help financially when I was old enough to get a job, but after-after...*you know*, I was let go." Alice's eyes had been fixed on her coffee cup, but now she was looking directly at me. Tears welled in her eyes and her bottom lip quivered as she spoke. "That's why I had to go. I couldn't burden my mom with another mouth to feed, someone else to provide for."

Before I could stop myself, I had gotten to my feet and was embracing her as she sobbed into my top with her arms wrapped around my torso. I rested my mouth on top of her head, "Alice, you have me, whatever you need..."

My words were muffled in her hair, but I felt her grip tighten around me. Her body molded to the natural curves of my waist, I felt her move slightly, almost too close to the bulge that stretched the crotch of my jeans. I gulped, *Did I want her to notice it?*

She smiled as a blush crept to her face. She unraveled her arms and moved away from me, her hands quickly picked up her cup, and her eyes avoided mine. *So she had noticed it.*

I took the seat beside her, pulling my cup closer to me. I shifted in my seat, stirring in a sugar cube just to distract myself from the fantasies of her.

"I used to want to be a nurse too, like my mom, that's why I never went on social media, I didn't want any distractions from my studies... all it is used for is gossip and who is hooking up." She rolled her eyes and her hand resting on her lap, slightly grazing mine. A long silence ensued as we sipped at our drinks.

"I'm going to assume you don't have a steady girlfriend," Alice suddenly said, as I took a sip of coffee. Her words caught me off guard and I almost choked. The coffee was hot on the back of my throat, and it burned as it slid down.

"No... um... I-." I spluttered, shame crept over me, knowing she knew about the long line of one night stands. I was always careful and I always used protection. I used to keep women at an arm's length, seeing how bitter my father had become, how he mourned for my mother by sleeping with various women half his age, until eventually one of them got pregnant.

My father never loved Josh's mother, but he married her out of obligation. I did not want that future. I took a deep breath, formulating my explanation in my head.

"It makes sense, why settle down when you can have anyone you want, whenever you want right?" Alice tried to smile, to put laughter into her voice as she let her hair out of her ponytail once more. I realized this was a nervous tick of hers, playing with her hair, twiddling with it, as if it was a comfort blanket.

I took hold of her hand, stopping her. "It's not like that at all Alice." I said, feeling my pulse quicken. "I just never found the right woman, someone who I saw a future with."

She bit her lip, "Perhaps you were looking at the wrong types of women... or in the wrong places"

Alice Bowers, you have no fucking idea.

"Did you want anything to eat?" I asked her, as the waitress headed back over to our tables, asking if we wanted a refill. "You should eat something."

She shook her head, "um, maybe later..." she said, one hand resting on her stomach, reminding me of her bout of morning sickness. I nodded as I watched her retie her hair in a ponytail. My hands reached out, allowing her curls to trickle through my fingers.

"I like it down." I whispered, noticing the crimson creep into her cheeks once more. She bit her lip, and let her hair slip through her fingers, crashing back town like a tidal wave. Alice smirked as she slid the hairband back onto her dainty wrist.

After I paid for the bill, we wandered aimlessly around the small village, eyeing up the boutique souvenir shops. I felt her hand slide into mine, her slender fingers interlocking with my own. My body thrummed with the urge to kiss her, to show her how I felt about her. Yet I remained silent, allowing her to dictate the pace, the ball was in her court. It was up to Alice to decide what it was she wanted.

The village was filled with sleepy, old wooden structures that looked as though they would collapse with a strong wind. Gimmicky souvenirs filled the windows. I could tell Alice was bored, her eyes were drawn to the sea.

"Do you want to walk along the shore?" I asked, unable to hide my smile when her eyes lit up and led the way. As we walked hand-in-hand I thought about how unfulfilling my life was before I met her, seeking solace and self-affirmation with one-night stands, and throwing every ounce of energy into the company. The long hours, the little sleep, the stress I put myself under unnecessarily, just to take my mind off of the bitter loneliness.

I watched as her hair billowed behind her on the sea breeze, completely unaware that her natural beauty had opened my eyes on the miserable existence I had lived. My father's voice cut through my thoughts. *"Money cannot buy you happiness, nor can it buy you love, son, but in this world, money is power."*

I thought that was all I had wanted: power. Yet as I walked hand-in-hand with Alice, knowing inside my bones I would do anything for her, I discovered what I truly wanted; *love* and someone who loved me, for who I was, not for what my money could buy them.

She stopped walking as our feet sank into the soft, dry sand. "Marcus, I'm glad that you are here." She rested her head on my shoulder, the roaring of the waves as they crashed into shore a few feet away almost drowned out her words. But I had heard them, they continued to echo in my head when we continued to idly walk on.

I knew time was running out; my absence would be noticed and the press would soon be out looking for where I had disappeared to. There was still much to sort out, still arrangements to make for Alice's new life. But being in her company, it made me wonder; *could I just let her walk out of my life?*

Isobel - FLASHBACK: One Year Ago.

"There is only one way to make cash... for yourself," my mentor, Crystal, had told me. "You have to go *freelance*." Her words echoed in my head, as I crept along the streets.

"Rule number one: never give them your real name. Rule number two: never ask them for theirs. Those are important." She had handed me a few items of clothing. Red. Leather. Sexy. I recalled being in her office as she gave me the run-down on how *freelancing* worked. I was shaking like a leaf, at least in the office I had some sort of protection, should things get too out of hand. In a motel room or a grimy alley freelancing for some underhanded cash, I was completely on my own.

I tottered past a kebab shop, the smell of grease and processed meat made me feel nauseous. Yet I continued to put one foot in front of the other, as I recalled the rest of Crystal's rules.

"Rule number three: never use main roads. Stick to the alleys. Police often patrol these areas and you do not want to be caught by them," she handed me a pair of knee-high PVC boots, heels taller than any I had ever seen in my life.

I trundled through the back streets and alleys as she advised, still off balance in the heels she had let me borrow despite the hours I practiced walking in them. The black PVC squeaked and the clicking of the heels echoed with every step I took.

"Rule number four: do not get caught, and I don't just mean by the police. Johnny likes the control; he wants to know when we are with clients, it's why he has such a regimented system... he doesn't want his girls *entertaining* without his knowledge."

She applied lots of layers of mascara to my eyelashes.

As the gentle wind blew, they felt too heavy to blink.

I was almost there at the 'pickup' point Crystal had arranged. She had set me up with one of her off-the-book regulars, apparently one of the gentler ones.

"Rule number five: never, and I mean ever, allow them to do anything that you are not comfortable with. If you are not into kinky stuff, bondage or any of that shit... you tell them. No still means no."

I rubbed my lips together, feeling the thick lipstick she had applied earlier that afternoon.

Rule number five made me smile. It was ironic because this whole situation was uncomfortable to me; selling my body for men's pleasure, ensuring I made the right sounds and moved the right way. If I adhered to rule number five, I would not be walking the backstreets to meet an off-the record client, nor would I be working for Johnny in the first place.

"Rule number six: stash the cash. Never take it back with you. Most of us spend it straight away. Others hide it in places no one is likely to stumble across it."

I just had to walk straight, along this backstreet, another few minutes as I would be there, the guy would be waiting for me in a red prius.

Crystal explained what he looked like in great detail though I could only remember small snippets. He was *mature* with thinning silver hair with a small goatee beard to match. He was well groomed and always wore expensive suits.

What I did remember was her stark warning, it had embedded itself in my brain. "He goes by the name of Harry, but that isn't his real name. He is a good man and pays well because he is stinking rich. If you recognize who he really is, pretend with everything you have that you don't. He is a well respected man, he doesn't want his *sexual desires* to be made public knowledge. So keep your mouth shut."

I remember the look, the scared but angry glare she gave me. I had sworn on my life I would never tell a soul if I recognized him and she had seemed satisfied.

As I walked now, I tried to imagine who was stinking rich and matched the vague description I recalled. My mind came up blank, ruling out the only person I knew who vaguely matched that description; Charles Morgan, the founder of Morgan Industries.

There was no way it would be him. He drove flashy sports cars, not a Prius-

There was a rustling noise in the small alley beside me, rooting me to the spot. My breath was heavy, I could see it linger in the frosty night air. My heart was beating rapidly. My eyes flitted from the direction I needed to go, back to the alley.

"Rule number seven: do not get yourself into a dangerous situation. Listen to your gut instincts." I stepped towards the sound. disregarding her last rule.

I had been on the streets long enough now to get used to the sounds of scurrying rats and stray cats, also scrounging for their next meal. But this was neither of them.

Curiosity got the better of me, I turned on my heel and walked into the small dark alley. The rustling immediately stopped the moment my heels did.

Someone else was here. I could feel eyes on me though I did not know where they lurked.

"Who's there?" I called, my voice trembling. "I know you're there." I stepped further into the alley, one foot at a time. The streetlight from the backstreet was dim, casting everything in darkness. Shadows and shapes. Blurred movement before me.

Emerging from the shadows, the dim light barely lit up his face, but his eyes were wide and glassy. His cheekbones were prominent and he stepped forward with a smirk on his face. He looked dangerous, feral even.

I scolded myself for my reckless courage, wishing I had followed through to the 'pick up point'. Instead, I had confronted this person in this alley, not even a mile away from my workplace.

This was where I was going to die, staring into the handsome face of my killer.

All because I did not stick to her last rule: Rule number eight: *run.*

TWENTY-SEVEN

My feet hurt and my back ached. I could not remember when I had walked so much. I only ever took a few steps around the house, my bedroom had been my preferred prison. But I did not want Marcus to see my struggle.

He paused as he felt his phone vibrate, with his other hand he slid it out of his pocket, checked the screen. I saw his eyes darken and the muscles in his body tense. I had almost forgotten that we were still holding hands until I felt his fingers squeeze mine. With a scowl he slid the phone back in his pocket.

"You can take that" I said, giving him a small smile. I pointed to a bench just along the path a little, still within sight but out of earshot. "I will wait there." In all honesty, I was grateful for the opportunity to sit down, rather than eavesdrop on his private conversation. Marcus looked at me, his eyes widened.

"Shit. Alice, are you hurting?" He looked mortified, looking behind us at the path we had taken, calculating how far we had walked. "Shit. I'm sorry, I... forgot".

"Marcus, it's fine. I was enjoying the walk." I told him with a smile. It was true, it had been beautiful, until moments ago when my legs screamed in agony. "I just need to sit for a few minutes," I added as we neared the bench.

His phone chimed once more, his jaw set, he reluctantly let go of my hand. "It will only take two minutes."

I watched him as he strolled away with the phone pressed to his ear. Whoever was on the other line, it was clear he did not want to talk to them. His fist clenched into a fist, before shoving it in his pocket. Although he kept his back to me, looking out across the shore, every few seconds he would glance over his shoulders, as if checking I was still where he had left me.

I took my opportunity to properly admire him. Marcus was broad shouldered with strong arms. His biceps bulged as he held the phone up to his ear. The white t-shirt in the sunlight was almost transparent, showing the dark pattern of his tattoo that spread across his chest and back, reaching up to his collarbone.

The jeans were tight around his muscular thighs and buttocks and he stood with a side profile. I could definitely make out the outline of his package. I had felt it earlier, my shoulder had brushed against the hard rod that was beneath his zipper, my heat had throbbed at the thought of it. My mind went into the fantasy of him, wanting him to take me, to be my true first, the guy who I would have given my virtue to, had Josh not stolen it.

I wanted to run my fingertips along his bare chest, feel it against my own. I may have been a virgin before, but I was not scared to know what I wanted, to know what positions I would have liked. But Marcus, I would let him put me in any position he wanted, as long as he purred my name-

"Alice," He called, "Sorry, I have to make another call. Two more minutes I swear."

I nodded, keeping my mouth shut firmly. allowed my fantasy to play out in my head, when Freyja rudely interrupted.

"He likes you," she giggled. *"I can see his thoughts... you should listen to them some time... phew!"*

Scowling, I blocked her out once more. Even if he does like me, it didn't change the fact that I was pregnant with his brother's child. *There could never be a future between us.* I would just become another one of the many women who jumped into his bed. *though I would willingly in a heartbeat.* I sighed as the tingling in my core increased.

He turned around to face me, his mouth in a wide grin, revealing his straight white teeth. He was gorgeous, handsome, and way too good for me. My stomach tightened, trapping the butterflies inside. I squirmed awkwardly as I tried to ignore their wings that fluttered uncontrollably.

I looked down to my bump, where my unborn baby was growing inside my body. Marcus had allowed the waitress to think we were an item, that this child was his. Considering we were holding hands across the table at the time it was not an unreasonable assumption to make.

"I told you; he likes you" Freyja piped up, her frustration for my doubt of her abilities was obvious in her voice.

I shook my head, dropping my eyes to the floor, saddened and embarrassed.

Perhaps he just feels guilty because of what Josh has done to me.

"How do you explain the bulge? Or the extra long shower?"

The thought of him thrashing his solid shaft in the bathroom next to me, that I had barged in on him. The heat rose to my face, my head felt faint.

Suddenly, Marcus' trainers came into view, stopping just before mine, his knees resting against mine. I looked up, feeling him lean closer as his arms stretched out on either side of me, our faces inches from each other. I wanted to kiss him, I held my breath feeling the heat radiate from his body.

"Alice..." he whispered, causing me to look up at him, our eyes locked. He opened his mouth to speak, but then closed it again, swallowing the words he had decided not to say.

"Um... shall we head back?" I asked.

He nodded, whoever was on the phone whatever the conversation had been about, it had shifted the dynamic between us. It had altered his mood. Moody and dark, like a storm, seemed to linger around him.

Slowly, we trundled back along the coast, retracing our steps in the sand, hearing the seagulls cawing overhead and the distant sounds of the waves crashing. Somewhere along the way, our hands found each other and our fingers entwined once more.

Crystal

Johnny *fucking* Malone. Every day another one of his parcels would arrive. 'Presents' taunting me of my failure so far to find him new recruits. Today it was a small glass timer with red sand inside. So far, I have received a clock with some very lewd images hand-carved into the wooden surround, as well as a calendar. They were everyday things - simple reminders that the deadline was fast approaching.

I felt a wave of terror wash over me. It was not for lack of trying. I had been frequenting every homeless shelter with fliers and business cards. Every day between appointments without fail, yet not one woman had taken the bait.

As I stumbled into the office, I heard his footsteps follow me, shutting the door behind him as quietly as possible. His zipper was already undone, his hard shaft already in his hand. I watched mesmerized as he stroked it as he approached me.

"I know you are not even *trying* Crystal, or at least not *hard* enough," his voice purred "You. Need. To. Try. Harder" he emphasized every word as he pushed me onto the bed, his knees straddling either side of my body, slowly shuffling along until his shaft was in front of my face. He smirked down at me, "Perhaps you can show my dick how hard you can work."

That was how sex with Johnny always started; he loved the way my mouth felt around his shaft, his guttural groans as I took his length, my hand working his shaft as my mouth formed a tight suction around him. He would be more erect than ever before as he was taken to the very cusp of his climax.

"That is why I charge so much for your blowies, Cryst" he sighed, as he pulled me to my feet, sliding his hand between my legs, tracing my entrance with his fingers.

He repulsed me yet there was something about him that I craved in a sadistic, self-destructive way. He scared me in the rough and brutish way he fucked, but over time I learned that fear could transform into arousal.

He had a penchant for going bareback, preferring to feel the tightness of my core without a rubber dulling the sensations. It was also rumored that he had also impregnated quite a few of his working girls in previous years. Their pregnancy turned him on more than anything else.

I could not afford another mouth to feed.

I made sure I stayed on top of my birth control tablets, because I could never reject him. Even if he did scare the shit out of me, my body craved him, needed him.

I only ever experienced real orgasms when he fucked me. I was fed up with giving men their pleasure all the time, faking it as loudly as I could, when I wanted to feel the real thing. I knew it was not right to get so aroused by a man that scared the shit out of me. I knew it was not normal to crave a man who would do things to me to cause pain.

But the pain would ebb away, and more often than not, it would turn into pleasure.

How could I resist him and deny myself of the desire my body so desperately wanted, craving my own release after granting it to countless others?

The moment he thrust me against the wall, his hand wrapped around my throat, and my leg raised as high as it would go, dangling over his other arm, any trace of rationality was erased. I bit down on my lip to stifle my scream as he sunk his shaft deep within my slit.

"Crystal, you filthy whore...so fucking tight... even after taking all those cocks," he groaned, his breath hot against my ear. His hips moving hard and fast, each one buried me a little deeper into the wall. Suddenly I was bent over, a vibration pulsated against my rectum.

I squealed as he pushed it deeper and harder against the resistance. "Your orgasms are mine, Crystal." He moaned as he reentered my heat slowly, purring at the sensation the vibrations made through my body and along his length.

His balls slapped against my sensitive nub as he drove into me, harder than before. His animalistic growls were fierce and frightening. His hands both grabbed my throat, pulling my body back to him so he could get even deeper, his words rang in my ear as he moaned.

"I don't want any of the fake bollocks 'I'm coming' shit you give the clients. I want to feel your nectar soak my balls. You have done it before, my little *slut* and I won't stop until you do it again *and again...*"

Prying my mouth open he forced his fingers inside, as his other hand tightened around my throat with each thrust. Involuntary gasping and choking noises escaped me. I felt my core quiver, as my climax neared.

"That's more like it, *Cryst...* Come for me you little *whore.*" He purred as his hand slid from my mouth down to my clit rubbing it in fast, circular motions. His muscles tightened as a shudder ripped through his body and his shaft pulsated inside me.

"Crystal... fuck...fuck..." he panted, as his hot load shot inside me, triggering my orgasm. My core convulsed against his shaft, milking every drop of his load as it mixed with my own, trickling down the insides of my thighs.

Panting and out of breath he spun me around to face him, crushing his lips against mine. "I fucking love you Crystal," he moaned as his arms wrapped around my waist and my body melted into him. Our hearts hammered in our chests as we stayed like that for a few moments before the shrill notification sound warned me of my first client of the day.

Johnny pulled away from me, checking his zipper was fastened before heading to the door. He paused, his eyes narrowed. "Don't let me down, Cryst... I want *more* of your time... not *less.*"

I stood watching him in silence, feeling our come dribble out of my entrance, my breathing heavy.

I knew I should get away from this, from him, but the ripple of the aftermath reminded me why I had stayed for so long, the reason that I hadn't tried to run like my little 'apprentice' had.

Aside from the fear of his wrath, I loved fucking Johnny. Or was it I fucking loved him? Was there even a difference between the two?

⚙

Isobel

Fire engulfed me; my lungs, my stomach, the blood that ran through my veins, even the tears I cried scorched my skin.

I stumbled to the loft, gasping for breath, crawling on my hands and knees up the stairs. I thought I was going to die as my panicked thoughts swirled around in my mind.

What would we do? Where would we go?

Then another more sinister thought gripped me, *Would Cole abandon me? Would I have to return to that world?*

I huddled into my sleeping bag, crushing Scruff to my chest with one hand and rolling the heart pendant in the other, until my breathing finally returned to normal, and the fire inside me subsided.

I felt like a burden, if I could get a job like Cole's, one where I did not have to sell my body, I would feel less like a lost cause. Yet I currently relied on everyone's kindness; Cole, Maxine, The Shelter, and now Alice.

I did not want to go back to turning tricks, but I was beginning to think I never had a choice,

Johnny's words had been right all along; *"I would never amount to anything without him."* My hand traced along my cheekbone, my fingers feeling the faint scar that he had inflicted in a moment of rage.

No, I can't go back.

I curled into the fetal position, wishing for death if that was what my life would become. The walls were closing in, my chest caught in a vice-like grip as the panic flooded through me once more.

If Johnny finds me then death will be the least of my concerns.

⚙

Cole

I found her circled up buried in her sleeping bag, her arms wrapped around her body and pain etched across her face. I instantly checked if she was breathing, sighing in relief when she stirred as my cold fingertips brushed her neck.

Her hair was different, pulled back into plaits. I did not like it. It was not the beautiful sea of unruly hair I was used to. The skin around her eyes was red and swollen. *Shit. She's seen the sign.*

I sighed, as I sat beside her, my eyes slowly moving across her face, following every line and curve of her features, as if committing them to memory. Tracing my finger along her cheekbone I noticed that her features were more defined, but also it revealed a small scar that was usually well hidden.

"Cole?" she gasped, wide eyed and panicked.

"I'm here" I replied snuggling beside her. My arm wrapped around her waist pulling her into my chest.

"What are we going to do? Are you going to leave me?" She said as the fear in her voice clutched at my heartstrings. She turned to face me, her eyes gazing up into mine. Glassy with tears.

I shook my head and kissed her on the forehead. "I'm not going anywhere without you Bel. You should know that." I felt her body sag in relief, as she exhaled deeply. Pressing her body closer to mine. "Unless you don't want me to?"

I felt my shaft twitch as her thigh brushed against it. I held my breath as she intertwined her legs and pulled her face level with mine. Her breaths were shallow, hot against my face. "Cole, I want you, always." She purred, as she wriggled to get comfortable. I felt her heat brush against my thigh, causing every muscle in my body to tense.

I moved my hand up to her face, smoothing her non-scarred cheek with my thumb. Resisting my urge to pull her on top of me, "Bel, no matter what, things will work out. We may need to leave here, go somewhere new-"

Her fingers ran down my lips, silencing me. "Wherever you go, I will go," she whispered, her words comforting me like a blanket.

Kissing her fingertips, I hastily moved to her nose, and her neck and then finally to her lips as I savored every moment. "Bel...I want you to be... my-" I exhaled, my voice shaking, my member rock hard and pressing against her. "Not just at this moment... like-"

Realization crept into her face as I felt her smile widen beneath my kiss. "Cole, I was always yours." She whispered, her hand stroking my shaft over the top of my jeans. "All you needed to do was show me you wanted me."

It was my turn to gasp, her hand so expertly teasing it through the fabric of my jeans. Every nerve ending was on hyper alert.

"I love you Bel" my voice came out as a whisper. "I just didn't know if you *wanted* the same thing."

"I love you too Cole."

Unaware of how such few words could inflict a mix of emotions within me all at once. Joy, hope and belonging, yet a sting of uncertainty burdened me.

What if I can't find somewhere else for us to stay?

Her lips were on mine, her arms wrapped around my neck, her kisses pushing away all of the nagging thoughts. All I could think about was her, and only her.

My hand firm on her back, I rolled her on top of me, her heat pressed firmly against the bulge in my pants.

"Cole" she whispered, her eyes piercing mine, as she stopped moving. "You need to know something" I looked at her, my desire burning like a fire within me as I removed the hair bands, and unpicked her plaits, watching as her hair cascaded down past her shoulders and rested against her breasts.

"I know Bel." I told her, my hand snaking into her hair, a smile of my lips as I guided her head down to me, bringing her lips back against mine. "and I don't care-" I told her between feverish kisses, as my lips explored her neck, feeling the cold necklace along the base of it. "You did what you could to survive... but you never have to do that again."

She dug her hips into mine, grinding against my member, I could feel myself losing to the desire that had been bottled up inside of me for so long.

"I'm still on birth control" she whispered, as her lips grazed my earlobe. "I want you to make me yours Cole. I want you to take me...to claim me as yours."

I slid my hands underneath her top, feeling the softness of her supple breasts, her taut nipples against my palm, fondling them as I have wanted to do for so long. I slowly removed it, bringing my mouth up to greet them, rolling my tongue over her nipples.

"Bel" I breathed, as I felt her hand run though my hair, holding my face against her breast, as her other one unfastened my jeans, before sliding inside and taking hold of my shaft. I groaned as I tried to remove her jeans, not wanting to break away from her, but the suspense was killing me. An unseen force drew me deeper and deeper to her.

I lowered Bel onto her back, my trembling hands slid her jeans off and her knickers, revealing her naked body before me. My eyes ravaged her body, until I noticed goosebumps spread along her body, I ripped off my jeans as she clawed at my t-shirt, until I was hovering over her, the heat of our naked bodies against each other as the thrum of our hearts beat against each other.

Her small moans were like a sweet song as my tip rubbed against her silky slit. She gasped when I slowly entered her, feeling her tightness embrace me, stretching to accommodate my rock hard member. Her moans beckoned me to go deeper.

I thrust in and out of her wildly as I unleashed my desires. I had thought about this for so long. I wished I had the balls to kiss her sooner, knowing I could have spent every night like this.

"Cole..." she gasped, her legs wrapping around my waist, allowing me to go deeper than before, her nails scraping along my back, "Cole... please don't stop."

I had no intention of stopping, and to prove it I increased my pace a little, feeling her writhe and squirm against me, feeling her thighs clench against my hips as she moved in time to meet me. Her moans grew louder as I took her over the edge, but I was not done yet. I drove my hips deeper, harder, until our bodies clapped against each other as they connected, my member filling her to the hilt, feeling her entrance dampen as she came.

She bit her lip once more, her fingernails digging deeper into my flesh as my name rolled off her tongue. That was the final straw.

No longer could I hold back my load, feeling it explode within her warmth. I rolled onto my back, pulling her quivering body against mine, our breaths synchronized as we recovered from the long-awaited release. I planted my lips on the top of her head, "Bel, that...that was-!"

I felt her adjust her head, so that our lips were pressed together once more, her tongue seeking mine. "That was the first time I have ever enjoyed sex." she murmured, filling me with indescribable elation and satisfaction.

"I love you Bel," I whispered. pulling the sleeping bag over our naked bodies, shielding her from the bitter wind that whipped through the loft.

My eyes scanned this makeshift home, knowing that she deserved better than this. I wanted to give her a better life. Her breathing slowed, as she fell asleep, her body still wrapped around mine.

I became lost once more to the dread that gradually crept up on me, the longer I stared at the ceiling, the more it dawned on me that I needed the higher power to align our stars, to grant me one wish. A way to make my dream a reality.

Fighting against sleep, my mind calculated a plan, unable to allow myself to think of where we would be sleeping, should it fail.

TWENTY-EIGHT

Marcus

I could not bring myself to speak the words back at the beach, but she had a right to know. Even though I knew deep down, it wouldn't change the outcome. She had already decided.

As we walked back along the beach, I was trying to think of the best way I could tell her, the most tactful way to tell her that one of her options was no longer available. It was too late.

We were almost at the B&B when a little boutique shop caught my eye. *Babies & Beyond*. I could see her eyes linger on the items in the window, confirming what I already knew.

"Do you want to have a look?" I asked, giving her hand a gentle squeeze. At first she looked reluctant, afraid even, but she eventually nodded, biting the nails on her other hand. A little bell chimed, marking our entrance. It startled Alice, and I thought for a moment she was going to bolt back out the door. I squeezed her hand and gave her a reassuring smile, watching as her lips curled at the corners.

A world of pastel shades surrounded us, making it difficult to concentrate on any one thing. Alice's eyes scanned them all, twinkling as she took it all in. Her gaze stopped at the small selection of neutral white and grays in front of us. Her hand roaming over the tiny outfits and miniature socks and hats.

Though I tried not to, I felt uncomfortable, I had never envisioned myself standing in such a shop. It was not that I never wanted children, I just did not feel I would make a good father figure. My own was not an exemplary role model to follow, and I feared I would become him.

I stood in one spot, grinning as she browsed the shop, walking among the clothes racks. Despite being well overdue for one, I knew from her medical records that her GP was unaware of her pregnancy, she had not had her baby's first scan, nor did she have a due date. I made a mental note to talk to her about it, and arrange a private one.

My eyes followed her every movement, unable to look at anything else other than her, as she looked through racks of maternity clothes.

I felt a hand on my shoulder. "How far along is she?" an older lady asked, as she too watched Alice flit around the shop "Um… just over thirty weeks" I mumbled.

The lady's eyes squinted as her smile spread across her face. "I bet you are both so happy. It's your first child, I assume?" She paused, her gaze expectant of an answer. I nodded, before she erupted in a little squeal. "It's so exciting, the miracle of life!" she cooed.

While we were talking, Alice had taken some items to the till, two pairs of maternity jeans and two long-sleeve tops.

"Please excuse me" I said to the lady, before I scrambled to Alice's side.

"I will get these" I offered, handing over my card for payment, picking up a white sleepsuit that had caught my eye beside Alice. It had a cartoon elephant embroidered on the front. Memories of my mother floated back, of the way she collected elephant ornaments and how she often spoke fondly of her favorite animal. So much so that from a young age it had soon become mine too.

"This one as well" I said, placing it on the counter, watching Alice's brows furrow.

I saw her eyelids flicker closed as my lips grazed her forehead, I felt her body relax into mine as her arms wrapped around my waist.

"Thank you," she murmured.

For a split second I had almost convinced myself that we were a regular couple, that for a fleeting moment she *was* carrying my child. It felt so natural, so easy to let my guard down around her.

"Can we, um… get something to eat now?" Alice asked in a soft voice after we left the shop, the smell of salted chips with vinegar and battered fish lingered in the air.

As we walked past a restaurant, I saw Alice's expression grow dark; it was crowded and loud. People sat in every seat and the bar area crammed. She scuffed her feet on the floor, her eyes cast down to the small stones that crunched beneath her shoes as her other hand pulled self-consciously over her stomach before chewing on her fingernail.

I recognized that look; shame, embarrassment and anxiety. I never wanted her to feel that way, I would have happily strolled in there proud to accompany her, but I would not force her into a situation she was uncomfortable with.

I pulled her into my embrace, "Alice, we don't have to go in there." I soothed, feeling her face turn up to me, her lips curved into a small smile, inches from my own. I wanted to kiss her, to feel those soft lips against mine.

"We can get a pizza," she murmured, turning her head away from mine, to the small fast-food place down the street.

I nodded, swallowing back my regret. *I missed my chance.*

⛬

Isobel

Through the small window opposite my sleeping bag I could see the sliver of the moon, the dark blanket of clouds still covered the sky, but my fear of losing him, losing our home had woken me.

I felt Cole's arms pull me in tighter to his side, encouraging me to fall back asleep, but I knew sleep would not come. I looked up at his peaceful face, finding myself reliving those moments, the warmth of his words and his acceptance of me washed over me. I smiled to myself in the dark, trying to soothe the fear that still gnawed at my insides, trying to distract myself by studying his peaceful face that still wore a small satisfied smile on his lips.

I knew with Cole it would have been different, my previous experiences being sordid, I was my client's *dirty* secret, they cared little for me, they were only there for themselves. But I had never expected that sex could be a sacred act, a special bond between two people who cared for one another. I had never anticipated that I would have ever been so lucky.

Cole's words *"I don't care..."* had eased my worries, and had cleared my mind from the unspeakable, disgusting actions I performed for a price. Those memories that I had failed to erase for the past year, those that trivialized everything I did, made me doubt that my life could ever be anything different, that I would ever amount to anything more than a whore.

I had been so worried about what Cole would have thought had I told him the truth of my past, the real reason I was in that alley the night we met exactly a year ago. I was scared he would have been repulsed by me, would have shunned me the way the rest of society did.

I had completely disregarded the possibility that he might have already known, I underestimated his perceptiveness. Looking back I was naïve to think he would not have at least an inclination from the start, considering how I looked that night. I shuddered at the recollection. All along I had been blinded by shame.

My heart thrummed when he said those words: *"You did what you could to survive... but you never have to do that again."* I knew he meant them, the voice was ladened with the truth. Though it still seemed surreal that he loved me, that he was able to develop these feelings for me despite my past.

I snuggled closer to him, feeling my heart swell, feeling like the luckiest person in the world at that very moment. I recalled his touch; gentle and considerate. Ensuring he pleasured me rather than it being solely about his own needs, his own release. I was taken by surprise by the first orgasm, allowing my hungry lust and desire to overcome me. Cole made me realize I could enjoy sex, rather than it be a deed I needed to tolerate.

As I traced my fingers along his naked chest, I felt the yearning grow inside my own, the fire in my core for him again, as I dared my hand to move lower.

Cole's lips crashed against mine before his eyes flickered open, revealing the same passion burning inside them. I felt the smile creep across his face as he rolled me on top of him. His shaft was hard and ready, as I felt it rub against my needy core.

I let out a soft moan. As it grazed my exposed nub, sending a ripple of pleasure through my body. I felt nervous, being on top, I knew what to do, but for a moment my mind froze. "Bel, relax..." he murmured, pulling my breasts towards him, his tongue flickering over my hard nipples, his breath hot against them as his hands slid down to my waist, guiding me down onto him.

I let out a small gasp feeling the familiar fullness from before, as his shaft entered my warmth, his hands easing me into a gentle rhythm. His breath quickened, deepening into groans as I ground my hips against his.

Hearing his pleasure drove me to increase my pace, ignoring the ache in my muscles as I worked them harder and faster than before. Small beads of sweat formed on my brow, trickling down the side of my face as I thrashed against him, feeling him buck underneath me to match my tempo, his hands holding onto my breasts as they bounced against my body.

I had learned to recognize when a client was close to coming, in that profession you wanted to get it over with. The sooner the better. So as soon as you felt the little twitches of their shaft, heard their breathing change into frantic grunts you knew you had to increase your momentum, but with Cole, I did not want it to be over just yet.

Going against all I had been taught, I slowed down, kissing him between each thrust, my lips planting kisses along his jawline, down his neck. "Fuck" he moaned, cupping a breast and maneuvering it to his hungry mouth.

He pulled my nipple between his teeth, the sensation drove me wild, made me cry out his name and made me increase my pace once more.

"Bel, I'm so close" he murmured, I too could feel that I was toeing the line of my climax. "Come for me," he whispered, taking my other nipple to his mouth, in less than a minute I felt my orgasm explode, my breath caught in my throat, as my body pulsated and convulsed. My inner walls gripping his shaft as my climax ripped through my body.

"Cole" I gasped, my body crashing against his, no longer having the strength to keep me up, feeling his shaft throb still inside me as his seed trickled down my thigh.

"Bel, you are amazing" he exhaled, as he ran his hands through my untamed locks allowing it to cascade over our faces as I kissed him, until my orgasm subsided, until his shaft went limp.

"Cole," I whimpered against his mouth, "thank you."

"What for?" He asked, his voice a gentle whisper, his hand stroked my cheek.

"For loving me," I sighed, "for making me feel like I belong," I kissed him again. "For proving to me that sex can be, and should be, *fucking amazing.*"

"You don't need to thank me," he smiled, his teeth grazing my bottom lip. "I have loved you for a long time Bel, I just never knew how to tell you." His voice was gruff, heavy as sleep threatened to consume him.

"I love you Cole." I told him as I slid off him, laying on my side, my eyes closing as I placed my head on his chest. Hearing his rapid heartbeat slow, feeling the rise and fall of his chest fade to normal.

"I never thought this was how we would celebrate a year of each other's company" He chuckled lightly. My stomach fluttered at his words, surprised that he remembered the significance of today. "I only wished I had told you how I felt sooner, so every night could have been spent like this." Cole added, his lips brushing my forehead.

My hand found his, lacing my fingers through them, "I'm scared Cole... these past months having found this place... I don't know-"

"Bel," he murmured, his mouth buried into my hair, feeling his breath flutter across my scalp. "I won't let us go back out onto the streets... I promise."

The darkness washed over me quickly as his words soothed me like a lullaby as they whispered softly through my hair. "Sweet dreams Bel."

Alice

Back at the B&B, an empty pizza box lay at the bottom of the bed by our feet as we sat leaning against the headboard staring into nothingness. The sleepsuit Marcus had picked out was placed on the chair opposite the bed. *It was cute, adorable even, but why did he buy it?*

I was so excited to show my mom; she loved babies and I knew she would be so excited to be a grandparent. But then it dawned on me, like a suffocating darkness, she would never meet my baby. She would never get the chance to be a grandmother. Tears pricked my eyes, threatening to fall at any moment.

I wiggled my toes, trying to distract myself, my poor feet were tired and achy, and my back was hurting.

I put my head on his shoulder, then changed my mind and sat up straight once more.

I could not fathom what, if anything, was going on between us. I just knew I needed to focus on my baby, yet I could not stop thinking about how it felt so natural to hold his hand as they walked along the coast. How easy it was to be myself in his company or admire how gorgeous he was. Even as we sat in this easy silence, I was unable to concentrate on anything other than how close his body was to mine.

"Alice, you can rest your head on me if you want to," he whispered, moving his arm around my shoulders to make it easier for me to snuggle into him.

I could have fallen asleep like this, but I needed to speak. I needed to clear the air, to know once and for all what it was he wanted from me. If he just wanted sex then I'd happily give it to him. But the way he acted sometimes, as if we were a couple, made me wonder if he wanted *more*. I had overheard the conversation he had with the woman in the shop, the way he allowed her to believe that he was the father, that this child I carried was his, *ours*.

"Al-"

"Marc-"

His eyes locked onto mine and we both chuckled. "You go first," I said.

"No, I insist, ladies first" he remarked, his eyes twinkling as he smiled at me.

Oh, I could play that game too. "Age before beauty" I said, turning my body so that I could face him, his hand falling from my shoulder.

"And a beauty you are," his words were so quiet, so low, I was not sure if I heard him correctly, or if I had imagined it.

He looked at me, for a moment I almost believed we *were* a real couple, but his eyes dropped to my stomach and the atmosphere between us changed in an instant.

"Alice, do you know how far along you are into your pregnancy?"

I nodded. I had known from the moment my bump started showing my time was running out, yet I continued to hide behind my bedroom door for weeks, months even. I calculated the dates, over and over, checking and then checking once more. I was well into the third-trimester. *In a few days I will be thirty-six weeks into this pregnancy.*

It was what had prompted me to leave that day, saying nothing to anyone. It was nearly time and I was not prepared, not in the slightest. My tears spilled down my cheeks as the raging hormones coursed through my body.

His hands came up to my face, wiping away the tears. "And this is what you want?"

"Yes." I asked, my voice harsher than I had intended.

He took hold of my hands as he studied my face. "Did you consider adoption?" he whispered.

I pulled my hands out of his, wrapping them tightly around my stomach. *No one is taking my baby from me.*

"No." I heaved up my bag that was now on the floor retrieving his envelope. "I will not give my baby away. Marcus, *this* is my choice."

I paused, gasping for breath "I know what I am giving up, what I need to do so no one knows who the fuck I am, or what happened to me..." I felt deceived, that this was all just some ploy. A lure for Josh to get his own way, *yet again.*

"I promise, I won't tell anyone..." I paused, trying to contain the sobs that were stored in my chest. "You can have your money." I said, shoving the envelope to his chest. "I don't want your *bribe* to give my child away."

My breathing was heavy, the great dam I had tried to build to contain the sobs broke. I refused to look at him. My eyes lingering on my bump, my hands cradling it.

"Why were you pretending in the shop that you cared? That this child was yours, if you were just here to convince me to give it away? Why buy that sleepsuit?" My eyes locked onto his. "Why did you really come here Marcus?"

I felt his arm pull me towards him, lingering on the small of my back as the other hand tilted my face up towards his. Feeling his lips graze against mine, soft like the brush of a feather.

"Alice," he whispered. "I came for *you*."

Freyja

A fragment of light.

A crack in the wall she built around me.

I saw brief glimpses through the gaps during her moments of vulnerability. The moments she let her focus slip on keeping me out.

The darkness inside her was weakening her, allowing her blockade to crumble.

I knew that soon, I would be free. Thanks to the child that was rapidly growing inside her. The key, the prodigy, my beacon of hope for a better world.

The child I want to protect at all costs. A child *he* wanted to raise as his own. If she would let him. He and I were alike where Alice was concerned.

We wanted to protect her, wanted to keep her safe and happy. We both had guilt that we needed her absolution so that we could continue on our Fated paths.

If Alice could stop being stubborn for a moment, to let me show her what the future could bring, what the man beside her wants her to know, perhaps then, she might actually be able to find peace and live happily.

Marcus and I wanted to join her on the journey of parenthood, to ease the burden of the grueling and demanding times, as well as revel in the most rewarding and satisfying ones.

If only she would let us.

How can I show her that there is only one thing stopping her dreams from coming true?

Her fear.

TWENTY-NINE

Marcus

What the fuck am I doing? The inner turmoil of my conflicting feelings and desires for her spiraled in my head. I had abandoned the plan the moment I got in the car to come here, I knew this was not how it was supposed to be, but it was what my heart wanted.

"Alice." I whispered, breaking the kiss. I cradled her face between my palms. Her skin felt so soft under my touch. "I don't want you to get rid of the baby." I could see the confusion wash over her face, the way her eyebrows would furrow into a frown, causing her eyes to squint and little wrinkles in her forehead become more prominent.

"But, but why did you say that?" She sniffed.

"Because...well...I," I stammered, my shoulders slumped as my hands slid down to hers, holding my hands over her stomach. "I didn't want you to rule out all the options."

She nodded, wiping her eyes with the sleeve of her cardigan. "There are no other options Marcus, I want my child, I want to show it the unconditional love it deserves, father or not, my child *will* be loved."

"Alice, you wanted to know why I bought the sleepsuit, it's because elephants are my favorite animals," my voice whispered as I picked it up from the chair and held it in my hands, examining it. 'They remind me of my mom, they were her favorite animals too. Big and strong, but fiercely loyal... a herd will raise an orphaned calf with just as much love as if it was one of their own."

I felt her hand on top of mine, both of us looking at the sleepsuit together. Her touch was so gentle and tender, like feathers tickling the backs of my hands.

"Alice..." I paused, lifting up her chin so that she could see in my eyes that I was being serious. My heart was beating uncontrollably, my hands were trembling as they held her closer to me. "You don't have to do this alone."

Her eyes widened and confusion flickered across her face. I felt myself succumbing to the warmth that flooded me, overwhelmed by the ideas that rattled inside my head, the one every legal advisor would be set against, the one where I would never have to let Alice go.

I took a deep breath before pressing my lips against hers once more. Never had I wanted anyone or anything more. "Alice, I want you both to become a part of *my* life."

Josh

"Where the fuck are you?" I snapped when the call was answered.

"None of your concern," he replied as the sound of seagulls pierced through the phone.

"You're with her, right now, aren't you?" I shouted, downing the glass of whisky in my hand. My hand was shaking so much the ice cubes clinked against the glass. "Another" I demanded of the girl behind the bar.

"What the fuck are you playing at Marc?" I asked, my tone of voice darkening in my anger.

"It is of no concern to you," he replied, cold, emotionless.

"Of course it fucking is!" I yelled down the phone, slamming my glass down on the table so hard it shattered in my hands. "She is still carrying my child, isn't she?" I hissed.

He hung up. *Motherfucker!*

I tried to call again, but it went straight to voicemail. I shoved my phone in my pocket. Staring at the barmaid who had cleaned up the fragments of broken glass. I glared at her, noticing she was still holding the bottle in her hand.

I licked my lips as I grabbed hold of her wrist, "leave the bottle" I snapped. My eyes narrowed slits as I stared at her, reveling in the fear that oozed from every pore in her body. She placed it down, her eyes pleading, begging me to let her go. I like that look. I thought as I let my grasp linger there, holding her for a few more seconds, letting her suffer just a little longer.

"Yes, we like it when they whimper, don't we?" Asmodeus' voice chimed in.

I let her go, watching her as she scurried away from me faster than trapped rats being released into the sewers. I felt repulsed by myself, feeling myself becoming like him, feeling his impulses, his desires taking over me.

"You should just stop resisting me, what is done, is done" he said. I put the bottle to my lips and drank, as my eyes scanned the bar. It was still early, so it was quiet now, but I knew I needed to leave here before it got busy. I did not trust him or myself.

"You have well and fucked my life up," I told him. "That is why I will continue to resist you until you fuck off..." Drinking from the bottle I wished every gulp would erase a little more of my memories, praying that they could change the past.

I needed her to get rid of the child, so that this secret could be forgotten like a bad dream. There was no way I could ever tell Effy the truth if Alice kept the child. It was what my brother was supposed to be doing, trying to convince her, bribe her, doing *something* to encourage her to get rid of the damn thing.

Yet Asmodeus' anger grew, the more I wished harm to come to the child. He saw it as a key to ultimate power. A way to reign over Hell. The more I thought about it, the more he would threaten to tell Effy the truth, or to continue the endless cycle of meaningless flings.

I held my head in my hands, *I love Effy, I could not lose her.*

Anger surfaced for my brother, *What the fuck is he playing at?*

I knew he was too soft to make the demands.

He is a disappointment to our father. He had taught him every lesson, yet he had not seemed to take any of it on board.

The sinking pit in my stomach, the throbbing in my head, the nausea in the back of my throat told me I was well and truly fucked.

Asmodeus' chuckle irked me, *"one way or another you're all fucked."*

Freyja

Humans are all faced with decisions in their lives. Sometimes they are minor and have no real impact, whereas others are the catalyst to a chain of events that can alter their entire future.

Humans never know at the time what their decision will lead to. Often fretting over the unimportant ones and making the crux decisions in haste.

I could hear Alice's thoughts, each one trying to convince her against falling for him. Yet what she did not realize was that this was her crucial moment, the decision she made now to accept his offer or refuse it, could alter her Fate.

Before her stood her soulmate, yet she was too blind or scared to see it.

She needed to be shown, I needed to encourage her to take that leap of faith. This was her chance to embrace her destiny, to allow her heart to rule her head for once.

I could see her resolve fading as Marcus deepened the kiss, as his hands slid down her body and held the sides of her swollen stomach. I could feel her apprehension, to allow herself to hope, to dream that this could work with every word he spoke.

"Alice… meeting you has opened my eyes to what I truly desire above everything else; *you* and the chance to have a *family* of my own."

THIRTY

Every day we went to the shelter, paying if we needed to so that we could have a shower, it was worth it, just we could fully enjoy each other's bodies.

Night after night, Cole's hands moved all over me, exploring every inch of it as if I was an unclaimed land and it was his first time discovering it.

Never before had I experienced this level of intimacy or sensuality before. It had always been regimented with a set time allocation and a set price. There was no time for passion or foreplay, so I savored every moment, reveled in the many orgasms Cole coaxed from my body.

"Bel" he groaned, as his kisses trailed down my spine, his hands squeezing my bare buttocks as I knelt in front of him. Feeling my core quiver as his mouth lingered over my heat, his tongue slowly teasing the delicate inner folds. I had squirmed the first time, never experiencing it before, but now I relished in the feeling of his tongue probing the entrance, curling along my slit, teasing my sensitive nub.

Tonight was no different, he had waited until my body stopped spasming before thrusting his shaft inside me. Our moans of pleasure reverberated off the walls of the loft, his shadow cast by the dim candlelight. Though he was taking his time, slowly and seductively, sliding his length in my warmth, it was not long until his tempo increased, his hips slapping against my buttocks and his hands firm on my waist, as he took us both to another happy ending.

Falling in a naked heap, we spoke about the future, dreaming of what our apartment would look like and what pets we would have. But I knew all of our plans were just dreams. We were not in a position to be too selective, we needed cheap and affordable and to be able to look after ourselves first. Yet it was nice, as I lay there, my muscles achy and exhausted, to know that Cole wanted a future with me.

"Bel, as long as I am with you, I don't care where we live, or what it looks like." He yawned, his arms cradling me into him. I could feel the darkness of sleep wash over me, as the gentle rise and fall of his chest calmly rocked me.

Another day over, tomorrow was another day closer to the demolition of our makeshift home. My chest tightened as our future was still unclear, it was the elephant in the room, we both knew it was there, but refused to acknowledge it. Whilst we spoke of our future, it was as if we had all the time in the world, not a little over three weeks.

I tried to remain calm, to allow Cole's soothing words to comfort me. "It will all work itself out."

But how could he be so sure?

Cole

I never wanted to leave her side, but I knew I had no choice. Our time was running out, and the savings I had scraped together so far was not nearly enough.

My determination to make a better life for us outweighed my reluctance to leave her warm embrace. As I gazed at her sleeping face, a picture of her serenity and happiness, I knew it would be worth it once we were in a proper bed, in our own place.

"Bel" I said in a whisper, as I slid my body out from underneath her, placing a delicate kiss on her forehead. "I will be back soon." She stirred but did not wake. I left her with another gentle kiss on the cheek before covering her naked body with additional blankets before zipping up her sleeping bag.

I threw on my discarded clothes from last night before making my way to work. The rain lashed down, relentless heavy bullets that saturated my clothes before I was even halfway there. Head bent low, I pushed through, grateful that for now, we had the loft to go back to afterwards.

I remembered the long nights under these skies, trying to seek shelter wherever we could from this weather. In shop entrances, under bridges, even those long nights sat in the shelter, unable to afford a bed each, I had opted for Bel to sleep, and I would wait for her in the lobby. Yet every time she refused, fighting back sleep like the stubborn person that she was, as we watched the rain lash against the window pane.

I smiled remembering the missed opportunities where I could have told her how I felt about her, the times where she had fallen asleep against me as we huddled together for warmth against the merciless winds.

"Ah Cole... come in!" My eyes snapped up, noticing I was at the front of the shop, Mr. Banerjee stood holding the front door open for me. I looked at him puzzled as I walked through the door. His chuckle resonated as he ushered me through to the back office. A spare pair of jeans and tshirt was waiting for me. "I figured, you may have resembled a drowned rat upon your arrival." He said with a smile. "They should fit."

I picked them up, noticing they were new with labels still on them. "Mr. B-" I said, about to thank him, but he was gone. I peeled off the sodden clothes that clung to me like a second skin, hanging them over the radiator to dry off, before entering the kitchen.

Stacks of plates were waiting to be put away from last night, I sighed knowing that in a few hours, I would be washing them once more. *Stop complaining, at least I have a job.*

I looked at the list Mr Banerjee left for me on the noticeboard; cleaning tasks he got me to perform each day before opening. Today's tasks included a thorough deep clean of the kitchen as well as changing the oil on the vats.

As I scrubbed every inch of the kitchen, my anxiousness consumed me, driving me to scour so hard my knuckles turned red and sore. I wondered if Bel would be awake yet, what she was thinking, what she was doing. My eagerness to be by her side as I recalled her naked body alone in her sleeping bag. I allowed my mind to drift to her naked breasts, feeling her soft, silky skin beneath my palms, her nipples solid against them. My member twitched as I moved to another section of the kitchen to clean, recalling the tentative moment my shaft entered her for the first time. Feeling her warmth embrace the length of it, feeling with each time her confidence grew, and her shame ebbed away.

At first, it had been hard to imagine her in these positions with someone else, my jealous mind would taunt me, make me question if any of her clients were bigger or better than me. Until her first orgasm ripped through her body and the words she purred after put my mind at ease. *"That was the first time I had enjoyed sex before."*

The thought of satisfying her like no other, giving her orgasm after orgasm with my fingers, tongue, and shaft, that was all I wanted. I did not want her to feel obliged to please me. I needed her to know I wanted her to be mine to love, not just to fuck. I wanted her to feel special, wanted her to know that I cherished her body and everything about her.

I used to envision intimate moments with her most evenings trying to focus on the book in my hands rather than the slender frame of her body, the cute heart-shaped face, imagining how good it would feel to be buried deep inside her. The torture of waiting until the dead of night drove me wild, struggling to remain silent as I used my right hand to jerk off over my fantasies of her.

"Cole-"

Mr. Banerjee's voice jerked me from my thoughts, my engorged bulge thankfully hidden behind the counter. My head snapped up in his direction.

"We need to talk," he said with a weary look. I gulped. Anxiety gripped my chest, and my breaths became short and shallow. I could feel it in my gut, bad news was coming, I did not want to hear it, fearing that he was about to cement my failure.

I could not let Bel down, especially not after a small unintentional kiss had blossomed into something that I would fight tooth and nail to protect. *How could I face Bel as a failure?*

He was leaning against the doorframe, trying to smile, for the first time I noticed his face was etched with more wrinkles, there were bags under his eyes. Mr Banerjee looked tired and drained.

"I'm getting too old for this line of work," Mr. Banerjee sighed, "and I have learned this morning that not one of my children intends to carry on the restaurant if I was to retire... *or die.*"

I watched him pinch the bridge of his nose with his thumb and forefinger, his expression pained. "Not a single one has any inclination to continue this business that I have worked so hard to build for them, so that I could provide them with stability for their futures."

I could hear the frustration in his voice. He was a proud man, though the past week or so he had been clutching at his back, and becoming forgetful with customers' orders. I tried not to pay much attention to the happenings at the front end of the restaurant. But I did care about Mr. Banerjee, he had given me a lifeline when he caught me out the back rummaging through his bins.

I watched as he walked over to me, the tension and anticipation of being let go from the job had made my member fall limp, so when he put his hand on my shoulder I did not feel quite so awkward.

"You're a good kid, Cole, I wish at least one of my children were more like you. Not afraid of a little hard work." he tried to chuckle, but even I could hear that it was forced. "Cole, I want to show you something".

I tore off the cleaning apron and followed him. *What could he want to show me in the stockroom?* I had never been inside of there before, I was never allowed.

The first thing I noticed was Mr. Banerjee was trying to move huge sacks of rice, and a racking of vegetables on his own.

"Mr. B- what are you doing? Here, let me help-" That was when I saw it, what that racking had been hiding, a brand new dishwasher, complete with cellophane wrap and Styrofoam padding around it. My shoulders slumped, it confirmed that I was out of a job.

"My eldest son, Ishaan, bought this about a month ago." As he spoke, he was looking at me, assessing my reaction. "You know me, I'm an old man. I don't like technology." He patted the top of the dishwasher "I fear these things don't wash items as good as by hand, you know? I like it done the traditional way. but my son was insistent that I had one." He clapped his hand on my shoulder. "You were doing a good job, so...I shoved it in here, out the way," he said, a slight twinkle in his eye.

He was silent for a few moments, the pair of us just stood looking at the dishwasher. *Why was he telling me all of this? Why isn't he kicking me out of the door?*

As if he had read my mind, he spoke once more. "Cole, I want you to help me with things around here, not stuck in there washing dishes." He paused; his small smile widened as he witnessed the shocked look that had spread on my face.

"You are a good man, an honest, hard-working man. If my children are not interested in this place, I figured, well, perhaps you could run this place for me someday when I am too tired to continue to do so myself."

I was taken by surprise. I knew that Mr. Banerjee's children had shown no interest in the restaurant since I had been working there. None of them came by, or when they did they just expected free food or wanted something from their old man. But I had no idea that this was where the conversation was heading.

"Mr. B- I'm shocked. I'd love that, but-" The reality that I would have nowhere to live crashed down on my happiness, my smile faltered as I looked at him.

"What is it Cole?" He frowned, causing the grooves on his face to deepen. His genuine concern was evident as he stared at me, waiting for me to speak.

"I am trying to find somewhere for me and my *girlfriend* to stay, where we are now... it won't be an option in the next couple of weeks." I sighed. "So, I don't know if I will be able to stay around here..."

Mr Banerjee's face turned into a smile as he looked up to the ceiling. "I think I may be able to help with that too."

Alice

The room was spinning, I could feel his arms holding me, but everything else was a blur. His words were circulating in my mind, *"Let me take care of you, both of you."*

Marcus' azure blue eyes were staring at me, expecting a response.

"Why?" That was all I could say. "Why would you want to do that?"

I felt his hands drop away from me, and I could hear Freyja shouting at me from inside my head.

My brain could not process what he was saying, "Alice, I care about you, more than I have ever cared about anyone. It's a big step I know…"

I was too stunned to speak, my mouth opened but there were no words. I failed to comprehend how Marcus would want me. I failed to understand why he would want to raise another man's child when he could have started a family of his own with any number of women. *Why would he choose me?*

"May I?" Marcus asked, his eyes on my stomach.

My heart was pounding, I felt small flutters in my stomach, as he kneeled on the bed, bending low so that his face was level with my swollen stomach. His fingers slowly lifted the fabric of my top to reveal the bare skin that stretched over my pregnancy bump.

I felt self-conscious, the silver stretch marks streaked across the sides, beneath his fingertips, reminding me of zebra stripes. I tried to pull the fabric back down, but his hand stopped me as he planted kisses along them, stopping just above my belly button.

My skin tingled beneath his lips, my breathing slowed as I watched him incredulously. It was such an intimate gesture as if he really was the father, as if he was genuinely happy for this child's existence. It filled me with a warmth that I had never experienced before, I wanted to kiss him, I wanted to believe he accepted me, accepted us both, but it seemed just too surreal. As if I was in the scene from a romance film my mother loved, rather than reality. *People like Marcus do not fall in love with someone like me in real life.*

"Alice... " he whispered, one hand still holding onto my belly as he raised the other up to my face. I sat there staring at him blankly, my mind still trying to process what was happening.

"Will you let me be this child's father? I promise to love and protect both of you..." His face moved closer to mine. I could see that he had let his guard down. His eyes were like a window into his soul; open, inviting, full of warmth and love.

A thrum of excitement coursed through my body as I wrapped my arms around his neck, pulling him closer to me, as I have wanted to do since he first arrived. My chest tightened as sobs threatened to erupt at any moment as tears welled in my eyes.

My mouth crashed against his, "Yes Marcus..." I whispered, my words dancing over his lips, before he deepened the kiss, my mouth was hungry for more and my body yearned for his touch.

"Alice" he groaned between kisses, as he pushed me back onto the bed, as he hovered over me. I could hear the purr of desire in his voice, his hands roaming over my body, as he kissed me with quick urgent kisses, I could feel my body tense, when his hands brushed over my thighs. He must have felt me stiffen, because he instantly moved his hands.

"I will never hurt you" he whispered, pulling away to kiss down the curve of my neck to my collarbone. The sensation tickled against my skin, my cheeks grew warm and my body arched into his kisses, welcoming them as a warmth spread in my core.

"We have all the time in the world Alice," he murmured, his lips still so close to mine. I could feel his breath hot against my face. "We don't have to rush-"

"Marcus, I want to-" I murmured as I grabbed a handful of his hair and pulled his face closer to mine.

My hands slid under his t-shirt, sliding it up over his chest and head, until his bare torso was revealed. My fingers traced every muscle, feeling slight goosebumps prick his skin. before following the outline of his tattoo. I could feel the warmth emanating from him, his heartbeat thumping under my fingertips. Out the corner of my eye I could see the bulge straining against his jeans,

I gulped as my hand slid towards it tentatively, he must have mistaken my hesitancy for doubt.

"Alice. We don't have to-" his mouth was saying, but I had ignored him, as my hand unfastened the button, and pulled down his zipper. My hand caressing his length over his boxers. He groaned and purred my name once more.

My insecurities and inexperience screamed in my head, but I refused to succumb to them, instead I pulled at the waistline, ripping his jeans and boxers off. I knelt on the floor, his shaft directly in front of my face. My eyes widened, taking in his size. *No wonder the women wanted him.*

"But he is yours," Freyja whispered. *"He is giving himself to you."*

My lips hovered around his tip, my tongue dancing around him, encouraged to continue by his groans, I took more of him in my mouth. I tried to keep eye contact, remembering reading it in a magazine about how men enjoyed it. I sucked in my cheeks, my lips forming a perfect seal as I moved my head up and down slowly building up speed. It twitched beneath my tongue, feeling my lips slide further down his length until I gagged and my eyes watered when it hit the back of my throat.

A deep groan rumbled from him, vibrating through every muscle, his voice muttering my name. As his hand held the back of my neck, his hips thrust against my mouth. Hearing his sounds of pleasure aroused me, encouraging me to carry on until his shaft twitched.

"Alice-" He was breathless, his hand weaved in my hair, slowly guiding him out of my mouth. "Come here." He moaned, using his hand to guide my face back up to his where his lips were desperate to crash against mine.

"Tell me if you want me to stop." he whispered as he slid my top over my head and unhooked my bra. I smirked, *not a fucking chance.*

Marcus' lips planted delicate kisses along my neck, gradually making their was lower, kissing the exposed flesh along the top of my cleavage before taking each one in his hands, slowly rubbing his thumb over my nipples until they hardened like bullets. His mouth ravaged them, licking and sucking them. They were more sensitive now than ever before, I gasped loudly as his hot mouth and exploring tongue devoured each one, my hands holding his head in place as I enjoyed the tingling sensation he evoked.

This felt right, as if this was how I should have lost my virginity. Marcus was someone that cared, who appreciated me and my body.

I tensed as he slid my pants down my legs, his fingers paused and his head snapped up at me. "Alice it's fine if you don't-"

I cut him off by pulling his face closer to me so that I could kiss him. "I'm just, you know, not very experienced" I whispered in his ear.

Within moments my lacy French knickers were revealed to him, damp from my arousal.

His nose nudged my cheek, his lips brushed against my jawline, encouraging me to look at him. I could see his desire burning like a fire in them. Something about this facial expression looked hungrier than his lips crashed fiercely against mine.

"Alice-" he gasped, "I can assure you, *that* is a good thing." His breath quickened, as I felt my desire deepen.

"It's just... " I gasped, "you're like my first... *everything*... apart from-" I moaned as his shaft pressed against me. A growl rolled off his chest,

"Alice-" he whispered, trying to steady his voice. "We don't have to, it's okay if you want to stop." I could hear it in his voice, the way he was holding back, fighting against his urges.

I arched my back so my lacy underwear grazed against his hand, I could feel his resistance breaking, as he understood what I was doing; trying to wriggle out of my underwear, he slid them off easily, his fingertips grazing my thighs, sending a tingling sensation along my body. I pulled his face down to mine,

"Marcus, I want you-" I whispered, aware that every nerve in my body was alert to his touch. His lips clamped down into mine, as he slid his fingers between my legs, teasing my slit.

"*Fuck* you're so tight." He exhaled, as he slid two fingers deeper inside. I moved against his finger, loving the way his thumb rubbed against my clit. I wanted more, I wanted his mouth to ravish every inch of my body, and I was not afraid to tell him so.

Effy

Can I keep doing this to myself? Can I live with being second best?

I hated feeling this way, in the quietness of my room, alone with nothing other than my own hurtful thoughts for company.

I knew I should have expected to feel this way as it had been my choice to accept being the 'runner up' for his affection, yet it still hurt when I would awake from the same recurring dream. My subconsciousness tormented me with images of them together; scenes of their bodies entwined, intimate and close. Skin against skin. Their mouths pressed against each other as they fucked. I was trapped, unable to do anything but watch, feeling sick, as my internal voice screamed at them. My pathetic attempt to try and stop them failed.

I had no evidence they had ever been together; he had promised that nothing had ever happened, but I struggled to shake the fact that he had called me by her name. That moment forever etched into my memories. Leaving a niggle of doubt that would eat away at me.

Why had Alice suddenly disappeared? Does it have anything to do with Josh?

My stomach churned as guilt clutched at my lungs with an icy grip. My best friend was missing, yet my sole focus was still Josh. *I am an awful friend. Prioritizing him over her, always.*

I thought back to the last time Alice and I had properly spoken, it had been before the Soirée, before Josh had asked me to be his date; but even then I had done all the talking, and it had all been about him.

Was I truly that obsessed with him?

The answer was always yes, despite my anger and jealousy that spread through me faster than a wildfire during drought season, I knew I could not walk away from him. I had wanted him to notice me for so long that I tried to convince myself that it did not matter, that he had settled for me after Alice had rebuffed him.

Was the disdain she showed for him just a cover-up for her true feelings? Was she just trying to be a good friend knowing I was obsessed with him?

I did not know the answers to these questions as they spiraled around in my head like a tornado, damaging what little self-esteem I had left.

I needed to be beside him at every moment, knowing that when I was there, he treated me as if I was the only one he had eyes for, that I was not his second choice but his first.

It was easy to be convinced by his passionate kisses and the way his hands caressed my body, the way he made love to me, that I was the only one he wanted, *even if I wasn't.*

But when I'm at home, alone, my imagination is my worst enemy, my mind my tormentor.

Even when I should be more concerned about the whereabouts of Alice, praying that she is safe, that she will come home soon. I secretly wondered if Josh knew where she was.

A nagging feeling in my gut told me he was hiding something from me, *they both are.*

Marcus

A smile flickered on her face, her eyes wide in shock as I sucked each of her breasts, the look of pleasure on her face as she experienced it for the first time. It had made my shaft stand harder than ever, my longing to feel her warmth wrap around it, as my fingers drove inside her tight slit.

I longed to bury it deep inside her, to thrust against her so hard she would scream my name, but I held back, *for now*. Her traumatic past experience made me want to take things slow, to savor the moment, our first time. I wanted to make her feel safe, to feel loved, as *her* first time should have been.

She needed to know that I worshiped every part of her body, that everything about her turned me on but also that for me this was more than just insatiable desire, that I wanted more than just sex. *I want her in every way.*

My lips moved over her stomach, until my face was buried between her silky thighs, hovering over her smooth mound. A smirk flitted across my lips, knowing I was the first to taste her, my member twitching as she moaned from the moment my tongue began to explore.

I curled it against her entrance, teasing her lips and delicate nub until she scrunched her hands into fists, clutching at the bedding as her back arched, I smiled as I buried my tongue deeper into her core holding onto her thighs to keep them open wide as her body squirmed under her first orgasm.

It had taken her by surprise, feeling her muscles tighten as the intense wave of pleasure ripped through her body, she bucked and thrashed beneath my tongue and her thighs tried to clamp against my face as she came.

I greedily lapped at her nectar, the sweet taste of it made me yearn for more, as I continued to work her slit with my practiced tongue, hearing her whimper and pant as wave after wave of pleasure crashed through her. Aroused further when her fingers clutched a handful of my hair, holding my head in place as she ground her hips and her pulsating core against my face.

I had been with more women than I cared to admit, but none of them had ever reacted this way to my touch, and none of them had driven me to want to please them beyond my own release. I wanted her to enjoy this, every single moment, while my member throbbed in anticipation.

She tugged at my hair, giving me a silent demand, so I moved to where she wanted me. She took me by surprise when she pulled my mouth down onto hers, her tongue slipping through my parted lips to taste her sweetness.

It was fucking hot; *she was fucking hot.*

"Please" she moaned, as her hand slid down to my shaft. Her tiny hand wrapped around it and worked its length.

"Marcus... I want you." she whimpered and guided it towards her heat. The tip slid against her nub, slowly prying open her tight entrance.

Slowly, I eased myself inside her, inch by inch, feeling her tight walls envelope me, squeezing it, making me want to thrust all of it into her tight warmth. She gasped my name as I felt the flesh of her mound meet the base of my shaft.

My eyes flew open, watching her bite her lip as she ground her hips against mine.

"You're so...*big*" she gasped, sending a shiver along my spine. I wanted to thrust hard and fast, to make her come over and over, but I needed to refrain. I was already teetering on the edge of eruption.

I was going to take it slow and steady for her, I wanted nothing more than to bring her as many orgasms as I could before succumbing to my own.

Her arms snaked around my neck, as I drove against her, our bodies slamming into each other as my desire for her overcame me, the self-restraint from moments before a distant memory as I was thrusting inside her with every inch of my shaft, as hard and as fast as she could take.

Her nails dug into my back, leaving crescent shaped indents in my skin as another orgasm took over her. I continued to thrust through it, sending another ripple through her body moments later.

I craved to hear her pant, to cry and scream in her breathless voice, I loved hearing my name roll off her tongue. She was taking me over the edge, I could feel my resistance slipping, bit by bit.

"Harder" Alice breathed, hot against my ear, as her nails scraped along my back. I greedily obeyed, sinking my shaft into her deeper, as my thrusts grew faster and my breaths became short shallow grunts.

I could feel her slickness, her warmth coating my shaft as she moved her hips to meet me with every thrust. Her full breasts bouncing freely until I trapped one with my hungry lips.

She cried out, as she came again, this time taking me with it. My load shot like a jet inside her. Our orgasms in perfect concert, and our moans of pleasure harmonious. I could only imagine how thin these walls were, how everyone would have heard us.

I collapsed beside her, holding her quivering body, as we relished in the heart-thumping aftermath of our orgasm, savoring the serenity and genuine happiness that engulfed us both.

I wanted to do this every night, to feel the closeness of her body against mine, to bury myself in her warmth over and over until nothing else mattered. I wanted my world to revolve around her, *because I love her.*

Even as the darkness spread in the room, I could see the surprise and shock on her face, I could feel her muscles relax as I held her stomach in my hands.

"Marcus" she said, wriggling her body even closer to me, her eyelashes flickering over her gorgeous piercing green eyes.

I allowed my lips to graze hers, a smile playing on both our lips. "I want to. Alice, I have never felt so sure about anything in my life." The moment those words had left my mouth, I felt the atmosphere change into a comfortable silence, as my words hung in the air between us.

I felt her nose rub against mine and her lips curl into a smile as she nodded, "okay."

That was how she fell asleep, naked and wrapped around me. A satisfied grin lingered on her lips as she succumbed to her fatigue.

I smiled to myself in the darkness, feeling our hearts beating as one.

THIRTY-ONE

Asmodeus

There were several reasons why I chose Josh, the main one was that he did not always need me to persuade him to make bad decisions. The darkness was already in him; his rage, his malcontent, his desire for destruction... his eagerness to seek revenge on his brother, Marcus, and sabotage the company and the empire his father had refused him.

Had he been included in the will and the inheritance, the darkness would have still been there, but there would have been different vices, different *opportunities* for the darkness to unfold.

I stumbled across him in Bangkok, his disturbed little mind seeking pleasures that he knew would be frowned upon in civilized society. Legs spread wide, his hands tied in ropes above his head, bent over the bed, his moans of pleasure muffled by the shaft shoved in his mouth. Behind him a woman stood, though she was no ordinary woman, with a five o'clock shadow and an Adam's apple, he knew when he picked her and her two friends up from the bar what they all had going on downstairs.

The thought of being taken aroused him, his rectum pounded by her while a third took his manhood into their mouth, milking him whilst the others and thrust into him until his body quaked and his load squirted so violently, the girl on the receiving end choked until tears streamed down her face.

The rigid shaft in his mouth twitched, but he was not ready for that *just yet*, it was his first time after all. He yanked his head back, just as the white streams erupted, coating his face in the warm stickiness, feeling the thick globules trickling down and dripping from his chin.

I could hear his thoughts, his sadistic, self-loathing thoughts that he deserved this; that he should be manipulated and punished. The final load filled his rectum, his knees buckled, his wrists bleeding from the rope ties as he came crashing to the floor.

I slid into his mind, his drunken and vulnerable state made it easy to manipulate, made it easy to direct his anger not at himself, but at those who violated him. Any one of them; the closest one he could reach. Using my inhuman strength he yanked at the ropes that bound him, tearing as if they were made of nothing more than paper. His mouth curled into a sadistic grin as he reached for the closest girl, catching her by her ankle.

I felt his enjoyment as he dragged her body closing to him, splaying her legs wide and rammed his hand so far up her anus that they begged him to stop, but he continued until he was hard once more. Taking her with the absence of lube, tearing them by the sheer brutality and rage he harnessed to pound them dry. Coming once again as one hand wrapped around her throat squeezing until they were on the verge of passing out, while his other fondled her shaft until it was erect and throbbing. Determined to make her shoot her load involuntarily, his fist tightened around it, pumping as hard as he was thrusting inside her ass. Within minutes his hand was coated in streams of warm, sticky cum.

He chuckled menacingly, holding no remorse for his actions. If the others had not fled, he would have done the same to them too.

That was the Josh I needed; the ruthless, demanding and villainous barbarian, not this lovesick, little lost puppy he had let *Effy* transform him into. His only concern was that she would discover the truth; that Alice carried his, *well my*, child in her swollen belly.

Soulmates, bleugh.

Though my need for him was done, my mission was successful. That child was going nowhere; that call to his brother confirmed it; there was more than just Alice and The Divine protecting that child now. His own brother was betraying him by helping her *keep* the child.

If only Josh knew what his brother truly thinks of Alice.

It was obvious from Marcus' voice that there were some underlying conflicts of interest going on in that brain of his; the battle between what he wanted, and what he should be doing. But Josh was too drunk to notice.

Sat in the seedy bar his father once owned, that *Marcus* now owned, drinking whisky neat from the bottle, it only ever led to trouble. Trouble I no longer wanted to be a part of.

He blamed me for his decisions, for his multiple flings and the thirst for virgins, and while this was partly true, we had been on the same page. Josh had reveled in the deeds just as I had. *So who is really to blame? The one who loses control when he has too much to drink, or the one who gives him the strength to fulfill his deepest, darkest wishes?*

Still we were at an impasse.

Josh's determination to remove the child, made it difficult to be complicit, when I had my own agenda. My part of the prophecy was done, but I needed to see it through to the end.

I was *not* going to let Josh ruin my chance of usurping the reigns of Hell and vanquishing Lucifer once and for all.

No. I no longer wished to use Josh as my vessel. I would find another easy target.

I just needed to bide my time until Josh was so drunk he would agree to release me from his body. I knew he would not do so sober; he relied on me more than he wanted to believe; for his charisma, his charm. *That is all me.*

Without me, he is nothing. A forgotten love child of a whore and an old man who paid for his mother's slit. Josh was a mistake, and he knew it, only his mother had shown him love, until she too perished in the clutches of addiction so soon after his father's abandonment of them in his will.

So that was what I was doing now, watching and waiting as the night unfolded, and with each drink, I felt his resistance slipping. Whispering encouraging and hateful snippets into his ears, like poking an already agitated bear, until I got the reaction I wanted.

Finally he snapped.

Rushing to the men's restroom and vomiting all over himself; he cried, he begged me to leave him alone so he could live his life, to be happy with Effy.

Chances are he is more likely to ruin it. But I shrugged, playing the merciful shadow in his mind and happily obliged.

That is after all what I wanted all along.

A chance to be free once more.

Alice

In those days we should have been making arrangements for my new life, my new identity, instead we filled it with exploring each other's bodies, learning about each other in a whole different way. Leaving the room only for a few hours each day to enjoy the coastal air and eat.

We talked and laughed as if we had known each other for years. We fucked like horny teenagers, giving into the spark that ignited an unyielding fire between us. Each time was explosive, leaving us breathless. We were like magnets, drawn to each other and impossible to separate.

Marcus was everything in a lover that I could have envisioned. It was as though he had stepped right out of the romance novels Effy would eat up. He was successful, rich, but aside from the material stuff he was kind, compassionate, and he was *very* handsome. He made sex enjoyable, always putting me first, making sure I was comfortable, trying different positions that would work around my bump.

My muscles screamed in agony and my core ached, but it had been worth every second of it. My fingers traced the small bite wounds on his shoulder, as my eyes took in the various lovebites that decorated his neck above his tattoo.

It had not taken me long to learn *exactly* what he liked, what turned him on and to realize that by surrendering my body to him fully, he would take me to ecstasy over and over again.

Even as he slept, my body was his, allowing his arms to wrap around me, his hands resting on the swell of my stomach. I was his. I felt his soft snores as his deep breaths flitted across my neck, hearing his soft murmurs of my name as he dreamt,

I felt Freyja gradually take control. Her entity slipped through my thoughts until she pushed me back into the depths of my consciousness.

I panicked at first but she quickly revealed why she had taken over. "*Look*" she whispered, guiding my hand to my chest and turning my body to face him, his hands, nos rating against the small of my back.

A rope of light connected Marcus and I, threading itself around his arms, and binding our hearts together. *"I have been trying to tell you that he is your soulmate, will you believe me now?"* she whispered, slowly relinquishing her hold over me.

As my vision returned to normal, the binding was gone, my heart dropped, I had been filled with warmth when I had seen it, my stomach flipped in excitement and my mind was cleared of any doubts.

"Your human eyes can't see it, but I can, and I have since he first arrived here Alice." Freyja chuckled, *"Though I needed you to see it for yourself for you to truly believe... you can be quite stubborn, you know."*

I smiled as my fingertips traced along his arms, where the rope of light had encircled him, "I wish I could see it." I sighed, my voice quieter than a whisper.

"You don't need to see it to feel it," she whispered, but she did allow me one more glimpse of it of the light that protruded from my heart, shining blindingly against his dark tattoos and sank beneath his chest. *"everytime it appears, it is brighter and stronger than the last."* Freyja added. *"because you are both accepting of one another, embracing the love Fate has helped you to find."*

For a few moments I just watched as the light slowly faded as Freyja shied away into the corner of my mind once more. Finally snuggling my head into his warm, muscular chest after he rolled over onto his back,

"Can't you go back to sleep?" he murmured, his fingertips toying with my hair, at the side of my face.

"Not really," I said, as my anxiety gripped me for what tomorrow held. We had discussed it before another wave of passion flowed through us. Marcus had explained that today was the true start of our relationship; for the world to see we were an item, that we were starting a family together.

My heart fluttered at the idea, though my doubt still niggled away in my mind. "Tonight is our last night here..."

His fingers brushed under my chin, tilting it up to face him; "Nothing will change when we leave this place Alice. I will still want this. I will still want you."

My heart fluttered, my doubts in my mind eased by his words. I had fretted as he integrated back into normality, away from the isolation of the cocoon we had here, his mind will change and I will be abandoned and forgotten, not able to fulfill all of his wants and needs. My insecurities were only intensified more by the abundance of hormones that overwhelmed me, as I tried to stifle the sobs that welled in my chest.

"Marcus... I'm scared - that- that-" I exhaled deeply. "That you will want your old lifestyle back; the carefree bachelor."

He slid from underneath me, his eyes narrowed as they locked onto mine. "I have what I want Alice, everything I want is right here." He purred, his lips pressing against mine.

Marcus' mouth trailed down my neck, along my breasts and lingered on my stomach. "Tell your mommy to stop worrying." He whispered, his breath hot against the taut skin of my abdomen. "I am not going anywhere, because I love her."

I wrapped my arms around his neck, pulling his face back up to mine. "What did you just say?" I murmured against his smiling lips.

"I love you Alice."

He did not give me a chance to respond, his rigid shaft pressed against me, my lips busy with his deep and passionate kisses. "Marcus..." I gasped, as his thrusts sent me to the brink of an orgasm within minutes, "I love you too."

Our moans rang out in unison as he drove his hips against me, his shaft filling me completely, and enveloping him in my warmth as we were designed for each other. Hearing his pants, his confession of love echoed through my mind over and over making each orgasm that little bit more intense.

All the women in the world, but Marcus Morgan loves me.

The sun was slowly filtering through the gaps of the drapes when we had finally finished, our breaths heavy drawing out the early caws of the seagulls beyond our window.

It was a little after lunchtime when we finally set off on the long journey, excitement and nervousness pumped through my veins as reality set in. Marcus filled the time talking about his house, The Meadows, situated in the countryside, far enough from the city to be isolated and secure, but close enough for his commute to work and for my mom to visit whenever she wanted.

I smiled, hearing how his advisors had already found a tenant for his city apartment, and his promise to be home every night by five-pm, without fail. "You will always come first," he smiled, a playful smirk on his face as his words held a double meaning. "I can't wait to show you my office."

My eyes lit up and I bit my lip, excitement flooded my body. "Is it soundproofed?"

Marcus' hand slid over to my thigh, *"not in the slightest."* he purred. I felt the fire ignite in my core, I could see the desire in his eyes.

I wished at that moment I was not pregnant, so we could pull over and fuck in his car, by his smirk he was calculating if it was possible. "As soon as we are at The Meadows Alice, you are mine," he said as he licked his lips.

"I'll hold you to that." I said, as a yawn suddenly overcame me, my eyelids suddenly feeling heavy.

"Try to get some sleep Alice. I know I have not given you much opportunity to do that recently" he winked, his hand hot on my thigh, sending small electrical currents to ripple through my body.

As I allowed the vibration of the car and the distant noise of the radio to fade away, a smile spread across my lips.

When his voice finally stirred me, we were not at a service station. There was so thrum of cars zooming along the freeway, or the clattering of fuel pumps in the background. Instead it was silent, luscious green rolling hills, lay beyond the windshield, and to the side of me was a large modern looking building; all clean lines of metal and glass.

As I peeled myself away from the leather seat, I felt the stiffness in my back and neck, the achiness of being cramped in the same position for too long. "Where are we?" I mumbled, turning around to look at him.

"Alice, do you remember our story?"

I nodded; the story we would tell everyone including my mom about our whirl-wind romance. How we had supposedly met in a coffee shop in town, during my free period and his lunch break, how we had kept our relationship a secret to stay out of the press for as long as possible.

I wished our story had been true, like a modern day fairytale, complete with a happy ending.

I bit my nails, wondering how my mom would react. *Will she be happy to be a grandmother?* Though I supposed that depended on if she had forgiven me, My letter had been harsh, playing on her insecurities, accusing her of being a terrible mother. My chest tightened as I thought back to my words, they were necessary to stop her from trying to find me. Yet, this strange twist of Fate had rendered them unnecessary.

Will she ever forgive me?

Suddenly Marcus was outside the car, opening my door and taking my hand to help me climb out. It was only then that I spotted the small sign on the outside of the building; *private hospital.* His eyes lit up as he led the way, his hand intertwined with mine, as we made our way toward the main entrance. "Are you ready?" He whispered.

The way my heart thumped, the warm glow that flooded me whenever he was near would never tire.

Marcus chuckled, tightening his grasp on my hand as we entered through the automatic doors. I could not imagine this moment without him.

Within moments of checking in at the reception desk, a young doctor called our names. "Daniel. This is Alice" Marcus said, his voice full of pride and his smile was sincere as he introduced me. Daniel uttered a small greeting, his eyes flickering up to me from a brown file open in his hand.

Patient name: Alice Louisa Bowers

"These are your GP and hospital records," Daniel replied, seeing me eye the file. "We ran a few precautionary tests, using your genetic profile, your family's medical history, you know, the usual, " he paused. "We needed to determine whether you were in a high-risk category, whether your baby was likely to be more prone to any abnormalities or any other health conditions we needed to be aware of."

"And?" Marcus asked, his hand gripping onto mine as we navigated through a labyrinth of corridors.

"So, glancing at the results..." Daniel said as he opened the door to a clinical room, "All appears to be good, healthy. But we will know more after your scan," he paused as he approached the ultrasound scan that sat in the center of the room.

Marcus wrapped his arms around my waist, his lips fluttering against my forehead. I felt as if my heart was going to explode.

As Daniel hooked me up to the machine in the center of the room, the first thing I heard was my baby's whirring heartbeat, before the grainy black and white images started to resemble an actual baby. I stared at it,

I could see Marcus' eyes glaze over as tears filled his eyes as they were transfixed on the screen.

"Measurements are all looking good..." Daniel said, as the ultrasound probe smoothed across my lower stomach. The gel was cold against my skin. "Would you like to know the sex of the child?"

I looked over to Marcus, shaking my head. *I don't care as long as my baby is healthy.*

"Here" Daniel said, holding out several scan photos printed on a thin strip. "As always, we uphold the strictest confidentiality." Marcus' jaw muscles tightened, but he nodded.

I glanced at the notes attached to the top, as my heart fluttered in response.

Patients name: Alice Louisa Bowers.

35 weeks and 5 days. Due date: 21-March.

Marcus

"Thank you" Alice whispered in a croaky voice as we got back into the car, her gaze fixated on the scan photos clutched in her hands, her smile made her eyes glisten.

Brushing a stray curl behind her ear, I placed a kiss on her forehead, "You don't need to thank me Alice," I told her, as I pulled away from the hospital.

Her smile was contagious as her eyes flitted from the scan photos up to the beautiful countryside that spread in front of us. Miles and miles of nothing other than green fields and blue skies.

"Marcus, is that... the house?" She gasped, as I pulled off the country road, the roof only just visible.

I chuckled, this house was huge, a converted farmhouse, complete with a long driveway that snaked its way through acres of land. I had grown up in flamboyant and egocentric houses all my life, it benefited my father because he loved the limelight, whereas I just wanted somewhere quiet to escape the hustle of the city from time to time.

Her eyes were wide as I switched off the engine. "I hope you like it." I added, pressing my forehead against hers.

Her voice was awestruck when she next spoke. "Marcus" she gasped, "It could be a crappy one-bed apartment and I wouldn't care."

Whenever I stayed in this house, I always felt like this place was missing something. Now, as I stood in its entrance with her, it felt like home, rather than an empty shell. It was then that I realized I needed to share this house with someone special, like her.

"Where would you like the tour to start?" I asked, I saw her eyes twinkle.

Her arms pulled me closer to her, her lips trailing kisses along my jawline and down my neck, her hand slithered down to my crotch.

I licked my lips, feeling my member stir, as I took her hand leading the way up to the bedrooms. This place was my sanctuary away from city life; the women and work.

Alice was the first woman to have been brought here, *the only one who I wanted to stay.*

THIRTY-TWO

ALICE'S DREAM

The world was full of color. The world was full of sounds; songbirds, chatter and children laughing. It was the height of summer when Earth came to life. When nature was enjoyed by all. The park was busy, small children running around, playing, smiles on the faces of those who did not have a care in the world. The sun was shining, not a single cloud in the sky. It was beautiful.

Parents were talking with each other, while watching over their children; laughing and enjoying moments like this. I felt a tug on my sleeve. "Please, mommy?" her cute little voice rang out. Her green eyes looked up at me as she pointed to the park.

"Of course you can, darling," a man's voice chuckled. "We will be waiting right here."

Her bright ginger curls bounced and swung as she skipped through the park. Her pink glitter wellies thumped hard on the tarmac until she entered the soft mulch that surrounded the swings.

"Push me daddy!" She yelled. I watched him as he strolled towards her, his muscles rippling with every step he took. His white T-shirt bulging, tattoos trailed down his arms. My sight focused on the tightness of his navy cargo shorts around his firm thighs.

"Higher!" she giggled "to the sky!"

Their laughter echoed above the other noises in the park causing my smile to spread wider as I watched them. *My life is perfect.*

ॐ

I woke up face down in the bar's "drunk cell," a holding room in the back of the club for those too inebriated to get a cab home. I did not care to admit how many times I had found myself there.

This morning though, I found the crushing weight that usually sat on my chest and the suffocation of my oppressive shadow was gone. *Asmodeus is gone.*

A smile flickered across my face, as the giddiness of elation swept across my brain. *I am free.* Yet, there was a sinking pit forming in my stomach, the flicker of fear behind my eyes, I no longer had him to blame for my actions, for the angry and irrational thoughts in my head, I had no one else to protect me from my irrational self than *him;* my brother. Marcus.

Where the fuck is he anyway?

The club would have called him, would have told him I was here to pick me up or at least send someone to do it for him. But nothing. No one had come for me.

The ticking of the clock tormented me, as I sat here until ten-thirty, my anger running wild, as I followed his GPS pin on my cell, using the last of my battery up, watching it travel back from the coast.

Is he still with her?

A warning popped up on my phone warning me my battery was low which I ignored. I watched as his orange dot stopped at a private hospital. Not just any private hospital, *dad's most trusted* private hospital, where he went to keep his illness out of the press.

My smile crept on my face as my phone died. There would only be one explanation why he would have been there; to follow through with the original plan. *Perhaps he is not as cowardly as I had thought.*

I rattled the bars, shouting at the top of my lungs, demanding someone to come here and let me out. Eventually someone heard me, a long-haired, bearded caretaker, with a mop and a bucket in tow.

Old, scrawny and grimy looking, his face covered in tattoos, and his skin sagging around his neck and arms, He looked like a walking corpse. Just the sight of him sent goosebumps along my skin, but as he rattled the keys on his chain attached to his belt, I could have hugged him.

The man smirked as he held the door open. "Guess big bro's gotten fed up of yer shit... finally."

I bit back my retort, knowing that for once, knowing my brother was taking care of my problem. "Can I use the phone to get a ride... I can't walk home like this."

He nodded, pointing to the old corded phone hung up on the back wall. I uttered my thanks before punching in the only number I had carved into my brain, my father's old chauffeur, unwilling to admit how many times I have asked him to pick me up from here recently.

Within five minutes the blackened windows of the SUV pulled up, I clambered in and kept my head bowed low. "Bad night huh?" The chauffeur known only to me as Barnes asked. "Results didn't go as planned?"

I grunted, thankful that the tinted windows held back the glare from the sun that was beaming down outside, but the sticky, stuffy interior made my nausea creep up along the back of my throat, burning as the bile ascended.

Shit. What is she doing here?

I spotted Effy standing in front of my house as the car rolled through the gates and drove up the path to the door. The sun reflected off her sleek blonde hair, her golden eyes squinted as she tried to look in the car.

Fuck.

I scrambled out, keeping my head low, shielding my eyes from the blinding sun as I fished out my keys from my back pocket.

"Josh?" She gasped, reaching for my hand, taking the keys from my fumbling fingertips and trying them all until she found the right one. The lock opened with a clunk, and never had I been more relieved to be home.

I collapsed on the cold tiles of the hall, allowing their ice cold bite to cool my head.

Effy's footsteps disappeared to the kitchen, returning moments later with an ice cold bottle of water and a damp towel. "Here," she murmured, placing it over my forehead. "Let's get you on the couch." Her hands took the brunt of my weight as we staggered to the lounge.

Flashbacks of taking her in every position possible raced through my mind; on the sofa, by the fire, against the sliding glass door that led to the pool. This woman was amazing, she did not recoil at the stench of stale alcohol that oozed from my pores, as many others would have. I collapsed onto the leather sofa, feeling its coolness numb by body.

"Josh... it's ok... we all *struggle* sometimes." She whispered, sliding closer to me, offering me the bottle of water. "Let me help you."

"Why?" I asked dumbly, taking the bottle washing down the bitter taste of bile with huge gulps.

"Because I love you Josh..." her hand raked away my hair from underneath the tower. "The good, the bad and *the revolting...*" She chuckled.

I felt my heart flutter when she smiled, the way her golden eyes creased in the corners and a small twinkle flickered across them.

"What are you smiling at?" She asked me suspiciously.

"Move in with me" I blurted, seeing her stiffen at my words. "Effy, clearly... I need your help."

She smiled, placing my head on her lap, her fingers running through my hair. "I think you're still drunk."

"Effy, I mean it."

Effy placed her fingertip over my lip, silencing me. "You know, everyone has their demons... the ones we try so hard to fight..." she exhaled deeply, "just we have to try not to let them win."

I noticed that her eyes had glazed over, no longer talking about me. I could see the hurt etched across her face, her mind still insistent upon Alice and I.

I wanted to hug her, to kiss her, to show her how much I cared for her, but I could barely move my heavy muscles, I could barely see straight, "Effy," I sighed, "I swear on my life nothing has happened with Alice."

Her amber eyes narrowed as she searched my face for a flicker of doubt, any tell-tale signs of a lie. Thankfully, I was still able to maintain my poker-face. For several moments she stared at me, before her lips fluttered against my cheek. My hand caught hold of hers, interlocking her fingers with my own. "Will you live here with me?"

"Ask me again when you're sober" She sighed, standing to her feet. I yanked on her hand, dragging her back down to me.

"I am *not* drunk, Effy. What I want will not change."

I watched as a smile curled at her mouth,

Ross

I needed something stronger than coffee. *What the fuck is Marcus thinking?*

Pinching the bridge of my nose, I poured over the contract once more, sat in the living room of the infamous country house he never stayed in. The white walls seemed too sterile, the room was free from ornaments, from any personal touches, the only thing Marcus cared about was the red-head asleep on the couch. The one still carrying his brother's child.

My eyes swept over her, her hair like a sea of flames draped over the arm of the couch, one hand tucked under her porcelain face while the other hugged her swollen abdomen.

I had been concerned when he called, when he told me to meet him here. I had expected bad news about the girl.

Not *the-end-of-his-fucking-life* news.

I took a deep breath, feeling his hawk-like eyes focused solely on me. "Josh will need to sign these papers." I insisted as I slid the contract into the manilla envelope and handed it to him. "Of course... *she* has a different contract to sign... a waiver of sorts... one you will also need to sign, to make this decision legally binding... of course that's when she eventually wakes up."

His eyes glowered at me, the muscle in his jaw tensed as he got to his feet. "It's been a long journey, she needs to rest."

"And I gotta get home to my wife and daughters... that too is a long drive."

I watched as he paced on the spot, contemplation crossing his face. "Fine." He huffed, sitting beside her, tucking back her long curls, his lips delicately placed on her forehead, hovering there until her eyes flickered open. "Alice... I'm sorry to wake you, but Ross, my family's lawyer, is here to finalize our *arrangement* before we go public... he needs your signature."

I watched as her top lifted revealing her stomach as she stretched, the sight was hypnotizing yet repulsive. I hated the pregnancy stage, the mood swings, the lethargy, there was nothing attractive about a pregnant woman. They were just one walking, talking bag of highly strung emotional time bombs, a sentence away from erupting at any given time.

Her piercing green eyes stared at me from behind her lion's mane of curls. She slowly nodded as Marcus helped her to her feet.

Even as she perched on the barstool opposite me, her face illuminated by the LED light, I could still not understand Marcus' infatuation. The way he looked at her as if she was a goddess, he had been with supermodels and actresses, healthy, petite and gorgeous, and then there was Alice; a wild mop of curls, and very pregnant. *With his brother's bastard child.*

What the fuck is he thinking?

I had known him his whole life, a friend of his father's, as well as the family's most trusted lawyer, for both business and personal matters. Never had he been so disconnected with the legal proceedings, he had no haste to get her to sign these papers.

"Marcus Morgan," I snapped, commanding his attention. "We need to meet with Josh. He needs to sign this contract." My hand slammed down on the contract in frustration. He looked at me, something stirring in his eyes.

He nodded. "So, once he signs this contract it will relinquish him of his rights as the paternal father?" He asked me, tearing his eyes away from the girl for the first time since she awoke.

I gave him a curt nod. "In the eyes of the law, he will have no rights to the child. No say in how he, or she, is raised. No visitation rights. Nothing. It is ironclad. Not even the slipperiest of eels could find any loopholes. Should Josh ever decide he wanted to find one."

"Good," he said, his eyes averting back to Alice, who fidgeted uncomfortably on her seat. "Um... sorry... I need to use the restroom." she squirmed, crimson flushing into her cheeks.

I straightened my tie and coughed. "Marcus. Are you sure that this is what you want?" I asked, as soon as she had waddled out of sight.

His brow furrowed, his eyes piercing mine. If looks could kill someone, with that look I knew I would have died a hundred different ways, each one as painful as the last.

"Yes." He spat. "What part of 'I want her and her child' do you not understand?"

I sat up a little straighter and motioned to the blank space where she had been sitting moments before. "This contract will bind you to her... All the responsibilities that follow in being this child's father. In the eyes of the law-"

"I know Ross. In the eyes of the law, I will be responsible for the child." He sounded bored, his tone flippant. Marcus leaned forward across the breakfast bar, his eyes locked onto mine and his hands splayed wide on the granite surface. "I know that by signing this child contract with her, the child, *our* child will be entitled to the Morgan empire. In the event of my death."

"Are you sure that she is not just going to use this for her own advantage? She is very young, Marcus. The substantial amount that your father entrusted in you-"

With a stern expression etched on his face, he interjected, "She is not a fucking gold digger" he snapped. "Here…" he slid the uncashed cheque we had discussed on the counter before us. "If she were a gold digger, this would have been cashed… and she would have demanded more."

I held my hands up in surrender, if he was anything like his father, it was wise not to anger the agitated bear.

"All I'm saying is…" I paused, trying to choose my words, not to anger him further but to persuade him to reconsider. "Your father worked hard to build this business. For you. I wouldn't want a rash decision based on impulse to jeopardize it all."

Rage consumed him, boiling his blood and clouding his thoughts. Though, I could see he was attempting to contain it. "Ross. My decision is final. I will sign on the dotted line without a shadow of a doubt," his blue eyes shone, "but I will be checking the fine print… I know how slimy a bastard you can be."

I had to give him credit for that, something he had learned from his father; "*always read the fine print, that is where your lawyer will have you by the balls.*"

"Ross, I love her, she means a lot to me. She is worth it" he paused, looking away as she shuffled back into the doorframe, "I know you might not understand it, but I don't need you to… all I need you to do is sort this out so that legally Josh is erased from her child's life."

I could have sworn I saw a small smirk curl her lips, but in the blink of an eye, it was gone. Her brows furrowed as her eyes flitted between me, Marcus and the contract before her. "So, where do you need me to sign?" she said.

ॐ

Isobel

At first, I thought he might have been on a high. he was bouncing around, buzzing as he launched through the door and hugged me in a tight embrace. In all the time I had known him, he had never succumbed to drugs, never lured by their temptation. He was one of the few people I knew who was not consumed by addition.

So, it was strange to see him so animated in this way. Shifting his weight from door to foot, his arms flailing around for emphasis when he started speaking. Words tumbling out of his mouth in incoherent, jumbled phrases.

"Whoa... Cole, slow down... breathe!" I said, as I lit the candles.

"Mr. Banerjee... my boss-" A tear rolled down his cheeks, as many more filled his eyes. "He- he has *saved us* from going back onto the streets."

I dropped the box of matches, the small wooden strands scattered across the floor at my feet, my hands trembling. *What did he just say?*

"Mr. Banerjee, he wants to retire... he wants me to run his company-"

"But Cole- how does that-"

"And he is willing to rent out the apartment above, for a third of the asking price... until we are in a position to pay him more." Cole's shoulders shook as his sobs overcame him.

"Why? Why would he do that, for you, for *us?*"

Cole chuckled, snot streamed from his nose. "I guess Fate gave him selfish children for a reason. Bel, he doesn't want them to sell everything he has worked his whole life to build. He wants me to take it on, permanently, once he is ready to retire... you can work in the restaurant, we can live independently away from the streets... *we can put all of this behind us.*"

My own tears began to escape as Cole's arms wrapped around me.

"Bel, I promised things would always work out for us. There is nothing stopping us now from having that future we have dreamed about... a real one... the two of us."

I looked at the empty Tupperware I had forgotten to give to Alice, I was holding onto it until the time had come to say goodbye, when Cole and I would need to leave before this place would have been pulled down to nothing but rubble and ash.

Perhaps now I will never have to say goodbye.

"Bel, we can leave the ghosts of our pasts behind us, everything we have done, every choice we have made... it has led us here... to Mr. B... to the fresh start he is giving us..." His eyes twinkled with excitement as his hands cupped my face, his lips inches from mine. "All you have to do is tell me this is what you want..."

My lips danced against his as our tears mingled, "I would love nothing else, Cole." Yet even as I said it, I still felt a sinking pit deep in my stomach, a fear that I could not shift.

I had outran my past for so long, *how long will it be until it catches up with me?*

THIRTY-THREE

Isobel's lips were gentle, as they trailed down my chest and met her hand that was around my rigid shaft. She was determined to show her gratitude, as her tongue slid over the tip, I had to fight back the urge to explode there and then.

Slowly her mouth inched along my length, her lips providing just the right suction as her hand worked towards them. Her other hand caressing my balls. I moaned loudly, uncontrollably as she increased her tempo, knowing if I come now it would be a little while until I would be able to enter her.

"Sit on my face, Bel." I murmured, my hands groping her thighs, shimmying her body so her heat straddled my face. Her entrance glistened in her arousal, the sweet aroma enticed my tongue to lap at her juices. My desire to make her come matching her feverish movements against my shaft.

"Soon Bel, we will have our own place, a proper bed, somewhere we can make love over and over without the chill of the concrete beneath us."

She purred as my words flitted over her core, before gasping aloud as my finger slid easily into her slick entrance. My tongue danced against her clit as her head bobbed over my shaft, until neither of us could hold back any longer.

Like a thousand fireworks erupting across my skin, my seed erupted, filling her mouth until small gagging noises echoed in the air. I felt her lips tighten around me as she gulped down my cum, gasping for air once my member fell limp against her tongue.

I knew she had orgasmed, but I wanted one last more, as I coaxed her into turning around to face me, so I could watch her beautiful face scrunch up in pleasure.

Seeing her figure loom above me, her soft breasts against her pale skin, my hands were free to cup them, to roll her nipples between my fingers as I buried my tongue deep inside her entrance, fucking her with it until her body bucked against me, her body shuddering under the orgasm that ripped through her body.

Her thighs clamped against the side of my head as her nectar flooded my mouth and dribbled down my chin. "How- how did you do that?" she whispered, bringing her face down to mine, her tongue running along my upper lip.

I smirked, "Bel, I think the first thing we will need to buy is a waterproof mattress protector, now that I know you can do that."

Her lips pressed against me, as her breaths came in hot and heavy. "Whatever you did - that was fucking amazing."

You are fucking amazing Bel, I thought. *I will walk through the fires of Hell for this woman if I had to.*

I glanced over at the book that was beside her sleeping bag, the glass angel ornament was still there, looking over us, but the flicker of the candles glinted off of the metallic keys for our new apartment.

I pulled Bel's body as close to me as possible, feeling her melt into every contour of my body. I inhaled the soap on her skin, tasted the salt of her sweat as I kissed her shoulder.

Our future is going to be perfect. I will not let anything ruin our chance at true happiness.

☸

Alice

I need sleep.

That was the extent of my mental capacity; exhausted from our journey, from exploring Marcus' home, of Marcus himself. More importantly, I was just overwhelmed by the sudden twist that happened in my life. I no longer needed to feel alone or scared - I was neither. So that left only one thing to overwhelm me; fatigue.

Yet as I sat there next to Marcus and opposite Ross, I tried to push the thought from my mind and swallow the yawns that kept trying to creep up on me. This was important to Marcus, this was important for our future. *I need to concentrate.*

"So this is like a prenup agreement?" I asked, as my eyes glazed over the words.

"Without marriage." Ross interrupted. "It's to protect Marcus' assets."

My face scrunched up, as I bit the top of the pen lid in anxiety, as I tried to make sense of the legal jargon. "You know I don't want your money, don't you?" I asked, staring at Marcus.

"Of course I do." He said with a swift kiss to the forehead. "Alice, please could you excuse us for a moment?"

His voice may have been neutral and his face looked composed, but I sensed the anger simmering beneath his calm exterior. I nodded and went upstairs, to the room we had chosen to be the nursery. It was empty now, but in my mind I imagined where we would place the crib and the changing station, how the nursing chair would be perfect near the window looking out onto the acres of green fields, the walls a soft gray and new plush carpet beneath my feet. Everything that Marcus and I had discussed hours previously.

Their words drifted through the open door, and as much as I tried to ignore it; I could not stop myself from hearing them.

"What the fuck is this Ross?" Marcus' tone was sharp, his voice was projecting rather than shouting. "You expect her to sign that?"

"But Marcus-"

"I am not making her sign this damn thing."

"There has to be some protection of your assets Marcus. Your father-"

"I said no."

"She could be using you, wanting only what you can *provide* for her and her child-"

I hadn't realized I had been slowly gravitating to their argument, but as I stood there in the door, tears running down my face, my anger flaring, I felt the compulsion to justify myself. To do whatever it took to prove to them both that Marcus' fame and money was the last thing I wanted. *I just want him, he could be poor and have nothing to his name - I would still want him.*

"I do not *want* Marcus' money..." I sniffed. "I will sign it."

Ross' face grew red, his gaze averted to the paper in front of him as his mouth tightened into a thin line.

"Alice..." Marcus sighed, rushing to my side before embracing me in his strong, muscular arms. I inhaled deep breaths to steady my sobs, allowing his cologne to fill my head, the fragrance mixed with the thrum of his heartbeat soothed me.

"*I* know you don't, Alice," he said, his forehead resting against mine. "Ross... he is very much like my father, he doesn't trust anyone."

He shot Ross a look who was holding the contract to Marcus. "It would put myself, and your *financial* advisors at ease, *and off your back.*" He smirked.

Snatching the document, Marcus read it over before scribbling his thin, calligraphic signature on the dotted line before reluctantly handing it to me with a small smile. There were chunks of text crossed out, with his initials next to it; some of the more obscure demands Ross wanted me to agree to. Marcus had almost redacted all of the bizarre stipulations ranging from receipt collecting and monthly allowances to paying my share of the bills to live in his country home.

My tired eyes took longer to read over it, pausing after each section, just to recollect my thoughts before signing. I was not being hesitant nor dense, I was just trying to absorb the information through the tired fog that clouded my brain.

I noticed Marcus had left in a line, that this contract would be reviewed *prior* to marriage.

"Do you want to read the contract Josh will sign?" Marcus asked me, once I put the pen down. "I've read it, and it is solid... Josh will have no legal right to your child, Alice."

I shook my head, kissing his cheek. "If you are happy with it Marcus, then I am too." I sighed, feeling my eyelids slightly drooping as my fatigue took over. Suddenly, Marcus was carrying me over to the sofa, placing a soft, plush blanket over me.

"Rest now." Marcus said with a fleeting kiss to the forehead, feeling the darkness wash over me. Their distant, voices filtered into my ears.

"Marcus, are you sure... you can change your mind now, but once I leave..." Ross' voice came as a hushed whisper. "If you are doing this out of guilt-"

"I will not hear another word against Alice or my decision... Or I will find another lawyer."

"I think you are making a big mistake."

"And I think you should get the fuck out of *our* home." Marcus said sternly.

My heart swelled with gratitude for his fierce loyalty and unwavering devotion, as I succumbed deeper into my slumber.

What have I done to deserve someone like Marcus Morgan?

※

Isobel

I did not recognize her at first, without the fake eyelashes, a thick layer of foundation and bright red lipstick. Yet it was definitely her, a ghost from my past I had tried to forget, my mentor, an old friend and she was walking toward me. My mood suddenly soured, I had been on my way to meet Alice at her house, the clean Tupperware tucked under my arm and a spring in my step.

Swamped in a loose, baggy jumper and flared light-denim jeans instead of the sexy ensembles I remembered her wearing. She appeared a lot shorter than I recalled, though I had always seen her in six-inch heels, instead of white trainers.

A flashback to this morning, seeing her face among the others at the shelter, I had not recognised it then, so I had not paid her much attention. But now, facing me in the street, I knew who she was. Or at least whom she used to be.

"Lilly?" Her eyes lit up, embracing me in a hug before I could say anything further.

In truth, I did not know whether to hug her back or punch her in the face. But one thing was I was certain of, if she was here, Johnny was never far behind.

I scowled at her, crossing my arms over my chest. "What are you doing here Cryst?" I asked her, my eye caught sight of a Red Ticket poster illuminated by the streetlight above. "*Please* don't tell me you are *recruiting*?" I asked her, my chest tightening and my stomach churned.

Her bottom lip quivered, "I must Lilz. Since you escaped, slipped under his radar, he has had all of us on lock-down. His supervision has been heightened. Every month you were gone, he increased security levels more, until-" she paused, her hands clasped together looking down at the floor. Tears suddenly sprung free from her eyes and her whole body shook.

"Three girls have OD'd in the last two months because there is no other way out now," she muttered, her voice as quiet as a mouse. "He knows where I live, about my daughter... *I have to," she* sighed. "*I have no other choice.*"

She looked at me then, studying me through her glassy eyes, "How did you do it? How have you escaped him for so long?"

I shook my head, refusing to answer her. *I will not fall into a trap.*

I knew I should have carried on walking and not acknowledge her. *Ignorance is bliss.* But not where Johnny Malone is concerned.

I have already put myself at risk of her giving him my location; at least I could get some answers, to know in which direction to run. I took a deep breath before speaking, "Does *he* know I'm here?" She shook her head feverishly, "Are you going to tell him you saw me?" She shook her head again.

I knew deep down, if it came to her own safety or mine, she would tell him. She had always been one of his favorite girls; the one he slept with more than the others. She pretended that she hated him, but it would not surprise me if she loved him, if she would tell him just to keep him happy.

Crystal never did like it when he became *obsessed* with her protégé; when he started visiting *me* more than her.

A vision of his face flashed in my mind; my skin burned as I recalled his hands groping me everywhere, bile rose to my throat and my scar on my cheek throbbed. I tried to shake my head to clear the image of the cold blade against my face, as his shaft thrust inside me. My hands bound above my head. The more I tried to move, the deeper the blade bit into my face. I had the stupid idea to refuse him, this was my punishment.

"Lilz?" Her voice interrupted my thoughts, but instead of bringing me back to reality, instead I sank into another memory. The first time I met Johnny.

I remembered that he looked like an average guy, nothing about him was distinctive enough to pick him out of a crowd. No tattoos, no scars, a generic haircut and never flashed his cash. His ambiguity made him invisible, like a ghost. It made him dangerous. It was what allowed him to run such an operation for years without ever getting caught.

The most terrifying thing of all was his personality; cold, ruthlessness, misogynistic. His pure, unadulterated brutality made him a monster.

If the devil does walk the Earth, he would be Johnny Malone.

"Lilz?" Her hand shook my shoulder, this time dragging me back to attention. "Are you- are you okay?"

I swiped the back of my hand against the corner of my eye, refusing to let any tears fall.

"Lilz, Johnny... He has bigger fish to fry at the moment... cops are rife over the latest overdose... it's why I am here; looking in new areas for talent."

"Well, I've not been in this area long, and I don't plan to stay." I lied through gritted teeth, my hands balled in fists by my side.

Recalling how I thought I was going to die, how lucky I was, to escape him by pure happenstance, by my meeting of Cole in that alley.

"I'm thinking of heading further north, there is not a lot around here. Those who have money keep it tight up their arse." I added.

Crystal nodded, taking the bait. *Good, perhaps I could avoid him coming here altogether if I fed her enough lies to relay back to him.*

"It's quite a sleepy town here, not much in the way of making cash." I told her, averting my gaze.

Crystal nodded her head, taking her cue to leave. "Lilz, I won't tell him you're here. *I promise.*"

Her words meant nothing to me, but I summoned a small smile to appease her, but my stomach tightened into knots and my dreams shattered before my eyes.

I have to leave before Johnny finds me.

ॐ

Bjorn: 893 AD – The Lament of a Viking King.

Many seasons ago, there was a family - a family that had it all. All the gold and silver, all the land they could ever dream of.

The trouble was, nothing that they had was ever enough. They wanted more land, so they invaded and took more. Then they desired more wealth, so they would steal and pillage what they could.

Until one day their father left to raid another foreign land, never to return.

Presumed to have perished at sea. The family crumbled, like the buildings and allies around them. Until all that was left was one son.

One son with a determination to keep all that he had worked hard to reclaim.

That son is me.

Problem was, I had no sons to pass on my title, as King of the Vikings.

I had a daughter, but no matter how strong of a warrior, how fair and loyal she was to our people, it would never be enough. She would never be accepted to rule in her own right.

I had no choice but to marry her off - to the victor of a battle for her love. Two other Viking clans; both with men who I could use to my advantage against the Saxons.

Erik had lands and ambition and was impressive with a sword. He had made short work of slaying Magnus in the bid to take my daughter as his hŭs-frŭghæ - his wife.

He offered protection and showed no mercy for our enemies. The gods had guided him to me as an answer to my prayers.

But I did not know it was Loki, the trickster god, who sent him to me.

Josh

Marcus' orange dot had not moved from his country home for the last few days. I frowned as the dot bounced on the spot relentlessly. *What was he doing there?*

Since he purchased the house, he hardly ever stayed there and not once had he taken *company* there. *So what the fuck was he doing?*

As the cogs in my mind twisted, the more paranoid I became; I knew it had something to do with Alice. It was too coincidental, and like my father, *I do not believe in coincidences.*

My eyes looked Effy over as she slept blissfully beside me, studying every curve of her naked body.

"Josh. What are you doing?" she murmured, her eyes heavy and her voice still thick with sleep.

"I have to sort a few things out, business matters while my brother is out of town." I lied as I shoved on a pair of jeans and a t-shirt. "I will be back later, okay?" I leaned over her and kissed her fully on the lips, feeling her body naturally react to my touch.

"Hurry back," she murmured.

Less than twenty minutes later I was walking up to the front door of his house, fiddling through the bunch of keys looking for the spare one I forgot to give back to him. He had a business trip in Hong Kong, and he wanted me to check in on the place, I never did, but I still kept the key.

The first thing that I noticed was that his car was not here. The Volvo he refused to upgrade, a clunky beast of a car. I frowned, perhaps I had read too much into this; he must have left his phone inside.

But when the lock clicked open and I realized the alarm had not been set I knew something was going on.

My brother was a stickler for security; paranoid by his sudden thrust into the spotlight after our father died.

The place still seemed sterile, empty, no different than it had been when he bought the place; apart from the two half-drunk cups of coffee sat on the counter. A pot of instant decaf coffee sat by the kettle.

He must have had company last night. But since when did he have decaf?

I flicked the kettle on and perched myself on the bar stool next to the breakfast bar. Intending to make myself comfortable while I waited for him; he was never without his phone, and he would never leave dirty cups on the side.

That was when I heard a voice; a muffled voice of a woman, coming from another room in the house. The soft shuffling of bare feet against the ceramic tiles, getting louder as they drew closer.

The sunlight glowed through the wall of glass from the room behind the door she opened, casting her only as a silhouette against the brightness. She stepped forward, and my jaw dropped and my eyes bulged.

With an audible intake of breath, I was not who she had been expecting either.

The glass of water she had been holding fell out of her grasp, shattering into thousands of pieces on the black slate floor. They twinkled like stars against the dark night sky.

Alice

Every night I kept having weird, vivid dreams. Dreams so real, so tangible, they were like memories, flashbacks from different lives that were not my own. They were Freyja's former vessels, but last night, it was different. I woke up screaming about Isobel.

I had tried not to think about her for such a long time, that the memory of her, the memory of losing her incurred a pain so sharp, so real, I had awoken thinking I had been stabbed.

My eyes were wide open, my head racing, panting as if I had run a marathon, beads of ice-cold sweat trickled down my spine. Marcus had held me in an instant, his reassuring words, his soothing tones had calmed me, until my breathing returned to normal.

"It's just a dream" he said over and over, as he embraced me. But it was not just a dream, I knew she was dead. I had envisioned her standing before me, as an angel.

It is just the hormones I told myself as I snuggled into Marcus' chest. Marcus had bought a load of pregnancy books, ones he and I would read together as we snuggled up on the couch late at night. Reading about the different stages of pregnancy, how the body changes to accommodate the baby, as well as how the hormones released can alter the way the mind words. Anything from typical forgetfulness to absurd and vivid dreams.

We stayed in silence, neither one of us able to go back to sleep, just enjoying the calm, peacefulness of each other's company, his hand resting, on my stomach.

"Alice, I love you" he whispered. I turned my head to look at him, to reply when I felt a sharp, prodding movement from within. "Did you feel that?" he asked, turning so that he could look into my eyes. "And again?"

I giggled, "I think this baby likes hearing you say that, almost as much as I do" I whispered, placing my own hands next to his on my stomach, seeing if we could feel any more of the baby's movements.

Marcus had leaned his face over my stomach, his lips grazing over it delicately as he spoke. "I love you too little one" he whispered, placing a kiss just above my belly button. His kiss was returned with another little kick under his lips. "Mummy and daddy can not wait to meet you."

My heart was melting, this moment was too perfect. The way he had called himself daddy was just the cutest, most heart-warming thing I had ever heard. *We are going to be a proper, loving family,* I thought, *like I had when I was a child.*

The baby within me kicked once more, his eyes lit up in delight, as his lips found mine. We must have stayed this way for hours until the sun peeked through the gaps of the curtains, and the alarm on Marcus' phone shrilled.

"I don't want to go" he whispered, curling his body back into mine after hitting the snooze button. "I wish I could stay here with you." A smile crept across my lips.

I kissed him, "I'll still be here when you get back" I told him, looking into his topaz-blue eyes, feeling guilty for causing the tiredness that lurked within them.

"You promise?" he smirked, deepening the kiss, his member hard against my inner thigh. I stifled a chuckle as I felt him slide inside me once more, his thrusts slow and meaningful, exciting every nerve-ending in my body.

"I promise."

THIRTY-FOUR

I could spend all my days at home with her, and yet it would never be enough. I procrastinated, taking 'sick' days just to stay here in this house with her, uninterrupted, happy and content.

"You are still the CEO" she whispered that morning. "You still have a responsibility to your role, to the company your father left you." I snuggled into her bosom, wishing to stay there forever.

"I'm going to miss you." I purred, kissing her collarbone, up her neck to her lips. "I will miss you too." She murmured against them.

I had been fortunate that those important meetings had been rearranged. I was lucky to get a second chance with Mr. Chang. It was a serious offense to be late for business meetings, in Mr. Chang's culture, let alone to cancel at the last minute. If I wanted this company to succeed in its global success I had to attend the meeting today. Failure to do so would be disasterous for the company's reputation.

That was how I came to be sitting in my stuffy office on the top floor of the office tower, rather than at home, where I wanted to be, with my pregnant girlfriend. *The love of my life.*

It still felt surreal; those past few days spent lounging around in the country house, talking, learning more about each other. It was all new to me, getting to know someone. Allowing myself to leap out of my comfort zone and plunge straight into the most serious relationship I had ever experienced.

It felt awkward at first, but she was amiable company to keep; conversations flowed, finding common ground, it felt as though we had known each other our whole lives. I had told her everything there was to know about me, about my past, my childhood. I did not want any secrets between us.

I was used to quick flings, orientating around my carnal desire, failing to remember their names in the morning, not caring if I ever saw them again. I was always safe though, protecting myself as well as the family business. A lesson my father had ensured he instilled within me.

"Son, women are snakes with tits. You want the tits, but you need to watch out for their bite. Their venom can destroy you and all that you have." I always kept them at a distance, never wanting to know anything about them if I could avoid it. But with Alice, it was different. I could not get enough of her. I wanted to learn more about her each day.

Without realizing it, Alice had entered my life and had changed me; made me become a better man. Being intimate, sensual without always leading to sex, was also new to me. I found that I enjoyed holding her and comforting her night after night almost as much as feeling my shaft deep inside her. *Almost.*

Our souls aligned as we kissed long, deep and meaningfully, holding her until she fell asleep. Being there to comfort her when she had a nightmare. From the moment I had met her at the B&B, as we meandered along the coast, well before we had been intimate, I knew I was falling for her.

My office line rang, breaking my attention. I snatched it up. "Mr. Morgan, the video call with Mr. Chang is being prepared in the boardroom in five minutes" my secretary announced.

I took a deep breath, finding the only thing that brought me comfort was the sound of her voice. I wanted to call her, just to speak for a few moments, just because I missed her, because I was feeling homesick.

When the realization hit me; my phone was still at home, sitting on the bedside cabinet, where I had accidentally left it after spending a few extra minutes with Alice, when I should have already been out of the door.

An ice cold grip squeezed the air from my lungs, I knew I was being paranoid, hyper-sensitive and concerned over nothing; but without my phone, I felt disconnected from her and I began to worry. *What if something happens? What if she needs me?*

Alice - FLASHBACK: Fourteen years old.

Isobel arrived almost forty minutes later than usual. It was a school night, and my mom was working a day shift so she would be home in an hour. I had my explanation, how I knew Isobel already figured it out; a friend from school.

But the moment I saw Isobel, I could tell by her skittish demeanor that she would not be staying long. She chewed on her bottom lip and picked at her fingernails, keeping quiet as she pushed around pieces of pasta from one side of the plate to the other.

She had barely eaten a thing. Neither had I, too engrossed in studying her face, trying to work out what was wrong. Her eyes were wide and bloodshot, surrounded by red blotchy skin, clear indications that she had been crying *a lot*. She kept her hands screwed up inside the cuffs of her sleeves and she cowered in the chair.

I wanted to reach out to her, to comfort her, but I did not know where to start, how to approach her change in behavior. *Had she been attacked?*

"Aren't you hungry?" I asked, after watching her spear the same piece of pasta with her fork over and over. She shook her head. "I can put it in the Tupperware for you to take and have later?" I offered, picking up the Tupperware that was beside her.

I watched her sea of brown waves swish from side to side as she shook her head slowly. "I'm- I'm..." she muttered, biting her bottom lip that had started to wobble. "I won't be around for a bit." she finally said, her voice so low I barely heard her.

My brow creased as I stared at her. "Oh... where are you going?"

"Away from here."

"Izzy- has something... *bad* happened?" I asked, endless possibilities running through my mind; she had been attacked, the police were onto her for stealing something; she had been refused help by the shelter.

"Alice... I want to tell you- but it's... it's best you don't know," she sighed, getting to her feet and stumbling to the door.

"Isobel, do you need money? I have some of my allowance upstairs-"

"Alice, thank you for everything, but it's best that I leave, before it gets too dark."

I felt sobs welling in my chest as I silently watched her walk down the street, becoming nothing but a blur, walking out of my life, as my tears blinded me.

I knew in my gut, that would be the last time I ever saw her.

Isobel

I cried from the moment I left Alice's house, glancing over my shoulder, weary of being followed.

The streetlights were just starting to come on and I knew Cole would be back soon. I took a deep breath. Walking away from Alice was difficult; she had gone out of her way to help me, feed me, and had given me clothes to stave off the cold. And I had repaid the favor by possibly leading a dangerous man to her home. The ghosts of my past were hot on my heels, and it was no longer safe for me to stay; to drag anyone else into this mess.

But the worst was yet to come.

As I walked along the streets, I tried to memorize every part of this place; the sights and smells, knowing that I would miss them. We had been here longer than anywhere else thanks to the sanctuary of the loft, and the promise for a life to stay here had filled me with hope.

Now it left a bittersweet taste in my mouth. *I could have a real future with Cole, but at what cost?*

Johnny was here; he will find me.

He will kill me.

The songs of unseen birds slowly quieted as the sky grew darker, the graveyard loomed ahead. I had not intended to come this way, to veer in the complete opposite direction of the loft, but I found myself sitting, wasting time, sitting on a piece of crumbling ruins of the old church looking at the two unmarked graves.

The fragrance of damp earth filled my nostrils as I gazed at the graves that had triggered an unlikely friendship. I found a strange sense of peace, as I sat here, watching one lone squirrel appear out from the thick brush of nettles to the side of the cemetery. It was the only sign of wildlife I had ever seen here.

I watched as it leaped across the sodden grass. stopping for a split second to look at me with its beady black eyes, before bounding back in the direction it had come. I took a deep breath as I looked up at the outline of the moon, becoming more prominent in the sky as the minutes passed.

I said a silent prayer, wishing for Alice's protection, for Cole's as well as for my own, before I set off for the last time back to the loft.

Cole

There was something wrong the moment I stepped into the loft. Not only was her sleeping bag missing from its usual spot, but her backpack was gone.

Isobel was gone.

I rummaged through what little stuff we had, trying to make sense of why she had a sudden change of heart. *She said she loved me.*

That was when I saw it, the necklace placed beside the small angel ornament on top of the book I had tried to read to distract myself from thinking of her every night before we kissed. Now it looked like a shrine.

I snatched up the necklace, it was still warm and the candle wax that pooled beneath the wicks was still liquid.

She had not long left.

I shouted her name as I tore through the warehouse, my heart pounding with every hurried footstep I took.

On the street I ran, though I was not sure if I was even going in the right direction. *Where would she go?*

I thought about the shelter, but she knew I would look there, so instead I headed to the main road out of the city. *Perhaps she would hitchhike to the next town.*

I almost could not believe my eyes when I saw her standing there, backpack bursting at the seams with her sleeping back rolled up under her arm.

"Bel!" I shouted, my feet running as fast as they could towards her, my lungs were burning, but I pushed through. "Bel!"

She jumped a mile, almost stumbling into oncoming traffic. I pulled her wrist just in time as a car honked its horn and swerved to avoid hitting her.

"Bel, what are you doing? Where are you going?"

She refused to look at me, standing in silence as I tried to hold her hand.

"Bel, talk to me." I sighed, my hand falling limp by my side.

"I can't be with you Cole." She sniffed, keeping her head low. "I thought it was best to leave before you got back."

"Bel, I don't understand... I thought- don't you-" My words failed me, as my eyes lingered on her. "I love you Bel."

Her head snapped up, her eyes streaming with tears, she no longer bothered to wipe them away as they fell too thick and fast. "I'm sorry Cole." she whispered as she turned her back to me and started walking along the road.

"Please don't leave Bel." I shouted out to her. "Whatever it is, we can get through it, *together.*"

She stopped momentarily, and my heart skipped a beat, thinking she had changed her mind. But the words that came out of her mouth shattered my heart into a million pieces. "No, Cole. We can't... because I- I don't love you."

⚇

Effy

Even with her gone, I could not stop thinking about them, the two of them together. I had become obsessed. Even as I moved in with him, spent every waking moment in his company and every night fucking him; it was all I could think about.

No matter how much he denied it, I was plagued by the fact that I would always be second best. Knowing that none of this would be happening if Alice had agreed to go with him to the Summer Solstice Soirée. She would be here instead of me; that was what he truly wanted.

My insecurities were eating me alive; stopping me from sleeping, checking his phone in the dead of night to see if he had been in contact with her.

This morning though, he had slipped out taking his phone and car with him. Even if he said it was business-related, I knew in my gut, he was going to her, wherever Alice was, Josh was going there.

Rage coursed through my veins as I tried to track his number through the 'find my phone' app, but it only picked up the last place his phone was switched on. Just as he had headed out of town.

I cursed as I threw my phone across the room.

Why would he do this to me?

Why would he invite me to live with him, promise me a future with him, if he was planning to go to her all along?

I hated Alice Bowers with every fiber of my being. I wished she never returned. No matter how close we had been in the past, I never wanted to see her again.

I wished that she was dead.

⊛

Marcus

My work mobile rang as I was in the middle of my meeting with Mr. Chang. I tried to ignore it, to carry on, but its incessant ringing made my heart race.

"I'm sorry, Mr. Chang, I have to take this." I stepped out of the board room, yanking my phone out of my pocket to see it was my security guard, wondering why he was calling this number instead of my personal one. My heart dropped.

Shit.

I instantly called him back. "Darwin? What's wrong?" The line was silent for quite some time; "Darwin... "

"Oscar didn't know... your brother's car... his eighty-five Chevy... it's at your home."

I growled, as I stormed through the office block, "Is it still there?" I barked. Noticing Julie gave me a weird look as I passed the desk. There was no time to explain.

"Yes... wait... shit - no... it's just left." Darwin said, frantic clicking of buttons sounded in the background.

"Shit. Darwin, how long was he there... Did he go into the house?"

"I don't know... Marcus... the alarm wasn't set so I can't be sure if he went in."

My tires screeched against the asphalt as I sped out of the parking lot.

"Check every fucking camera, the house, and traffic cams... I need to know where he is and who is with him."

The line was quiet for a moment. My heart thumped wildly in my chest, deafening in my ears.

I heard a gasp, and a lot of curse words in the background.

"Marcus. We think he is heading to the hospital."

My blood ran cold, ice gripped my heart and lungs, I struggled to breathe.

"Marcus, the camera has him carrying Alice into the passenger seat of his car. It- It doesn't look good... Alice-I think she's hurt."

No, no, no.

"Where is he now?" I choked, trying to hold back the tears, I needed to get to her, I needed to get *him* away from her. He's already hurt her once, and now possibly again.

My mind flooded with scenarios, none of them were good, I had this sinking feeling deep in the pit of my stomach. *If he has hurt her, I will kill him.*

THIRTY-FIVE

Cole

All I could do was watch as she walked away without a word, head tucked low against the crisp night air. She never looked back. Not once.

Did I really mean nothing to her? Was she scared she would change her mind if she saw my crying?

My shoulders shook as tears and snot ran down my face. I could not believe she was walking away from the future we had planned. One that was within our grasp.

A few days was all it would have been, then we would have been in our own place.

Was she scared?

Slowly I made my way back to the loft, but I could not bring myself to go inside. Instead, I sat at the bus stop, hoping that she might change her mind. My hand clutched the glass angel and the necklace tightly in my pocket.

What has happened for her to suddenly leave?

☸

Isobel

I wanted him to tell him, I wanted to believe that we would fight Johnny together. But it would only end in bloodshed. Johnny would kill us both.

I saw the pain flicker in his eyes before I carried on walking, forcing one foot in front of the other as I kept my head low and sobbed. My words had felt like razor blades in my throat, slicing every part of me as I said them.

I never had a choice. It is either I hurt Cole, or Johnny does.

Johnny would not be in the mood to *talk*, he saw my escape as a humiliation, saw my continuous evasion of him for the past year as a loss, and Johnny never liked to lose.

With each step I took, I replayed the scene over in my head, wishing I had been honest, wishing I had told Cole that I loved him, that I still wanted a future, *a real one.* But it would have done more harm than good.

As I got to the next junction, the hypothetical scenes began playing in my head; *what if I had just stayed in the loft and not met Alice, would I have been safe? Or what if I had pretended not to know her, to carry on walking and pretend she had mistook me for someone else, would I have been safe?*

I glanced across to my left, the tip of the warehouse's roof barely visible.

What if I had just been honest with Cole from the beginning, so that he knew what he was getting himself into before he had a chance to fall in love with me, would he still have helped me?

I sat on the metal barrier beside the road, staring out at the warehouse, as silent tears rolled down my eyes and cars whooshed along the road behind me.

I smelled it before I could see it.

Thick black smoke billowed in the air. Suddenly I could no longer see the top of the warehouse roof, surrounded by an orange glow. *Cole!*

I ran and I ran, until I could no longer feel my legs beneath me.

I uttered a silent prayer, praying that he was not in the building.

Cole, I love you... I'm sorry.

Bjorn: 894 AD – The Battle of Blood.

Logi fell from the sky above. A rain of fire.

They had used our own technique against us. Arrows ablaze punctured the night sky in a wall of light, littering our camps. Wreaking chaos among our sleeping men. We had been surprised, our attack was to happen when they were most vulnerable, in the early hours of the next morning.

My men were positioned carefully along all the roads in and out of the fortified city. They ambushed their deliveries of grain, of crops, raiding the supplies and any other loot that they carried, using what we could, in order to feed our own men, as well as commandeering their horses for the other men that were soon to join us.

We had the advantage, our bellies were full, our minds well-rested, by attacking in the early hours of the morning, we would have had the perfect natural soft sunlight, but it had meant needing to move our camp closer to them, under the cover of nightfall.

My daughter's hūsbōndi, Erik, had become a hersir, a fierce commander of my warriors, his information so far had proven true.

Until the moment fire poured from the sky like hundreds of shooting stars.

We wanted this city for the land, it was the only city left that stopped us from going further, from expanding our lands deeper into Saxon territory.

I was led to believe that they were in no position to attack, or defend their beloved city. Far too weak, to wield their clunky armor and shields. They were supposed to be quivering in fear, waiting for starvation to claim them before we breached their walls... but they had struck first.

They knew we were coming.

A shield wall was formed, to defend ourselves from the onslaught of fire-headed arrows, as we proceeded to push forward. My men armed with a battering ram, created by the strongest tree nearby, sure to force open the gates with their brutish force behind them. The doors rattled and creaked and shards of wood splintered away as they hit the same weak spot over and over again.

On the horizon I could see our reinforcements, our allies, silhouettes against the rising sun., approaching to help us with our battle.

That was when a sea of molten fire cascaded over the top of the wall, pouring down onto my men below. The field of battle was filled with their screams as they melted and burned, until most were nothing but blackened and charred flesh. The stench assaulted my nose, made my stomach heave.

"Kill these heathens!" A loud bellow came from behind the stone walls. "Send them straight to the depths of Hell, where they belong."

It was too late to retreat now, the gates flew open, and a swarm of armor clad men charged at us. Our shield wall crumbled. Footsteps and metal clashing together drowned out the last of the cries from the burning men.

I could see the ships, many of them with, their masts broken and sails aflame. We had been outwitted on the waters as well as on land.

Every move we made, they seemed to expect, already having counterattacks in effect or striking first.

All hope of winning this battle was lost. All we could do was try to retreat with our lives. I glanced to my side, Erik nor Freyja was beside me, instead they were fighting among the others who had stood proud and honorable to face Valhalla.

But they were not fighting the Saxons. They were fighting among themselves.

I swung my blade, hacking as many Saxons as I could to get closer to them, their shouts drowned by the noise all around them. Metal clanged as our axs hit their armor, and shattering of wood as their swords broke through our shields.

The sun glinted off her blade, her green eyes shone with a fierce determination. Her face was contorted with pure, unadulterated rage.

Erik's blade thrust through her chest.

I yelled her name, reaching out for her, unable to move to her fast enough.

She knew she was going to die, but with her remaining life force she swung her blade, taking Erik's head from his shoulders in one clean sweep. His head rolled along the ground and his body crumpled in a heap.

I scrambled to her, dragging her away from the continuing onslaught of our men. Tears stinging my eyes as a trail of crimson followed us. "Valhalla awaits you" I trembled, removing the sword that protruded from her body, and laying her on the ground, as the battle continued to wage on around us.

I placed her sword back in her hands, as I spoke out loud to the Gods. "Odin, our All-father hear my plea, please make my kin to your hall of Valhalla, may her journey be safe and swift, Freyja goddess of love and of battle receive her into your open arms, may the Valkyrie's guide her to Fólkvangr."

I stared into her eyes as the light of her life ebbed away. My kin, the rightful heir to my people, had taken from me. Taken by none other than by one of us, the traitor amid us.

I knew in my bones why she fought against Erik, she had figured out quicker than I that he had been warning them of our plans -r he was the mastermind behind them all.

I do not know what he stood to gain from his betrayal, but I refused to die a cowardly death on the battlefield. My daughter was at one with the gods, no amount of tears would bring her back.

But I could see her again.

Grasping my ax, I returned to the battle, knowing I was going to die this very night; but I was going to take as many Saxon bastards down with me as I could. *May they rot in their feared Hell.*

I had nothing left to fear. I had nothing left to lose.

"Where are your gods now?" A loud voice boomed. I swung my ax with all my strength at the voice that seemed to boost these Saxon's morale. My target moved, I had been led into a trap, rope strung me upside down above them. Too far away for the swinging of my ax to hit anyone.

I growled.

His beady black eyes stared up at me, he wiped at the drops of blood that splattered his face from the spray of my warrior's throat he had just slit.

"You have lost, heathen" He smirked at me, taunting me as I dangled by single foot, the blood slowly rushing to my brain.

I heard the ripping of flesh, felt the rush of blood gush down my face, before I embraced the darkness, clutching my ax with every morsel of strength I had.

Alice - FLASHBACK: Fourteen years old.

A bright orange glow filtered in through the bedroom window, as blue flashes of light whizzed past the house. The acrid stench of smoke filtered into the bedroom from the open window.

Fire!

I could not believe my eyes as I rushed to the bedroom window. Black billows of smoke blanketed the sky, smogging up the street until I could barely make out the flats. They were as tall as they were wide, engulfing the abandoned warehouse in a blazing inferno.

I watched in horror as the fiery tendrils danced through the building as piece by piece parts of it began to fall. The strong jets of the water cannons desperately tried to put it out, to no avail.

Even though Isobel had never expressed that was where she slept, where she lived, I knew she did, I watched her come and go, I could never see her full journey, but it was always from that direction whenever she did visit.

A sudden pain tore through my chest, forcing the air from my lungs as all I could think about was her. Praying that she was not caught up in there. That for once, my instincts were wrong and she was staying elsewhere.

Freyja stayed silent.

"You must help her... we must do something!" I sobbed, pulling at my curls as I crumpled on the floor, my shoulders shaking with my violent sobs.

We had only known each other for a short while but Isobel had become my closest friend. I looked forward to her visits, I enjoyed her company, and I even made her a friendship bracelet but I had forgotten to give it to her earlier.

No one else knew of her, not my mom and especially not Effy; she would not understand my want to help her, her jealousy would compel her to say horrid things. I knew Effy too well, she did not like competition, she would not handle being second best; especially to a homeless girl.

I scrambled back to my feet, watching as more flashing lights flooded the street, police cars and fire engines, ambulances.

Ambulances?

Freyja stirred, but remained silent.

My TV flickered to life by itself, a LIVE News broadcast showing on the screen. *"The cause of the fire in the city's historic warehouses is still unknown. As you can see behind me, this fire is destroying everything in its path. Once the fire has been put out, there shall be a thorough investigation into the cause of the warehouse that was set to be demolished in the upcoming weeks."* The news reporter's voice spoke in a matter-of-fact tone, as she stood well away from the burning warehouse, in the background. Occasionally she glanced over her shoulder, as more teams of firefighters rushed onto the scene behind her.

All of them were struggling to put out the fire.

"Police are cautious to reveal too much prior to the full investigation, as firefighters are making every attempt to control and diminish the flames. We have had some anonymous tip that a few of the local homeless members of society would frequently use this building, which was why it was condemned to be demolished in less than a weeks' time.- "

I could hear her words, but they were not registering, the room was spinning and once more I was a heap on the floor, clutching at my chest struggling to breathe.

"It has not been confirmed at this time if anyone was in the building when the fire started-"

The TV screen went black cutting off the reporter.

Freyja and I both knew it, we could both feel the truth resonate through my bones.

Isobel was dead.

Josh

Time seemed to stand still, my eyes wandering over her. The tumble of her red hair cascaded down like a sea of fire over the white fabric of Marcus' robe. Noticing how it was unable to stretch around her fully, revealing her very swollen stomach, and bare porcelain skin of her cleavage and legs.

My eyes were unable to move away from her being half-naked and pregnant in my brother's home.

What the fuck?

I opened my mouth to speak, but no words would come out. It was as if my tongue had been cut out of my head. In my momentary paralysis, I saw a flicker of movement as she tried to run for the door to the side of me.

It all happened so fast.

I caught hold of her wrist trying to stop her from standing on the broken glass barefoot, but her foot slipped on the water.

She fell.

She screamed.

An ear-splitting, inhumane cry left her mouth, before a chorus of sobs and whimpers as she curled up on a ball. A spot of crimson appeared through the white fabric of Marcus' robe.

Shit.

I tried to make a call, but my phone was switched off, and I didn't have time to wait for it to turn on. *Fuck!*

I knelt beside her, ignoring the shards of glass embedding themselves into my legs, "Alice, can you stand?"

She flinched away from me, screaming at me.

"Alice, we need to get you to the hospital." I panicked, scooping her up into my arms, trying to hold onto her tightly as she tried to resist me. Tears pricked in my eyes, she had every right to be scared of me, to not want me near her.

But I had no time to explain, I had no explanation to give, not one that she would believe.

"My baby-" she sobbed, as I kicked open the door, and cradled her out to the passenger seat of my car. "My baby-"

The crimson stain grew bigger with each second and I knew it was not good.

My heart raced, as I quickly clambered into the passenger seat and sped off down the drive.

The electronic gates opened an eternity too slow. My hands thrashed against the steering wheel, my mind a chaotic mess.

I glanced over to her, she was quietly sobbing clutching at her stomach, as blood stained the passenger seat as well as the robe. There was too much blood.

This is really fucking serious!

I replayed the scene over and over as I sped through the streets, not stopping for anything knowing I needed to get to the hospital, before both their lives were on my conscience.

This is all my fault. All Asmodeus' fault. Where is he protecting this child he so desperately wanted?

I gritted my teeth, all this pain and suffering, for what? He was not even here to save her.

We were going over the bridge, we were less than two minutes away from the hospital.

My heart was pounding, glancing over at Alice, to check she was still breathing when her eyes suddenly snapped open.

That was when I lost all control of the car.

I saw us swerve off to the side, the engine still accelerating even though I tried to hit the brakes, the barrier buckled and finally broke.

We were free falling, for at least five meters before the ice cold water of the river below crashed against the windshield.

The watery depths were dragging the car down, until we were surrounded in the murky water. I tried to unbuckle my seatbelt and Alice's too, before the cracking of the windscreen caught my attention.

The glass exploded, I felt shards fly at my face as the water flooded the car.

The last thing I saw was Alice's curls floating lifelessly, its color slowly fading like a flame being snuffed out.

❀

Crystal

I had followed her from the shadows, as she approached the abandoned warehouse. Watched her as she scurried into a little makeshift entrance in the building's side.

This is not her first time coming here.

I did not want her to know I was stalking her, knowing she would have made the wrong assumption behind it. I had no intention of informing Johnny of her whereabouts, I had been proud of my 'prodigy,' that she had spread her wings and flown away from the nest we were all trying to escape from.

All I had wanted to know was that she had somewhere to go, that she was not all alone. My memories of how I had found her seeped into my consciousness, as she slept rough on the streets, using an old cardboard box to lie on, newspapers balled up inside her clothes to keep her warm.

I knew she would not want to come back into the game, into the life she had spent over a year running from, I just wished that she was not still turning tricks on her own to survive.

I never intended to lead him here, to lead him to her. I was not even aware that he had followed me here. But I should have guessed that he would be checking up on me.

I shuddered, fully aware of the extent of his abilities. I knew how furious he was at her, his cash cow, his plaything, for escaping.

He made me sick, yet he still found a way to pleasure me.

I am sick too.

By the time I found out he was behind me, it was too late.

"So, this is where that *whore* is hiding, is it?" His voice, as cold as ice, made me freeze on the spot. His wrist spun me around so fast I almost fell.

"Johnny? What, um...what are you doing here?"

"Do you think I was stupid, *slut*?" he asked. I shook my head frantically. "Did you think I was going to let another one of my *whores* slip out from under my nose?" He pushed me against the brick wall, as he made his way closer to the warehouse.

I tried to grab him, my hands grabbing thin air. *Fuck.*

"I know what you are trying to do Crystal... trying to find a way that you too can leave me." His eyes glinted dangerously; he launched himself at me, his hands around my neck.

He was not playing nice anymore.

Johnny was going to kill me.

Think Crystal, think! How can I distract him? What is Johnny's weakness?

"Johnny," I gasped, feeling the blood being starved from my brain. My hands trying to reach for his shaft, knowing it would be hard. He was always hard when he was angry.

My hands managed to grasp it, to squeeze it tightly in my hands. His grip loosened a little on my throat, a smirk curled the corners of his mouth.

I gasped for air, trying to put on my best seductive voice, as my whole body trembled in fear. *If I fail, both Isobel and I will die tonight.*

I thought about my daughter, snug at home asleep as Tanya looked out for her. When the parcels started arriving, I knew I needed to make a plan, a will to ensure my baby did not go into foster care. Tanya looked puzzled when I asked her to sign the legal document a client compiled for me, but she signed it nonetheless.

It was a peace of mind that whatever happened to me, Roxanne would not end up in care.

My hands reached lower under Johnny's pants, my cold hands found his warm shaft. For the first time, it did not send a tingle through my core.

I forced my lips onto his, taking advantage of the lack of pressure against my windpipe. I purred at him as I broke away, hoping that my last ditch attempt would bide Isobel some time to escape.

"Johnny... you're so sexy when you're angry."

THIRTY-SIX

"Help!"

A voice called from within the building, muffled over the deafening sound of the inferno as it ripped through the warehouse. A deafening scream pierced my eardrums as I approached the main entrance. "Cole!" I yelled out his name. "Cole!"

I entered the warehouse, feeling the heat, the intensity of the flames as if I was walking through the depths of Hell.

"Cole? Are you there?" I shouted, panic creeping into my voice.

I felt a hand on my wrist, I turned around.

Crystal!

"Get out" I yelled. Pushing past her, shoving her towards the exit. She shook her head, her eyes wide, pleading.

"Lily, how nice of you to come." The voice sent a shiver along my body, despite the sweat that trickled along my forehead and down my cleavage.

Johnny.

Despite the thick smoke suffocating us all, I could just make him out, a few feet in front of me, separating me and the steel steps to the loft. *Separating me from Cole.*

"Alas, the wanderer has been found." Johnny chuckled, flicking his lighter open so that I could see his face among the thick smoke. "Face it *Lily*, you have nowhere to run, you cannot disappear from me this time."

"What have you done?" I cried. Trying to see past him, to see any signs of life behind him. The loft had not been engulfed in flames, but the wall of fire was dancing steadily closer to it, as well as closer to us all.

"I want what is *mine,*" he growled, lunging towards me. He caught me off guard, I stumbled backwards. His weight pinned me to the ground, flames less than three feet away from my face.

"You're going to kill us all Johnny!" I screamed trying to wriggle underneath him, as the fiery tendrils crept closer by the second, closing the gap in which I had entered. Isolating us from any means of escape.

Johnny's face contorted into a snarl, his teeth bared as his hand slid down to my crotch. "Well, I had better fuck you one last time then-"

I heard a slick squelch, before a gurgle of blood spilled out from his mouth and splattered over my face.

I screamed when I saw a knife jutting out of his throat.

"Bel!"

"Cole!"

He coughed, scooping me off the floor, a wet blanket draped over him. "Hold the blanket to your face!"

I heard a crack as a ceiling beam fell from the roof, landing on top of Crystal. The fiery beam struck her head, before tearing through the skin on her face.

I screamed again.

"Don't look, Bel," he soothed, his voice shaky but trying to remain calm. "Concentrate on me. I will keep you safe. We will get out of here *alive.*"

I held a piece of blanket up to his face too.

"I'm sorry Cole," I sobbed. "Th-this is all my f-fault."

"Shhh," Cole said. "Just breathe..."

"I -I should not have l-left. I s-should have t-told you e-everything."

He remained silent, as he continued to navigate another exit as the smoke thickened and the heat was becoming unbearable.

"I l-lied to you Cole" I sobbed, still holding the blanket up to his face. His eyes stared at me, but he had not slowed his pace.

"Cole, I don't want to die with you believing my l-lie" I sniffed, "I do love you."

His arms tightened around me, a small whimper escaped him as flames licked his arms as he squeezed us through a gap in the wall.

Tendrils of fire reached for us, like hands trying to pull us into their fiery embrace, gripping onto the leg of my jeans, causing me to cry out. I flapped at it with the damp towel, inhaling thick black smoke just before we got out into the open air.

"Bel, why did you go into the burning building?" He asked, his face serious as I coughed and spluttered. I could feel myself losing consciousness.

"For you... Cole... I would walk... through... Hell... for you." I struggled against the blackness that was creeping into my vision, I stared at his face as he carried me through the smoldering grounds surrounded by walls of unyielding flames.

"How will...we... leave?" I asked, my head spinning, my vision was now like looking through a tunnel – small pinpricks of light was all I could see.

"We will always find a way, Bel, *together.*"

Alice

My baby is gone.

I knew it as soon as I had fallen in Marcus' kitchen. A slicing pain shredded my insides, as if my baby was being ripped out of my stomach. Hot, damp, liquid pooled between my legs at an alarming rate.

Not only was he a rapist, but he was now also a murderer.

I could think of nothing besides the pain, wanting it to end.

The world rushed past the windows, nothing but blurs, I did not want to be in a world without my child. For months I had kept this secret; I had grown to love it, to care for it, to protect it.

I had failed.

I can not live my life knowing I failed as a mother.

Freyja was frantic, but I was determined. If my baby was dead, I no longer wanted to live. Nor should he be allowed to live either. For all his sins, he more than anyone deserved to die.

I drew in her strength, harnessed her powers, using telekinesis on the steering wheel and telepathy on Josh to make him think he was hitting the brake when instead it was the gas pedal.

We were all going to die.

It would all look like *his* fault.

The car seemed to stay suspended in midair for several long moments after it rammed through the barriers. During the freefall, I tried not to feel scared; I tried to embrace the justice that once the river's depths embraced us. Josh will go to Hell, and I will be reunited with the child I never got to meet here on Earth.

This cruel, cold Earth.

Promising so much, but delivering so little.

Our future had been bright, happy. *Marcus.*

I tried not to think of him, my soulmate, despite Freyja's persistence.

He will love another. He will move on. I cannot.

The roaring of the water as it embraced the car was deafening, Josh was trying to unbuckle our seatbelts, trying to break the glass to get out.

I need to break the glass, I thought, focusing on it with all my remaining strength. The windscreen cracked, one long line that branched out across the whole screen in minutes.

Any second now-

I heard him take a gasp of breath as the glass shattered, I felt shards fly at me like a thousand needles, I did not take a breath, I allowed the water to fill my lungs. I was not going to resist.

Josh was fighting, but it was a losing battle, the will of the water too strong as it dragged the car further to the bottom of the river.

I wanted Josh to suffer, and I wanted to die.

Freyja screamed my name, over and over, but the water muffled her voice.

She grew distant from me, until I could no longer hear her, or anything at all.

Marcus

There was traffic everywhere. No matter what turning or alternative route I took there was more traffic.

"As the streets remain gridlocked all emergency services have been called to the bridge known to the locals as 'Angel Bridge' as rescue attempts are made to recover a driver and passenger from what appears to have been a silver Chevy Impala. It is not known yet why the car lost control and careered over-"

Silver Chevy Impala.

Angel Bridge.

No. Shit... No, no.

I called my security detail again using the hands-free in my car, the call was answered straight away "Please tell me they are at the hospital... please don't say-" My words were getting lost by my sobs as I fought to hold them back.

"Marcus-" Darwin said, I could tell by the sad undertone of his voice he was bearing bad news.

"Don't say it-" I sobbed. "Just... don't."

He was quiet, too quiet. For a moment I thought the line had cut off.

"We caught his car on the cams, and we sent a team to intercept them. but before our guys could- Marcus, man... *I- I'm so sorry.*"

My blood ran cold, my stomach tightened. "No!" I shouted. "Run the plates!"

"Marcus, we're sorry. We did."

"Was she in the car?" I asked, crossing my fingers, my toes, everything in the hope that he was alone.

"Yes Marcus, Alice was in the front passenger seat."

☪

Freyja

One drop of rain is all it takes to cause a ripple in the sea. One small action can alter the course of someone else's Fate. The only reason why accidents happen, is because for that one split moment, attention is diverted elsewhere.

In that moment, in Marcus' kitchen, I had been fascinated by Asmodeus' absence within Josh. I was too intrigued and concerned by the demon's whereabouts to look at the bigger picture to anticipate how the scene would unfold.

I had not seen the fall coming, if I had I would have stopped it by any means possible. But an accident happened, and a devastating loss resulted in my momentary lapse of attention.

I wanted to protect the child, to protect Alice, but my own despair at failing them had allowed her to harness my strength, my powers, *all* of it.

There was no stopping her.

The collision was far from an accident. It stemmed from her malicious intent to inflict pain, to eliminate them both entirely. Unwittingly, she had unleashed a catastrophic series of events that not only changed her destiny but also impacted the very fabric of the Earth itself.

Everything I had created over the last few millenia would be gone.

I failed them; every last one of them. All because of my one small mistake.

I had lost her, now I was losing myself along the way.

Cole

My foot caught on some debris that lay scattered on the ground. I could feel myself falling; both of us tumbling to the floor with a crash.

"Bel" I yelled, crawling to her. A huge cut on her forehead. Her eyes closed. "Bel, can you hear me?"

Moments passed as I sat there, cradling her head on my lap. Tears falling down my soot-covered face. "Please wake up!"

Her pulse.

I could still feel her pulse, her heartbeat against my fingers as they hovered under her chin, at the top of her neck. We were outside, but not far enough away from the burning rage of fire behind us. I had to move her, and fast. Not knowing what was on this site that may be flammable or worse yet, explosive.

Her eyes flickered open, the sense of weightlessness against gravity caused her eyes to flicker. "Cole?" she asked, her voice slurring. "Cole is that you?"

"Yes Bel. I'm here." I said cradling her in my arms once more.

"Are they- "

"They are dead Bel. They can not hurt you anymore."

"Where are you taking me?" she asked, unable to lift her head from my shoulder.

"Some place safe, Bel," I murmured, kissing her forehead. "I'm taking you *home*."

She shook her head, trying to point behind us. My heart raced, as adrenaline surged through my body, that guy's blood still on my hands.

The wall of fire was unrelenting, as I leaned over her as much as I could, I pushed through the flames, breaking through the blackened fence on the other side. We tumbled through the long grass. I looked around, we had managed to come out of the back of the warehouse. The damp, earthy aroma made a refreshing smell from the smoke that had clogged my throat.

I stumbled over to Isobel, wiping at her cut on her forehead, the scuffs on her face and arms, the singe marks on the clothes.

I was thankful not to face the police and fire crews that were at the front of the building.

Though I was not sure what guided me to her, it was like an unseen force dragged me to her.

Whatever it was, I was thankful. If I had been a moment too late I'd have lost her forever.

THIRTY-SEVEN

"Hello?!"

"What should we do?"

"Hello?!"

"Why don't we try- "

"Hello?!"

"Do you think we should - "

"HELLO?!"

I did not want to wake up. Ever.

My child was gone. Dead.

Doctors and nurses surrounded me. Marcus was trying to shout over them, trying to be heard. My heart ached for him, but I never wanted to wake up. I did not want to face the world without my baby. *I am a failure.*

There was nothing they could do, nothing anyone could do to bring back my child. *So why would they not let me die?*

I just wanted to be at peace, I wanted to be free from any more pain.

I watched my body from overhead, watching Marcus cry as he grasped my hand at the bedside. My mom stood in the doorframe, beside herself with grief.

But I still stepped aside.

This hospital was full of pain and suffering, as I strolled down the corridors, invisible and unseen, I could feel all their pain, I could hear their prayers.

Why did Freyja let so many of her creations suffer this way?

I felt the white hot fire surge through me, seeping out of my fingertips as I continued along the corridor, the flames crackling in my wake.

The world outside was no better, I could see the smog of evil like black billows of smoke choking the atmosphere.

I am going to rid the world of evil. I will do what Freyja was too scared to do herself.

No longer could I appreciate the beauty of the world she had crafted; it felt tainted, ensnared by the tendrils of evil.

As I moved past her creations, I let slip the whispers that echoed in my mind, conveying the singular thought, a straightforward command and my only desire; *destroy.*

Marcus

I was struggling to keep it together. I was crumbling under my grief and succumbing to my rage. Daniel told me that there was no chance of saving the child. The placenta had become detached by some kind of trauma, his words echoed in my mind: *"it appears that it may have occurred before the crash."*

Everything was spinning. The world from beneath my feet was crumbling, the future that we had envisioned, the vision that I wanted was slipping out of my grasp. fading into nothingness.

I needed her to wake up. I loved her, needed her. I could not bear to lose her too.

The machines beeped and whirred, monitors flashing everywhere. The public hospital was teeming with press, now even more so since I was involved.

This was not how it was supposed to be.

Why did I go to work instead of staying at home where I wanted to be?

My heart stopped as I watched the wires and tubes intertwine and enter her body, I was paralyzed.

Flashbacks of the last moments spent with my father, hearing the ECG beep plateau in front of me.

No, Alice, she has to wake up!

I clutched at her hand, my tears falling down my eyes as doctors failed to give me information. Time stood still.

Alice will not die. I kept telling myself. *She will come back to me. I need her.*

Emily

I received an urgent message on the radio, but the first time the words came out as static noise.

"Emily?" The voice on the other end of the radio said, his voice was unfamiliar.

"Yes?"

"You're needed in the ER department."

I looked at the rota on the wall, I was not scheduled to be in the pediatric ER department today.

"Are-Are you sure?" I responded.

"It's your daughter... she was involved in the Angel Bridge crash."

The radio slipped from my hand, shattering like my whole world. Fear gripped my chest, holding my lungs hostage.

I rushed through the corridors, dodging around doctors, narrowly avoiding a fellow nurse who was too busy looking at the clipboard to see me flying towards her.

My mind was on Alice.

I wanted to see her again, but not like this. This was every parent's worst nightmare.

Please keep my baby safe! I prayed, hoping that this time someone would listen.

I had to fight my way through the crowds of people; flashes of camera, and endless whispers, until I saw her and a primal scream escaped me.

Isobel

His eyes were the first thing I saw when I woke up. Glassy brown eyes, narrowing at me with concern.

"Cole!" I gushed, trying to sit up, but the room was spinning too much.

"Bel." He whispered, laying me back down, so that my head rested on his chest. My body curled into him.

"I'm so sorry Cole" I started, reaching for the necklace that always hung from my neck. The realization dawned on me, I no longer had it. I had given it back to him, in the loft.

"Bel, you broke my heart back there" he sighed, pushing some stray curls out of my face.

"I know" I choked back a sob, I did not deserve his forgiveness. "Thank you for saving me" I started, I could feel my sobs welling up in my chest, threatening to escape. "I never did deserve you, Cole."

He kissed me with every ounce of strength he had left. "Never. Do. That. Again," he gasped, breaking apart to say those words.

My arms locked around his neck. I never wanted to let go. "I love you, Cole." I whispered, breaking our kiss. "Walking away from you was one of the hardest things I have ever had to do."

I felt his head rest on my forehead; his chest heaved heavy sighs as he fought back his sobs. "Bel, I want you to trust me... no matter how big or small. I will always fight beside you."

"Johnny- he's-"

Cole's head nodded, his lips buried deeper into my hair. "He can't hurt you anymore Bel." His voice was tense, he was hurting. *Cole had killed someone to save me.*

I tilted my head to look at him, scared that he would hate me, for making him carry out such a villainous deed.

"I'm sorry Cole. I'm sorry that you-"

He pressed his finger to my lips, silencing me. I noticed his hair was streaked with blood, ash and cuts covering his face. Blood, *my* blood smeared on his cheek.

"Bel, I would do *anything* for you. I would do it all over again in a heartbeat to keep you safe." He sighed. as his finger traced along my face. "Everything I have done, has been everything within my power to prevent you from going back to a life like that." His lips brushed mine. "Please promise me you will never do anything like that again."

"I promise Cole" I sobbed, unable to hold it back any longer. "I am sorry...I love you."

He fell silent for a moment; "I love you too Bel," he smiled back in response.

It was only then that I took in our surroundings. The smell of fried chicken and curry lingered in the air. "Where are we Cole?" I asked, bringing my gaze back to his face.

"We are home." He smiled.

A sliver of coldness slashed against my neck, images of the knife sticking out Johnny's neck flashed before my eyes. I held up my hand, feeling the familiar shape under my fingers. My necklace. Cole's necklace, being fastened around my neck. I savored the familiarity of it against my skin.

"Bel, this is the start of our future together."

⚄

Like a fish trapped in a net, I looked for a way to escape. Ashamed and unwilling to admit defeat.

"It is not too late to fix this," his words sounded soft and soothing, almost like a hushed lullaby. My first creations surrounded me. I had created these like any manufacturer would create their prototype models, learning from the process, understanding the strengths and opportunities to improve on the next model.

These angels held superiority over all others. Yet they were not without their flaws. Flaws which I had used to my benefit. Using them to forge them as protectors, binding them to a superior, their loyalty bound to stop anyone or anything trying to cause humanity damage. Me included.

"It is too late," I retorted, trying to force my authoritative stature upon them, "this is their Fate." He shook his head, his eyes showed his disappointment in his master.

Shame washed over me as I felt the sting of his pity.

"Alice may have decided to do this...but you are Freyja The Divine," he gestured to the desolate land. Debris of destruction was disregarded all around us. "You know you can manipulate Fate. Only you can reverse what has been done."

Buildings nothing more than mountains of rubble, skeletal remains carpeting the ash-covered land. She could have been one of them.

He stretched out his hand toward me, encouraging me to take it. "Together we can make this right."

I glanced around at the Earth around me . It was destroyed, only the embers smoldered in the distance, the wind carrying the ash in the air, thick and heavy like fog. There was nothing at all in this barren land; no trees, no grass, no wildlife.

All of it had been wiped out, eradicated into complete oblivion.

Earth had been damaged beyond repair, never had it suffered such devastation before, and it had all been caused by one pair of hands - my hands.

Is this the true Fate for my creations and for Earth?

☸

Effy

I had seen it happen, every single moment forever imprinted on my brain. From the moment the car went over the edge of the bridge, to the moment they were being dragged out of the river. I had been outside of the city, in search of a pharmacy that did not know me or my mother, I knew they had to abide by strict patient confidentiality, however I was not taking any chances.

Josh and I never used condoms, not only did I find them uncomfortable, but he also claimed they dulled the experience, that he could not feel my tight entrance when he used one. I had allowed this to happen, relying solely on my birth control tablets. Although it was not until this morning, after a night full of rampant, lustful sex with Josh, that I discovered to my horror, that I had forgotten to take it yesterday morning.

When I saw that small white tablet staring up at me from the blister pack, yesterday's pill still there beneath the intact sealed foil, I felt as if I had been hit with a ton of bricks. Never had I forgotten to take it before.

I knew I needed to go to take the morning-after pill, but I wanted to avoid talking about it to anyone that I knew, or who knew me and my mother. It was only as I stepped out of the pharmacy, preparing to cross the road, when I recognized his car heading towards me on the street. My stomach tightened fearing that he would recognize me as he drew closer to me. But he never.

He was going too fast to have noticed me, but not fast enough. I caught a glimpse of *her* sitting in the passenger seat. I could not make out her face, as her head was bowed, her copper coils covering her face, but I knew it was Alice, no one else around here had hair remotely similar to hers – a crown of fire.

I felt sick to my stomach, my worst fear than he and Alice had been seeing each other, fucking each other, behind my back had been confirmed. Anger flared within me, as I hailed the taxi that was not far behind them to follow them. We had been tailing them while stuck in traffic with no issues, but when the road cleared, opened into multiple lanes across the bridge, the taxi could not keep up. I watched his car grow into the distance. "Miss I can not keep up. They are going too fast."

"I don't care!" I snapped.

That was when it happened, when I watched the accident happen from our vantage point ten cars behind them, all of them screeching to a sudden halt. My taxi driver was unable to stop in time, colliding with the car in front of him. Like a domino effect, each car was shunted into the ones before it.

My driver hit his head on the steering wheel during impact, splitting open the skin just above his eyebrow. Blood trickled down his face from the open wound. He was cursing, but I was not listening, I was too horrified by the cause of their emergency stops. We all witnessed the car swerving across the lanes, hurtling through the safety barrier and fencing before plummeting to the watery depths below.

All I remembered was screaming out his name as I scrambled out of the taxi. Rushing down the three flights of concrete steps that took me onto the public footpath that ran the length of the riverbank.

I had little in the way of coherent words as I called the emergency services. I tried my best, through my shock and sudden outburst of sobs, to give them the location and a brief explanation of what I had witnessed. It had not taken them long to arrive, but the car had already disappeared below the surface, neither of them had resurfaced.

All my hatred and jealousy had left my body, instead being replaced with total fear and uncontrollable panic.

Please, please, please... let them be alive!

THIRTY-EIGHT

Emily

When I reached her, she was surrounded by machines, doctors and nurses. My eyes glued to her as she lay lifeless and pale on the hospital bed. Her hair once so vibrant now hung dull and flat on the hospital pillow. Intravenous fluids being forced into her body. Her heart rate was slower than the normal range.

It was only then that I spotted them. Effy and a man in a suit. Not talking, just staring at her as the doctors and nurses busied themselves around her, like flies on shit.

"What the fuck happened?" I yelled to no one in particular, but to them all. "What happened to my daughter?" I cried.

Effy was the first one by my side. Embracing me in a bear hug, her sobs made her whole body shake. "The. Car. They crashed. River" were the only words I could make out.

I had heard about the accident on the bridge. We were always informed of accidents as they happened, and warned in case we were needed by other departments to help deal with the aftermath. "I'm sorry to tell you Mrs. Bowers, but we will need to perform surgery to remove her child."

I gasped, staring at him stunned, *"what the-?"*

"Your daughter was pregnant at the time of the accident, a little over thirty-seven weeks, we have managed to stabilize Alice for now though she remains unconscious. But the baby-" he broke off, unable to look me in the eye "the baby was dead when she arrived here."

My entire world came crashing around me. Effy was the only thing holding me upright.

"Alice should pull through," he added. Placing a gentle arm on my shoulder. "She is a fighter." I felt another pair of hands support me, as my knees buckled. The gentleman in the suit. I had never seen him before, but I was thankful for his help as they took me over to the chair beside her.

"Oh Alice!" I sobbed clutching her hand.

☙

Marcus

Tears streamed down her face as she tried to compose herself. She had every reason to be upset. She had found out that she was a grandmother in the worst way possible, as well as finding out that her own daughter's life hung in limbo. Her daughter whom she hadn't seen for a few weeks.

"Are you... are you the father? I mean, *were* you the father... of her child?" she asked, her voice distant, detached. I nodded my head. The plan stayed the same, everyone was to believe the child was mine. Ross had issued a statement for the press, for social media inquiries, it was bound to appear in the news. The unborn heir to the Morgan Industries perished in a fatality.

"We kept our relationship a secret," I started, my hands still trembling, clasped on my lap. "It was my decision, to keep it a secret, wanting to protect them, both of them from the sharks and the pariahs of the media." She shook her head, still not taking it in. "I am the owner of Morgan Industries. I had inherited the title when my father Charles died" I sighed. "With that title, sadly, comes little privacy."

"How did you two meet?" She asked a question that both Alice and I had expected, our answer concocted between us. *"It must be believable; she will not be convinced. We must take advantage of her working so much."* I remembered her saying when we were discussing it.

"We met by happenstance. Right place and the right time." I paused, my voice low, soft, "I had popped into a coffeeshop for a coffee and a sandwich for my lunch hour, and I saw her sat in a booth opposite the counter, typing on her laptop. I was intrigued by her, who wouldn't be with her wild red hair, and her bright green eyes!"

I glanced at Alice as she lay there unresponsive and tangled with wires. A lump formed in the back of my throat, I coughed, trying and failing to clear it. "I had approached her, asking what she was writing about, that was when she told me she was writing her notes for college. I did not want to distract her, but she insisted she needed a break, needed more caffeine and a distraction for a few moments, anyway. So, we had sat and drank coffee together."

"When was this?" she asked.

"About a year or so." I lied. Alice and I had agreed on an appropriate timeline, even a date we supposedly first met, to make our story more believable. I hated lying, especially as I could see more tears well up in her mother's eyes, but for Alice I would do anything. "Mrs Bowers, I was, *am*, in love with her. Alice is remarkable, funny, and beautiful. Unlike anyone I've met before."

I took a breath, trying to steady my nerves, keep my voice from trembling. "Not long after that first encounter, we began dating, meeting in secret, a few stolen hours here and there. Making the most of our time together, while you were at work." I placed my hand over the top of Emily's and Alice's hands. "I love your daughter Mrs. Bowers, and I know she loves me too." I sighed, my shoulders sagged, "we just wanted to keep our relationship a secret, our child, a secret from the world."

Both of us trembling, our fear coursing through each other. In a way it was calming, being able to share the emotion, the burden with someone who loved her just as much as me. "She did not want to keep it from you, she knew you would be upset, but that you would understand. If you want to blame anyone, Mrs Bowers... Please blame me."

I could see more tears swimming in her eyes "I always worked too much, after her father died, money was...well," she sniffed. "It would have been easy for me not to notice," she tried to blink back tears. "I knew something was wrong, in the weeks leading up to her disappearance. I was not there when she needed me the most."

I nodded; I knew that feeling too well.

⛬

Effy

I did not understand. "Why was she in the car with Josh?" I asked.

He shrugged at my question. "My brother was doing me a favor, Alice and I were supposed to have lunch together, perhaps do a little of shopping for the baby," his voice cracked, "but I was still in a meeting, so I asked if he could pick her up, as he was coming by the office anyway."

I got to my feet, "excuse me for a moment" I whimpered as I left the room. Leaning against the wall in the corridor, trying to make sense of it all. The next thing I was aware of was him standing beside me. "I thought Josh liked Alice... I thought they were together, after he-"

"He what?"

I shook my head embarrassed, but his eyes narrowed, expecting me to answer. "He, um... he called me by her name one time, during sex. Everyone always saw her as the beautiful one in our friendship, so I shouldn't have been surprised he was more attracted to her than me."

I saw him stand a little straighter, his claw clenched. "Sorry, I shouldn't have said anything, he was your brother, and I imagine it must be hard to hear that they were having an affair-"

"They were not having an affair Effy," he told me, there was a tone of truthfulness in his voice. "I know nothing ever happened between them." His eyes were piercing mine. "So, you need to stop saying things that are not true, that you have no evidence of."

I nodded my head, feeling stupid, wiping my eyes with the back of my "I... I loved him too." I replied, as my voice broke into sobs once more. My thoughts were with Josh as he lay in the hospital's morgue.

"My brother was many things," he sighed, "he was far from perfect. But he was loyal to those he loved, and while he may not have loved many, I know he loved you. He had played a big role in keeping mine and Alice's relationship a secret, perhaps you had mistaken that for a secret of his own."

"Why would he say her name during sex?"

He shrugged his shoulders "That, Effy, I do not know." he replied. "But when you are keeping a secret for someone else, it is more common than you think to get distracted, to slip up, especially when you are not in full control of your senses."

$$\text{☙}$$

Marcus

I did not want her to remember my brother in a bad way. I may have despised him, but she was the one person who loved him, who never saw his dark side. It was best for her to remain that way.

I left her in the corridor, approaching Alice on the bed once more. Her mother still sat by her side holding one of her hands. I ached to stand next to her, to hold her other hand.

"Marcus, they are going to take her down to surgery" she whispered, letting go of her hand, allowing me a few moments to be with her. I kissed Alice's forehead, while placing her hand between both of mine.

"I love you Alice" I whispered. "Please come back to me."

$$\text{☙}$$

Freyja

I was being given an opportunity for redemption. A chance to make things right. Though the question was; *how far back do I go?*

I saw her life flash before my eyes; every single moment like cinematic reels, each one highlighting a moment I could change. Each one resulting in a different Fate.

I wanted Alice to be happy, to find peace and love with her soulmate, but that only happened after Josh's attack.

The clock was ticking, as I contemplated my choice; *am I doing the right thing?*

The angel's hand was outstretched, his eyes cast upon me, encouraging me to take it.

I glanced around at each one, tears stinging my eyes, I needed them to know how sorry I was, that even The Divine can make a mistake.

My creations were based on myself after all; flaws and all.

Lucifer.

I want to hate him, and for as long as I can remember, I have run from him, scared of his darkness. But through the fiery flames, I had seen the truth, the shadows that lurked inside me which had breathed life into him.

He still needed to be destroyed; that child was our only hope.

I tentatively took his hand, feeling the warmth emanate from his touch. Their wings started fluttering, pulsing like a heartbeat, mesmerizing and hypnotic, until I could no longer concentrate on anything else.

I made my choice, I only hoped it was enough.

THIRTY-NINE

Marcus

A shrill cry sounded from down the corridor. I thought my ears were deceiving me. It was a baby's cry, loud and piercing.

I looked around yet here was no one else here on this floor. It had been my request to be separated from the members of the public. This event was traumatic enough without the press being all over it like vultures picking the rotting flesh of a corpse.

An image of his face flashed into my mind. My brother; Josh. *He is dead.*

I bit my lip to stop it from trembling, until I tasted the bitter and metallic blood. I did not want to mourn him, instead I wanted to hate him. After everything he had done, not just to Alice, but for all he had ever put me through in the past. Yet, he was still my brother. I still loved him, despite it all, and as much as I did not want to admit it, I would miss him.

If my father treated him better, in life and in death, perhaps Josh would not have turned out the way he did.

I pinched the bridge of my nose, the sound of a baby's cry was tormenting; knowing the child Alice had carried; that we had both intended to raise together, was gone.

"Marcus?" Daniel's voice choked, his eyes were glassy, a confused expression etched across his face.

I got to my feet, grateful that he was able to pull strings so he could be here; I knew why Josh was bringing her here; in theory it would have been quicker. *But the bridge-*

"Marcus, I- I don't know how to say this..." His eyes were wide, incredulous, there was a tone to his voice I could not fathom; shock and something else.

"Alice, is she okay? Is she awake yet?"

Daniel nodded frantically, his Adam's apple bobbed up and down as he tried to formulate the words in his mouth. "Marcus, Alice is awake... but-"

"But what?" I growled clutching onto his shoulders. The baby's cry suddenly sliced the silence once more. My brows furrowed, listening to the cry, to the closeness of the sound.

It sounds like its coming from-

I ran down the hall, Daniel hot on my heels almost crashing into me as I skidded to a stop inside the door. My breath caught in my throat. I rubbed my eyes, unbelieving the sight before me.

I span on my heel to face Daniel, "you... you said-"

Daniel took off his glasses, wiping the corner of his eye with his sleeve. "It truly is a miracle Marcus- in all my years..."

His words drifted into silence as I walked towards the bed in a trance. Tears ran down my face, as I tentatively approached Alice. I wanted to embrace her, but she was still connected to the machines, her face covered in bruises and cuts.

My chest tightened as I saw her eyes flicker up at mine, her smile spreading across her face as she sobbed. "I thought I lost her." she whispered, "I thought I had lost everything."

As I stood beside her, I gazed down upon the baby bundled in a pink blanket, my heart swelled as her shrieks shattered the silence.

A laugh escaped me, a choked, amazed and shocked laugh.

So did I.

"Alice..." I sighed, planting a kiss on her forehead, her hair still damp at the roots. "I love you."

It didn't seem enough; those three little words, they could never express how much she meant to me, how much I would have lost. Not just my future, not just my happiness. Alice was my world, my everything. I did not want to imagine my life, or the universe, without her in it.

For over two hours I had been expecting the worst, holding back my tears; trying to follow another one of my father's rules; *"Men don't cry, it's a form of weakness... Us Morgan men are not weak."*

As my tears flowed, I did not feel weak; I felt elated, relieved, *and joyful.* I had been so prepared for the worst that the sudden rush of happiness took me by surprise. It had knocked the air out of my lungs, like a swift kick to the family jewels.

"Do you want to hold her?" Alice asked, her hand reaching out for mine.

For a few moments I stood there, our fingers intertwined, feeling her soft, silky skin against mine. Smiling as if I had just won the biggest jackpot in history.

Of course I wanted to hold my daughter, but I wanted to hold her too. My arms wrapping around them both, as my sobs quaked through my body, I wanted to hold onto them both and never let go.

"Marcus... we're going to be fine," she whispered, her lips kissing my cheek. "We will be out in a few days; they just want to do some observations."

I inhaled her scent, the blood and the silt from the river water, but also the faintest hint of her favorite floral perfume and the scent of the newborn baby in her arms.

"Alice, I came so close to losing you both..." I sobbed, my arms tightening just a little bit more.

"But we are here, Marcus, *both* of us. Our family, our future... This is just the beginning."

Slowly my arms slid from them, but my eyes never left hers. "Alice... I-" Her fingers brushed against my lips, before pulling my face down to hers, and feeling her lips grace them instead. Her tongue parting them to deepen the kiss. My heart fluttered, as I kissed her fiercely, abandoning every negative thought that had plagued me back in the waiting room. *Alice is here, she is safe, she is mine.*

The baby screamed again, both of us broke apart chuckling softly as we gazed down at our daughter.

"Have you thought of a name?" I asked her, as I stroked my daughter's face. Noticing the small wires that were connecting her to the monitors. My mind flashbacked to the many baby name books that sat on her bedside, remembering how she liked the name Elizabeth, and I smiled when I told her that was my mother's name.

Alice bit her lip and nodded slightly. "I don't know if you will like it though. "

I felt Alice's breath hot against my ear as she whispered the name she had decided. It brought another rush of tears to my eyes as it fell softly like a lullaby. Instantly it became my newest and most favorite song.

As I cradled my daughter wrapped in the pink blanket, her cries quietened as I spoke. "Welcome to the world; Freya Elizabeth Morgan."

Alice

My eyes flickered open at the sound of the familiar cry that stirred me from my slumber. It was the wails of a baby.

My heart leaped at the sound of it, as it had since the moment I laid my eyes on her small round face. My heart filled with joy as I felt a movement stir beside me, as I watched Marcus pick her up from her cot and carry her over to me in the hospital bed.

I watched through blurry eyes as his strong muscular arms wrapped around her, protective and firm, as his lips nuzzled the top of her delicate hair, a streak of orange so vibrant against her porcelain skin. It was easy to see that Marcus was smitten with her; a true, doting father.

My heart swelled looking at them; tears had formed in my eyes as he slowly placed her in my arms, his lips grazing against mine the moment he let his hands slide out from underneath her back.

He took out his work mobile and snapped a few photos.

"I probably look awful." I groaned, looking at the IV drip still attached to my arm, and feeling the cuts still tender and sore on my face. My body ached, more than having the child torn from my stomach, the crash landing in the river had battered and bruised my body.

Everyone said I had been lucky; everything had worked out perfectly. It had, but it was not by sheer luck, and it certainly was not supposed to be my Fate.

The moment I had slipped in Marcus' kitchen was the moment Freyja had turned back the clocks of time and altered the course of my Fate. She protected my baby, she ensured that throughout the fall and the car plummeting off the bridge, that my daughter would be delivered to me; safe and healthy.

I do not know how she managed to traverse time and space, nor do I want to, all I wanted to do was thank her. Yet, she was no longer inside me. I felt her emptiness the moment I woke up from surgery. I had not been expecting her to leave me, even though throughout these past few months that was what I had wished for.

Visions of a scorched, desolate Earth haunted me; my true fate. The one Freyja had veered me from by keeping my daughter alive. It was so tangible and real, I still could smell the charred remains and the thick billowing smoke.

I looked down at my daughter, knowing I would have destroyed the whole world for her; in revenge for her existence being ripped away from me.

"Alice, don't cry..." Marcus cooed, as he perched beside me on the bed, his arms wrapping around both of us, as my tears fell silently.

The smell of him, his signature cologne and the salt in his sweat soothed me, as I leaned my head against him. *This is perfect.* Despite the dull ache of emptiness that Freyja left behind.

I knew she had given me a new beginning, had given me the opportunity of having the future Marcus and I had dreamed of, but I now had to discover who *I* was without her.

FORTY

"Freya!" I cooed, "shall we meet your baby sister?"

I could not contain my happiness, my love for my daughter and her children. Her life seemed to be complete. Marcus was a perfect gentleman, and he carried flawless genetics. Their second child, another girl, had been born in the early hours of this morning. Calling me to look after Freya while they went to the hospital, much more prepared than when Freya entered this world. That day was a whirlwind, a bumpy roller-coaster. Unexpected twists and turns around every corner, evoking every emotion known to man.

I turned up to work that day as a broken mom with an estranged daughter but came away a proud grandmother. *Freya.*

Her name seemed familiar even back then in the hospital room, like I had heard it, used it, before. But I could not explain how or why I recognized it. I tried many times over the years to recall the memory, but always drawing a blank.

I knew Freyja was a goddess of love and fertility in Norse mythology. The name was fitting considering the way she entered this world, a miracle baby, presumed dead, conceived and born out of the genuine love my daughter and Marcus shared.

I looked at the beautiful toddler before me, her copper curls bouncing up and down as she jumped with impatience. Her green eyes were striking even for her young age.

"Up, Nana Bowie" she tugged at the sleeve of my jacket. Raising her arms as a gesture to be carried. I obliged, scooping her up into my arms. I could not imagine a world where she was not in it, as we had all initially feared.

I held her, giving her an affectionate squeeze. Her green eyes glinted as she giggled.

If only her grandfather, whom she inherited the green eyes from, was here to see them now.

He may not have been a great husband, but he was a great father. I knew in my heart he would have been proud.

☙

Freyja

My only hope to rid the world of Lucifer and his creations rested solely on *Asmodeus*.

It was ironic that a demon would be the one to cure the world of the evil that infiltrated it. I may have been blind from seeing it, reveling in the delights of the Earth I had once created, but I could feel it slowly suffocating.

With each year that passed the tendrils of darkness slowly strangled the light that had once been there. My angels were not enough to stave it off much longer, we all knew they were fighting a losing battle, yet they refused to release me.

I knew Lucifer had escaped the moment the Angels imprisoned me here. It was my tether to Earth that kept him bound to the confines of Hell. But now he was let loose to run amok, knowing it was only a matter of time before he found them; Alice and the child I had desperately tried to protect.

Asmodeus needed to act fast, before it was too late.

EPILOGUE

Four Years Later
Alice

The world was blanketed in darkness, thunderous and ominous gray clouds rolled across the sky, blocking out all the light. A fog so thick you could cut it with a knife lingered in the icy atmosphere. A storm was coming. Loud claps of thunder, a quick flash of light.

We had been in the fields beyond our house taking our dog Rover for his daily walk to tire out the energetic nature of his breed, a beagle. When we got him as a puppy so active and animated in his movements that we appreciated the vast lands that surrounded The Meadows, so that he could exert his energy chasing squirrels and trying to catch butterflies.

Freya and Rover were inseparable, wherever she went, so did he. Her personal protector. They had run on ahead, as I carried her sister, our most recent addition, Isabella, or as we all called her Izzy. Her little legs had grown too tired to walk any further. At that moment I found it hard to believe that Freya was now six years old, Rover was five years old, and Izzy was almost three years old. Time was going too fast.

The day had started, as it always seems to nowadays, the four of us having a lovely breakfast together. My perfect family: my perfect husband Marcus, always made the best pancakes. The smell of them still lingered on my clothes, as we walked towards the house.

Suddenly Izzy erupted into tears. Sobbing and shrieking as if she was in physical pain. Piercing cries at the top of her lungs, deafening and hysterical. I tried to console her, but her arms kept hitting mine away. I did not know what was wrong.

Rover started barking at something in the distance. I snapped my head up to see what had garnered his attention. He had never barked or growled like he was now. His teeth bared; canines revealed.

"Frey!?" I called, no longer able to see her figure among the fog. "Freya, sweetie, where are you? Wait for mommy."

I heard her call out for me, just one word, *"mommy"* before a loud blood-curdling scream. "Freya!" I ran as fast as I could with a still screaming toddler in my arms, trying to find where the sound had come from.

The wind seemed to hiss my name. *"Aallliiiiiccceee"* over and over, sending shivers along my spine and goosebumps to spread across my skin.

It was not Freya my daughter, nor was it Freyja the being that once inhabited my mind. The being that I had lived with since birth, whom I had grown to love and miss as well as despise, leaving me now with only emptiness; a gaping void that could not be filled. I missed her, despite everything. If it had not been for her I never would have ended up living this perfect life with my perfect family.

A branch snapped to the left, I turned to face the sound. "Alice...we meet at last," his voice, smooth as melted chocolate began. "What a great pleasure this will be."

"Who are you?" I shouted, putting my body forward, trying my best to shield Izzy "What have you done with Alice?"

"Oh nothing. She'll be fine. Just entertaining my hell-hounds." His voice was familiar, but also unrecognizable.

I bit my lip. "Please, don't hurt her," I pleaded. "Who are you? What do you want with me?"

"Well, where do I start?" he pondered, still only seeing his silhouette outlined in the fog.

His eyes snapped open, they shone like neon warning lights in the dark. It was all I could make out at this distance as darkness blanketed us. They were deep crimson, and my skin burned under his intense glare, as if he was trying to invade my soul.

He stepped forward, his face slightly illuminated by the silver glow of the moon. My eyes opened wide in shock, shaking my head in disbelief. *No, it can't be.*

"Alice," he purred, his voice familiar, tugging at my heartstrings. "Surely you know who I am by now?" He licked his lips, those lips I have kissed a thousand times over the last few years.

"Marcus?" I whimpered, cradling my daughter tightly into my chest.

"No Alice, I am *Lucifer.*"

ABOUT THE AUTHOR

Raven has been weaving narratives that traverse a myriad of genres and topics since childhood. Through her journey as a writer, Raven has honed a distinctive voice that resonates with readers, spinning tales of adventure, romance, mystery, or of fantastical realms and ethereal entities. In each intricately crafted page of her books, she embarks on journeys to places afar with lovable and relatable characters, inviting readers to escape from the reality and monotony of everyday life.

As a wife and a mother of two, life can be chaotic, yet Raven still dedicates as much of her free time as possible to bring to life ideas from her vivid imagination, in the hopes her readers find her stories transformative, inspiring and entertaining, with the aspiration to share this gift with audiences far and wide.

When she is not outside tolerating the unseasonable British weather, you will find Raven as a consistent online presence on most social media platforms, where she offers regular updates and new insights for upcoming releases. She is always happy to chat with her readers and followers.

Website: https://www.ravenleitheharlow.co.uk/

Facebook: https://www.facebook.com/ravenleitheharlow

Instagram: https://www.instagram.com/ravenleitheharlow.author

Twitter/ X: https://x.com/RavenLeithe

Printed in Great Britain
by Amazon